WHAT THE HEART
REMEMBERS

DEBRA GINSBERG

NEW AMERICAN LIBRARY

NEW AMERICAN LIBRARY
Published by New American Library, a division of
Penguin Group (USA) Inc., 375 Hudson Street,
New York, New York 10014, USA
Penguin Group (Canada), 90 Eglinton Avenue East, Suite 700, Toronto,
Ontario M4P 2Y3, Canada (a division of Pearson Penguin Canada Inc.)
Penguin Books Ltd., 80 Strand, London WC2R 0RL, England
Penguin Ireland, 25 St. Stephen's Green, Dublin 2,
Ireland (a division of Penguin Books Ltd.)
Penguin Group (Australia), 250 Camberwell Road, Camberwell, Victoria 3124,
Australia (a division of Pearson Australia Group Pty. Ltd.)
Penguin Books India Pvt. Ltd., 11 Community Centre, Panchsheel Park,
New Delhi -110 017, India
Penguin Group (NZ), 67 Apollo Drive, Rosedale, Auckland 0632,
New Zealand (a division of Pearson New Zealand Ltd.)
Penguin Books (South Africa) (Pty.) Ltd., 24 Sturdee Avenue,
Rosebank, Johannesburg 2196, South Africa

Penguin Books Ltd., Registered Offices:
80 Strand, London WC2R 0RL, England

First published by New American Library,
a division of Penguin Group (USA) Inc.

First Printing, September 2012
10 9 8 7 6 5 4 3 2 1

NAL REGISTERED TRADEMARK—MARCA REGISTRADA

LIBRARY OF CONGRESS CATALOGING-IN-PUBLICATION DATA:
Ginsberg, Debra, 1962–
What the heart remembers / Debra Ginsberg.
p. cm.
ISBN 978-0-451-23700-2
1. Heart—Transplantation—Fiction.   2. Self-realization in women—Fiction.   3. Psychological
fiction.   I. Title.
PS3607.I4585W47   2012
813'.6—dc23
2012007809

Set in Adobe Garamond Pro
Designed by Catherine Leonardo

Printed in the United States of America

PUBLISHER'S NOTE
This is a work of fiction. Names, characters, places, and incidents either are the product of the
author's imagination or are used fictitiously, and any resemblance to actual persons, living or dead,
business establishments, events, or locales is entirely coincidental.
     The publisher does not have any control over and does not assume any responsibility for author
or third-party Web sites or their content.

For Dr. Michael C. Martin

Forward-thinking physician, old-fashioned healer

WHAT THE HEART REMEMBERS

Praise for
WHAT THE HEART REMEMBERS

"A cross between Laura Lippman and Kate Atkinson, this novel is complex, original, and utterly intriguing. Will stay with you long after you've stopped turning the pages."

—Deborah Crombie, *New York Times* bestselling author of *No Mark upon Her*

"A tense, twist-filled ride that knocked the breath out of me more than once, but what I found most compelling was Ginsberg's nuanced depiction of the relationship between two complicated women. Part friendship, part rivalry, part cat-and-mouse game, the deepening bond between Darcy and Eden kept me guessing—and reading—far into the night."

—Marisa de los Santos, *New York Times* bestselling author of *Falling Together* and *Love Walked In*

Praise for the Novels of
DEBRA GINSBERG

"Keen and ruthless observations of human foibles."

—*The New York Times Book Review*

"The suspense and tension keep tightening and building to a shocker at the end, which shows that home may be where the heart is, but it's also where the secrets are." —*The Boston Globe*

"The kind of reading that'll keep you up all night . . . If there is any literary justice, Ginsberg soon will be a huge star."

—*The Dallas Morning News*

"Debra Ginsberg grabs the reader from the first pages and without letting up delivers a well-written novel full of interesting characters. She proves without a doubt that you can never really know what goes on behind closed doors." —*The Post and Courier* (SC)

"A gripping suburban suspense novel with real people at its core. This will appeal to fans of . . . Mary Higgins Clark [and] Lisa Gardner as well as Tom Perrotta." —*Library Journal*

"Ginsberg smoothly sketches captivatingly flawed characters."

—*Entertainment Weekly*

"Wicked fun and suspense from a talented new writer with an original, clever voice."

—*New York Times* bestselling author Lisa Scottoline

"Ginsberg's writing is clever and seductive as she spins this tale of psychological peril and illumination."

—*New York Times* bestselling author T. Jefferson Parker

"A fresh voice and story, with a winning heroine. Another triumph for Debra Ginsberg, who clearly has many gifts of her own."

—*New York Times* bestselling author Laura Lippman

PROLOGUE

Del Dios Highway was a bitch in the rain.

Actually, it was a cruel mistress under the best conditions, but at least when it was dry and clear, this road showed off all its beautiful charms. The twisted asphalt ran through crazy-rich Rancho Santa Fe, past sparkling Lake Hodges, and into the dry, mall-infested brush of Escondido—all of it on the edge of a cliff. There was a reason its name translated to "God's Highway," after all—it was breathtaking. Didn't matter how many times you'd driven it or how jaded you were about scenery. Of course, there was another reason for the name too. Del Dios was lovely all right, but just like a wrathful god, it also had a very real ability to punish. Beautiful and treacherous—a familiar combination. Especially in the rain—this unexpected but somehow perfect deluge. Of course it was raining.

1

A bucketful of water pelted the windshield, as if she herself had read those thoughts. And maybe she had. Maybe psychic ability was one more trick in that woman's already-full bag.

He turned the windshield wipers on high, but they shuddered and stuck. He cursed and fiddled with them, turning them from low to high and back again, but it didn't seem to help much. Now they were on low. But there wasn't enough clearance to make a difference. The rain had turned into a full-on flash fury, and there was nothing to see out the windshield but bleared shapes in green and gray. He took his foot off the gas and barked out a laugh. The inside of the car rang with the sound of it.

Crazy and dangerous this drive was. But he should have thought of that before he got involved with her. It wasn't a stretch to know that at some point he'd end up here, begging for purchase on a rain-slicked grade. He could have avoided all of it if he'd chosen not to go back to her. But he had gone back. Inevitable. Karma. Call it what you will.

As happened so often lately, *her* image materialized—a mirage in full color, beckoning and soft, that come-hither whisper always playing around her Cupid's bow lips. There was something about her beauty that set her apart—made her different from all the other cat-eyed California demigoddesses. She had that perfect body and the long golden hair—and none of it fake or enhanced—but that wasn't all of it. There was the money, of course. It was so much easier to be beautiful when you had money—people didn't realize how true that was. But there was more. There was something inside her steely core that made her special. She was fantasy made real—a bewitcher of men. *He* knew that—he knew he'd been spelled—but he'd been powerless in her sway just the same.

He still loved her.

The thought came snaking in, unbidden and unwelcome.

He would always love her.

The rain had become torrential—a freak storm—and the wipers had quit altogether. It was essential now to get off this road, but here, on God's forsaken two-lane highway, there was nowhere to pull over and nowhere to go but ahead or down. He was a skilled driver, and it wasn't in his nature to panic, but fear was pulling at his face now, clamping the muscles of his jaw.

The road, the rain, the fear. The first two were manageable. The fear, though . . . It was getting very difficult to stay calm.

Visibility had become so poor, it was impossible to see the oncoming SUV until it was almost on top of the car. The space between them could be measured in horrifying inches as the vehicle swerved past, leaving the terrible sound of a near miss ringing in the breath-damp car. Too close.

Goddamn her, goddamn her. The words were like a song. Damn her to hell. It was *her* fault—all of this.

He was peering through the bleared windshield, hunching over the wheel. The mile markers were indecipherable, and the landscape was dissolving. Impossible to tell how near or far the next turnoff might be. Numbness was setting in, a sort of dull, hypnotic fear.

There was a patch of clear sky in the near distance, glowing like a benediction. The cloudburst was moving overhead. In a minute, in a mile, it would be dry.

He punched on the CD player, and the car filled with a song in midplay—their song. *Her* song. But it was just a fragment of a lyric— ". . . water on the moon . . ." —and it wasn't even there long enough to sing along. Because in the space of a second, all sound, touch, and smell were drowned in the sudden vision of lights—the shining beacons of an oncoming and out-of-control eighteen-wheeler dead ahead.

Brake—the natural response—foot to pedal. No thought in it, just pressure and the search for resistance. He was hitting the brakes hard, the muscles in his leg straining from the force. But the car was unresponsive. The car was going faster. He swerved and spun. No use. Impact was coming.

It was her fault—all of it. The thought flashed and splintered. Darkness.

Then the scream. *Her* name—the very last sound.

PART

1

CHAPTER 1

PORTLAND

Eden had already left her building and was halfway to the restaurant when Derek called.

"I'm running a little late," he said. "Sorry, Edie."

"Okay," Eden said, "how late?" The light breeze that had been following her through the South Park Blocks had turned, without warning, into a brisk wind. Dry fallen leaves rustled past her on the street.

"I don't know," he said. "A half hour?"

"That's not really *a little* late, Derek. What's up?"

"Just some stuff I have to take care of here."

"Do you want to—"

"No," he said, reading her thoughts, "I don't want to cancel!"

She laughed into her cell phone. "Okay. No need to sound so militant."

"Won't be more than a half hour, I promise," he said. He paused for a moment. "Forty-five minutes, tops."

"Derek—"

"Why don't you just wait for me at home? I'll come pick you up, and we can walk over to Soleil Bistro together."

Eden hesitated. A strong gust pushed against her back. She was dressed up and hungry. She'd skipped lunch in anticipation of this early dinner, and her stomach was growling. She knew that if she went home now, she'd start rummaging through the kitchen for something to eat.

"Eden?"

"Okay, Derek. But you should know I'm hungry."

He made a noise that was part growl, part moan. "Me too, love. Wait for me. Won't be long. I promise."

Eden ended the call. The light was fading, and the air was getting cooler. She turned around and took a few steps in the direction of home, but then she stopped, staring ahead into the urban green of the South Park Blocks. Eden didn't like to change direction once she'd decided on a course of action, even if it was something as simple as this. It would be easy enough to go home and wait for Derek, but she just didn't want to. She turned around again and, picking up her pace, continued walking, a smile forming on her face. If she hustled, she could easily reach Derek's office within half an hour. She'd surprise him. Yes, that was a much better plan.

Eden felt a flicker of trepidation as she blazed past Soleil Bistro. For several reasons, she suspected Derek was planning something big for tonight. For one thing, he'd been specific about wanting to dine at that restaurant, where they'd first met just over two years ago. For another, he'd chosen this odd not-lunch-or-dinner time for their date, which could mean that he wanted to make sure the place wasn't humming with people. And he had been adamant about not wanting to postpone or cancel. She didn't want to ruin it for either one of them by showing up at his office instead of staying home as she'd said she would, but . . .

What did he have planned? Eden wondered. Derek's athletic-shoe company, which he'd started in his living room not long before he'd met Eden, was growing, and Eden knew he'd been romancing a couple of big accounts. So maybe he had news on that front. But Eden thought it was likelier to have something to do with the two of them. They'd been talking about *the future* often lately, and the conversations invariably had the word *we* threaded throughout.

So, Eden thought, maybe he was going to propose to her. Public displays of affection, or affectation for that matter, weren't really Derek's style, but he was a romantic at heart—more so even than she.

Eden smiled, marveling again at her luck in finding Derek. He was exactly the man she'd envisioned for herself when she was a little girly-girl doodling hearts and arrows in the pages of her unicorn-covered purple diary. He was that classically handsome boy-next-door type; blond, blue-eyed, and effortlessly muscular. Of course, as soon as she'd entered high school, Eden revised her opinion about what made the perfect man. Then it was the skinny, philosophy-spouting goth types she went for. Well, faux-goth, really. She might have been aiming for fashionable, but Eden still liked clean edges. In college, her tastes changed a little more to include the brooders, the sensitive guys who claimed to be feminists and proved it with their creative spellings—*womyn* and *wimmin* and so on. She avoided the clean-cut ones, the blonds, and, usually, the athletes. At some point, probably over another bottomless caffè macchiato with another scrawny-armed dilettante spouting his opinions about the state of the environment and the role of government, Eden woke up from what had been a decade-long romantic slumber and went back to where she started. You had to know yourself before you knew who you wanted to be with. That was what Eden finally figured out. The girl who had lovingly pasted shiny heart stickers into her diary was at her true core—the reason she'd never thrown that diary away. She met Derek almost immediately after that revelation. She literally ran into him. It was her first marathon, and something (fate, Derek said later) tripped her after the fifth mile; she tumbled onto him, pulling them both down to the ground. He hadn't taken offense, and, after one look at him, she didn't want to get up. They'd been together ever since. Eden's parents, who'd always had faith in their daughter but who had become increasingly irritated with the strays she dragged home for the holidays, were as happy with Derek as she was.

Sometimes, she thought, things just worked out the way they were supposed to.

Eden was still smiling when she reached Derek's office, but, in spite of her best efforts, she couldn't keep it on her face once she walked in. Derek's staff (or coworkers as he liked to call them) consisted of three: Charles, Xander, and Wendy. Eden knew and liked them all—odd bunch that they were—and they had always seemed very comfortable with her. But as she entered the outer office, both Charles and Xander glanced at her, guilty looks on their faces, and then both flicked their eyes over to Derek's glassed-off space inside. Following their gaze, Eden could see Derek and Wendy (a beautiful Nordic blonde) huddled together, their faces practically touching. The stab of jealousy she felt was so sharp and unexpected, it took her breath away. It was the look on Wendy's face that troubled Eden the most. She was staring intently at Derek, who was looking down at something in his hand, with a look that Eden could only describe to herself as *lovelorn*. Eden took all of this in over the course of a moment because, when Derek looked up, the expression on Wendy's face changed immediately, as if she'd rearranged all of her individual features to reflect a professional composure. But then Derek gave Wendy a big, satisfied, and so help him, *intimate* smile, and Eden felt heat rush to her head.

"Hey, Eden, how are you?"

It was Charles, speaking, it seemed to Eden, from across a great distance. Eden wanted to answer him, but she couldn't look away from the scene in front of her. Then, as if they could feel her stare, Derek and Wendy both turned their heads toward her at the same time. Eden didn't like the twin expressions of dismay that formed instantly on their faces.

I should have gone home.

"Is it raining out there?"

Finally, Eden was able to break her gaze and turn to Charles. She felt as if she were speaking to him from underwater. "No," she said. "It isn't raining. Windy. It was windy on my way over here."

The smile Charles gave her then looked painful for him to produce.

"How's it going, Eden?" Xander had finally found his voice, but Eden didn't get a chance to answer him because at that moment Derek came striding over to her, Wendy in tow; that implacable expression returned to her lovely face.

"Edie! I thought you were going to go back home. What—"

"Changed my mind," Eden said. "Hello, Wendy," she added frostily. "Hope I didn't interrupt anything."

Derek caught her tone and seemed genuinely surprised by it. Wendy didn't move a muscle in her face, but Eden thought she saw a shadow pass across her pale blue eyes.

"No," Derek said. "I'm just winding it up here, actually. Hang on a minute and we can go together." He gave her an odd look. Eden put it somewhere between perplexed and annoyed. "Now that you're here," he added.

"Okay," she said.

Derek went back to his office, and Eden thought—a moment too late—that she should have followed him, because the atmosphere in the office had become thick and unpleasant. Nobody seemed to know what to say, so no one even tried. *No small talkers here*, Eden thought. After giving Eden a tight, preemptory smile, Wendy turned around and went back to her desk, where she sat down at her computer and began typing as if her life depended on hitting the right combination of keystrokes. Eden was so uncomfortable that for a moment she considered walking out of the office or shouting an obscenity just to break the tension. But before she could do either of these inappropriate and tempting things, Derek came out, jacket over his arm, and took her elbow.

"Ready?" he asked. He seemed nervous now. Eden's unease was turning to something darker, blossoming inside her like a toxic flower.

"Yes," she said.

"Good night, everyone," Derek said to the room at large, and received a few murmurs in response. He didn't say a word to her, nor she to him, until they had clattered their way down the metal stairs, exited the building, and were striding down the wind-swept street. It was fully dark now, and the streetlights winked orange overhead.

"So," Derek said, "dinner it is." His voice sounded cramped somehow, and he was walking fast—too fast even for Eden.

"Derek, what's the damned rush?"

He stopped so abruptly, she almost ran into him. *Again,* Eden thought.

"Are you *angry* at me, Eden?" There was a note of disbelief in his voice. He held his hands out in a kind of supplication. "What is it?"

There was no point in not coming out with it, Eden thought. Even if it upset him—upset them both—and ruined the eve-ning. Letting it fester would be worse.

"Wendy . . . ," Eden started, and faltered. What she was going to say suddenly seemed ridiculous. The way Derek was looking at her now, rattled but with eyes full of love for her, was all the validation she really needed. Wasn't it?

"What about Wendy?"

"What were you doing with her? When I came into the office? It looked weird, Derek, I have to tell you. And Charles and Xan-der gave me these looks like . . . I don't know what. Like there was something going on that I shouldn't know about."

"You know," Derek said after a pause, "I told you to wait for me at home. I'm sorry I was late, Eden, but I did tell you."

An icy feeling crept up Eden's back. Why was he speaking in that soft, sad voice? This night had already taken so many left turns, she didn't know which way she was facing any longer. "And . . . ?" she said, her voice trembling a little. "I didn't. So, Derek?"

"I wanted to show Wendy . . ." He stopped and ran his hand

over his head. He always did that when he was trying to work out a problem, Eden thought. "You *did* interrupt, but it's not what you think. I had a whole thing planned, Eden." He sighed.

"What are you talking about? I'm confused."

"I *know*," Derek said. "Okay, I wanted to wait, but . . ." He reached into his pocket and pulled out a little red box. "Come here," he said, ushering her under an alcove lit in hues of red and gold by a string of Christmas lights. "I want you to have this," he said, and faltered. "No, that's not what I meant." He hung his head for a second; then he looked up, smiling sheepishly, opened the box, and pulled out a ring. "It belonged to my grandmother," he said. "She gave it to me when I was a kid. I know it's a strange thing to give a grandson, but for some reason she just skipped right over my mother . . . She never liked my mother much, to be perfectly honest. She was a strange one. Did I ever tell you—"

"Derek?"

"Sorry," he said, and smiled at her. Even in the low light Eden could see the slight tremble in his hand. "I love you, Eden, and I want to be with you always. I want you to marry me. No, not *want*—I mean, of course I want you to . . ." He reached for her hand, held it open, and placed the ring in her palm. It was a Claddagh ring—two golden hands holding a crowned heart—simple but delicately cut and very pretty. "Will you marry me, Eden?"

Eden felt the swirl of many emotions competing for prominence. There was love, of course, and passion too. She was surprised but not surprised, and she felt guilty for suspecting him—for allowing jealousy to snake its way into her brain, if only for a moment.

"Derek—"

"I'm going to get you a real one," he said. "A real diamond

engagement ring. But this . . . I think maybe my crazy grand-mother knew I'd find you one day. I think she meant for you to have it."

"I think it's beautiful, Derek," Eden said, and kissed his mouth hard. She put the ring on the fourth finger of her right hand with the heart pointed inward. *Spoken for.* "I will marry you. Yes, I will."

"Happy," Derek said, grinning. "I wondered. You had me go-ing there for a minute."

"I'm sorry," she said, wrapping her arms around him and pull-ing him close. "It was stupid of me to think . . . whatever. But it really didn't help that Charles and Xander gave me those looks when I walked in. As if they'd been caught at something."

Derek took Eden's hand and started walking again, more slowly this time, but with purpose. "They knew about . . . I was nervous, Eden, what can I say? I didn't tell them everything—just that I had something big planned. And then I showed Wendy the ring. I wanted to know if she thought it was good enough for you."

"What did she say?" Eden asked. She tugged at her scarf, pull-ing it tighter. The wind had died down a little, but the air was downright cold.

"She said it was beautiful and that . . ." Derek chuckled and gave Eden's hand a squeeze. "She said the whole institution of marriage was a vestige of the patriarchal enslavement of women, but she was sure you wouldn't see it that way."

"What?!"

"She's a feminist."

"I think she's into you, Derek."

"Wendy? Are you kidding? I do *not* think so."

"I saw the way she was looking at you." Eden leaned into

Derek as if to reassure him. "I'm not jealous, I'm really not, but I know what I saw."

Derek grunted in assent, but Eden could tell he wasn't really listening. He stopped walking and turned to her. "Babe, are you really, really hungry? Because I just want to take you home right now and take all your clothes off. Please?"

"I can wait," she said. "To eat, I mean."

"Oh," he said, exhaling heavily and picking up his pace. "Thank you."

Eden laughed and raced ahead of him.

CHAPTER 2

It was almost midnight by the time Putterman and his wife, the last guests to leave, finally said their good-byes. But even after Darcy had thanked them for coming *at least* three times and Peter had walked them to the front door, the two of them lingered for another fifteen minutes, Peter regaling them with one more story (which was either about golf or the new tax code—it was all the same to Darcy), while a draft from the open door blew in and reached Darcy all the way in the living room. As she gathered as many wineglasses and brandy snifters as she could carry, Darcy could hear Putterman guffawing over some bon mot or other and the shrill tone of his wife's voice as she chimed in. Putterman's first name was Larry and his wife was Anne, but

17

Darcy only ever thought of them as *Putterman and his wife*, just as she thought of all their guests tonight as *Peter's friends*. And that was odd, Darcy thought as she set the dirty glasses down on the kitchen counter, because this little soiree had been her idea.

It had been a successful dinner party as these things went. Darcy had cooked almost everything herself. The theme (because one had to have a theme) was *Mad Men*–inspired retro, which meant that there was a roast and a green bean casserole and several appetizers stuffed into pastry. The Baked Alaska had taken some doing, but Darcy had pulled that off too. She'd put a modern twist on everything, of course, and had enjoyed trussing the meat and torturing egg whites into a meringue, but midway through the process she'd been struck by the irony that of the ten people at the party, she was by far the youngest and the one who had no memory at all of the era from which she was drawing her culinary inspiration.

"Sounds like fun," Peter had said when she'd first floated the idea of the party. "Invite whomever you'd like."

But when Darcy drew up the guest list, she could think of nobody of her own to put on it. Unlike her husband, Darcy had never had a wide circle of friends. She had dated away most of her college years (which didn't really matter, since her communications degree was fairly useless anyway), too busy to form any close relationships with any other women. Then, when she'd gotten her real estate license and dived into the piranha tank that was the San Diego market, she found that friends were much harder to come by. In fact, before she met Peter, there were only two people Darcy felt she could call in the middle of the night if she needed to be bailed out of jail or talked off a ledge (her own definition of what constituted a real friend). The first was Maxine, another real estate agent in her office. The second was Josh, a drinking buddy who lived in her townhouse complex. Neither relationship had survived her marriage to Peter.

Although he never said so explicitly, Darcy knew that Peter didn't like the idea of her being so chummy with a guy—especially one with whom she'd downed many a shot. And while Maxine had been Darcy's maid of honor, their friendship was already fraying before the wedding. Maxine resented Peter or rather what Darcy was getting with Peter, and she didn't make a secret of her feelings. It was true that Peter was much, much wealthier than Darcy. And it was also true that she was younger than he, but not so much younger that they fell into a dirty-old-man-meets-brainless-bimbo cliché. There were seventeen years between them. It wasn't an unreasonable difference. She'd been a grown-up—twenty-seven, to be exact—when they married, and he'd treated her as one. She'd never thought of herself as a trophy wife, even though she could see how it would appear that way to Maxine. And to Josh. And to Peter's friends.

Darcy had made an effort to stay in touch with both Maxine and Josh after the wedding, but there was so much to do setting up the house and settling in to her new life that maintaining the relationships had been difficult. And she'd quit her job after she married Peter, which irritated Maxine even more. Darcy hadn't given it much thought then—she was happily wrapped up in Peter—and the years, six of them now, had just passed.

For a long time it hadn't mattered to Darcy that she'd brought neither friends nor family of her own to her marriage with Peter. Her parents had divorced when she was a girl and then rediscovered each other just after she'd turned twenty-one. They had remarried and moved to Belize, where they could "live as one with nature," happily spending whatever Darcy might have one day inherited. They'd shown up for her wedding but only because

Peter had sent them plane tickets and put them up in a nice hotel. Nonplussed by her parents acting younger than her husband, Darcy hadn't had the urge to see them since. And Peter seemed just fine with that, just as fine, in fact, as he felt about Darcy's lack of friends. He had assumed, as had Darcy, that his friends would become hers.

But it hadn't exactly worked out that way. Yes, she played tennis with the wives occasionally and had worked with a few of them on various charity events. There were plenty of dinner parties and even, one year, a joint Hawaiian vacation with Putterman and his wife. But none of these social connections had evolved into personal friendships. And as Darcy had served her martinis and canapés, she realized that aside from Peter, there wasn't a single person in her elegant dining room with whom she'd choose to spend time. Peter hadn't yet reached his mid-forties when they married. And the forties were a damned sight hipper than the fifties were looking to be if his friends were any indication. At least, she thought as she refilled her own snifter with the last of the Armagnac, her knowledge of real estate provided a slim overlap of interests with her guests and gave her something to talk about.

"Gone! I thought they'd never leave."

Darcy turned to see Peter approaching her, a large and only slightly drunken grin on his face.

"You mean Put—" She caught herself. "Larry and Anne? They did seem quite dug in, didn't they?"

Peter took the snifter from her hand and took a sip. "Don't get me wrong—he's a great guy, but . . ." His smile turned lascivious. "I've been waiting to get you alone." He pulled her closer to him and kissed her, biting her lips a little at the end. "Baby, you did an amazing job tonight," he said. "Gorgeous dinner, gorgeous hostess." He slid one hand down the back of her black cocktail dress and grabbed her backside as if weighing it out and reached into her upswept hair with the other. "Let it down," he murmured. "You know I like your hair down."

"Peter," she said, smiling, "the house is a mess. I mean, a *real* mess."

"Hell with it," he said, kissing her neck. "Let's go upstairs." He pulled gently at her hair, and Darcy obliged him by removing the clips that were holding it in place. All at once it fell—a blond waterfall cascading over his hands. "Mmm," was all Peter could say. He stepped back for a moment and appraised her, his eyes full of lust and appreciation. Darcy flushed with pride and pleasure.

"You're so beautiful," he said. "I'm a lucky man."

"So you had a good time?" she asked

"Of course I did. Not to mention that I have the most beautiful wife in the room, the city, the county. You make me look good, Dar."

"Well . . ."

"Let's go upstairs," he said again. "I have something special for you." He laughed. "And I think you know what it is."

"I feel like I should at least tidy up a little."

"Come on, Darcy." He was still smiling, but there was an edge creeping into his voice. Darcy knew that edge well. When he wanted her—and he wanted her often—Peter was unlikely to be put off. Perhaps it was naive, but Darcy had never worried about her husband cheating on her. He just seemed so passionate about her, and she couldn't imagine how he'd find the energy to match it with anyone else. His ardor was that consuming and one-pointed. Still, she hesitated. There was a cleaning service scheduled to show up in the morning (Darcy wasn't masochistic enough to saddle herself with the cleanup), but she hated the idea of coming downstairs in the morning to a trashed kitchen and dirty living room. If she could at least pick up the plates . . .

Peter slapped her behind just a tiny bit too hard. "I need you, babe." He pushed her in the direction of the stairs. "Don't make me go all caveman," he said. "I mean, I'd take you right here, but the floor's kind of hard and, well, my knees ain't what they used to be."

Darcy didn't like being pushed, but she liked Peter's attention and his need. A flame inside her ignited and began to burn. She moved toward the stairs, Peter following so close behind that his hands could roam her body and his lips could brush her hair.

"The lights," she said. "We should at least turn—"

"Fuck the lights," he said hoarsely. And then he picked her up—just hoisted her in his arms and carried her up the stairs. It was exciting, if not entirely comfortable, but Darcy worried a little about the effort it was costing him. He was red-faced and wheezing slightly when they got to the top of the staircase.

"Okay, okay," Darcy said. "Okay, Peter. Put me down."

"Thank you," he panted, almost dropping her.

Darcy led her husband into the bedroom, unzipping her dress as she walked. Peter had already shed his shoes and shirt and was unbuckling his pants by the time he fell onto the bed, grabbing Darcy and pulling her down with him.

"Thought I was going to die," he mumbled into her hair. "All night . . . looking at you . . ." He ran his tongue down the side of her neck and clutched at her dress, pulling it, clawing at the bra underneath. "Take . . . it . . . off."

Darcy took it off, all of it. For a moment, Peter stopped to watch her, his eyes blazing. His longing was palpable. It crashed over her, overwhelming and dragging her under like a riptide.

She felt a tremble go through her naked body; then he was on her, twining his hands into her hair, pressing his mouth against hers until her lips parted, and driving his body into hers so hard and fast she gasped with both pleasure and pain.

"Dar . . . ," he moaned. "Mine . . ."

You're hurting me.

"So . . . good."

Too rough.

Peter gripped her shoulders, shuddered, and collapsed on top of her. His breath was hot in her ear. He lay so still and became so heavy that Darcy thought he had fallen asleep. But when she shifted under him, he tightened his grip on her. "I love you, Darcy," he said.

"And I love you, Peter." She had to move; she had to get out from under him before she suffocated.

"I'm sorry," he said after she'd managed to slide herself and move him to the side. She took a deep breath.

"Sorry for what?" she said.

"I know that wasn't great for you." He traced his fingers along her sternum, then cupped her breast with his hand. "But I couldn't wait. I'll make it up to you." He rolled over and away from her. Darcy shivered as cold air hit her bare skin. Peter drew her back in to him, wrapping his arms around her. Protecting her. After several minutes, she thought again that he'd passed out, but he started laughing.

"What?" she said into his chest. "What is it?"

"Larry," he said.

"Larry what?"

"He gave me a late fiftieth-birthday gift." Peter sat up and leaned over the side of the bed, rooting around until he found his pants. Digging into the pocket, he pulled out three blue diamond-shaped pills and slapped them down on the bedside table.

"Viagra," he said.

"That's funny?"

"It is," Peter said. "It's funny because he thinks I'd need Viagra with a woman like you in my bed. If he could have seen what just went on—"

"Peter, that's an awful thought."

"You know what I mean," he said. "But I guess I'll hold on to it. You never know. Right, Dar?"

Darcy sighed, feeling exhausted but wired at the same time. "You don't need Viagra, honey," she said. It was what he wanted to hear, and, well, it was true.

Peter lay back down, spooning himself against Darcy. "Did I tell you how amazing you were tonight?" he said.

"Mmm."

"You could do that, you know. Party planning or consulting. Or whatever. I'm sure there's a business in it. You'd be good at it."

"I don't think so," she said. "I've already spent too much time in other people's houses over the years."

"You should do it," he said, as if she hadn't spoken. "I wouldn't mind."

"You wouldn't what?"

"It would be okay with me," he said.

Darcy felt something shift and sink inside her as if she'd ingested a stone. There was a change in the air; it was colder suddenly, and her body felt heavy. Peter leaned over her and kissed her lightly on the cheek. His hands were tender now, stroking her back, her hair, the curve of her hip. "Think about it," he said. "My Darcy darling."

He sighed into her hair; then, suddenly, he *was* asleep, his arms encircling her, keeping her close, even in unconsciousness. Darcy grew warm in his embrace, his breaths coming slow and regular against her back.

Darcy closed her eyes and waited for the release of sleep.

CHAPTER 3

PORTLAND
One year later

Eden was running. Her muscles were loose and her legs moved easily through the morning mist. She felt good—really good. She was wearing her new shoes—the special ones Derek had designed and named just for her. They were a pale pink with a scripted *E* embroidered just a couple of shades darker on the side. She looked down at her feet, at the barely pink blur moving across the flat gray of the pavement. She could feel the concrete on her soles as distinctly as if she'd been barefoot. But it didn't hurt to run—that was the difference. She loved these shoes. And she loved Derek for creating them, for knowing that pink was her favorite color and never making fun of her for it.

Eden headed away from her apartment and down to Waterfront Park, to the edge of the Willamette River, turning the corners by instinct. She'd taken this route through the city so many times, she could do it by muscle memory alone. She was still chilly, which was strange because it seemed as if she'd been running for quite a while. She should have warmed up by now. The sky was gloomy—not so strange for Portland, but it did seem to have become grayer and heavier since she'd been out. Eden breathed in but couldn't catch enough air. She coughed; it felt strange, choked off. The next breath was shallow too, even though she made the effort to draw in deeply. She slowed her stride, tried again—she was fine now, just a creeping feeling of weirdness. Something was not quite right. She was perspiring, her body sticky but cool. Her heart skipped a beat, and she coughed again. There was moisture on her face.

No, not now. Not again.

Eden turned right on Yamhill and headed down toward the water. Pioneer Courthouse Square was so busy today, even in the gloom. The sound of the fountain was loud in her ears as she passed. And something else too. Children? Eden thought she heard their shouts and laughter although she couldn't see them. Why weren't they in school? Were they on a field trip? She kept running, though her legs were already starting to feel tired. Eden wondered whether it was the shoes or whether she just hadn't stretched for long enough. She hoped it wasn't the shoes. Derek would be so disappointed.

The park and river were both in Eden's sight, mere blocks away. The bridges arching over the water looked particularly grim and foreboding under that slate-colored sky. But Eden was quite winded now and realized for the first time since she'd set off that she might actually have to stop and catch her breath before she got down to the park. She became dizzy, the buildings spinning and merging into one another. And then her heart went wild—crazy, irregular beats with no rhythm—fast, faster, too damned fast. What was happening to her heart? What was—

Take it easy. You're fine. Don't panic. Keep running.

Slowly, the city stopped spinning and came back into focus—cars running over manholes, the whoosh of TriMet buses, a clutch of yellow dandelions in a small corner of green grass. Eden could breathe again. Relief flooded her body, and her knees almost buckled.

Now the water came into view, gray like the sidewalk and blending into the gray of the sky. So many shades of gray. Eden glided through them all, running without effort once again. Her body felt weightless, almost airborne. It was good—it was all right, no need to worry. She would be fine. She and Derek would be fine. They were going to be married in the Rose Gardens, and it was going to be beautiful. She just needed to keep running. If she kept running, it would all be fine.

Then the landscape changed abruptly even as Eden stared straight at it. The water was no longer in front of her. She had gotten turned around somehow and was running uphill, back in the direction of her apartment. At least that was where she *thought* she was headed, because the street she was on now looked unfamiliar. Eden felt a tremor of fear. She should know this place; she had been here before. She was still running, but now her strides had slowed. There was something in her way.

Something was wrong.

But over there—Eden knew the buildings now coming into view; there were the tan and chrome structures she recognized, the modern ones that had grown up around her own old brick apartment building.

But where was it?

Eden felt a crushing need to get home. Her legs had started to strain, her feet sticking. She looked down. The ground had turned to sand, dunes of it all around her. But she pushed on because she could see it now just over a ridge that had never been there before—her building. Home. She kept moving, every stride hurting her now, her teeth grinding and her calves cramping. Somehow she was still running. She couldn't stop running.

Eden was standing at the entrance to her apartment building, at the big glass doors that were supposed to open into the foyer, but something was wrong. The engraved plate set into the brick above the entrance was supposed to read THE MIDLAND APARTMENTS, but it didn't. Instead it stated OUR LADY OF THE SACRED HEART CHURCH. The letters were black, thick, and calligraphic.

When had they put a church here?

Eden leaned forward and pressed her face up against the glass. There were shelves and shelves of board games stacked precariously, as if someone had just shoved them in without thinking. The boxes were all red, and she couldn't read any of the titles. She moved her eyes to the left and right, looking for the door. They must have moved it because it used to be right there where that announcement board was standing. It was the old-fashioned kind, spongy and charcoal-colored, the sort you had to press white plastic letters into. Eden squinted at it through the darkening glass until she could make out what it said.

In Memoriam
Eden Harrison
Viewing and Services: four o'clock p.m.

Eden's hands fell heavily to her sides. Her chest bloomed with pain. She didn't go to church. She didn't know this place. She didn't belong here. She started to cry, and the tears burned the sides of her face. Everything hurt. Where was Derek? She should have called him. If only she had thought to call him, none of this would have happened. And now it was too late.

She was already dead.

"Eden, it's okay. I'm here."

She could hear Derek's voice, and she turned toward the sound of it even though she didn't expect to find him. She was already dead.

"Eden? I'm here, honey."

Eden opened her eyes. She could see Derek's face now through the fading colors of her dream, and he was as real as she was. She was still alive. Or was it *not dead yet*? Her broken heart seized and shuddered—*symptomatic arrhythmia*—making her cough. The effort exhausted her, but not enough to prevent anxiety and adrenaline from surging through her body. Every time it happened now, she thought it might be the last time.

Not yet.

She hated herself for being so afraid.

"I was dreaming about . . ." Eden had to catch her breath. "I had the running dream again. But . . ."

"Just take it easy, Eden. It's okay; it's okay." Derek fussed around the bed, his hands smoothing the blankets and pillows, his fingers coming to rest in her hair and brushing it from her face. His eyes, creased with the strain of caring for her, looked like crushed blue ice. There was love there, Eden could see it, but there was also fear and the kind of sadness that comes just before real grief sets in. He was already mourning her—his eyes were saturated with it. She reached over and took his hand in her own. His was warm—*alive*—and hers was cold and clammy. She avoided looking at her bloodless fingers, their nails colored lavender from lack of oxygen, and kept her eyes fixed on his—on that sad, fractured blue—and waited for her breath.

"I miss it so much," she said finally, hearing the tremor in her voice.

"I know," he said.

"I think that's why I keep dreaming about it. I just want to run again."

"You will, Eden."

"Derek—"

"No, don't—"

"The other part of the dream—"

"Eden, you—"

"I'm sorry, Derek. This isn't the way it was supposed to be. I hate that you have to do this."

"Do what?" Derek leaned back, a flicker of something—annoyance? distaste?—shadowing his face for a moment. "I don't *have* to do anything. I'm *not* doing anything." He sighed, blinked hard, looked away from her. "I wish there was more I *could* do." He caught himself then, gave a quick shake of his head, and set his jaw.

"Can I get you something, Eden? Anything you want . . ."

Eden sat up in bed, disgusted with how much effort it took. The dream was almost gone now, just a few dark tatters lingering on the edge of her vision.

"How long was I out?" she asked. "I don't even remember falling asleep."

"Not long." He was lying. He'd gotten better at it lately, Eden thought, but not quite good enough.

"I'm going to make some tea," he said. "Want some?"

"Sure. That would be nice."

Derek got up and walked in the direction of the kitchen, then stopped halfway as if he had forgotten something and stared out the window at the gathering Portland gloom. She'd fallen in love with him right there at that window three years ago—the big oak creaking in the wind and rain lashing the glass. It hadn't been a special occasion—just grilled cheese sandwiches and tomato soup for dinner and the two of them watching TV. She'd gotten up to look outside at the shiny black pavement and winking orange streetlights.

"Looks like a storm," she'd said, and suddenly Derek was there behind her, lifting the hair from her neck, the soft touch of his lips on her skin.

"I'm so glad I'm in here with you," he'd whispered.

She'd grabbed his hand and squeezed, too choked with emotion to answer him. That was it—the moment she knew. There was never any question that she and Derek were good together and were probably in it for the long haul, but in that second she felt love come in heavy and sweet and fill her completely.

Watching him now, Eden wondered if Derek was remembering the same thing. She was going to ask him, going to get absurdly and inappropriately romantic, but he saved her by sighing again and moving into the tiny kitchen to put on the kettle.

This place was too small, but they'd been very happy here. *She* had been happy here. In a way, she'd grown up in this apartment—had gone from being a naive girl to, well, a woman, for lack of a better word. It had been her first place on her own out of college and here, inside these ivy-weakened walls, she'd become acquainted with herself and figured out what she liked and what she didn't. She'd started running. She'd gotten her job at the Columbia School. She'd become comfortable with herself and her own rhythms, discovering that she could trust her instincts and that she actually *liked* spending time alone. She'd become emotionally self-sufficient. And then, when the time was right, she'd met Derek.

Derek had kept his place even though they ended up spending almost all their time here. But as soon as they announced their engagement, they started looking for a bigger place. They'd found one so quickly that Eden suspected Derek had already scoped it out—a lovely little house in the Pearl District, a "starter home," so close she could stroll down and visit this old building if she wanted to. And then, and then, and then . . .

They weren't going to get there, Eden thought. They weren't going to make it to the starter home. *She* was going to stop before *they* could start.

Eden could hear Derek rustling in the kitchen. He must be trying to find things to do, she thought, because it didn't take that long to pour hot water over a tea bag. Maybe he was afraid to look at her and show her his own fear. But no, Eden knew that wasn't true. Sometimes she did this—tried to think of reasons why Derek was getting irritated or fed up with her or reasons why she didn't want to be with him anymore; yet it was pointless and silly—*childish*—because she always came back to the same conclusion. He loved her. She loved him. And that was going to remain true until she died.

She was going to die.

She heard Derek's words in her head: *Sooner or later, we're all going to die. It's not your time yet.* He'd said that at least a hundred times since that first horrible day in the hospital. And she'd believed him, hung on to his words, *internalized positive energy*, but it was getting so hard to do that now. The fact was she needed a heart—a live, beating, human heart that wasn't her own—and as every day went by, that prospect seemed less and less likely.

Don't give up, Eden. Derek had told her that too. She could feel the tears now, wet and sticky in the corners of her eyes. She'd always felt so lucky, so *fortunate*. After all, how many girls wound up with Prince Charming? It was one of the most pointed ironies of her situation now.

But it wasn't just Derek. Until the day she'd collapsed in the park, Eden felt she'd gotten more than her fair share of good fortune. It was part of the reason she'd dedicated herself to working with special-needs children. It was hard work, but Eden had always felt a strong sense of responsibility about the providence that had been showered on her. You had to make good use of what you were given, she thought. You had to pay it forward. And it wasn't as if she didn't like what she did. As hard as it was, Eden liked her work and loved her kids. Of course, she was no good to them now, was she? She remembered how, in the early days of this illness, when everyone still thought she was going to recover quickly, her friends and workmates at the school had the kids make her little cards and projects—all kinds of brightly colored construction paper hearts—with sweet messages enclosed. It had been a while since she'd heard from anyone there, though just how long Eden couldn't tell anymore. Her world had shrunk down now to inside these walls. How she missed her kids. She could see their little faces and dirty hands now, outstretched. Their hands were always dirty. It didn't matter how many times you took them to the sink; they always managed to find something grimy to play in . . .

"Honey?" Derek was standing over her with a steaming mug

in his hand. She hadn't even seen him come back into the room. Had she fallen asleep again? "Do you want to just rest a little more?"

There was a new furrow above his eyes. When had that happened?

"No, it's okay. I'm going to get up. I'm going to get out of this bed."

"Let me help you—"

"No, Derek, don't." She wiped at her eyes. "I'm sorry. I didn't mean . . ."

"I know. It's okay."

"No, it isn't." Eden moved herself slowly, laboriously, catching an unwelcome glimpse of herself in the full-length mirror as she got out of bed. Sickness was so ugly. They didn't tell you about that part of it. She'd been pretty not too long ago; long, shiny hair, clear dark eyes, a fit runner's body . . . That was all gone now, replaced by this skinny, pale woman who looked twice her age. Vanity. Her sorry sight was the least of her worries, but it was still hard to take.

I'm not even thirty, Eden thought.

It had started to rain. Eden could see small drops on the window, and the sky outside looking heavy enough to fall right on top of them both. Derek followed her to the table and sat down next to her, just a little too close, as if he expected her to tip over at any moment. She laughed a little because the whole thing seemed suddenly absurd, and it made Derek smile.

"I'm all right, you know," she said.

"Yes."

"For now, Derek."

He pushed the tea toward her, and she took it, warming her hands on the mug. The smile had vanished from his face. Her fault. Again. Add crushing guilt to the list of things they didn't tell you about when you got sick like this.

"I think we need to talk about what's going to happen," she said. She tried to breathe deeply, fear gnawing at her again, but it was impossible. She could never get enough air anymore. Worse, she was starting to forget what it felt like to be able to just open up her lungs and feel the oxygen flooding her body.

"What do you mean, Eden?" He used to call her *Edie* all the time, she thought. Now it was always *Eden*.

"You know . . . about . . ." She cleared her throat, stalling. "I keep having these dreams, Derek. Not just about running." She wanted to tell him about the church, about how she knew what it was like to be dead already, but those were hard words to pick and she was so tired of hurting him. There was a scraping sound against the window. Branches? The wind was picking up outside, and that oak really needed to be trimmed.

"Look," he said, "I know what you're going to say; I do." He tucked a strand of hair behind her ear—such an intimate, sweet gesture. *Heartbreaking.* "And I know how you feel. I mean, no, I don't know exactly how you feel; how could I? But I know what I feel, Eden, and I know what's true. You are going to have the transplant. It *is* going to happen."

"Derek, you can't know that. And you should—"

"I can't explain it to you," he said. His eyes were fierce now, burning with need. She felt herself fading under their heat. She couldn't do this anymore—couldn't keep up this losing game. "It's not false hope, Eden. It's not. I know about all the difficulties and the challenges and . . ." He leaned forward and brushed his lips against her cheek. He smelled like lemons. "I can *feel* this. You have to believe me."

"Okay," Eden said, and she had to wait a moment to catch her breath again. "So I don't have to go through that whole speech about how you should date other women once I'm gone?" She tried to punctuate the line with a wry smile, but the effort it took to be flip had exhausted her. Derek smiled. What a trouper he was.

"Actually, I think I might like to hear that speech," he said. "Could be interesting."

"I love you, Derek," she said.

She expected him to answer her, to tell her he loved her too, more than anything and forever and always, but he didn't. He kissed her, not lightly as if he feared she would break, but with passion and desire.

She leaned into him, sighing, and let him wrap himself around her. She remembered how, when they were in the first, hottest flush of their romance—that time when every lyric of every love song was written expressly for them—she had lain in his arms on a cold rainy day just like this one and thought, *I can die happy now.*

Maybe it was wrong—a dangerous slap at fate—but Eden couldn't help thinking it would have been better if it had happened right then. Dying happy was no longer an option.

She missed him already.

CHAPTER 4

SAN DIEGO

Darcy stood in front of the mirror, wasting time by playing with her hair. She wasn't hungry—hadn't been hungry for months, really—and didn't feel up to pretending to go into a rapture over a plate of *linguini ai funghi* or whatever tonight's "made special for you, signora" offering was going to be. But Peter would notice if she seemed anything less than ecstatic over dinner, and he would get "concerned" and comment. Then she would have to go into some endless explanation of how she was feeling and what was wrong and fabricate yet another story about her hormones being out of whack or cramps or something else that veered deeply enough into *women's issues* that Peter was turned off and changed the subject.

But, she thought, that kind of parry probably wouldn't even

work now. Lately, Peter had been soldiering through his distaste of such things (he was so *not* the kind of man who would run out to the store for tampons if you needed them) so that he could talk to her about them in an informed way. He'd been doing some research, he said, and he'd decided that it wasn't normal for her to be experiencing so much distress with her cycle. He was worried, he said, and thought maybe she should see a doctor.

Of course, what he meant by *worried* was, *Why are you coming up with excuses to avoid sex?* Because if there was one thing Darcy had never avoided before, it was sex with her husband. He'd counted on that; for a long time, so had she. It had been one of the cornerstones of their relationship. *Had* been.

Darcy sighed. Once Peter started doing research, all bets were off. He was like that about everything outside the topic of money, his particular calling. If he didn't have direct knowledge of something—be it roof tiles, the potential health hazards of cell phones, or, in this case, the secrets of the womb—he *researched* it. Extensively. And then he became his own expert, and you couldn't tell him anything. She had once found this quality of his endearing. But now she was either going to have to put on a better game face or be prepared to start discussing what he'd learned about the delicate interplay between estrogen and pro- gesterone and how it affected mood. Because once he got started, Peter was unlikely to stop. And that was especially true lately.

"There's this thing called premenstrual dysphoric disorder," he'd said the last time she'd begged off a roll in the hay. "It's this condition where you literally go crazy before your period. It's documented! Who knew?"

"Every woman knows, Peter," she'd said. "It's something we live with constantly. There's just a new name for it now. And I've been lucky to have missed it all this time. But our bodies change."

"No, honey, I'm not talking about regular PMS," he said (as if he knew anything about *regular* PMS). "It's a whole other thing. I read this journal where it says . . ." and then Darcy had drifted off, as she had so many times before, to the small, protected space inside her own head where nobody else could enter.

Anyone listening to that conversation or any of the similar ones they'd had would have been impressed by the depth of Peter's concern and love for her. And he did love her. Darcy knew that love well, had depended on it, and had returned it too. But there was so much more to it than that. Peter's love was inextricably tied to his need to control, to *manage* everything in his life, including her. It was subtle, and nobody who hadn't experienced it directly would have been able to understand it; yet she felt it in every comment and gesture that Peter made. His notion of who Darcy was—an ideal, something he had created in his own imagination—with every passing day had less and less to do with the flesh-and-blood woman he had married. Darcy would never be able to convince anyone of this, but the truth of it was that Peter wasn't a good husband—at least, not anymore. There were the little things (though not so little, she supposed, if those had been the *only* things), such as his not being tuned to her. He didn't understand her very nature. Not that this stopped him from trying to shape that nature—forcibly if he had to—to one that suited him. But what was worse, he felt completely justified in his lack of understanding. His reality was the only one that mattered.

And then there were the big things. Well, *one* big thing. Darcy didn't want to think about this—couldn't, in all honesty, really wrap her mind around it. Because if she called it what anyone else would call it . . . But no, it wasn't abuse. Because if Darcy were being *abused*, that would make her sad and stupid and low class. And that was not who she was. What Peter did—that specific roughness of his—wasn't really abuse. He didn't hit her. Not really. There were never *events* or fights that ended in situations where one might leave or call the police (heaven forbid *that* ever happening). And he was never apologetic about those times when he got physical with her. If it were abuse, he would say he was sorry. He would promise never to do it again. There would be a look in his eye—something, some admittance of wrongdoing. She'd seen enough movies-of-the-week, she'd watched enough *Oprah*, and she knew how it worked. The thing was, sometimes, afterward, Darcy wasn't even sure anything had actually happened at all. It was just who he was—an extension of his need to control her.

Darcy felt a cold shiver run up her back. Control—that was the problem. It had begun so slowly, Darcy hadn't even noticed at first. At the beginning of their marriage, the seventeen years between them hadn't seemed to matter—Peter was . . . youthful and an equal in spirit, if not financially. But then, by degrees, he'd become more and more like her keeper. That was a terrible word, but that was what it felt like sometimes. He made suggestions that weren't really suggestions, gave hints that were more like commands. She went along, able to shrug it off until about a year ago. That dinner party they'd had—as innocuous as it seemed at the time—was a turning point in Darcy's mind. And the more Peter pushed, the more he tried to shape her or . . . change her, the more she retreated. So it wasn't abuse. She felt a flutter in her throat—as if she'd swallowed something small and winged—and she coughed reflexively.

But, Darcy thought now, maybe control wasn't the real problem at all. Maybe it was just that he wasn't her soul mate. On some level she'd always known this, but it hadn't mattered before because, well, because she hadn't really believed in the concept of soul mates then. One's soul was one's own—one was born alone; one died alone. It wasn't a pessimistic worldview; it was practical. But now . . . Now she knew differently.

Darcy felt her blood surge and tingle—an automatic response every time she thought about—

Stop it, she told herself.

She *had* loved Peter; it was why she had married him. She'd never been one of those women just out for the cash—it wouldn't have worked for her. She had to have felt love—if not a raging fire, at least a flame. And she had. Even now, she had feelings for her husband. But it was love of a very different sort. Because if Darcy knew nothing else at this moment in her life, she finally understood what real love was. It was huge and painful, ecstatic, dangerous and all-consuming.

You couldn't help whom you fell in love with.

Darcy stared at the sullen image in the mirror. That old wives' tale was true; if you frowned long enough, your face would freeze in an ugly position, and you'd be stuck with it for life. She couldn't remember the last time she'd seen herself smiling in this mirror. Was she even capable of it anymore? There was a line—right there between her eyes—faint, but getting deeper. She made a conscious effort to relax the muscles in her face and soften her expression, and she studied the effect. It worked—almost.

Darcy twisted her long hair into a knot and clipped it with a large turquoise and silver barrette. Her reflection said too severe, and she let it down again, shaking it loose, watching it ripple in yellow waves around her face. Maybe if she lifted up just one side . . . No, now she just looked like some teenaged half-wit. She ran her fingers through it, tossed it, and brushed it one more time. What to do with it? The possibilities were almost limitless and could keep her standing here all night.

She picked up a lipstick from the vanity. It was the same bright red as her "I'm Not Really a Waitress" nail polish and the piping on her black halter dress. The combination set off her blond hair and just-bronze-enough skin very nicely. She pursed her lips and dabbed, leaning into the mirror and seeing, behind her own reflection, that of Peter, who was standing in the doorway, smiling. He was leaning into the doorjamb, arms crossed. Darcy wondered how long he'd been there and why she hadn't seen him before. A tremor of guilt twitched at her eye. She put the lipstick down.

"Beautiful," he said. "As always."

Darcy attempted a smile—made it happen.

"Are you almost ready, honey? I'm getting kind of hungry." His smile broadened. He was overdoing it on the golf course, Darcy thought, because his face was looking way too tanned and was starting to lean toward being leathery. It gave him an almost simian appearance that wasn't flattering. Set against those unnaturally white teeth of his, the overall effect was almost ghoulish; yet he was still a good-looking guy. Even now, Darcy had to admit that and, in some perverse way, took pride in it. The tangy orange scent of his Hermès cologne wafted over to her on a gust of air.

"Almost," she said. "I'm just . . ."

"You know," he said, "I read somewhere that Eric Clapton wrote 'Wonderful Tonight' while he was waiting for his wife to get ready for dinner. She couldn't decide what to wear, so he started strumming and came up with a masterpiece."

"Yes, well . . ." Darcy hoped he wasn't going to go off on an

Eric Clapton or Beatles or, worse, a Rolling Stones tangent now. She didn't think she could stand it. It just made him seem older and the gulf between them wider. And he still thought he was being hip—even after she'd told him, repeatedly, that her own *father* listened to those old fossils and that the Stones had long been considered a family act.

But Peter didn't seem to care about that. There was a time when she'd tried to get him to listen to music that was happening *now*, but it was an oil-and-water proposition. He just wasn't interested. Darcy would never know if things might have turned out differently if he had been. But now, watching him lean toward her as he got ready to serenade her with lyrics that were decades old, she suspected it wouldn't have made any difference at all.

"Honey," he half sung, "you look wonderful tonight."

"Peter . . ."

"No, really. You're gorgeous, Darcy."

He meant it, Darcy knew.

"I just have to fix my hair," she said. "It'll just take me a second."

"Leave it down," he said. "Please leave it down." Peter pushed himself off the jamb and walked up behind her. She watched him in the mirror. She saw his hands go slow motion into her hair and lift it, his fingers sliding through it and the strands falling like a shining, collapsing web. She felt the warmth of his body behind her, his breath on her neck. He was like a man hypnotized. It was the same now as when they'd first started dating. Peter wanted to wrap himself in her hair; he wanted to tie his wrists together with it. He loved to touch it, to feel it on his skin. Darcy thought he'd never forgive her if she ever decided to cut it. "Mmm." He breathed in deeply. "Sister Golden Hair, you are."

"Peter, no. Don't sing it—no."

But Peter couldn't stop himself. "Come on, it's a classic, honey." He hummed a few bars of the America song and let the hair fall through his hands.

"Well," she said, "at least you're in the right key."

He started laughing—just a chuckle at first, but it blossomed into full-throated glee.

Despite herself, Darcy laughed along. She couldn't help it.

"Where are we going?"

They were driving west on Del Mar Heights Road, the ocean before them in the near distance—a sparkling blanket made silver and gold by the setting sun. Darcy had expected him to make the turn north and head to Il Giardino, the new restaurant he'd recently discovered and was now obsessed with, but he'd kept going straight, which could only mean he had something else in mind.

"Peter?"

"Relax, honey."

"I am relaxed. I'm just . . . Thought we were going to—"

"The Plaza," he said. "We haven't been to Poquette for quite a while." Darcy stole a look at him. His hands were easy on the steering wheel, but she couldn't read the expression on his face. A momentary panic clutched at her gut, and she felt her shoulders tense. But no, there was no way he knew anything. No way he *could*.

"I've missed it," he said. "Been thinking about that mustard-crusted catfish of theirs."

"Okay."

"You've no objection, right?" He gave her a smile, a quick flash of teeth. "I thought you loved that place."

"I do."

"Okay then. All good."

But it wasn't all good, and Darcy knew it. If there was one thing that marriage had taught her, it was how to interpret her husband's rhythms—all the little gestures and tics that made up his personality—and Darcy could feel a discordant note hanging in the air between them. He was too quiet, just a little bit too reserved. Anxiety rippled through her as he guided the car down toward the ocean and turned right onto the Coast Highway. Then, as they wended their way through picturesque Del Mar (or "Olde Del Mar" if you were a tourist paying extra for the view and the T-shirt to go with it), that anxiety turned into dread—knotted and cold at the base of her spine. She found herself unable to banter, to make the kind of light conversation the evening seemed to call for. Her tongue was heavy and her mouth dry. And Peter wasn't helping. His eyes were fixed straight ahead, calm and still. He was holding something back.

By the time they arrived at the Plaza, parked the car, and walked upstairs to the restaurant, the silence between them had become thick and uneasy. Peter put his hand on her arm just above her elbow, a gesture both chivalrous and proprietary, and guided her toward Poquette. Darcy's stomach fluttered and flipped. There was no way she was going to be able to eat with any kind of gusto tonight. She simply wasn't that good of an actress. A drink would have been more than welcome, but here, in this place, she wouldn't trust herself with more than half a glass of wine.

The big glass doors opened with a rush of air bringing with it the aroma of lemon, rosemary, and expensive perfume. They were inside. Darcy kept her eyes cast down on the blue-and-white tiles of the entryway. The controlled din of the dining room was loud in her ears—laughter and conversation, glasses, plates and silver-ware clinking, and then the maître d' welcoming them. "So nice to see you back," he said.

Peter remained quiet until they were seated at "their" table on the patio—best view in the house that had so many beautiful ones to choose from—and they had their water poured and their wineglasses filled. She had barely heard him order the wine and had no idea what it was other than white and, she was sure, costly. When the bread basket arrived, Darcy kept her focus fixed on it, as if the fate of nations depended on her maintaining eye contact with a slice of rustic sourdough.

Peter lifted his wineglass. "So," he said, "I have good news."

Darcy looked up at him, the glow of another beautiful California sunset shimmering between them. She knew in her heart that this moment was a before-and-after dividing line and wished she could freeze it, turn everything off, and just go home. She forced a smile. The bright red lipstick felt heavy and slick on her lips.

"Yes?" she said.

"We're moving!"

No. No, we're not.

"What?"

"I'm going to explain all of it in a second, love." Peter took a long swig from his glass. He was no idiot—he knew she'd hate the very idea of moving—but he didn't care. This much Darcy did not have to be told. "But first, I just want to say that this is a really good thing. I know you love it here—we *both* love it here—but it's time to move on. I've gotten an offer . . . and even if it wasn't the kind of offer that only an insane person would pass up, I've still been thinking that it's time to leave California."

Time to move on? No, it isn't time to move on.

"Where, Peter?"

"That's the best part—we're moving to New York!"

Darcy shook her head, unable to stop herself. "No, Peter. I'm not going to New York. I'm not moving." She was trembling, her body turning into water. She had to stop. She couldn't stop.

Peter sighed, and Darcy could hear the impatience in it. He had probably been hoping she'd be easier, and now he was going to have to do some work. But work or no work, it wasn't going to make a difference. "Just hear me out before you snap the lid on it so fast," he said. "There are several *million* reasons to move. And we are going to live in the most beautiful place. I'm going to show you the photos—"

"You've picked out a *place*? Without asking me?"

"Listen—"

"Peter, no. I'm not moving." Her stomach churned. Her heart raced, and she could feel a flush spreading across her face. Peter picked up his butter knife and turned it around in his fingers. His color had risen too, darkening his cheeks and jaw. He waited a beat, opened his mouth, then closed it. He placed the knife back on the table.

"Darcy," he said, "you have to understand something. This isn't a question. I'm telling you. I'm not asking."

His voice was hard, heavy, and warning in a way she didn't often hear. But they were in a public place. *This* public place. He hadn't even talked to her about it—not even a mention. When had it come to this? Had she been *that* removed? She panicked, thinking about what she might have said or done, anything that might have given her away. But New York? No, it couldn't happen.

Only then, when the full weight of what he was saying finally settled, did Darcy raise her eyes and look beyond him, across the dining room and over to the bar. The two bartenders stood with their backs to the dining room, but Darcy knew that the one on the right sensed exactly where she was sitting and could feel her presence as keenly as she felt his. Her senses sharpened, Darcy thought she could see the dark hair curling at the nape of his neck and feel the curve and solidity of his shoulder under her palm. Silently, she begged him to turn around.

She wondered again if this was all some elaborate way of telling her that she'd been found out. But no, Peter would never . . . It just wasn't in his nature to be so subtle. She felt the touch of her husband's hand on hers, and she shivered, desperate to pull it away.

"Do you understand what I'm saying, Darcy?" Now his voice was cold. He'd made up his mind. Of course he wasn't asking.

Turn around. Look at me. Darcy's heart lurched in her chest. *Help me.*

CHAPTER 5

Darcy regretted cutting her hair the second she left the salon. Or maybe before, but while she was in the chair, the overly enthusiastic stylist chattering on about how wonderful Darcy was going to look after she was finished—about how her very life would change with this new cut—Darcy couldn't hear the voice in her head telling her that it was a big mistake. *It's only hair,* she kept telling herself. *It will grow.* Besides, there was the excitement of a change and, more importantly, of being able to control that change. All of this took her away; it transported her. She sipped her complimentary mint tea, watched the flash of the scissors, and, for an hour or so, she listened intently to the mindless chatter of the silly girl wielding them.

But then, as soon as she'd shelled out more money than any haircut was worth and stumbled out of the dim, perfumed interior of the salon into the glare of reality, the thrill evaporated. Despite the warmth of the midday sun, Darcy shivered when the air hit her newly bare shoulders. Peter was going to hate it. Of course he was. Wasn't that why she had done it in the first place? Why she'd slunk off to a salon all the way in Pacific Beach that she'd never been to before?

Yes, Darcy thought as she surveyed herself in the bathroom mirror, and yes. Technically, it wasn't even that short—the blunt ends grazed the top of her collarbone—but that flowing net of golden hair was gone.

"I like it," she said out loud to her reflection. But she wasn't even fooling herself anymore.

It had been two weeks since their disastrous dinner at Poquette, but she and Peter hadn't had a real conversation about moving since then. Darcy knew he hadn't changed his mind—Peter was immovable once he'd decided on something—but he hadn't given any outward indications that he—they—were going anywhere either. The tension of not knowing his plan or his timeline was eating at Darcy, but she couldn't bring herself to do the simplest thing, which was to just ask him. Some part of her held to the irrational belief that if she said nothing, if she just pretended he'd never even mentioned moving, she could erase the evening at Poquette and carry on as if it had never happened. Not that this was working. In fact, her magical thinking was failing miserably, and she had only to look in the mirror to find evidence of that. Darcy knew she was going to have to do something much more definitive than cut her hair if she wanted to stop Peter from going ahead with moving, but she was stuck—frozen in time, space, and her own head.

She thought again about that terrible dinner, and angry tears stung her eyes. She'd kept looking over to the bar, willing him to turn around, desperate to see his eyes, but either he couldn't or wouldn't, and Darcy had been afraid to attract too much attention to herself. After Peter's announcement, she'd tried to make it seem that she was just staring into space, but she felt as if every staff member in the restaurant could read her thoughts. The maître d' stared at them across the dining room—always so anxious to make sure Peter was happy—and the waiters and waitresses peered at them as they passed between tables. Darcy was used to this. She and Peter were an attractive couple, but it went way beyond the physical. It was no secret that Peter had plenty of money and that Darcy belonged to him. The waiters and waitresses at Poquette, never obvious or rude with their glances, always gave her a surreptitious once-over. But that night it felt as if they were all either ignoring her or glaring at her—especially the waitresses, a few of whom Darcy could even name. It was almost as if they *knew* something. Still, *he* wouldn't turn around—wouldn't look in her direction. Peter went on and on, his questions becoming more rhetorical and accusatory. Why couldn't she be more supportive? Why was she acting as if he'd just told her he was moving her to Siberia instead of to the lap of New York City luxury? Why did she always have to act so *wounded* about everything?

At some point, Darcy got up and told Peter she had to use the restroom. As she rounded the bar, her heart started beating hard enough to make her head hurt. He was there, ice and tall glasses in his beautiful, capable hands. He looked up as she passed—finally—and smiled because it would be rude not to. She was a customer, after all—a regular. There was so much she tried to convey in what must have been the look of desperation she gave him.

Help me. Please help me.

She had to walk by quickly. It was all so dangerous. Then it was just her, alone, crying in the cinnamon-scented bathroom, holding her fingers to her eyes, and trying to keep her makeup from smudging. By the time she came out, he had vanished from behind the bar. Her eyes scanned the dining room and couldn't find him. There was a moment, as she wove unsteadily back to their table with all those eyes on her again, when she thought perhaps it was a signal. He was waiting for her out back, in the kitchen, *somewhere*. She wanted to run, but she kept walking.

"What took you so long?" Peter asked when she sat back down. He'd ordered dessert for both of them. He didn't even like dessert.

She couldn't remember anything else they'd said to each other or even if they'd exchanged any more words. She couldn't remember the drive home. All she remembered was the feel of his hand on her shoulder as he escorted her out of Poquette. It was firm—too firm—his fingers digging slightly into the soft space above her collarbone, just this side of painful. And she remembered the crazy and desperate thought flying across her brain that perhaps if she made love to him—seduced her own husband— he'd magically relent. She hated herself for even entertaining such a notion, because just as quickly she knew it would never work. Not that she was capable of it. Not then. Not after seeing *him*. But in any case, screwing herself into Peter's good graces wasn't much of a plan.

But, she realized as she stared at her short-haired reflection in the mirror, neither was this.

Darcy ran her fingers through her new hair one more time, turned around, and walked out of the bathroom just as the front door opened. Peter was home. She was seized by a momentary and ridiculous panic over what he was going to say. There was probably some kind of psychological term for this, Darcy thought—misdirected guilt or something like that. He was whistling; the sound bounced off the tile in the entryway. It was new tile and had cost them plenty. Italian blues and greens— Peter had picked it out himself. It was quite beautiful, but ever since it had been laid, the house seemed full of echoes.

"Darcy!" he called out. "You home?"

He sounded in a good mood. Darcy struggled to remember what he'd said he was doing today—where he'd been while she was busy transforming her look. She couldn't even remember whether or not they'd spoken this morning. Was there another dinner plan she'd forgotten about?

"I'm here," she called, and walked toward him.

"Hey, babe," he said, following the sound of her voice, "I was thinking—" He stopped short when he caught sight of her. She waited, too many beats for comfort, and watched as the expressions danced across his face. Surprise first, then alarm, disappointment, and then, finally, what she'd been expecting—anger that spread and hardened across his features.

"What was it," she said, "that you were thinking?"

"What the hell, Darcy?"

Despite herself, she put her hand to her hair again. Guilty as charged. "You don't like it?" There was an edge in her voice, and she didn't like the sound of it.

"No, I don't. I think it looks like shit."

"Peter—"

"Why do you want to look like every other stupid, fake housewife on the block? Because that's what I see when I look at you now, Darcy."

She'd known he was going to dislike it, but somehow hearing

the contempt in his voice now surprised and angered Darcy. "It's just hair, Peter."

He shrugged, his mouth turning down at the corners. "You're a big girl," he said. "You do what you want to do. Doesn't matter what I think, right?" He brushed past her on his way to the kitchen. For the first time, Darcy noticed he was carrying a bag from his favorite wine store in Solana Beach.

"It matters what you think, Peter. Of course it matters what you *think*. I just don't know why you're so upset. You can't tell me it looks bad, because I know it's a good haircut. It's just *hair*." There was a note of hysteria in her voice now, and she tried to control it, tamp it down before he picked up on it.

"Not upset," he said, his voice fading into the kitchen. "Whatever you do . . ."

Darcy thought about going upstairs, shutting herself up in the bedroom, and blocking everything out, but she knew it wouldn't work. That kind of swoon had never been in her repertoire. Anyway, at some point he'd come looking for her and make sure she participated in whatever domestic activity he had in mind for the evening. It was their way. No, it had *become* their way.

He was already uncorking the wine by the time she walked from the hallway into the kitchen. She recognized the Merry Edwards label. It was an expensive wine for a quick pickup, even by Peter's standards. So there was surely some kind of occasion he was commemorating.

"Get me a glass, will you?" he asked without looking at her. "And one for yourself if you like." He was still angry. There were dark clouds in his face and something barely controlled and dangerous in his tone. She'd never heard this before, or if she had, she hadn't paid attention.

Darcy took her time with the stemware, held it up to the light, checked for water spots. The tension in their happy yellow gourmet kitchen was getting thick. Suddenly Darcy felt exhausted. "Yes, I would like," she said. "A glass of wine would be nice."

Peter poured, swirled, and stared at the red wine in his glass, letting it breathe. If only he'd do the same for her. "I was going to wait until later," he said, "but what the hell, right?"

"What's happening later?"

"Nothing's happening. Just thought we could celebrate." He paused, aerated his wine a bit more, and took a tentative sip. He made a sound of satisfaction. Darcy waited for the other shoe, but ultimately she had to help it drop.

"What are we celebrating?"

"Our new lives," Peter said, holding up his glass in a half toast. "I thought the market was going to work against us, but I don't think we're going to have any trouble with the house. I spoke to—"

"Peter?"

"Mmm?"

"You're talking about selling the house?" It was what she had dreaded and known was coming; yet it still shook her. He was so casual about tearing into the fabric of her life.

"Gotta sell, Darcy. I don't want to leave it empty when we go, and I'm certainly not renting it out."

"I don't understand," Darcy said, and cleared her throat. "I don't understand why you aren't even talking to me about this. Why you don't even consult me. This is my house too, Peter. And it's my life too."

"I know how you feel about it," he said coolly. "You made it very clear at dinner that night. You don't want to go, and I get it. But, Darcy, what's the point in going over this again? It's not something I'm going to turn down. Have you got a better offer? I don't understand *you*. Anyone else—any other woman—would be *thrilled*. You're with me, and we're a team, no? Aren't we, Darcy?" He smiled, and the sight of that smile sent ice crawling down her back. But no, he didn't know anything . . . He was just doing his thing, just being her *husband* in that overly proprietary way he seemed to have been perfecting since that night at Poquette.

"I can't do it, Peter." She took a long sip of wine and felt it warm her all the way down.

"Can't do what?" He was almost at the end of his glass and was pouring himself more. She hadn't even noticed how fast he was drinking.

"I can't move to New York." As she said it, Darcy knew it to be true. It just wasn't going to happen, though she had no idea what would take its place instead.

"Why not? I mean, *really* why not?"

Again, Darcy's senses prickled. But it was a legitimate question. "My life is here. I don't want to live anywhere else."

He glanced at her, pursed his lips, took another sip.

"Don't be a brat, Dar."

There was something about the way he said it—something so dismissive—that captured everything that was and might ever be wrong with their marriage right there in those few little words, in that shortening of her name. A spark caught inside her and burst into flame. She couldn't stop it—couldn't halt the words that were falling out of her mouth.

"Fuck you, Peter."

He finished the wine he was drinking—drained the whole glass—and slammed it down. The stem snapped, and it fell, shattering, to the granite counter. Darcy's stomach flipped. His eyes were blazing, and his lips were stained purple. There was something wrong, something completely out of place in his expression. Maybe he'd been drinking before he got home, she thought, because—

Darcy stopped thinking and just watched Peter raise his fisted hand and swing it toward her face. The kitchen flashed white, and then there was nothing until—

She was lying on the couch, her entire head throbbing with pain that originated on the left side of her jaw. It took several seconds to put it all together—the glass, the fist, the explosion of pain. Those were just the physical details. The rest of it was taking longer.

He hit me in the face.

It hurt too much to cry. The pain was enormous and seemed to come from everywhere. Had he broken her jaw? She put a hand to her face. It was cold and lumpy and . . . plastic. There was a bag of something frozen on her face. Through her clearing fog of pain, Darcy could see that Peter was crouching beside her, holding it in place. Her eyes popped wide with sudden terror, and she startled.

"Darcy . . ."

He knocked me out.

"Don't . . . Don't . . ." Her voice worked. Her jaw worked. Her head was still pounding.

"I'm not . . ." He bit his lip, as concerned and solicitous as she had ever seen him. Emotion flooded her body, drowning her. Tears sprang and rolled. "You're okay."

"No," she said.

"No, I mean . . . You're going to be okay."

Why was he telling her this? Darcy's vision wavered. So many thoughts were cramming her brain, now mazy and chaotic. Had she fallen? Maybe he hadn't hit her, after all. Maybe she'd projected the whole thing. If not for the pain, she could convince herself it had been a dream. She sat up too fast and had to lean over to keep from spinning right off the couch. But she gave it a second, and the world righted itself once more.

"Darcy, I am so sorry."

He hit me in the face—knocked me out.

It was true—all of it. There was something inevitable about it. She'd been so stupid. That fist had always been there, raised; she just hadn't seen it until now.

"Honey, please." His voice was sweet, almost begging. "It will never happen again, Darcy."

No, it won't.

"Baby? Never again. I promise you."

He's sorry. Sorry sorry sorry.

"I need . . ." She stood up, surprised at how easy it was. A wave of nausea crashed through her and receded. "Bathroom," she finished.

It was a bag of peas; she could see that now. He was kneeling, holding it in his lap. She walked around him to the stairs. He didn't follow. She climbed them, and he stayed where he was. She fished her cell phone out of her purse and took it into the guest bathroom upstairs. She locked the door, turned on the bathtub faucet, and faced away from the mirror.

She punched in the number. *His* number.

CHAPTER 6

Darcy had never been to a funeral before, which was strange. Even more unusual, this realization didn't dawn on her until she was seated on a polished wooden bench in the sanctuary, staring into the obscenely large flower arrangement that only partially obscured a nearly life-sized portrait of herself and Peter. There were other blown-up photographs too, almost all of them featuring Peter *with* someone, but this one seemed—at least to Darcy— to be the most garish. No, not garish—ghoulish, that was the word. Then again, it was difficult to tell. Having never experienced this kind of event before, she had no idea what was appropriate, what was normal, or what might seem odd . . . How had it happened, she wondered, that nobody close to her had ever died before now?

Peter's sister, Lisa, put her hand on Darcy's shoulder and gave it a gentle squeeze. "How are you doing, honey?"

Darcy attempted a smile, grateful for the warm tone in her sister-in-law's voice. "I don't know, Lisa," she whispered. "This is . . . I don't know if I can get up there and talk." Tears spilled out of Darcy's eyes, splashing on the front of her dress. She lifted her fingers to her eyes, catching the tears before they fell.

"Yes, you can," Lisa said, her own eyes filling. "You don't have to be strong. You can cry." Lisa stifled a quick sob. "Nobody is going to care if you cry."

Darcy nodded and reached into her purse for something more suitable to dry her eyes than the balled-up Starbucks napkin she'd been using. She'd been worried about this moment. Lisa and her husband, Bill, had advised Peter against marrying her; though they'd accepted her eventually, they'd never really liked her. But she'd been surprised by how sweet Lisa had been. Even at the moment, when Darcy called to tell her what had happened, Lisa could easily have turned her grief into anger at Darcy. But she was supportive, concerned, even *protective* of Darcy.

"I—I don't know what to do," Darcy remembered wailing into the phone. "I don't know where to go."

"Don't worry, honey," Lisa had reassured her. "I know how hard this is, but we'll be there to help you."

And she'd been true to her word, Darcy thought, flying out from Minneapolis almost immediately, taking care of the arrangements for this very service, even planning the reception that would follow. In the days they spent together—or perhaps weeks, since the dawns and dusks were beginning to blend into a single half-lit palette—Darcy kept waiting for the other shoe to drop, for some kind of subtle dig or resentment from Lisa, but none ever came. There was only one moment of tension—so brief Darcy wondered later if she'd imagined it—when Lisa realized that Peter's body had already been cremated by the time she arrived in San Diego.

"I'm sorry, Lisa; it was what he wanted," Darcy had told her then. Lisa was standing in their kitchen, her tired brown eyes gazing out on the jacaranda tree just beyond the window. Peter had loved that tree. It bloomed only once a year, he used to say, but it was worth it for those beautiful lavender-blue blossoms— that distinctly Southern California bloom. Lisa turned to Darcy, something like anger clouding her face, and said, "Are you sure about that?"

"Yes, I am," Darcy said with conviction, because here she had right on her side, one hundred percent. Peter had always been adamant about cremation, going so far as to specify it in his will. He had a phobia of being suffocated, of not having air to breathe, and he was Poe-like in his fear of being buried alive. He'd told her stories about eighteenth-century safety coffins with attached bells that revived corpses could ring to signal that they were still alive. He had sworn, "That will never happen to me because you're going to burn me back to the ash I came from, babe." She was prepared to tell Lisa all of this, even the frankly weird details, but she didn't have to.

"I believe you," Lisa said, "but I wish . . . I wish you could have waited."

"He wanted . . . ," Darcy repeated, but caught herself. "I'm sorry, Lisa. I'm not . . . I'm trying . . ." And then, despite thinking better of it, Darcy began to cry again. Lisa turned back to the window, and the two women wept silently until the very air between them seemed thick with tears.

Now Darcy patted her cheeks with a napkin she'd found in her purse and fixed her gaze straight ahead at the stage (was it called a stage?) where she'd be called up soon to talk about Peter. Lisa had told her that it wasn't necessary, that others would gladly step in (Bill had some sort of big speech planned), that it was perfectly understandable if she didn't feel up to it. But Darcy had said that she owed it to Peter and that she wanted to make him proud, and so now she was committed. She regretted that decision now.

The Klonopin she'd taken this morning was wearing off, and Darcy was feeling her nerves. She had more in her purse and two refills when she ran out of those, but Darcy was trying to be careful with the pills. It would be so easy to become dependent on the blurry, edgeless sensation they gave her. They helped her sleep, but they also emptied out her thoughts. Now, without them, her stomach was unsettled, and the muscles of her shoulders were getting progressively tighter. The room was hot and airless too, heavy with the cloying scent of all those flowers. Darcy fought a sudden queasiness. She could hear the murmurs and greetings of people as they entered and took their seats, their sighs and sniffs enveloping her. She felt as if she'd been sitting here for hours, not minutes. She looked down her aisle past Lisa to Nick and Jeremy, Peter's nephews, seated between their mother and stoic Bill, both of them looking borderline fidgety and uncomfortable. They were only ten and eleven. Lisa, in her fifties, had waited a long time to have her boys.

"We're late bloomers, Peter and I," she'd told Darcy once. "It runs in the family. But it's all for the best, I suppose. Never too late."

At the time, Darcy had thought this was a pointed reference

to the age difference between her and Peter (Lord knew she'd gotten plenty of those), but now she believed that Lisa had been talking about children. Despite coming late to the parent party, Lisa was a fiercely devoted and dedicated mother, and she'd asked, more than once, when Peter and Darcy were going to produce kids of their own.

She'd had to avoid that question because there'd never been a real reason. Although he seemed to enjoy his nephews (and had provided for them nicely in his will—one reason Darcy suspected Lisa was being so kind to her), Peter's basic nature was selfish. He didn't want to share himself—or Darcy—with anyone else, even if that person had sprung from his own loins. Maybe *especially* a child, Darcy thought. He'd never laid it out quite like that because he probably wasn't even aware of his own selfishness (there were, in fact, a great many things Peter wasn't aware of), but Darcy understood what Peter really meant when he told her that they had plenty of time, that Darcy was young and should enjoy her life before giving it over to a child who would demand so much of her energy. And now it was too late.

But . . . maybe Lisa was right, after all. Maybe it was never too late.

As soon as the thought entered her head, Darcy could feel him, all the way in the last row, his eyes burning a hole in the back of her head. He was sitting with the contingent from Poquette; so many of them were here today. Rather than sending an invitation, she'd gone into the restaurant herself, draped in black and wearing sunglasses like some kind of celebrity trying to hide her plastic surgery.

"He loved it here," she'd told Jacques (not his real name, she knew for a fact), "and so I thought it would be nice . . ."

"But of course," Jacques said. "It is so very kind of you to ask, and we are so, so sorry to lose him. Such a wonderful man." Yes, Darcy thought, and one who single-handedly secured Poquette's bottom line some nights and provided college-fund starters for the children of a couple of favorite waiters. She was sure that accounted for a good portion of Jacques's sorrow.

Quite a few of them had shown up—Darcy had been a little surprised. They shuffled around uncomfortably in front, wearing black pants, so faded they were almost charcoal colored, and too-crisp shirts still with the package fold creases in their sleeves. Jacques wore the sharkskin suit she'd seen many times at Poquette. There were waitresses Darcy recognized as well—Jess-something and Lulu (you couldn't forget a name like that—or the perpetual pouty look that went along with it). There were also the waiters she knew even better who greeted her, saying, "Hey, Mrs. Silver. We're so sorry." And the bartenders. The bartenders were here too. That was, after all, why she had invited any of them in the first place. It was stupid, perhaps, but she'd wanted him here, even if she couldn't talk to him. And she really couldn't talk to him except in the most cursory way. She was so afraid of giving herself away, and there was so much swirling emotion in this room. Just seeing him was enough to set her heart racing.

The service was starting now in earnest, so Darcy literally pulled herself together, gathering the folds of her oversized silk scarf and wrapping them around her shoulders. She'd debated wearing something bright this morning—that red dress Peter had liked so much—and weaving the story of it into her speech; something about how Peter used to like to serenade her with cheesy songs of yesteryear ("The Lady in Red" being only one of many), but in the end she hadn't felt confident enough in her own storytelling abilities. So it was black all the way, complete with a hat, scarf, and pumps. Peter, she thought now, would have liked that too.

"And he was an especially generous man . . ."

No, Darcy thought. *No, he wasn't. He pretended, but in the end he took away everything he gave.* Fresh tears stung the corners of her eyes.

Joe Lightman was talking. He was one of Peter's oldest friends; the one Darcy disliked the most. There was no love lost on Joe's end either. Joe had always treated her like a high-priced whore. She'd said as much to Peter, but he'd just laughed her off.

"I remember when he asked me to be best man at his wedding . . ."

Darcy felt her cheeks flush and burn. The man had been awful at their wedding, she remembered. He got drunk and gave a way-too-vulgar speech that mentioned Viagra more than once. And there was something about the tone of Joe's voice now that scraped at her brain. She didn't dislike him, no. She hated him. Without even looking up, Darcy could feel the man's stare trained on her like gun sight crosshairs. In spite of her resolve to stay present and aware—never as important as it was now—Darcy felt herself retreating mentally to that warm, dark place in her mind where she was adored and caressed and safe. It was dangerous to be there now—to let herself imagine his hands on her skin, the shiver down her back when he touched her—but for one second, just for a moment . . . This was Darcy's real drug, and it was better than any pharmaceutical.

There was a rustle next to her as Lisa got up to speak. Nick and Jeremy both looked a little stunned now, uncomprehending. Jeremy looked over at her with the big dark eyes all those Silvers seemed to have, opened his mouth as if to ask her something, and then quickly turned away. He'd been schooled, no doubt, on how to treat Aunt Darcy at this most difficult time. A childish urge to giggle rose up in her throat, and she only just managed to choke it back down.

She turned her mind back to *him*, trying to capture his image behind her eyes, to feel his hand sliding slowly up the side of her leg, little shivers of excitement running down her back . . . But it wasn't his face she saw now; it was Peter's, alive and smiling, dark eyes full of admiration and pride. She would catch him like that sometimes, just looking at her. He almost always woke up earlier than she did in the mornings, and often she'd open her eyes and find him close to her on the pillow, that love-struck gaze on his face.

"Ah, you're awake," he'd say then, and reach for her.

He'd never stopped wanting her, never stopped reaching for her. It made being with him both easier and so much more difficult. Once, early in their courtship, he'd said, "You always close your eyes when I kiss you. Why won't you look at me?" As a way of getting him to trust her, to *love* her, she'd made it a point from then on to keep her eyes wide open. Old habits died hard. She'd seen that fist as it swung toward her face, hadn't she?

They had talked once, had gone to concerts together, had gotten drunk on expensive champagne and had sex in the car in the middle of the driveway. Darcy could remember these things, even now. She could feel the fizz of the Veuve Clicquot on her tongue and the pain in her knee as she'd jammed it into the gear shift. She could hear the echoes of her own drunken, lustful laughter as it mixed with his grunts of pleasure. But these recollections, as clear as they were, felt borrowed—as if they belonged to someone else and had been planted in Darcy's memory. Because what Darcy could *not* summon was the closeness she'd felt to Peter then, nor the passionate love he'd felt for her. The gulf between them hadn't opened overnight; it had happened gradually, widening incrementally and as inexorably as the wearing away of rock by the ocean. By the time Darcy realized what had happened to their marriage, the shape of it had been forever changed.

Lisa was struggling. Tears were running down the sides of her face, and she had started hiccupping. She was almost completely incapacitated and unable to finish her speech about what a wonderful kid brother Peter had been, an inspiration for her boys, but she was still trying, ungracefully, to get through it.

Darcy felt herself rising, though she'd made no decision to do so, then walking up the three short stairs to the podium and putting her arms around Lisa. There was a sound from the crowd—some kind of fluttering out of breath—which Darcy could now see was much larger than she'd thought, a black sea of mourners, and then an expectant silence so profound, Darcy thought she'd gone temporarily deaf.

"It's okay," she whispered to Lisa. "I'll take over. It's okay."

Lisa clung to her for a moment, her fingernails digging into Darcy's arms as if she would fall down without the support, before letting out a loud, wet sob and stumbling back to her seat.

"Peter would have been so happy to see all of you," Darcy began. There was a tremor in her voice. Darcy struggled to control it. "I'd like to think that he's with us right now," she continued, "but that would be selfish because it would mean he wasn't in a better place. And . . . I hope so much that he is in a better place." She drew a breath, and the scent of her own perfume wafted into her nostrils. She was perspiring. She dared to do it— to look back all those rows and meet his eyes with her own. Yes, there he was. The force of it nearly knocked her backward, but somehow Darcy kept talking. She had split herself entirely now—her physical body standing there, every black-clad blond inch of her a grieving widow and her astral body floating down the center aisle toward him as he beckoned, bright eyes flashing, mouth held loose and ready. *Safe,* she thought again.

"It sounds silly to say it," she carried on, "but when I met him . . . When I saw him, it was love at first sight."

Yes, it had been, but it wasn't Peter she was thinking of now. She hadn't been looking for it; she had done nothing to invite it, but he was placed before her anyway. Who knew it could really happen like that? Fate, if you believed in that kind of thing, had put him there, her name already written on his hands, on his mouth. It wasn't her fault. It wasn't. In a way, she'd had nothing to do with it at all.

"He always said he didn't believe in that," she said, "with one exception—us. And you know Peter—he was so good at making exceptions to things . . ."

A soft wave of laughter rippled through the room.

She'd gone in there for lunch—alone. Peter always thought it was strange that she ate in restaurants by herself, but Darcy had grown up an only child and was content with her own company. She'd decided to eat at the bar—a great spot to watch people. She'd never seen him before—he'd only just started working at Poquette. He put the cocktail napkin in front of her and smiled, flirting in a practiced way. She was going to play the game too—banter, wink, and quip—but then she really saw him, looked straight into those hypnotic amber eyes of his, and the air around her cracked like glass. It was the same for him, she could tell. Sometimes . . . sometimes you just knew. Later, when she couldn't justify staying there any longer and they both needed a reason to see each other again, he asked her if she ever went to Club Sahara.

"Should I?"

"I'm playing there on Saturday night," he said. "You should come."

Darcy was still talking, the words coming as easily as the tears that were running in silvery streams down her pale cheeks. Hardly anyone knew about Peter's charity work, she said, because he didn't want to make a big deal about giving. It made him a hero, she said, in her eyes and in those of everyone he helped.

She'd never been a sucker for a musician before. It was the kind of cliché she hated, but when she saw him on stage singing about love and pain, she felt as if her insides had been scooped out and her knees were dissolving. You couldn't help whom you fell in love with. It had never been in her control. She shouldn't have let him come here today—the stakes were too high—but she'd needed to see him. She needed to prove to herself that this *love was real and that it was worth what she'd risked for it.*

She stopped listening to herself, her brain finally allowing her to split fantasy and reality completely, and didn't tune back in until the last sentence fell from her lips.

"I wish he were here," she said. "I wish he could see you all. I miss him so much."

They were all crying, every single one of them. But there, all the way in the back row, the tears were for her alone.

The reception line had taken forever to get through. Darcy had been lost in a swarm of people, each with his or her own recollection of Peter that had to be shared at that very moment. They all thought her speech was beautiful and so touching. They all said the same things: "You must be devastated, Darcy. He was such a young man. It was such a huge loss. I had no idea Peter gave so much to charity, and if there is anything you need, anything at all . . ." Her hands and cheeks felt chapped from handling, and the afternoon sun was scorching the top of her head. She was again grateful when Lisa started rounding people up and directing them to the reception. The promise of food, Darcy thought, could move people like nothing else.

She'd insisted on bringing her own car to the service, something both Bill and Lisa had advised against, but which they both gave in to, accepting it as another indulgence to make in the name of grief.

"I need the time," Darcy had told them. "I know it sounds strange, but it will help me just to have those few minutes by myself in the car."

But as she walked across the grass to the parking lot now, her spike heels sinking into the soft dirt, Darcy wished she had a girlfriend with her—someone she could trust with everything. Only another woman could understand how she was feeling at this moment.

She was almost at her car when he came up behind her. She was so caught in her own thoughts that he had to call her name, although not loudly; she gave him that. Still, it was an error in judgment—a big one—to come after her like this. She thought he'd have been more careful.

"Darcy, wait."

The smell of jasmine wafted over to her from somewhere across the grass. She had to get home. She was the widow. They'd notice if she was even a few minutes late.

"Adam," she said, stopping, turning around, and trying not to look at him too closely. It was too difficult, and her heart was beating so fast. "You can't do this," she breathed as soon as he was close enough to hear. "Not now. People can see."

"Relax, Darcy," he said. There was something she didn't like in his tone—something proprietary and hard. A sliver of apprehension worked its way under her skin. "My guys are right over there. I told them I was going to come over and say good-bye for all of us. And give you our sympathies."

"I have to go, Adam. There's a whole . . . *thing* happening at my house, you know. I have a long night of this ahead of me."

"That was some speech you gave. You even had *me* convinced."

"Of what?"

"How much you loved him. How sad you are that he's gone."

"I did love him, Adam. He was my husband."

Darcy watched the emotions play quickly across his beautiful face—amusement, anger, and, finally, concern. "You're not serious," he said.

"Of course I'm serious. I loved my husband. He loved me." Darcy could hear her voice as if it were coming from another source. She sounded completely sincere, and that was because . . . because she *was* sincere. It was as if Peter's wife and Adam's girlfriend were two people residing in the same body and both had something to say at this moment. Yes, she had loved Peter, and they *had* been happy once. She could see Peter now—as clearly as she'd imagined Adam only hours before—a smile on his face, a dinner plan at the ready. There had been so much going on, so much strain, Lisa, the arrangements . . . But now the reality of it rippled through her. She was going to miss her husband.

"Stop playing with me, Darcy. Nobody can hear us out here."

There it was again—that wrong note in his voice. For a moment, Darcy wondered if Adam was going to threaten her. But no, it wasn't possible—not the way he was looking at her now. That longing for her was so strong and deep, she could feel it in her own body. It was pulling her in. Peter's wife—the same one who'd never said a word to anyone but Adam about the things Peter did to her—receded once again.

"He punched you in the face, Darcy."

"Yes." Darcy lowered her eyes, her face burning with the memory of it, her cheeks hot.

"He could have killed you."

"Yes." She was going to cry—she could feel the sharp sting at the backs of her eyes.

"This is me you're talking to, Darcy," he said. "You don't have to . . ." He took a step toward her and stopped. Was it her imagination, or could she feel the heat of his skin on hers? Her eyes blurred, and her toes curled inside her high-heeled shoes. She wanted to touch him so badly, her bones ached with it. Her mouth was desert dry; her hands clutched at the fluttering ends of her scarf. She licked her lips, willing herself not to move any closer to him and sniff at him like a dog.

"Adam—" Her voice was hoarse with desire, and he could hear it.

"When am I going to see you?"

"Adam, please. We're at his *memorial service.*"

"I *know*, Darcy. I'm not stupid. But it's been—"

"I know what it's been, Adam. You don't have to tell me. I've felt it too." She allowed herself to look at him full on, to search those almost-golden eyes of his for rage or madness. Maybe it had been unforgivably reckless of her not to have worried about him—about how he was going to react—until this moment, but he'd never given her cause. She forced herself to think now, to separate her mind from her wild, flailing emotions, and to choose her words carefully.

"It's going to be a while—and you know it—before we can, you know, before we can be—"

"Why?"

"Because . . ." She lowered her voice to a whisper, even though there was nobody else standing close enough to hear them. She wanted to touch him so badly, her body was vibrating with need. "Because I don't want anyone to know . . . to think that we—"

"But what about—"

"Adam, don't!"

"Baby," he said so softly, she wasn't even sure she heard it. "Tell me you don't miss me."

"I can't," she said quickly. "You know I can't tell you that—it wouldn't be true."

His shoulders relaxed a little, and his mouth started to curve into a smile that didn't quite form. "How long?" he said.

"I don't know, Adam." The words actually hurt coming out of her mouth. She couldn't stand to think about an open-ended time apart.

"Don't make me wait, love. Please." The yearning at the end of his plea made her heart flutter.

"I have to go," she said. "You have to go."

What did he want her to say? What did he want her to do?

He gave her a look that was searching, intimate, and knowing all at once. She felt as if every cell in her body had begun to shake. "We're playing on Friday night," he said. "We'll be at Zulu's, so not the usual place. It wouldn't be . . . You should come, Darcy. You should be there."

"I don't—"

"Don't forget, Darcy."

He wasn't asking. No, it was much more of a command than that. She'd heard those kinds of commands before. *This isn't a* question. *I'm telling you. I'm not asking.* Still, she couldn't stop herself from answering him, from giving him what he wanted. He backed up a few paces, his eyes still boring into her, and then turned, headed to the parking lot where his friends and coworkers were waiting for him.

"I'll try," she whispered, and then, just a little louder, "Adam, I'll try."

CHAPTER 7

PORTLAND

Eden was on a twisted highway on the edge of a cliff in pouring rain. The sky was heavy and dark—a warning. She had been here before and knew enough to be afraid of the turns that were coming, but still this road was unfamiliar. There were no markers here. She was far from home and shouldn't . . . She shouldn't be here at all.

It was beautiful—pink and rust rock on one side, sparkling blue water on the other, a big complicated sky overhead—but also a slick wet slide. There was something about the name, she thought—the name of this highway—that translated to beauty and punishment. It was on the edge of her brain as the car sped up, *too fast*, but she couldn't quite get at it.

A bucketful of water pelted the windshield, blurring her vision. The windshield wipers shuddered and stuck in the middle of the windshield. Whose car was this?

It was all *her* fault.

She had to get off this road, but there was nowhere to go. Cold dread clutched at her. She had been here before. Though she knew what was going to happen, she couldn't stop; she couldn't see.

Goddamn her.

She had to wake up; she had to get out of this dream before it killed her—before it killed her *again*.

The lights flashed in front of her—then darkness.

Eden was screaming. She could hear the sound in her ears, but when she opened her eyes at last, the room was still. Nobody was at her bed, no nurses had come rushing in, no doctors, no—no doctors.

Eden blinked hard, that stranger's heart beating overtime in her chest. She was home, in her own bed. Derek was . . . somewhere. She looked around, getting reoriented once again. Bedroom, hall, kitchen, window . . . It was beginning to feel like an endless cycle—waking up and feeling out of place, as if she didn't belong, and then needing several minutes to remember where she was and find herself once again.

The dreams didn't help. She could still see the colors of this last one—the pinkish rock face, dark chaotic sky—and that terrible feeling that she was going to die. She'd dreamed about death and dying before the surgery, of course, and those dreams had been vivid too, but they hadn't been anything like this. This one had terrified her so completely that her new heart lurched and pounded. She put her hand to her chest and touched the scar, long and thick under her fingers. She'd never get used to the feel of it between her breasts.

But, oh, what a fashion statement next time she stepped out in a bikini. Check it out, boys.

Eden startled as if those words had been spoken out loud by someone else instead of having come from inside her own mind. It was a strange thought—alien—and Eden didn't know where it had come from. She propped herself up in bed and pushed the hair off her face as if that alone would clear her head.

She could hear rattling in the kitchen and smell fresh coffee. So that was where Derek was. She felt a stab of pure envy. The rich taste of fully caffeinated coffee was one of the things she missed most about her pretransplant life, which was odd because she hadn't even been that much of a coffee drinker to begin with. She'd stuck mostly to herbal teas—they were less demanding somehow than coffee—and had filled her kitchen cabinets with them. But she'd lost her interest in tea now, as she had in so many other things. Eden told herself it was because tea reminded her of being sick (she'd swilled gallons of it in those last couple of months—making tea was one of the things Derek did to feel useful), but she didn't really believe it. The tea, the coffee, the antipathy toward colors (pink) and foods (tomatoes) that she'd once loved and the pieces of songs she didn't recognize but heard playing in her head—all of these were just a few of the ways she was fundamentally different.

And the dreams. The dreams were the most unsettling of all.

It was early, only five ten a.m. according to her bedside clock, and the light outside was still dim and gray. Eden wondered if Derek was planning to go for a run and decided no, not possible; he wouldn't drink coffee before a run. So why was he up so early? There were hours to go before her doctor visit (doctors, plural, she reminded herself—she was due to see that new shrink today as well), but Eden pushed away the sheets and got out of bed anyway, failing as she did so to avoid the mirror. She needed to move that thing or just take it down and smash it, she thought. The white tank top and underwear she'd slept in only served to highlight the weight she'd gained. She wasn't overweight—not yet, anyway—but definitely more plush than she'd ever been in her life. It was there on her hips and thighs; even her face had become much rounder than it used to be. They'd warned her about this, of course; they had told her to expect it. The pounds and puffiness were a function of all the immunosuppressant drugs she was taking and would have to take forever.

Because he couldn't possibly deny that the weight was there, Derek did the next best thing and said it suited her, made her even sexier than she'd been before. But Eden couldn't tell if this was the truth. The fact was that neither she nor Derek really knew how he felt about her new body, because he hadn't touched it in any kind of intimate way since before her surgery, though not for lack of trying or wanting. It was Eden who hadn't allowed it. That was another thing. Eden wondered how much longer she could get away with making *those* kinds of excuses.

She grabbed the pink silk robe Derek had bought for her when she came home from the hospital and wrapped it around her body. She would have been so much happier if he'd just gotten her something serviceable instead of this thing that looked as if it had come from Barbie's Dream House. It was too delicate—too *pink*—for her, but Eden wouldn't risk hurting his feelings by not wearing it. She was doing enough of that already just by being herself. Or, more accurately, *not* being herself.

Lucky to be alive.

The thought pinged through Eden's brain even though she

tried to ignore it. Yes, she was lucky—she was reminded of that every day—but only because someone else hadn't been. The math was devastatingly simple. For perhaps the thousandth time, Eden wished she knew even the smallest detail about the person whose death had given her life—age, hair color, anything. Hell, she would have settled for an astrological sun sign. But, just as she had been repeatedly warned, Eden hadn't been given the merest scrap of information about the donor. She had a good, strong heart pushing blood through her body, and that, according to the world at large, was more than enough.

But it wasn't, and Eden knew it never would be.

Derek was drinking his coffee at the tiny café table Eden had managed to squeeze into the undersized kitchen, staring at the lemon-colored wall and so lost in thought that it took him a moment to look up at her. He quickly adjusted his brooding, sad expression to something more neutral, though he couldn't quite summon happy.

"Sorry, hon," he said. "I didn't mean to wake you."

"It's okay—I was up anyway." He hadn't heard the screaming, obviously, which only served to confirm her belief that it had all been in her head. She wasn't going to tell him about the dream either. He was too concerned as it was; besides, she was tired—exhausted, really—of trying to adopt the positive spin Derek insisted on giving everything.

"I'll make you some breakfast."

"Not yet, thank you. Way too early."

"Eden, you have to—"

"I know, Derek. Please, let's not go there." She squeezed in next to him at the table. It was impossible to sit without legs and arms touching. Eating together here was an exercise in futility—it just couldn't be done without knocking forks and spilling drinks. This used to be kind of sweet, but now it just felt uncomfortable.

"Coffee smells good," she said, making a real effort to sound light. "I'd love to join you in some of that."

"There's that special decaf I got," he said. "Why don't I—"

"It's not the same." She pulled the robe tighter around her body to stave off the chill. The characteristic Portland damp was another thing that hadn't bothered her until after her surgery; yet now it grated on her senses. "But never mind. Why are *you* up so early, Derek?"

"Couldn't sleep. I've been thinking . . ." He drew in a deep breath and scratched at an invisible spot on his coffee mug. "I don't want to push you, Eden; you know that." He smiled for punctuation, morning stubble darkening the dimples in his cheeks. Almost sure where this was going, Eden wanted to interrupt him, but she held herself back. "And I know how incredibly hard it's been for you these last months, but I just think . . ."

A tremor rippled through Eden's body. Was he about to *break up* with her? The thought had never occurred to her, but, to her astonishment, she didn't find it entirely unpleasant.

"I think you'd be happier—no, I think we'd *both* be happier in a different place."

"Derek—"

"No, hear me out, honey. I know how much you love this apartment, and I know we can't go back to where we were before . . . you know."

"Oh." Eden sighed, feeling all the air leave her lungs.

"That house in the Pearl probably wasn't right anyway," Derek continued. "But I've been looking at others, and I think I've found one you'll love."

"I'm not ready to move," Eden said. "It's too soon." This was a lie, and Eden hated herself for saying it. She was more than ready to move, just not with Derek and not—Eden's eyes widened with the sudden realization—to another place in this city. She wanted to leave Portland with a desire so intense, it was sometimes all she could think about. She wanted sun and sand. She wanted . . . California.

"You're doing really, really well, Eden." There was just the faintest accusatory note in his voice. "Everyone says so. I'll be honest—I didn't think you'd recover this quickly. I don't want to make it sound cheap, but it *is* a miracle. But I can tell you've been struggling. I'm not stupid." His hand clenched and unclenched around the coffee mug as if he wanted to reshape it. "I know you, Eden. You have to let it go. This apartment is our old life. We have to move on to the new one."

Eden waited, letting his speech hang in the cold air between them while she searched for the right words or gesture to give him. But after several moments, she could see the hurt start to spread like a dark stain across his face, and it made her throat tighten with shame. Then, all she could think to say was, "I'm going to see the shrink today. I'm going to try, Derek."

"All I can ask." He got up and put his mug in the sink, then flipped the OFF switch on the coffeepot. He kept his back to her long enough to wipe at his eyes without her seeing the tears that had formed there and then turned back to her, a crooked half smile on his face.

"You're shivering," he said, and Eden realized she was. "Let's go back to bed for a bit and warm up."

She let him take her hand and pull her up; she let him lead her the short distance to the bedroom in silence as if they were trying their best to hit their marks in a grand cinematic love scene. When they climbed into the unmade bed, she let him slide the robe off her shoulders and kiss the hollow of her throat. She let his hands move slowly up her sides, to her breasts, avoiding the scar, trembling. She felt him sigh, press his body into hers—urgent, needy. His hands moved lower, clutching at her flesh, forgetting to be careful.

"Derek . . ."

He made a sound—a sob or a grunt, she couldn't tell—and stopped, his lips moist against her neck. "Eden, please . . ." He lowered his head then, putting it down on her chest, on top of the scar, on top of her alien, unwilling heart. "Please," he said again, this time his voice heavy with love and frustration and a thin, dark trace of anger.

So Eden closed her eyes and let him, the sound of blood rushing in her ears and images of rain, sky, and cliff splintering behind her closed lids.

PART

2

CHAPTER 8

SAN DIEGO
Nine months later

Eden hadn't anticipated how jammed up the Coast Highway would be with people headed to the San Diego County Fair. She was still getting used to this place—its weather, traffic patterns, and almost complete lack of public transportation—but that wasn't going to be an acceptable excuse if she showed up late for her first solo shift at Poquette. Trapped between the buzz and hum of the fair on her left and the waves crashing on the beach to her right, Eden could do nothing but crawl along with the long snaking line of cars whose drivers had made the same mistake as she in choosing this route. The air was cool, both inside the car and out, but Eden was perspiring. She didn't want to be late—

didn't want to give them *any* reason to fire her. Other than staying physically healthy, keeping this job was the single most important goal in Eden's life. In a bizarre way that she didn't really understand, she felt as if her *emotional* health depended on it.

Eden had applied for a job at Poquette almost immediately after moving to San Diego. And although she'd told her family— told *everyone*—that she was planning to look for education-related work, waitressing was the only thing she'd even considered. Even if she'd wanted to work with kids again, which, like so many other things, no longer held any appeal, it was too risky to expose herself in her immunocompromised state to the huge and frightening array of viruses and bacteria kids carried around with them. The argument could be made that waiting tables wasn't the most sterile of professions either, but Eden had done it in college and knew it wasn't exactly dangerous. Besides, she wasn't sure that she even had a choice. Very little of what she'd been doing since her surgery seemed to come from conscious decisions. Her actions— and even her thoughts—were guided by something else. Eden had felt *compelled* to move to San Diego. And then, as soon as she had her bearings, she headed straight for Poquette.

It was a beautiful restaurant with an epic view of the ocean and the potential for her to make quite a bit of cash, but that wasn't why Eden found her way up the marble steps and through the vine-covered awning. Though the truth was she didn't know why she'd driven around North San Diego County until she saw the Del Mar Plaza with its clean brick and high-end shops and decided she needed to stop *right there* and get out and walk up the stairs. It was as if something or someone had been pushing her. A few short months ago, Eden would have said it was her heart or, more accurately, *the* heart—that foreign object pumping blood through her body. But not now. She was tired of trying to convince people, including herself, that her heart (or its previous owner) was responsible for the changes in her thoughts, feelings, and behavior.

Every cardiologist and psychiatrist she consulted had told her some variation of the same thing; that it was impossible for a donor's organ to exert some kind of influence over a recipient. There were some stories to the contrary, they told her, and if she skimmed the Internet, she'd be able to find plenty of them (she had and she did), but these were all anecdotal at best and specious at worse. There was no scientific basis—none at all. Eventually, Eden just gave up trying to prove it, but that didn't mean it wasn't happening. She hadn't been hired right away. When she'd first walked into Poquette, the manager on duty— some kid who barely looked old enough to shave—didn't even want to give her an application.

"We're not hiring, and, to be honest with you, there probably won't be an opening any time soon," he said, and sniffed. "This is a very well-known restaurant."

Despite wanting to lean over the polished marble host stand and smack him, Eden ignored the officious tone in his voice and smiled. "Which is why I'd really love the opportunity to join the team," she said. "I understand you don't have anything right now on the floor. But maybe a hostess position or—"

"I really don't think so." The annoying manager, whom Eden felt she had already loathed for a lifetime, folded his hands and looked as if he were about to bounce her, when a sweet-smelling and highly tailored man swooped in from somewhere behind her and said, "Just give her an application, Steve."

With great lip-pursed resentment, Steve reached into a drawer within the host stand and extracted what looked like a pamphlet, which he then pushed toward her with one finger.

"Thank you so much," Eden said. "And thank you," she said, turning to the well-attired man and offering her hand. "I'm Eden Harrison," she said.

"Jacques," he said, and a voice in Eden's brain immediately whispered, *Not his real name.* He shook her hand and took her full measure within the space of a second, all without appearing as if that was what he was doing. Impressive, she thought. She could feel her color rising a little as he stared right into her, seeming to search for something. Her hand moved instinctively to her chest, to make sure that her shirt collar covered the scar. She was very careful about that now—only high necklines for her—but sometimes the fabric slipped, making it possible to glimpse the puckered skin beneath. She couldn't afford to let anyone find out—not now or, maybe, ever.

"We are fully staffed at the moment," Jacques said, "but things can change, and our busiest season is coming up. You have experience working in this kind of restaurant?"

"Yes."

"And, I assume, references?"

"Yes—I've recently relocated," Eden said, "from Portland. So my references are not local."

Jacques tipped his head like a bird, a flicker of amusement dancing across his smooth, tanned face. "Very good. Just fill out the application and bring it back. You never know." He smiled at her while Steve made a big show of answering a ringing phone and enunciating every syllable of the standard greeting.

"Thanks so much," Eden said.

She didn't wait for Jacques to call her. Something about his manner convinced her to go back in person only a few days after she'd left the application in Steve's unwilling hands. It was late in the afternoon, between the lunch and dinner shifts, and Jacques was sitting at the bar, drinking an espresso.

"Oh," he said, "I'm so glad you came back. It turns out some-one just left us . . ."

Almost effortless, Eden thought now. She'd spent the last week training, following other waiters and waitresses around, doing all the sidework they hated (polishing spoons, folding napkins, re-stocking butter dishes) and making no tips, but she was happy to be there. There followed two tests about various menu items (both written and oral and administered by Steve, who went from of-ficious to unctuous as soon as he realized that Jacques had taken a shine to his new hire). Eden passed both easily, and then she was given a schedule.

"I can only give you lunches to start," Jacques said, "but you'll do well during racing season. And then we'll see."

Eden was grateful for more than just the job and Jacques's kind attitude toward her. She was also happy to learn that the server uniform consisted of a white dress shirt, black necktie, and snug blue designer jeans. Jeans were all the rage in these upscale places now, but Eden didn't mind if people stared at her ass—it was her chest she was worried about keeping safely covered up.

After fifteen more excruciating minutes at a dead stop, during which Eden had time to note the names of several cheesy, dangerous-looking rides (Crazy Mouse, the High Miler . . .), she finally found a break in the traffic and arrived at Poquette with less than five minutes before her shift was due to start.

The time clock was located deep inside the kitchen, wedged between the dishwashing station and the salad prep area. Eden had to make herself small to avoid being swiped by heavy pans and trays. It was loud—the running water, shouting, cursing, chopping, slamming, laughing, and clinking silverware all blending into a bass-heavy rush of sound—and it was very warm.

"Hey, hey, hey."

Eden turned to see another waiter practically on top of her in the tight space. She replaced her time card in its slot and slid out from in front of him. He was blond and full-lipped, his hair carefully gelled into looking as if he'd just fallen out of bed, some almost-stubble on his rakish face, and pale blue eyes shot pink. Stoned, Eden thought. She could smell it on him even in the multisensory overload of the kitchen.

"You're the new girl," he said, and started singing. It was a Chris Isaak song she recognized, "Except the New Girl." Cute. "What's your name, new girl?" he said as they moved through the kitchen and out onto the floor.

"Eden."

"Right on. First day?"

"I've been training. First day solo."

"Cool. I'm Jojo. Let me know if you need any help." He gave her a wide, flirty smile, which she tried to return. He wasn't finished. "Live around here?" he asked as they checked the whiteboard to see which tables they would be responsible for. Jojo, she saw, had a five-table station in a prime location—on the patio with a view. Eden had three tables, inside and closest to the restrooms. Well, she was the new girl.

"Pretty close," she said, and straightened her tie.

"Traffic's a bitch, huh?"

"Yes, it was."

His smile dimmed a little, but he carried on with the small

talk as they headed into the dining room. Was she from around here? *No.* Did she have another job? *No.* Had she ever been surfing? *No again.* He was making a real effort, Eden thought, and though she knew where he was headed ultimately, she couldn't fault him for trying. There was something amusing and maybe even a little sweet about him. *Not the sharpest tool in the shed, but he's harmless.* Eden almost looked around before realizing the words had come from inside her own head.

"So, Eden, are you married?"

Although she tried to stop it, Eden couldn't help but see Derek in her mind's eye, and it pained her because she never imagined him anymore as the happy, relaxed guy she'd met, but as the confused and angry man she'd left. Derek wasn't the only person she'd disappointed, but it was about him that Eden felt the most guilty.

"No," she told Jojo, "I'm not married." They were in the cool hush of the dining room now. Service would begin in twenty minutes, and setup would take at least thirty minutes. "But I'm not available either," she said. Jojo gave her a last look—his expression somewhere between *I didn't ask if you were* and *We'll see about that*—then took off for his own section, whistling the Chris Isaak tune as he went.

Good old Jojo, Eden thought, though she had no idea why.

It was four o'clock before Eden was able to think in a straight line again. At that moment, Eden's only thought was that she was very glad she didn't have to work the dinner shift. The restaurant had been packed as soon as the doors opened, and Eden had spent most of the lunch rush in the weeds. Jose, her busboy, was helpful to a point, but he wouldn't go much beyond his own duties of setting, clearing, or delivering water, bread, and coffee. Jojo, so full of bonhomie before lunch began, wasn't even willing to show her where extra creamers were kept after the prefilled stash evaporated. It occurred to Eden that he was annoyed by her unwillingness to flirt with him, but he seemed just as buried as she was.

She'd just been starting to get caught up when those servers working double shifts went off the clock, so Eden had to finish a couple of extra tables. It was madness. But, she thought, it was only her first day. Things were bound to get easier. None of her customers (or *patrons* as Jacques had insisted she call them) seemed unhappy—at least outwardly. And in restaurants, people didn't tend to hold back when they were upset about something, so that was good.

She'd also been worried about how she'd feel after several hours on the floor. It had been a year since the surgery, and Eden felt fine; yet she hadn't gone back to running, which she'd been told was not really recommended, but possible. But Eden had lost interest in running—too many bad memories of collapsing in the park unable to breathe—and hadn't really done any other kind of rigorous exercise. Besides, she remembered how physically demanding restaurant work could be. Her new cardiologist, Dr. Morgan, wasn't concerned (though he seemed to find her choice of work puzzling), but he told her to monitor how she felt and, of course, if there were any signs . . .

But Eden felt great; tired but revitalized. The decent wad of cash shoved deep into her jeans pocket didn't hurt either. Though she'd been a little panicked at first, Eden was pleased—even a little surprised—that she'd been able to hold her own on the floor. It was a good thing she'd had that college experience wait-ing tables, she thought, because it had obviously resulted in some kind of muscle memory.

Eden took her first break of the day and walked over to the bar. "Hey," she said to the burly bartender who'd introduced himself earlier simply as "Sticks," "I don't suppose you'd mind making me a refreshing beverage?" She smiled broadly. *Never hurts to be on his good side.*

Sticks gave her an odd look, one eyebrow raised, as if she'd said something strange or discomforting. "What did you say?" he asked.

"Can I have a drink? Is that okay?"

He shrugged. "Sure." Still giving her the side eye, he mixed up a fresh lemonade with crushed mint and handed it to her. Eden thought she'd never tasted anything quite as satisfying. "You re-ally know how to make these," she said. "So good."

"I've never made that for you before," Sticks said.

"I know," Eden said too quickly. "I just meant . . ." She trailed off, not knowing at all what she meant and feeling very awkward. "Thanks," she finished, and headed back into the kitchen.

The dinner shift waiters were starting to come in. Two of them, Melissa and Marisol, hovered in the kitchen, picking at a desultory-looking staff meal of random seafood bits tossed with rice. Eden had trailed both of them last week. They looked scrubbed and fresh, their long dark hair gathered up into identi-cal ponytails. They could be twins, Eden thought. The uniforms were slightly different for dinner; instead of white shirts and black ties, they wore black shirts and white ties along with the same designer jeans, which both Melissa and Marisol filled out nicely.

"How'd it go?" Melissa asked Eden.

"Pretty good, I think," Eden said.

"Good for you."

"Thanks. And thanks for the training. It really helped."

"I'm just about ready to come on," Marisol said, "so you can turn your tables over to me. Got anything big working?"

"No, not really," Eden said, only mildly resentful that she was expected to give up tables she'd already started. "One couple on dessert on twenty-one and three girls just having appetizers on twenty-three." She peered outside the kitchen into the dining room. "Looks like a new table's just being seated."

Marisol put down her fork and went out to the edge of the dining room. Eden watched her watch a single woman being seated out on the patio—at the best table in the house, in fact—and saw Marisol's entire body tense.

"It's Mrs. Silver," Marisol said, coming back to her meal but not eating it. She looked as if she needed a stiff drink. Melissa flicked her eyes briefly toward the dining room and said nothing.

"What's wrong with Mrs. Silver?" Eden asked. "Is she a difficult customer? I know there are a few—"

"No, she's fine," Marisol said. "It's my table; I'll take it. Would you mind just getting her started, Eden? Just some bread and a drink order? That would really help me out."

"Okay," Eden said, "sure." She arranged a basket of the exotic flatbreads and muffins that Poquette was known for and placed it on a tray next to a ramekin filled with butter roses. Marisol whispered something to Melissa. For the first time in a long while, Eden felt the sting of being an outsider. She swept out to the dining room, aware suddenly of the red wine stain on her cuff and the wisp of hair that had come loose from her braid.

When she got to the table, Charlie, the day host, was still

there, leaning over the woman in a fawning posture, a beseeching look on his face.

"Ah," he said, seeing Eden, "and here is your bread."

"Thank you, Charlie." Her voice was surprisingly deep, Eden thought, but not mannish. It was rich and a little playful. Sexy. *A woman with a lot of money,* Eden thought suddenly and with surprising bitterness. But, she argued with herself, one could hardly hold *that* against the woman. *So why am I?*

She placed the bread on the table and the butter just so, trying not to lean, not to get inside the woman's space. She was so preoccupied with getting these details right that she didn't even give Mrs. Silver a glance until Charlie said, "This is Eden. She's new, but she'll take great care of you." Then he walked away.

Mrs. Silver said, "Pretty name, Eden."

"Thanks."

Eden looked at her then and froze halfway to a smile. Despite everything she knew about manners and politeness, Eden couldn't stop herself from staring or bring herself to look away. The moment grew long and extremely uncomfortable. Eden's eyes fixed on the luxurious sweep of gold hair, the unsmiling red-lacquered mouth, and then from under extremely expensive sunglasses, the exotic pair of eyes—long lashed and catlike, glittering with the reflection of the sun.

You look great, she thought and wanted so badly to say, but she didn't know why. Nor did Eden understand why she felt such a strange and roiling mix of emotions—admiration, sudden anger, even a faint sense of desperation. It was all so odd, so inappropriate. She'd only just met this woman, so why did she feel as if she'd seen her before? Why was there a sense of danger snaking its way into the pit of her stomach? Eden felt a jolt of anxiety run up her spine and settle at the base of her skull. The woman was beautiful and youthful and something else . . . Eden grasped for it . . . *Familiar*—that was it. She was saying something now and Eden was supposed to answer, but she was lost. She felt light-headed, blood pounding at her temples. *Say something, anything.*

"I'm sorry, I didn't . . ."

"I asked if we've met before. Have you worked somewhere else around here? Maybe Zu—"

"No, I'm new," Eden said. "I mean . . . I've just moved here." *Why was the woman looking at her like that—as if she knew something? As if she recognized the person standing in front of her?* "Can I get you something to drink?"

"Um . . ." She gave Eden a long look, and her expression changed again. Eden watched as slow surprise bloomed behind her cat eyes, and something like fear or concern flitted across her face. She lifted her hand—long, delicate, ringless fingers—to tuck a few wayward strands behind her ear. *That lovely golden hair,* Eden thought. For a moment the woman looked as confused as Eden felt and seemed unable to find the words she needed. But then she seemed to shake herself inwardly, to come to some sort of decision. She smiled—warm and wide.

"I need a glass of wine," she said. *Need.* "But I have to take a look at the wine list first."

"Sure, I'll—I'll let your server know."

"Oh? You're not my server?"

She was disappointed.

"I'm off shift."

"Too bad," Mrs. Silver said. "Maybe next time?"

"Okay."

"My name's Darcy, by the way. It's nice to meet you, Eden."

"You too . . ." Eden hesitated before adding, "Darcy."

After another long moment during which the two of them played some strange game of chicken—neither one able or willing to look away first—Eden finally turned and walked away from the table, across the dining room, into the kitchen, and all the way back to the time clock. She stood there, steam and noise enveloping her, until her heart slowed and the rush of blood in her ears had quieted. But even then, after several minutes in that small safe corner, Eden's hands were still trembling.

CHAPTER 9

Derek poured himself a glass of water from the liter of Evian the waiter had brought and tried to settle himself at his table. He'd been seated smack in the middle of Soleil Bistro's cavernous dining room, and even though it seemed particularly dark and gloomy today, he felt overexposed, as if he were on some kind of display. He hadn't been here since the last time he'd come with Eden—seemed like a lifetime ago—and he was beginning to feel both uncomfortable and slightly angry. He shouldn't have chosen this restaurant—a really stupid mistake—and now that he was here gulping his overly chilled designer water and trying not to remember the night he'd met Eden in this very spot, he realized he shouldn't even have made the plan in the first place.

Eden's mother, Patty, had seen through it right away. She knew there wasn't a burning need for him to return "some things Eden left" at his place to her. There were hardly any things to speak of anyway. He looked down at the small canvas bag at his feet. There was a notebook—the cheap kind you could get at any supermarket—that had a shopping list written on the first page and then nothing else. There was a small collection of barrettes that Eden probably hadn't worn since he'd met her, a couple of tops that she'd long forgotten about, a pair of flannel pajamas that she'd *never* worn, and . . . well, there were the shoes.

He'd put those light running shoes—the prototypes he'd designed just for her—at the bottom of the bag where he couldn't see them. Because the shoes hurt more than anything else. She'd been wearing them when she collapsed in the park that first time. Bad, bad luck. She'd loved those shoes. But she'd loved him too. Hadn't she? He wasn't so sure anymore. The Eden he *had* been sure of had vanished by degrees—by heartbeats. And in the end, she'd left both him and the shoes behind. She didn't want them, and Patty knew it. He hadn't fooled her or himself with that stuttering call he'd made, lying about stumbling across those items and making it sound as if he'd only just thought of returning them instead of obsessing about them and her and clutching onto everything he still had left of her.

Still, Patty had agreed to meet him for lunch. She'd agreed to take the things. Derek could see the pink edge of one running shoe beneath the clothes he'd piled on top, and his throat started to close. He wasn't going to get over Eden any time soon if he kept doing stupid things like this. He knew Patty felt sorry for him, but he also believed (well, *hoped* if he was being honest) that maybe she—and the rest of Eden's family—missed him a little. They liked him very much, of that he *was* sure, and he sensed that they were as baffled as he by how completely Eden had removed him from her life. In the end, of course, they had to support her.

She was their blood, and it was thicker than ever because they'd come so close to losing her. They'd disagreed with her decisions—didn't understand them at all—but ultimately nobody tried to stop her. Not really. Derek shook his head in disgust. He'd actually run interference for Eden after her surgery. He'd told her family how it was natural for her to feel different after such an incredibly traumatic event. He'd pulled out statistics, recommended therapists, and remained unflaggingly optimistic. *Give her time,* he'd told them. *She'll come around.* She came around all right—*all* the damned way around.

It didn't make Derek feel any better that Eden felt so clearly guilty about breaking up with him. Those looks she'd given him, especially when she *allowed* him to touch her (there was really no other word for it), as if she were trying desperately to locate her love for him and just couldn't find it . . . It had just made him feel worse. It might have been better if she'd just turned into a straight bitch with no trace of the old Eden. If not better, at least easier.

"Hi, Derek. Have you been waiting long?"

Startled by the sound of Patty's voice, Derek stood up too quickly and bumped the table, rattling the silverware and making the water tremble.

"Sorry, Patty," he said. "I didn't even see you come in." He pulled out a chair for her.

"You were so deep in thought," she said. "I waved at you from the door, and you looked right through me!" He leaned down so that she could give him a kiss on the cheek (Patty was by far the most petite of all the Harrisons) and a quick, hard hug. He held on for just a second longer than he should have. There followed a few minutes of grace, when it was okay to talk about the weather and what looked good on the menu, pour more water, push the bread basket around, and pass the butter. But there was only so long either one of them could keep it up, and Patty was the first to sigh, put her warm hand on Derek's forearm, and say, "How are you, honey? Honestly?"

"I'm . . ." He had every intention of telling Patty he was fine, things were good, the usual nonsense that he knew she wouldn't believe but that would be better than breaking down, but when he looked at her—her pretty face *so much like Eden's*—he felt his throat grow tight again, and the words just couldn't squeeze through. He swallowed hard and looked away for a moment. The worried concern in her eyes warmed him, but its very presence was a reminder of what had put it there in the first place.

"I've been better," he said finally. "It's been harder than I thought to . . . you know . . ."

Patty gave his arm a squeeze. Her hazel eyes blurred for a moment, but she blinked and the tears went unshed. Derek wondered who or what she was crying for—what part of it caused the most pain. Even though she still looked great, Patty had aged at least a decade while Eden was sick. They all had for that matter, but those months of walking the edge of despair, of not knowing whether Eden would survive, showed in every line on Patty's face. And she didn't even know how convinced Eden had been that she wasn't going to make it. Those dreams of hers . . . Derek could still feel the cold fear in his gut when he remembered them. It had been so difficult to stay hopeful when Eden seemed so sure she would die. He'd never told Patty about the dreams Eden had shared with him—those visions she'd had of her own funeral and then, later, of dying again.

"I understand," Patty said now. "I sometimes think that all of this must be hardest for you. I wish there were something we— something *I* could do. You gave so much to her."

Derek bristled. Though he was sure she didn't mean to, Patty's voice had just a trace of that same pity/guilt combination he'd heard so often in Eden's. He'd never expected or demanded that anyone—Eden least of all—repay him for the time and effort he'd spent taking care of Eden. There was no balance sheet that had to be reconciled here. It had always been about love.

"It's not as if she owes me anything," he told Patty, instantly regretting it when he saw her expression change to one of embarrassment.

"I know," she said. "That's not what I meant."

"I'm sorry, Patty."

"No, don't be. You have nothing to apologize for."

This meeting really had been a mistake, Derek thought again. What could he possibly have been hoping to accomplish by making Patty come out here? All it was doing was reminding her of those terrible days when Eden was sick and reminding him of everything he'd lost. He'd always felt close to Patty—never had any trouble talking to her. But there was a big difference between those intimate conversations he'd had with her at Eden's hospital bedside and the awkward one they were having now. He'd gone from soon-to-be-son-in-law to jilted boyfriend. Pathetic. He was more grateful than he wanted to admit when the waiter approached their table to take their lunch order and interrupted what had become a tense and uncomfortable silence.

After they'd ordered—Derek purposely selecting a dish he'd never tried before in a ridiculous effort to chase away at least one memory—Patty seemed to brighten up a little. She asked him how things were going with his business, saying it seemed like the economy was improving—had he noticed that too? He tried to fall in with the microscopic small talk, offering bland answers and posing a few more equally banal questions about the family he'd come so close to marrying into.

Patty had picked through half of her salad and he'd managed to get down some of his seafood linguini before he buckled again.

"How is Eden doing?" he asked. "Is she . . . Is she feeling okay?"

"You haven't heard from her?"

"Not recently," he lied. It had actually been weeks since he'd gotten any kind of response to the calls and e-mails he'd sent Eden. "But I've been so busy. And I'm sure she has too."

"Yes, of course," Patty said, going along with it. "She seems to be doing fine. She's working, spending a lot of time going to concerts—or shows, I guess, that's what she calls them. She says San Diego is gorgeous."

"She's working?"

"In a restaurant," Patty said. "A really nice one. They have—"

"Is that a good idea? You know, for her health?"

Patty gave him a quick look. There was much in it he didn't really want to see. "You know she has a great medical team down there," Patty said. "And she wouldn't do anything to put herself at risk, considering everything she's . . . well, you know."

"I do know. I was just wondering—"

"Look, you know I don't understand why she felt the need to uproot her whole life any more than you do, Derek. But if this is all part of what has to happen for her to heal, then I can't keep questioning it."

"No, of course not."

"I just hope . . ." Patty trailed off, plucking at her napkin and pursing her lips as if she didn't want to let too much escape from them. "I hope she isn't still trying to find—I mean, trying to find out more about the donor. No good can come of that." She sighed and pushed her plate away.

How many times had Derek told Eden that very same thing? So many that eventually she'd stopped talking to him at all about the dreams she was having in which she felt—no, she was *sure*— that she was experiencing the same things her donor had, that she *was* her donor for those moments. He'd discouraged her from thinking that way as much as he could. The closer Eden felt to her donor, the further she moved away from Derek. There was selfishness at the bottom of his efforts when you got down to it. He didn't believe—not really—that Eden's new heart was capable of reincarnating its previous owner, but her feelings were undeniable all the same. If you really broke it down, the whole concept of being able to put one person's heart in another person's body was a supernatural Frankenstein-type thing.

"Do you think that's what she's doing?" he asked Patty.

"I don't know." Patty hesitated, brushing a few crumbs off the tablecloth. "No, I don't think she is. But I don't know if it will ever really leave her mind."

"How could it?" he said, realizing as the words came out just how true they were.

"She isn't seeing anyone, Derek." There was something like a warning in her voice, and he couldn't quite figure out why. And then the other shoe dropped. "Not yet. But she will, Derek. At some point, she will."

"I wasn't asking—"

"I know you weren't, but . . . you have to stop worrying about her. You deserve to be happy, Derek."

He had no response to that—none that would be in any way appropriate at least—so Derek just bent down, lifted the canvas bag from the floor, and handed it to Patty. It felt heavier than it had when he'd brought it in, but somehow that didn't surprise him. His own body felt as if it had gained ten pounds since the start of this lunch.

"These are the things I told you about," he said. "Thought she might need them or be missing them or whatever."

Derek thought it was to Patty's credit that she didn't even bother looking in the bag. She just folded the top over to cover the contents and placed it on the table. "Thanks, Derek. I'll make sure she gets this." She reached for her purse and for a moment, Derek thought she was going to get up and leave, but she put it on her lap, sighed, and turned to him with something beseeching in her eyes.

"I've brought something for you too," she said, "but I'm so sorry to have to give it to you."

What could she be talking about? Derek's mind started whirling around impossible guesses.

"I want you to know she never meant to hurt you, Derek."

He forced a smile onto his face that likely looked as grotesque as it felt. "You're making me nervous, Patty."

"Sorry, sorry. I'm just . . . This is hard." She reached into her purse then and pulled out a small red velvet box. Derek recognized it immediately. He hadn't thought it possible for this meeting to end on a worse note, but he'd just been proven wrong. Of course, it was his own fault for forcing this get-together in the first place. Nobody to blame but himself.

"She asked if I would give this back to you. She doesn't feel right keeping it. I'm sorry, Derek."

He wished she would stop apologizing and almost told her so, but managed, for once, to keep his mouth shut. Patty put the box down on the table between them. He picked it up, pushed it open, and looked inside. There was his grandmother's Claddagh ring—hands, crown, and heart—gleaming at him like an indictment. Despite his protests that he didn't expect her to return it, Eden had given him back her engagement ring many months ago. It still sat in the sock drawer of his dresser. What else was he going to do with it? They'd called off the wedding, so it was fair enough that she should give him back that ring, but this one . . .

She'd worn it on her right hand, hadn't taken it off—ever—until the day she went into surgery. He didn't remember if she'd ever put it back on again afterward, but then there were so many of those kinds of things that escaped his notice around that time. But the night he'd given it to her—he remembered it so clearly it hurt—they lay with their limbs entangled, the sweat of their passion not yet dry, and she'd whispered in his ear that she'd wear the ring always, that *his heart* was safe with her. There was no reason for her to give this back to him other than to make some kind of statement. She might as well have stabbed him with a dull knife.

"Wow," he said, and cleared the thickness from his throat. "I can't say I ever expected to see this again."

"I'm sor—" Patty caught herself, then looked down at the table. "I promised her I would make sure you got it. That's the only reason I brought it with me today. She said it was a family heirloom. Is that right, Derek?"

"Right." He knew Patty felt bad about this, but Derek was suddenly in no mood to try to lift her spirits. She could have held on to the ring a little longer—or forever. It wouldn't have killed her. "Well, thanks," he said. He shut the box with a muffled snap and slid it into his pocket.

"You know, Derek . . ." Again, Patty seemed reluctant to

speak. "It might be better if . . . well, if . . ." She took a drink of water from her glass. Derek noticed the crimson lipstick stain on the rim. Eden had stopped wearing makeup after the transplant. She said it made her face feel "heavy." He wondered if she'd gone back to wearing it now. And then he wondered if he was ever going to get the chance to see her and find out.

"Maybe you should make a clean break from Eden. For your own sake, Derek." He raised his eyebrows in surprise. Had Eden said something?

"That's not coming from Eden," Patty said, reading his thoughts. "At least not directly. It's something I've been thinking. It's so clear how much you love her, Derek—how much you've always loved her—but the kind of change she's gone through . . . It's just that I think—we *all* think that it would be better for you if . . ."

"If I left her alone? Permanently?"

"That's not what I meant."

"I know," he said miserably. There followed a pause so strained that Derek wouldn't have minded a fire alarm or gunshots or the earth to just open up and swallow them both.

"Look, it's okay, Patty. I'm fine. And I know it hasn't been easy for you either. It's good advice, and I'll take it to heart." He cringed inwardly over his choice of words. "Thanks for meeting me here today—you didn't have to, and I appreciate it."

"Derek, I—"

"Not to worry, Patty."

He covered her hand with his own for a moment and threw enough cash on the table for lunch and the tip. Now struck with an intense need to leave the place, he couldn't wait for the bill. "I have to get back to work," he said. "Can I walk you out?"

Patty gave him a small tight smile and got up from her chair. "Thanks so much for lunch, Derek. It's been wonderful to see you."

She wasn't any better a liar than her daughter, Derek thought. More was the pity.

The chivalrous thing to do would have been to escort Patty to her car and make sure she was off safely, but when they emerged from the restaurant, both of them blinking in the sudden daylight, Patty insisted she was fine and told him she was sure he needed to get on with his day. It was all true, but Derek didn't go back to his office after giving Patty a quick peck on the cheek and leaving her there outside the restaurant. Instead, he turned and walked up Park, trying to fool himself about his direction but knowing exactly where he was headed.

Eden's old apartment.

Minutes later, he stood outside, looking up at the ivy-covered brick to the window the two of them had looked out of together so many times. As if to torture himself even further, Derek put his hand in his pocket and closed it around the small velvet box. Patty was right, of course. Eden was gone—in more ways than one—and he needed to get the hell over it. But there was the other thing Patty had said too that just kept bouncing around in his head. *I hope she's not trying to find out about her donor.*

What if finding out about her donor was the only thing that would allow Eden to be happy finally? What if that was keeping her from him? And what if someone actually helped (instead of hindered) her in her quest to understand those dreams—to make peace with the person who had given Eden the gift of a heart?

This is a bad idea. Derek could hear the voice in his head, but it was small and much too soft to shout over the other one that was screaming out how Eden might love him again, might be *herself* again, if only he could help her with this.

Now he walked fast—almost running—back to his office several blocks away, the idea blooming huge and hopeful inside him. He was sweating and felt grimy by the time he got to his building, but he didn't even bother to stop for a glass of water.

He pulled the little red box out of his pocket and placed it next to his computer. It was a fixed point he could look at—a talisman he could touch. His fingers hesitated above the keyboard for just a moment—just long enough for him to debate whether or not he was really doing the right thing and decide it didn't matter—and then he began typing words into the search box.

CHAPTER 10

Eden took a last look at her reflection and hurried herself out the door. She'd already spent way too much time in front of the mirror trying to decide between the faded jeans and the black pants, the blue blouse or the red T-shirt . . . So much attention to detail—to the way she looked. It was as if she were going out on a romantic date, not a casual get-together with a new friend. But for some reason Eden had not been able to figure, it was important to her that she look attractive (*beautiful* even) for her meeting with Darcy. She supposed it could be explained at least partially by simple female competition, the desire to look as good as the other woman (though Darcy was already so lovely that such an attempt was futile), but Eden knew that wasn't all of it. There was something else behind her almost-frantic attempts to outfit herself—a kind of niggling concern for her appearance that wriggled around in the back of her brain, irritating her consciousness like a splinter under a fingernail. Eden couldn't define it because she didn't know exactly what it was or where it came from. She knew only that this hyperconsciousness she had of Darcy's beauty and her own inability to match it in any way had been present from the moment she'd laid eyes on the woman in Poquette.

"What's wrong with you?" Marisol had asked that day when she came upon Eden at the time clock, still in a weird state of shivery almost-dread after her initial encounter with Darcy.

"Nothing," Eden had snapped, quickly reaching up to tighten her already-buttoned blouse with that instinctive response. Nobody could know. Nobody could see that scar. The mere thought of having to explain what it was exhausted Eden. And although having a heart transplant wasn't something to be ashamed of, deep within her metaphoric heart, the one that *hadn't* been replaced, Eden still felt as if she'd been rewarded for something she hadn't earned. No amount of therapy seemed likely to change that.

"Well, you look all rattled," Marisol had said, her eyes narrowing. "I just thought maybe you'd—"

"No, I'm fine," Eden had said. "First day, you know. Just catching my breath is all."

Marisol looked suspicious, and Eden worried that she was already making an enemy. *And you know how easy it is to offend Marisol.* The thought dropped in—again—as if someone else had spoken it.

"Did Mrs. Silver give you a hard time?"

"No," Eden said. "She was . . . fine."

Something shifted in Marisol's face then, as if she were putting something away—storing something for later use—and Eden had no idea what it was or how she was supposed to interpret it.

"She *is* fine," Marisol said. "I mean, it's not her. Sometimes they just get overly . . . She has a lot of money. She and her husband used to come in all the time and spend big bucks, so they want us all to take care of her now when she comes in. Special attention, VIP, all of that." There was undeniable irritation creeping into her tone. "It's never *her*, really."

"Her husband?" Eden asked, in spite of herself.

"He's dead," Marisol said. "We went to the funeral. It was fucking weird, actually." And with that, Marisol turned and walked away from Eden.

Something about that statement and the absurd offhand way Marisol had delivered it had struck Eden as impossibly humorous, and she was appalled by her own sudden urge to laugh out loud.

Only moments before that encounter with Marisol, Eden had experienced the odd shock of almost-recognition in meeting Darcy. But then, just as suddenly, it morphed into a whole new feeling of intrigue. And below the intrigue, there was an indefinable unease. Very much, in fact, what Eden was feeling right now.

Eden couldn't resist checking her face one more time in the rearview mirror as she started the car. She'd developed a nice glow—one couldn't quite call it a tan yet—from living in San Diego, even though she'd spent very little time walking the beaches and none at all sunbathing. Just the presence of the perpetual sun in this part of the world was enough to give a person that gold-kissed look, apparently. Before her surgery, Eden had never minded Portland's gray skies and rain—she'd even found them romantic and had enjoyed the way they blurred the landscape, giving it softer edges. Like so many other things, though, her feelings shifted radically after she had received her new heart. One of the first things that had come to mind as soon as she was thinking straight, in fact, was how depressing she found the rain and how much she craved sunlight. That feeling only grew stronger over the months of her recovery. It was one more reason to leave. *But see,* Eden thought now, *it suits me.* She looked better than she had for a long time. She looked *healthy,* but still—there it was again—not as lovely as Darcy.

My new friend, thought Eden.

Darcy had come back to Poquette very soon after Eden's first day, again at the tail end of a lunch shift, and this time Eden, who was working the closing shift and feeling much more confident, waited on her for the duration. The same sense of familiarity washed over Eden when she arrived at Darcy's table, bread basket at the ready, but it ebbed quickly, leaving just edgy curiosity in its wake. Darcy had left her sunglasses at home this time, and her long blond hair was pulled back in a pony-tail. Even though she was wearing jeans (albeit very expensive ones), a plain white oxford shirt, and high-heeled sandals, Darcy looked as if she'd come from a workout. Or, maybe, Eden specu-lated later, it was a look meant to telegraph "sporty." At any rate, she seemed somehow more approachable than she had the last time, at least to Eden. Marisol had been right about the fawning management, however. Once again, there was bowing and scrap-ing as if Darcy were a head of state. Not a celebrity, Eden thought. Celebrities got a crasser kind of attention—a sort of leering obsequiousness. This was about money, Eden decided—well, money and beauty.

For some reason, though, Darcy treated Eden as if she were in on the joke—as if they shared some kind of isn't-this-all-so-silly secret. As if they were already friends.

"So, what's your story?" Darcy had asked her sometime between the soup and the salad (both of which Darcy barely touched, Eden noted). "You're not from around here, are you?"

"How can you tell?" Eden shrugged off a sliver of annoyance at a question that seemed a little too personal, telling herself this was how conversations between patrons and waitresses often went.

"Something about you . . . ," Darcy started, and smiled. "You seem . . . not out of place—that's the wrong phrase—but . . . Oh, I'm sorry, that sounded terrible. Don't mind me. I rarely know what I'm talking about." Her tone, thought Eden, implied the opposite. She assured Darcy that she wasn't in any way offended, but the woman kept apologizing, ending finally with, "I should make it up to you. Let me buy you a glass of wine or something."

And now, here she was, on her way to that "glass of wine or something." They'd planned to meet at a little coffeehouse just north of Poquette. Darcy had mentioned something about it being a good place to hear local bands that were just starting out, which gave Eden a small thrill. Her appreciation for live music—preferably of the bluesy rock variety—was new, another on the list of postsurgical preferences that she'd begun to accept and fold into her new self. As she pulled into the parking lot of the place—Zulu's, it was called—excitement tickled the base of her spine. She didn't know whether this was because of Darcy or just because she was finally going out somewhere to have fun as if she

were just an ordinary girl (*woman*, actually) and not some freak-
ish shut-in with someone else's heart beating inside her chest.
Either way, Eden thought, she was going to roll with it.

Darcy was sitting outside on the patio, underneath a
bougainvillea-entwined trellis (another one of San Diego's bo-
nuses was that there was almost no event that couldn't be con-
ducted outdoors), wearing artfully faded blue jeans and a simple
but striking black pullover that highlighted the gold sweep of her
hair. It was an almost identical outfit to the one Eden had come
up with after all those combinations in front of the mirror. And
although it could be argued that jeans and a black top were an
extremely common combination, there was something about the
similarity—something about the way Darcy held herself in her
clothes—that once more sent an anxious ripple through Eden.

"Hey, there you are!" Darcy smiled when she caught sight of
Eden and stood up, waving.

Why is she so happy to see me?

Eden gave a little wave in response and made her way across
the patio. There was a half-full glass of white wine on the table
already, so either Darcy drank fast or had been waiting awhile.
But Eden wasn't late—she'd made sure of that. Yet the very first
thing that Eden said—as if the words were pulled out of her
mouth—was, "Hi, Darcy. Hope I'm not late!"

"No, not at all," Darcy said.

"Oh, goo—," Eden started, but before she could finish the
sentence, Darcy had pulled her into a hug. Eden could feel herself stiffen and pull away and tried to compensate by leaning
back in, but the whole thing felt weird. Eden had been skittish
about being touched since her surgery, but that wasn't all of it. It
seemed odd to her that Darcy—someone she barely knew—

would already be so familiar. But there wasn't time to analyze it within the two seconds it took to embrace and release. There was only time to feel the ends of Darcy's hair brushing her shoulder and inhale her scent of wine and white flowers. Eden fought the urge to cover her chest with her hands and wondered if she would ever stop feeling so self-conscious about the scar. She fumbled, smiled, and sat down with a total lack of grace. But if Darcy noticed Eden's awkwardness, she gave no indication.

"I'm so glad you could make it," Darcy said. "You look great! It's so nice to see you out of that uniform. Must be nice to *be* out of it too, I'm guessing." She gave a little high laugh and flicked her hair off her shoulders with the quick and expert motion of someone who repeated such gestures many times a day.

"Yes," Eden said, her voice sounding much slower than Darcy's to her own ears. "It is. But I don't mind it much. The uniform, I mean."

"Shall we get you something to drink?"

Eden wondered if the fact that it was still light outside qualified as an excuse not to drink wine and decided it didn't. "I'm just going to have some tea," she said. "I thought this . . . I thought there was only coffee and tea here."

"It used to be alcohol-free," Darcy said, her eyebrows slightly raised, "but they started serving beer and wine a few months ago. Popular demand, I guess." As if to underscore the point, Darcy took a swig from her wineglass. "Have you been here before?"

"No, not really," Eden said, and realized instantly how ridiculous that sounded. The truth—much too complicated to explain to Darcy or even to herself—was that she *hadn't* been here before, but she was having another one of those inconvenient and uncomfortable déjà vu moments.

"I ordered a couple of snacks," Darcy said. "There's a band

playing in a bit and it gets kind of loud, so I like to get my order in before they start. I didn't know what you liked, so I just got—"

"That's great," Eden said. "Thanks." She was suddenly parched and grateful for the glass of water sitting on the table.

"Do you listen to much live music?" Darcy asked. "I used to get out more often to hear local bands—there's something really great about hearing people when they're still working out their sound, you know? But I haven't done it as much lately."

"Too busy?"

"Um . . ." Darcy flicked her hair again. "Yes, I suppose so. Busy and . . . other things."

Eden was about to ask what kinds of *other things* had interfered, but a waitress appeared at Darcy's side at that moment, bearing a tray containing a basket of bread, stuffed grape leaves, a bowl of strawberries and cream, and a miniature pizza. It was a combination of items that only someone who had no idea what she wanted could have put together. Darcy quickly ordered another glass of wine, and Eden managed to ask for an herbal tea before the waitress—unsmiling and somnambulant— disappeared again.

"I know," Darcy said, reading Eden's expression. "There isn't much of a theme here." She laughed again and pointed to the food. "It's a bit crazy, really."

"Kind of," Eden said, smiling. She picked up a strawberry and bit into it. Something gave way, and she felt her shoulders relax. The ice, she thought, was broken.

"I didn't know what you'd like," Darcy said, "so I got something from every category."

"Thanks," Eden said. "It looks good, actually." Darcy was smiling—pleased with herself, Eden thought, or maybe it was the wine. Either way, she seemed to have softened a bit. Her lips looked a little less tense, smudged even. She took another sip from the glass, tipping and then draining it. She really was a strikingly beautiful woman, Eden thought. She could also tell that Darcy was comfortable in her own beauty—had never doubted it and so never needed to flaunt it. She was understated about it—Eden could see this in every gesture she made—and that made her even more alluring. *It's no wonder . . .* , Eden thought, and then stopped herself cold. No wonder what? Darcy was talking, and Eden had missed the beginning of the sentence. She pulled her focus again, shaking her head slightly as if to clear it of these odd, wandering thoughts.

"Have I asked you that already?" Darcy was saying.

"Asked me . . . ?"

"Where you came from. You said you moved here, didn't you?"

"I don't think . . . I might have," Eden said. She liked Darcy, who was smiling and radiating warmth, so why didn't she want to tell her anything personal? It was time, Eden thought, to get over her need to keep everything so private and secret. Eventually it would drive away anyone who wanted to have even the simplest conversations, let alone anything deeper.

"I moved down here from Oregon a while ago," she said, taking another sip of her heavily chlorinated tap water. Darcy, she noticed, hadn't touched her water glass. "From Portland."

"Oh, really? People say they love it up there—that it's such a nice, civilized city. Why'd you come down here?"

It wasn't as if Eden didn't want to unburden herself—to just spill all the ugly details on the table in front of this lovely, attentive woman; it was that she just couldn't. The thoughts, feelings, and words to express them were stuck firmly in her throat. "You know, it rains a lot there," she said lamely. Darcy smiled, waiting for the rest of it. "My parents . . . When I was little, we used to live near the ocean," Eden went on. "I needed to be near the water again. And the sun. I needed that too." It was so ridiculous to lie about something so trivial; yet Eden couldn't stop herself.

"Where'd you live when you were a kid?" Darcy asked. "I mean, which ocean?"

"Um . . . Santa Monica," Eden said. It was the first name to come into her head.

"Really?" Darcy said, "That's so funny because—"

"You grew up there too? Don't tell me."

"No, I—"

"Where *did* you grow up?" Eden was perspiring. Where was the tea already? She needed something to do with her hands, and her water glass had been drained down to the ice.

"I'm one of those rare people who actually come from San Diego," Darcy said. "I was born here."

"Oh, so you—"

"Didn't grow up here," Darcy said abruptly. "Went to college here and just stayed. Which does make me like most San Diegans, I guess. Everyone here is from somewhere else."

"That sounds like a good name for a CD," Eden said, relieved beyond measure to be off the topic of herself. "You said you used to listen to local bands more often. You were about to tell me why you don't anymore." Another lie. They were coming fast and easy.

Now it was Darcy who seemed uncomfortable. A shadow passed across her eyes, and her hands picked unconsciously at the wet edges of her cocktail napkin. It was odd, Eden thought, how her eyes seemed to change color even as you looked right at them.

Eden could have sworn they were cat green a minute ago, but now they seemed almost golden.

"Some things in my life changed," Darcy said. "I've sort of been going through a period of adjustment. I guess that's what you'd call it." Her mouth turned up into a small, mirthless smile. "I stopped going out so much, just in general."

Eden remembered what Marisol had said about Darcy's husband and how strange it had been to go to the funeral. What kind of woman invited restaurant staff to her husband's funeral? It was suddenly a question that Eden had to have answered.

"Why?" Eden said. "If you don't mind my asking." Darcy's gaze had become a bit misty, and Eden didn't think she was going to get an answer. The sleepwalking waitress returned at that point with wine that Darcy welcomed and tea that was, at best, lukewarm. It didn't matter—it was a useful prop, and Eden wrapped her hands around the mug as if warding off a chill.

"I don't mind that you asked," Darcy said after the waitress had departed once again. "And I don't mind telling you. But I haven't really . . . I don't really have that many friends. Well, close friends. Or . . . I don't know, girlfriends, I guess." She sighed and took a long drink from her glass. The wine was cold—too cold by the look of the frost on the glass—and the color of straw. Eden's heart gave an uncomfortable thump. It did that sometimes now, as if to let her know that it wasn't really hers and didn't really belong in her body. Her doctors had assured her that there was nothing to worry about—that this kind of "extra" beat happened to everyone, and it was just because of her heightened sensitivity that she noticed it. Eden accepted the explanation, but, as with so many others, she didn't quite buy it.

"Anyway," Darcy continued, and Eden sensed that she'd made

up her mind to go on—to reveal something she'd been holding back. "My husband died," she said. Eden didn't know how to interpret the look that crossed Darcy's face then—a strange spasm that could have been grief, disgust, anger, or none of those things. Nor could Eden explain why her own cheeks flushed and her blood seemed to lurch in her veins.

"I'm sorry," Eden said, although she wasn't. Quite the opposite. She was appalled by her own sudden lack of any kind of sympathy for this widow. The presurgery Eden would never have been so cold.

"Thank you," Darcy said. "We weren't like some couples. I mean, some couples do things separately—have different interests. We spent a lot of time together, so when he died . . ." She'd started tearing tiny pieces off the napkin and rolling them up between her fingers. "I just changed the way I did things. I stopped going out so much alone. It felt strange."

"That must have been difficult," Eden said. Her voice sounded hard and cold, not at all what she intended. She drank her tepid tea and cleared her throat. "How long . . . I mean, when did he . . . ?"

Darcy pursed her lips, looked down, noticed the shredded cocktail napkin and balled-up bits of paper for the first time, and swept them to the side of the table. "It's been a while," she said. "What can I say? Maybe it should have been easier, or maybe it should get easier at some point, but it hasn't for me." There was a note of bitterness creeping into her voice. "I haven't been able to get on with it, you know? Or something like that. And that's probably more than you want to know." She attempted a laugh that didn't quite work.

"No," said Eden, "not at all. I mean, I did ask. I can't understand how it feels to lose someone like that . . ." Here Eden trailed off, unable to finish the thought because this too was untrue. She *did* know how it felt to lose someone. She'd gained the life that someone else had lost, and in the process she had lost a good portion of herself.

"We used to go to Poquette often," Darcy said. Eden managed to keep herself from saying, *I know.* "My husband liked that place a lot," she continued. "Sometimes I wonder if they expect me to tip like he used to. I can't, you know."

Eden watched her, wondering what kind of response she wanted.

"It's not that I don't want to, but he was so lavish. I can't afford . . ."

"You tipped me very well," Eden said.

"Yes, he was very generous," Darcy said, as if Eden hadn't spoken at all. Her voice was starting to slide into monotone, as if she'd said this before or was trying to convince herself of it. "I'm too young to be on the shelf, don't you think, Eden?"

"I don't know," Eden said, smiling. "How old are you?"

"Suppose I had that coming," Darcy said, returning the smile.

"I didn't mean it that way. I don't know that there's a time limit for grieving, is there? Everyone thinks there's some kind of period where you're supposed to get into your head and work everything out, and then suddenly you're just supposed to emerge all fresh and clean as if nothing's happened. It doesn't work like that."

"It sounds like you've been through this," Darcy said.

"No, I haven't. I just—I understand how people can be."

Darcy tipped her head to one side and gave Eden a strange little half smile. *She doesn't believe me,* thought Eden, and it made her unaccountably nervous. "I wasn't sure you were going to agree to meet me," Darcy said. "I'm glad you did."

"Why's that? I mean, why would you think I wouldn't meet you?"

Darcy shrugged. "You're new over there, but I know people talk." She tucked a length of hair behind her ear. "Do they talk about me when I come in?"

We went to the funeral. It was fucking weird, actually.

"No, no."

"Really? Of course they do." Darcy's tone was light, but the lightness sounded strained.

"Only in positive terms," Eden said. "Nobody's ever complained to me about you or anything."

"A few of them came to my husband's funeral," Darcy said. It was just this side of creepy, Eden thought, the way Darcy managed to read her thoughts. "He was really popular there. Do they ever talk about him?"

"No," Eden said.

"It's really the last thing I have that we used to do together," Darcy said, as if apologizing.

"Was it . . . ," Eden started, then stopped, realizing there was no tactful way of asking if Darcy's husband had been sick or old or had had an accident or had simply just woken up dead one morning.

"I miss him," Darcy said. But that wasn't what it sounded like to Eden. What it sounded like was *I hate him.*

There was a sudden clanging followed by the sound of instruments being tuned. Eden and Darcy turned at the same time to a small stage at the far edge of the patio where three musicians were warming up. They were young, but not too young—two guys and a girl—all dressed in the same studied casualness of black jeans and T-shirts. They were pierced and tattooed in all the right places. The girl's hair was cut asymmetrically, short purple on one side and a long black curve on the other, and she looked as if she'd been starving herself for at least a week. One of the guys was sleeping with her, of that much Eden was sure, but she couldn't tell yet which one. By the end of the set, it would be obvious.

Darcy was saying something about the band, but Eden couldn't make out the words. A wave of the most intense déjà vu she'd ever experienced had broken over her, and Eden felt as if she were drowning. She'd been here—this place, this table, this moment with the sun sinking and the ocean just over there across the Coast Highway. She'd heard this music, the sound of Darcy's voice in her ear. She knew what was going to happen next. It was . . . right . . . there. Eden started to see little points of colored light dancing in front of her, and her heart began beating wildly. Her throat felt scratchy, as if it were about to close up, and her palms were sweating. *What is happening to me?*

"Eden, are you okay? You look a little pale."

"I—I just . . ." The sound of her own words echoed, distorted, in the air around Eden. She felt panic rise in her chest as she tried to decide what to do. She couldn't fall apart like this in front of Darcy. What would happen? They would have to call a doctor or an ambulance, and they'd come and see her. They'd open her shirt. No, she couldn't let that happen. She was fine. Fine, fine, fine.

Darcy put her hand over Eden's. It was cool and soft, and something about its weight brought Eden back to her senses. Her heart, though, wouldn't stop. "I'm okay," Eden said. "But I think I should go home. I'm sorry, Darcy."

"Are you sure?"

"I might have . . . I might have eaten something. I don't know."

"Not at Poquette, I hope." Eden stared at Darcy, confused. "I'm kidding, Eden! Please."

"I'm really not myself," Eden said. "I don't know what it is." She stood up. The worst of it had passed now, but she still felt as if she were both in and out of her body at the same time. It was too much to try to negotiate. She had to leave. She needed to be alone.

"Let me walk you out," Darcy said. "Are you okay to drive? Do you want a ride?"

"I'm okay, really," Eden said. She was moving fast, weaving through tables. She had to get out.

"Is there anything I can do for you?" Darcy asked. "Do you need anything? Are you sure?"

"Thank you, Darcy. Hey, I'm really sorry to run out on you like this. I'm just—"

"Maybe you should see a doctor."

"I'll be fine."

Darcy had followed Eden so closely that when Eden stopped short in front of her car, she almost tripped into Darcy's arms. Darcy didn't seem to notice that she was blocking Eden's entry and was staring at her full in the face. Her eyes were now glowing hazel in the setting sun. Eden didn't know what to think when her new friend reached out and gripped both her arms.

"I'm going to call you to make sure you're okay," Darcy said.

"Really, I'm—"

"Let me, will you?"

"Okay."

"So I'll need your phone number."

"Right."

There was a long moment where neither of them seemed to know what to do. It took Darcy what felt like an unreasonably long time to release her strong grasp of Eden's arms and reach for her cell phone. Eden recited her phone number, and Darcy punched it into her phone. "Where do you live?" she asked Eden.

"Close," Eden said. "Ten minutes."

"I'll give you twenty and call you to make sure you made it home okay. Okay?"

Eden smiled in spite of herself. It was something her mother would have said. "Yes, okay, Darcy."

Eden was in the car, keys in the ignition, when Darcy leaned over for a final word. She was so close that Eden could feel the heat of her skin and the winey puff of her breath. "I don't know why, Eden, but I trust you. It's been so long since I had someone to talk to. I'm not wrong, am I? I mean, I can trust you, right?"

Eden thought Darcy might have been a bit tipsy, but it still seemed an odd question at the end of what had already been an odd encounter, and Eden was suddenly exhausted. She was too young to feel as if she couldn't do something as uncomplicated as having tea with a friend, and yet . . .

"Yes," she said. "Of course you can trust me."

"Okay," Darcy said. "Twenty minutes. I'm calling you."

Darcy watched Eden pull out and waited until she turned the corner onto the Coast Highway headed north. No more than five minutes later—Eden was debating whether or not to pull over and inhale some ocean air—her cell phone buzzed with the sound of an incoming text message. Could that be Darcy already? If so, she was crossing over from concerned to stalkerish.

But the message wasn't from Darcy; it was from Derek. It had been a while since he'd contacted her, and seeing his name on the small screen brought guilt and regret flooding back over Eden. It wasn't fair. Why wouldn't he let her go?

Call me, the message read. *Please.*

Unwanted tears stung Eden's eyes, blurring the road. She blinked hard and took her foot off the gas. The ocean was exactly what she needed right now—the sound of surf and the feel of sand under her bare feet.

She erased Derek's message with one hand and with the other, she steered her car toward the water.

CHAPTER 11

PORTLAND

Derek stared at his computer screen, his mind spinning. He'd typed **heart transplant cellular memory** into Google more than two hours ago and had roamed from one personal story to the next of recipients taking on the characteristics, likes, dislikes, and even the spouses of their donors. Every story was suffused with emotion and conviction. It was real. It had happened many times. There was a crawling sensation at the base of his spine, and a dull headache starting to throb at his left temple. These headaches had been coming more frequently over the last couple of months, and it bothered him. Before Eden left, he'd never had headaches. These days he kept a variety of analgesics, everything from acetaminophen to ibuprofen, stashed within easy reach wherever he went. Sighing, Derek picked up his coffee and took a long sip, screwing up his face in disgust as soon as the liquid hit his tongue. It had gone tepid and bitter from sitting too long; the same thing, he thought wryly, that was happening to him now.

The stories he'd read bothered him deeply and not in a way he could easily define. There was always a rational explanation, most often the power of suggestion, for why heart transplant patients so often felt such a close kinship with their donors, but Derek wasn't sure. A small part of him thought—no, *knew* unequivocally—that it was the heart itself. It wasn't just a pump or a senseless lump of muscle. The heart remembered. He hadn't believed it—or maybe he'd just decided not to—but he now felt that Eden's heart too had its own memories. And those memories had led her away from him.

Derek shook his head as if to rid it of its annoying thoughts. He hadn't meant to spend so long surfing the Internet for transplant stories. No, he'd come into his lovely steel-and-glass office with his extra-large coffee, fully intending to attend to business. There was a manufacturing issue with his latest design, and there were indications that the "barefoot technology" he'd invested so much in was already waning in popularity. His was a small business, but his clientele was fiercely devoted; he needed to be spending more time taking care of it—and of his clients. He couldn't let everything fall apart just because he'd been dumped by a girl.

But, as resolute as he was about carrying on, Derek couldn't convince even himself that Eden was just a girl.

After his lunch with Patty, he had been in a fever, determined to find out everything he could about heart transplants that he didn't already know from his months taking care of Eden, and trying his best to ferret out any information about the donor who had made it possible for Eden to live. He hadn't gotten very far. If a donor's family wanted to remain anonymous, it was extremely difficult, even for the recipient, to get any details. Not to mention that everyone, from doctors to therapists, recommended against going down that road. For someone who wasn't even *related* to the recipient, it was impossible. Even so, he'd crafted a letter to be forwarded to the donor's family. His fiancée, he'd written (although she no longer was his fiancée at that point), was over-whelmed with gratitude for the gift she'd been given (although sometimes he didn't know if that was true at all) and wished nothing more than to be able to express that gratitude to the people who'd lost a loved one so that she could live.

At that point he'd stopped, unsure how to continue—unable to articulate why he needed to have any morsel of information that they could spare and at a loss as to how to go about begging for it. He looked down at his company stationery—he'd gone completely old-school with the whole process, figuring that maybe the formality of it, the fact that he was an upstanding member of his community, might have some effect—and stared at the curling ink lines on the cream-colored page until they blurred. He was a moony ex who'd practically been left at the altar and was trying anything he could to get Eden back. That was what it came down to, he thought. And that was no reason to further disturb the lives of some family who'd already encoun-tered a much greater loss than he had. The whole thing seemed ridiculous.

He threw out the letter. Then, for good measure, he erased the search history relating to transplants on his computer. And he took the two books he'd purchased, but not yet read, about cel-lular memory (the only two books he could find on the issue, it turned out, and one of which was a memoir by a woman who'd actually had a transplant) and stashed them on the top of his bookshelf behind a large set of leather chess piece bookends.

He couldn't forget the look of pity on Patty's face as she'd sat across from him at the table—it had made him want to rip out what was left of his own heart. Winning Eden back by discovering the identity of her donor had seemed a good idea at the time, but he knew what he was doing was only prolonging the inevitable final break from Eden. So after that first, hot flush of a discovery quest, Derek gave up. Or at least he thought he gave up. He couldn't stop himself from calling her entirely or sending her e-mails or text messages. She averaged, Derek thought bitterly, about a twenty percent response rate, and most of those were perfunctory at best and lacking in anything he could interpret as warmth. Still, she did respond once in a while, and he could live with that.

But then he decided to bring up the ring.

Yes, in retrospect, it was a stupid thing to do. But Derek couldn't fault himself for it, even now. Not once, through everything that had happened with her illness, transplant, and recovery had Derek ever wished that he hadn't devoted so much time to Eden. At her lowest point, when she was barely able to do anything for herself, Derek could see how much it pained Eden to be so helpless and what a burden she felt she was. But Derek never felt there was anything owed to him. It was never about saving up favors to call in for later. Even before the marriage vows they hadn't ended up taking, Derek had accepted Eden exactly as she was—in sickness and in health—so he hadn't been trying to cash in any emotional chips by bringing up the ring. He would have done it whether or not he'd spent months on end at her bedside. At least that was what he told himself later.

"Your mother gave me the ring," he'd told her during one of

their rare and oddly distant phone calls. There was a long pause on the other end. Eden was so quiet, Derek thought he'd lost the signal.

"Okay," she said finally. She cleared her throat, and he waited, sure there would be some explanation forthcoming, but no, just another long silence.

"You didn't have to do that," he said. There was a tremble in his voice that he could not control. "I never intended . . . I wanted you to keep that, Eden. It was a gift."

"It was your grandmother's ring," she said. "It wasn't right for me to keep it."

"It stopped being my grandmother's ring the minute you put it on your finger. It's . . . It was your ring."

"I just felt it would be better," she said. There was no sadness in her voice that he could detect. How he wished he could see her so that he could at least find some hint of the pain he was feeling in her eyes. But she would never have allowed a video call. She barely tolerated phone contact as it was.

"Better for what?"

"For . . . because, Derek. Because we have to . . . I have to . . . I'm sorry if it hurt your feelings," she said. "I didn't mean to do that; I really didn't."

How many times had he heard her say that? It had rankled before, but this time it was impossible to swallow.

"Was it such a chore," he asked, sarcasm sharpening his tone, "to look at it? Or even know that it was in your possession? Was it so *burdensome* for you to hold on to that ring even if you never wore it? After all we've been through—"

"Derek, I have to go. I said I was sorry. We shouldn't even be talking. It's a bad idea. Just leads to . . . to . . . I have to go. Bye, Derek."

It had been very difficult to get in touch with her since then. He'd blown whatever chance he'd had at . . . at *what*? Reconciliation? As if she were anywhere near something like that. He picked up the small box containing the ring that he'd kept on his desk since Patty had given it back to him. The velvet was beginning to get worn from his constant rubbing at it as if it were some kind of rabbit's foot. It was true that he could have phrased it differently, he thought. And perhaps he should have tried not to sound quite so desperate, but he didn't want to take back the words. Giving back the ring, especially the way she'd done it, was a pointed statement, and she deserved to be called out on it.

Of course, if he were a rational man, Derek would have interpreted that statement the same way everyone else did—Eden's way of saying, *Leave me alone*—but common sense seemed to have deserted him at more or less the same time that Eden had. So Derek decided to interpret the action of giving back the ring a different way. Perhaps, he rationalized, it was Eden's way of getting a rise out of him—of forcing him to act, to find a way back into her life. It was a long shot, Derek knew, but it was possible. Otherwise, why would she have bothered? She could just have thrown the damned thing away or buried it in a drawer somewhere. But no. She was making a point.

And that was when Derek started once again to research the literature on heart transplants. Like an addict justifying his habit, he told himself it was casual—just an article here and there when he had time; it wasn't that important; it didn't really matter; he *could stop anytime*. But here he was, back in the thick of it, tying other transplant stories to Eden's and already pondering how he could inveigle his way into discovering the identity of Eden's donor.

Derek stared into his coffee cup, debating how badly he wanted to start all over with a fresh cup and whether or not he should go and get one himself or stick his head out the door and ask—no, actually beg—one of his staff to get one for him. He knew what would happen. Charles would raise one eyebrow and lift one corner of his mouth into a sneer. Wendy would give him a shocked you-can't-possibly-ask-a-woman-to-get-you-coffee-because-that-is-a-completely-sexist-and-borderline-discriminatory-thing-to-do stare, and Xander would simply ignore him. Derek would then have to sweeten the deal with the offer of beverages for everyone in the office and also, why not, the pastry of his or her choice. It was extortion, but he didn't mind. In fact, the little dance he did with his employees, all of whom were extremely snotty but highly intelligent, effective, and so fiercely loyal to him that he often thought of them as coworkers, was one of the things that had kept him sane throughout his breakup with Eden. He hadn't discussed all the details with them, wanting to keep at least some kind of professional distance, but they knew enough about what was going on. Despite their attitudes of superiority, he knew they not only respected him but cared about what happened to him. Then again, Derek thought, their jobs did depend on his ability to stay at least halfway competent.

He pushed his chair back and stood up. He needed a break. As satisfying as it would be to have a sparring match with them, a walk around the block would be better for him. When he opened his door, Derek was greeted by an immediate and unnatural hush as all three turned quickly to their keyboards. They'd been talking about him. He was bemused. Usually, these three had much more pressing issues on their minds—new apps, bad films, and food of all kinds—than the personal details of their boss's life, but Derek supposed it wasn't surprising. He *had* been distracted lately. And normally his door was always open—literally and metaphorically. He'd been closing it often lately.

"What's going on, guys?" Derek forced a smile. His eyes scanned the outer office. It was large enough that everyone had a decent amount of space to work, but also open enough that nobody could disappear from view. He could see Xander and Charles exchange a meaningful glance; Wendy could barely look at him. He felt awkward, a slight heat rising to his face.

"It's all good, all good," Xander said. At twenty-two, Xander was the youngest person in the office and also the most pierced and tattooed. A red and black snake hissed at the base of his throat, and the steel ball from his tongue piercing clicked against his teeth as he talked. "You need some coffee, D.?"

"Are you offering?" Derek asked, incredulous. Clearly, he'd been more distracted than he'd known if Xander was offering to actually do something for him without being bribed.

"I can get it," Wendy said. "If you want."

Despite her placid blond beauty and relative youth (she was only in her early twenties), Wendy had the bluest vocabulary Derek had ever heard. She knew words and turns of phrase that he was sure had even escaped some maximum security prisons. As a rule, she was utterly immune to embarrassment, so he was shocked to see a red flush creeping up her pale cheeks.

"What's going on?" Derek asked. "Did something happen that I don't know about yet? Are we declaring bankruptcy or something?"

"Just trying to be nice, boss." Xander's clicking tongue sounded amplified in the too-quiet office.

"Okay," Derek said. "I'm going to run down to the Koffee Klatch myself. Anyone want anything?"

"No, thanks."

"I'm cool."

"It's already lunchtime." The last comment came from Charles. At forty-five, he was the office's elder statesman and the one Derek trusted the most with personal information.

"Well, I guess I'm running behind," Derek said. "I'm still on breakfast time. But feel free to take lunch whenever. But if you all go at once, please lock up, okay?"

"I'm not going anywhere," Wendy said. Derek was absurdly touched, pulling all kinds of double meanings out of those four short words. Suddenly he was desperate for more. He needed someone to tell him he wasn't a lunatic, that what he was doing— or at least, what he was trying to do—had some merit. He hesitated, then perched himself on the edge of Xander's desk.

"Let me ask you guys a question," he said.

Three sets of eyes turned to him. They were wary, but they were listening.

"I've been researching this thing . . ." *This thing.* Derek sighed. He really needed to work on his delivery. "There's a phenomenon called cellular memory," he restarted, "that I've been looking into lately. Which is why you might have noticed that I've been a bit more, um, distracted than usual."

"A bit," said Wendy, adding, under her breath, "Fucking understatement, that."

"I can still hear you, Wendy. Anyway, what cellular memory is—"

"This about Eden?" Charles asked. Derek looked hard but couldn't find any trace of his usual sneer. And both eyebrows were level. If anything, Derek's "money guy" looked concerned.

"Kind of," Derek said, and looked down at his hands for a moment. When he looked up again, he could see that Wendy's blush had deepened, turning her entire face and neck a deep red. "Yes, it is about Eden, but not . . . Anyway, the thing about cellular memory—"

"People take on the characteristics of their organ donors," Charles said, interrupting again. "They suddenly like different foods, sometimes have different skills. Sometimes they can even experience a change in sexual preference."

Now the eyebrow was up. Good grief, was *that* what they thought? Derek wondered. That Eden had left him for a woman? Well, that would explain all the blushing from Wendy, though he wouldn't have thought she had it in her to get embarrassed over something like that.

"Yes, that's it," Derek said. "Do you know much about it, Charles?"

"A little," Charles said, and cleared his throat. Derek suspected Charles had been doing some research of his own.

"Well, I've found out some interesting things. When Eden . . . Well, you know a little about what went on during that time. Her doctors were really firm on this point, that there was no way her heart—her new heart—could retain any memories from the person it came from. And, you know, I believed that too for a while. But I started reading up about it. There's a story—just happened a few years ago—about a guy who had a heart transplant, found the widow of the donor, married her, and then committed suicide in exactly the same way as the guy who donated the heart." Derek paused for a moment, gauging the reactions, realizing he'd weighted the story rather heavily in the direction of cellular memory rather than the wife both men shared. Nobody said anything, and Derek wondered if he'd made a mistake by bringing up his old/new obsession.

"But that's just one story," he continued. "There are a lot more.

There's a book by a PhD who's kind of made cellular memory a pet project of his, and he's done all these studies and questionnaires. Of course, it's not scientific, but . . ." But *what*? Why was he suddenly incapable of finishing a coherent thought?

"Totally," Xander said, breaking the short silence.

"Totally what?"

"It makes sense," Xander said. "How could you, like, just take a major organ out of one person and put it in another person without there being some kind of major reaction? It's not like the body is that stupid. If it were, how could it be capable of performing such complex tasks every millisecond of the day? The idea that cells remember trauma isn't such a stretch. What about phantom pain in amputated limbs and things like that?"

"The act of giving birth is so traumatic that a woman's brain has to secrete chemicals to induce a sense of amnesia, both physically and mentally," Charles added. "Otherwise women would never give birth to more than one child."

"Bullshit," Wendy said.

"No, really," Charles said. "Look it up. But what's this about, Derek? You said you wanted to ask us a question?"

"Yes, I did," Derek said, smiling at Charles's newfound knowledge of labor and delivery, a topic he'd never have assumed the childless and staunchly single Charles would be interested in. "What I wanted to ask is if you agree with me that there's validity to the concept, because I think that something like this has happened to Eden. I mean, of course something like this happened to Eden—she had a heart transplant; you all know that. What I meant is, I think she's . . . I think there is something about her new heart . . . something about whoever it was who donated that heart . . ." Derek cursed himself inwardly. He'd never been this tongue-tied before. He sounded like an absolute fool. He cast his eyes around the room, looking for help.

"You think she's taken on the personality of her donor?" Wendy said.

"Well, yes."

"And you want to know if we think that's a crazy idea?"

"In so many words."

"Well, I don't," Wendy said. "It seems pretty reasonable to me—to all of us." Xander and Charles both nodded in agreement. Wendy coughed—a short, polite cough that indicated she was about to say something unpleasant. "But even if it is reasonable— even if it's one hundred percent true—what do you hope to get out of all this, Derek? I mean, what's the endgame?"

"Not to put too fine a point on it, Wendy."

"Sorry, I didn't—"

"I know what you meant," he said quickly.

"I think Wendy's just saying that even if Eden is different because of her donor's heart, *knowing* that won't change anything," Charles said. "She's still going to be whoever she is now. But you don't know, things might not have worked out anyway. You know, even if she hadn't gotten sick or . . ." Charles trailed off, avoiding Derek's gaze as he looked down at his hands.

"The thing is," Derek said, feeling as if he'd set himself up and would now have to work mightily to avoid looking pathetic, "it's not only about *me*. I don't think Eden is entirely happy, and I think part of the reason for this is that her heart is not happy. Literally. Do you know what I mean?" He looked over at Wendy, who had found a spot of great interest on her computer keyboard.

"You should go for it," Xander said. Wendy and Charles turned to him, their eyes narrowed. Derek wondered if they'd all previously come to some sort of agreement to discourage him from pursuing anything to do with Eden that Xander was now violating.

"Go for what?"

"If you really feel that there's something wrong or that her heart is trying to tell her something, then you owe it to her and yourself to find that out and to tell her."

"What if she doesn't want to know, Xander?" Wendy sounded irritated. Derek decided that his hunch about an agreement among the three of them was right. "What if she just needs to get on with her life?"

The skin on the back of Derek's neck prickled. Wendy's words were too close to what he'd already heard way too many times.

"But maybe what she doesn't want to know is hurting her in some way," Xander said.

"Like what?" Wendy snapped.

"I don't know, but think about the story Derek just told us—about the guy who shot himself in the head just like the guy whose heart he got."

"I didn't say he shot himself," Derek said.

Xander shuffled his feet under his desk. "Yeah, well, I've seen that story too."

Somebody sighed—Derek couldn't see who—and the air in the room seemed to change, to lighten somehow. They'd all been in on this with him. He'd been so preoccupied since Eden had left and involved in his own thoughts, he hadn't been paying attention to them. But they had been paying attention to him and his, well, *obsession* was such a harsh word . . . and had picked up the torch themselves. Another person might have found this creepy, but Derek took comfort in it. For the first time in months he felt as if he had support. As if someone was actually on his side.

"Well, then," Derek said, "you understand."

"Just to come back to what Wendy was saying a minute ago," Charles said, "what is it that you're trying to accomplish?"

"Well, I thought if I could find out anything about the donor, it might help. At first, after the surgery, Eden really wanted to know who it was, but everyone came down so hard on her about that. I did too. I should have let her . . . But it seemed right at the time. It was important to be able to move on. And then she kind of gave up. At least I think she gave up. But she had nightmares. And there were so many things about her that were different. Not just the way she . . . felt about me."

"What kind of things?" Charles said softly.

"Not just the food preferences," Derek said. "That would almost have been a good thing." He stopped, on the verge, he thought, of saying too much.

"Have you found anything out yet?" Wendy had crossed both her arms and legs. Her body language said she was shutting down, but her tone had softened a great deal.

"No," Derek said. "It's very hard. The donor family really wanted to stay anonymous. They're really strict about these kinds of things. And I'm not even family." He was going to add, *I'm barely a friend* but thought better of it before the words could escape his throat.

"Do you want some help?" Charles had dropped his voice down low, as if suggesting some kind of illegal activity. He'd been watching too much *CSI* or something, Derek thought.

"What kind of help, Charles?" Derek was smiling, despite himself. "Do you *know a guy*?"

"I'm serious," Charles said. "I know we'd all help out, right?"

"You know," Wendy said, "whatever you need, boss."

"For sure," Xander said.

"Four heads are better than one," Charles said.

Derek slid off Xander's desk. His headache had receded for a few minutes, so much so that he hadn't even noticed it, but now it was back stronger than before, banging out a drumbeat from hell against his temple. "Thanks, guys," he said. "I can't tell you how much I appreciate your kindness. I didn't want to drag you all into this—even before when Eden was recovering—and I know I probably haven't been the easiest person to work with at times, so I apologize. This isn't the kind of thing you guys should get involved with. Hell, maybe I shouldn't either."

"But you just said—," Xander sputtered.

"I know, and, believe me, it's good to know you don't think I'm crazy. But I don't want you to think you have to do anything you aren't comfortable with. You know that, right? I'm not asking you—"

"Of course you aren't," Wendy said. "But Derek . . ." She faltered, at a loss for words. Derek realized this was the first time he'd ever seen her in such a fix. She looked up at him, her light blue eyes luminous and filled with something he couldn't define. "We just don't . . . What I mean is, all of us . . . We don't want you to get hurt. Again."

Staring at her, Derek was momentarily stunned into silence. He'd always known Wendy was attractive even if he hadn't paid much attention to it, but now it was as if he were seeing her for the first time, and he was astounded by how beautiful she was. A memory washed over him; Eden kissing him, putting that ring on her finger, telling him, "I think she's into you, Derek . . ." He'd been so besotted with Eden, he'd let that just skip over the surface of his consciousness like a pebble on water. But now—now it was sinking in. There was a spark in the air between them, but Derek was so jumbled, he didn't know whether or not he wanted to fan it into flame.

"I appreciate that, Wendy," he said, and before he could stop himself, he gave her what he knew was a seductive smile.

"She's right," Charles said. If he'd noticed any of the byplay between the two of them, he wasn't letting on. "And we know you aren't asking us to do anything."

"Okay." Derek gave them a quick, tight smile. He was heading for the door now, rattled and needing that coffee so badly, he could already taste it. He'd turned away from Charles, but, out of the corner of his eye, he caught a quick glimpse of Xander looking in Charles's direction. It wasn't exactly a wink he saw, but some kind of tacit agreement that flicked across the younger man's face.

"You know, I think I will have a coffee if you're getting one," Charles said. "I'm going to take lunch here today."

"All right," Derek said. "Pastry?"

"If they have one of those cinnamon spiral things."

"Check. Anyone else?"

"I might have a macchiato," Wendy said.

"Xander?"

"Latte and a blueberry muffin. If you don't mind."

"Not at all," Derek said.

He couldn't stop them, he thought as he headed down the artfully painted metal stairs that led to the ground floor. If they wanted to start their own investigation, they'd do it whether or not he asked them to or told them not to. What the hell, it was a damned sight better than looking at porn during work hours, wasn't it? And they were smart. If anyone could turn up a bit of useful information, it would be one of them. Wendy's white-gold, blue-eyed image appeared in his mind's eye for a moment. *Bad idea,* he told himself, but before he could consider it further, Eden overtook his thoughts again.

A thermal breeze hit his face as he walked outside. It had been much warmer than usual in Portland over the last few weeks and dry as a bone. The kind of weather the "new" Eden seemed to crave. She'd developed such an odd disdain for the city she'd loved so much before her surgery. She'd always said she loved the sound of the rain—that it made everything softer and that everybody looked better in Portland's "diffused" light. After the surgery, it was all so oppressive to her—all so depressing. And that was just one thing. He hadn't wanted to tell Charles about the others— about how she developed a hatred of everything pink (the color she'd always claimed as her favorite), of anything feminine or frilly. How she'd suddenly acquired an interest in the guitar, going so far as to price a couple before she gave up on that. How she cringed when he touched her. How it felt that every cell in her body—not just those that made up her heart—was rejecting him.

He could see the look in those golden brown eyes of hers—the war she had with herself when she finally let him make love to her for the first time after the surgery. She wasn't embarrassed about her body, which had undergone its own battle and had the huge scar to prove it; it was her mind, her heart, that didn't want to let him in. She had tried to hide it, he'd give her that. But she couldn't quite pull it off.

He felt his cell phone vibrate in his pocket with an incoming text message. He reached for it carefully, as if by handling it delicately, he could determine the caller. He could make it be *her.* He could see her face, the hint of freckles that ran across the bridge of her nose, the easy way she smiled—used to smile. He missed her so much, it actually stung his throat, his solar plexus.

D., Wendy wants muffin 2. Tx, boss.

Derek wanted to laugh. And he gave it his best shot, but what came out sounded more like a wounded bark. It matched well with the wet streaks on his cheeks. It was a good thing he was out of the office. He couldn't let them see him like this. He couldn't *be* like this.

Derek was going to put the phone back in his pocket. He was going to dry his eyes and keep walking. The Koffee Klatch was only a block away, and he was closing in on it. But he did none of those things. Instead, he found Eden's contact in his phone and composed a text message to her. Cell phones had made this so easy, he thought. The ways you could humiliate yourself were now almost unlimited.

Eden, please call me. Or at least answer my call. Just want to say hi. Just want to see if you're okay.

He hesitated, rethought, and hesitated again. Finally he added it—*xox*—and hit the SEND key before he changed his mind.

CHAPTER 12

SAN DIEGO

Waiting made Darcy nervous. She'd opted to drive over to the office of Lawrence Putterman, Esq. (as his old-fashioned letterhead proclaimed him) rather than accepting the lawyer's offer of meeting her at her home, and now she had to wait in his overly plush anteroom while one of his assistants copied some documents for her to take home. Why the documents weren't already copied when she got there, Darcy didn't know. She didn't trust "Call Me Larry" Putterman as far as she could throw him. He'd been Peter's lawyer—*one* of Peter's lawyers—and a member of the group she always thought of as his asshole friends who, to a man (because they were all good old boys) had been cool, condescending, and dismissive of her when Peter was alive. It had never seemed worth it to make the effort to try to warm any of them up. She'd kept her distance, never thinking that she'd need to be in any of their good graces and never foreseeing a scenario in which she'd have to deal with any of them in a professional capacity. How could she have?

She couldn't have known or predicted any of the things that had happened. She'd been too smug, maybe, but that was all. And she was being punished for it now, having to kiss Putterman's ass so that he'd be kind enough to fill her in on the details of Peter's real estate acquisitions—specifically the apartments in Paris and New York City that she hadn't even known existed before he died—and the status of the trust he'd set up for Lisa's boys, which had her name on it too and which her sister-in-law had not so subtly been inquiring about. It was true that if she'd let Putterman come to her as he'd wanted, she wouldn't be standing here staring at the ostentatious hummingbird feeder he had installed in his office garden (that he even had an office garden was somehow offensive to Darcy) and paying about five dollars for every minute she waited for Jenny or Susie or Connie to finish copying forms. But the alternative was unacceptable. She didn't want Putterman inside her house.

It was a cliché to think of a lawyer as unctuous, but that description fit Putterman perfectly. He practically slimed on her when she walked in, leaning over to kiss both her cheeks in some faux-European attempt to appear sophisticated as he embraced her just a little too tightly and his hands spread just a little too broadly across her back. He was a few years older than Peter, but he didn't look it. He was tall, trim, and still had a full head of salted blond hair. Darcy might have considered him attractive if she hadn't found him so repulsive. Her skin crawled as she remembered again how he'd slipped Peter that long-ago Viagra.

"You look wonderful, Darcy," he'd said when she managed to separate herself from the uncomfortable hug. "It's great to see you."

"Thanks, Larry."

"How're you holding up?"

It had been so long—months, or a lifetime, depending on how you viewed it—and yet every time she spoke to him, Putterman acted as if Peter had died yesterday and that she should still be in a state of frenzied grieving. And she never failed to hear an indictment in his tone. He probably thought she should be wearing a black veil.

"I'm fine, thanks, Larry."

"You know, you're welcome over anytime or if you need anything. I was just telling Anne the other day . . ." Darcy had tuned him out at that point, stifling the urge to ask him what it would cost her if she happened to "need" anything. She didn't know why he even bothered with the pleasantries—he so obviously meant none of it. And getting legal information out of him—in language she could understand—was almost impossible. But the man was an executor of Peter's will, so she was stuck with him for as long as it took to get it all . . . executed.

Their session hadn't been as long as she'd feared it might be, but every minute of it was torturous. Darcy couldn't stand to talk about Peter with anyone, least of all with someone who'd been on his side and not hers. Funny, she thought, that it ultimately came down to sides. Theirs was supposed to have been a marriage, not a boxing match. Yes, well . . .

To make it worse, Darcy felt she was being perpetually grilled by Putterman, even when he was ostensibly explaining some legal matter or making small talk. He didn't trust her either; that much was clear. He never had. Feeling she was being interrogated, however subtly, made Darcy even more paranoid than she already was. And the more paranoid she got, the twitchier she started to feel. And if she *felt* twitchy, there was no question that she *looked* twitchy. It took all of ten minutes in Putterman's excessively decorated office for her to feel as if she were being drawn and quartered. He could sense her discomfort, she was certain. She was sure that was why she was still being made to wait—so he could draw it out even longer.

The door of Putterman's office opened, and he peered around the door. "Darcy? You're still here? Did we forget something?" His musky cologne wafted in her direction.

"You—I mean, someone was copying those documents for me. The trust . . ."

"She hasn't given you those yet?" He made a *tsk* sound and disappeared back into his office. Darcy fidgeted. A hummingbird lit on the feeder and danced nervously around the food for a moment before taking off again.

"I'm so sorry, Mrs. Silver!" A skinny, harried twentysomething materialized from behind some unseen door, clutching royal blue file folders. "I thought you'd been given these already. I apologize for making you wait. I had no idea you were—"

"That's fine," Darcy said. "No problem." She took the documents from the assistant, thanking her, and turned to leave. But she wasn't fast enough. Putterman appeared at his door again.

"Great to see you, Darcy. Remember, if you need anything . . . And I'm more than happy to come to the house next time; it's no trouble."

The house. Not *your* house.

"Thanks, Larry."

"No problem." He smiled, and a chill ran up Darcy's sweaty spine. "You might give Lisa a call," he said. "She's been in touch. I told her we'd be meeting today."

"Lisa?"

"Peter's *sister*?"

He might as well have had fangs, Darcy thought. Fucking bloodsucker. And why was *Lisa* calling him?

Darcy mumbled her thanks once more, managing to avoid looking at either Putterman or the assistant as she finally got the hell out of the office and into the safety of her own car. She'd put the files on the passenger seat next to her, started the car, and pulled out of the parking space before she realized that both sides of her pink silk shirt were stained dark red with perspiration from underarms to waist. Add bad choice of wardrobe to her sins.

She took the long way home, through the village of La Jolla, along Torrey Pines Road, and to the Coast Highway. It added at least twenty minutes to her drive to go this more scenic route, but Darcy needed the blue-green peace of the ocean in front of her eyes to balance the chaotic landscape behind them. She was passing the State Reserve, where the leaning pines waved out over the water and wind caves pockmarked the cliff face, when she realized that she was angry at Lisa. What could Lisa possibly want from Putterman? Why would she call *him* and not her own sister-in-law? She gripped the steering wheel a bit tighter. She'd spoken to Lisa plenty of times in the last few months. It wasn't as if she'd been ignoring the woman. It was true that she didn't have every single detail of the trust, and maybe she hadn't been quite as diligent as she could have been about signing off on certain papers, but for God's sake, Lisa and her boys had gotten plenty of money already. It couldn't be the money, could it? There was no reason for Lisa to call Putterman unless . . . Darcy hadn't even thought that Lisa knew who Putterman was, but of course she did. They'd all met at the funeral at the very least. And there had been all those documents. So many signatures. He had left such a huge and endless stack of paper behind. Nothing was ever simple.

Lisa's conversation with Putterman—what could they possibly have discussed?—worried Darcy's mind like a rock in her shoe. She took a left turn on Ninth Street in Del Mar, followed it down to the edge of the bluff, and parked. She had no doubt that an irritated resident would appear within minutes and ask her to move her car, but she wasn't planning on a lengthy conversation. She needed just long enough to get some information out of Lisa. But she couldn't talk and drive at the same time. Her hands were shaking too badly.

Darcy calculated the time difference as she punched in Lisa's number, but it didn't really matter—whatever time it was in Lisa's world, she'd be busy taking care of her sons. She'd always been a devoted mother, but since Peter's death, she'd gone into a sort of maternal overdrive. Every moment, it seemed, was spent in their service. And Darcy wasn't just guessing at this—Lisa updated her regularly with photos and e-mails. There was Nick at science camp; there was Jeremy at a swim meet; there were both of them in their baseball uniforms. And there was Lisa, perpetually behind the camera, making cookies and loading up the goddamned SUV. Darcy didn't know what part Bill played in all of this. He seemed to have taken a backseat to Lisa's Mother Superior act. It was easy to cede, Darcy supposed, when you had the kind of financial cushion Peter had provided them all to lean on.

"Hello?"

"Lisa? Hi. It's Darcy."

"How are you, Darcy?"

"I'm okay." Darcy listened intently for any warning signs in Lisa's voice, any undertone of suspicion, but she couldn't hear any. She couldn't hear *anything*—Lisa's voice was neutral to the point of colorlessness. "So, listen. I've just been to see Lawrence Putterman."

"Did he tell you that I called?"

"Well, yes, Lisa, and that's why . . . We went over those trust documents, and I have some papers for you to sign as well. Look, I'm sorry I haven't gotten back to you sooner about this, Lisa, but I've been . . ."

"Is something wrong?" Lisa asked. "Because you've really gone quiet lately. It's not just the trust; you haven't responded to my last few e-mails either. I was starting to worry."

"Really, Lisa?"

"Yes, really, Darcy. Why wouldn't I?"

Darcy wondered if Bill was in the background somewhere. She wondered if anyone else was listening. She rolled down her window. Eucalyptus-laced marine air filled the car. Darcy breathed it in. "Why would you call him, Lisa? I mean, if you have a question about something, can't you just call me? I'd rather not have Lawrence Putterman involved in my family business. More than he is already, I mean."

Darcy couldn't even hear Lisa breathing in the pause that followed, but she could feel her own heart quicken its pace by half.

"I tried to call you, Darcy. You've been really hard to reach lately. And what do you mean, your 'family business'? What business are you talking about? Is there something you don't want him to know?"

Darcy was holding her breath. She wanted to speak, but she just couldn't let it out.

"He's the executor of Peter's will. He has to be involved,

doesn't he, Darcy? Is there some reason he shouldn't be? I don't understand. Hello? Darcy?"

Darcy exhaled, sighing into the phone. "No, there isn't. Even if there was, there isn't anything I can do about it, is there? I mean, I can't exactly take him off the case, can I? I'm incapable, it seems, of determining the course of my own life." Darcy felt her face flushing despite the ocean breeze. She'd said too much. Damn it.

"What are you talking about, Darcy? You're not really making much sense now. And I don't understand why you're so angry." Lisa's voice was soft in the way you'd use to calm a tantrum-throwing child, and it made Darcy extremely nervous.

"I'm not angry. I just wish you had called me instead of Lawrence Putterman."

"I didn't think I had to consult you before I made calls to the executor of my brother's will."

Passive-aggressive was not a good color for Lisa, Darcy decided.

"Let's not argue about this, okay, Lisa? I just called you to let you know that I did go there today and I do have the papers and I'm going to sign whatever it is that needs signing. I'm still dealing with the other things too—those apartments. It's gotten kind of complicated. I wish . . . I don't know why he didn't tell me about those. It's kind of a mess now."

Lisa went quiet again for a moment. In the pause, Darcy's anxiety rose again and with it, a kind of desperation. Talking to Lisa now had brought those last days back all too clearly. She felt again the stark fear she'd experienced when Peter had told her they were moving—fear that came not just from the thought of leaving Adam, but from being so completely controlled by another person. And then, that terrible night replayed itself in her memory over and over again. It was never his fist Darcy saw in the repeating scene but the glass smashing on the granite counter. It was like an eternally rewinding clip—the clink, the slam, the shattering of glass.

"What do you mean, a mess?"

Darcy had to work to remember the last thing she'd said. The apartments. Yes, that was it. "It's complicated," Darcy said. "The taxes . . . Peter wasn't very organized about it, which wasn't like him."

"Well, I don't think he was planning to die," Lisa said. Darcy's breath caught again in her throat. It was unlike Lisa to sound so sharp or irreverent about her brother—especially now. He'd become something of a hero to her in death. "I mean, why would a man in perfect health make sure his papers were all in order? He was probably planning to surprise you with the Paris apartment, Darcy."

Yes, he had all kinds of surprises up his sleeve. Like that fist of his. Darcy's stomach flipped, and her hands were trembling. Had Putterman said something to Lisa, or had she embarked on this fishing expedition all by herself? And why now?

"Darcy? Are you still there?"

"I don't think that was it, Lisa. I don't think he was planning to surprise me. At least not in a good way. And you know that Peter was very careful about his *things* and about his financial affairs. That was what he did. So there wasn't any reason for him to leave that particular piece of it such a mess."

Darcy kept seeing that glass smash on the counter. She just couldn't wipe out the image. And now it had come with the memory of pain. That feeling that her whole head had been split open. The bruise had been terrible—the color of a tornado-filled sky. Tears had come to Adam's eyes when he saw it. He'd looked away, but she'd seen them shining there.

"I don't know what you're trying to say, Darcy."

"I'm not *trying* to say anything—I am saying what I mean. I don't know what it is you blame me for, Lisa. But there were things about Peter you don't—didn't know. Things about our marriage." Now her voice was trembling as well. Well, too bad. She couldn't stop now. "You shouldn't judge—especially not me. You don't know, Lisa."

"What don't I know? And why don't you tell me?"

Slam, smash. Slam, smash.

"He wasn't a goddamned saint, Lisa. I know you think he was. But he . . ." She hiccupped and put her hand to her cheek. It was wet. At some point during the conversation, she'd started crying.

"He what?" There was a note of warning in Lisa's voice. She didn't want to hear it, Darcy thought. And what was the point of telling her? It was over—done. But only in the most surface of ways. There was still so much darkness bubbling underneath. She'd never said the word *abuse* out loud—not even after Peter knocked her unconscious—to anyone. Not to the doctor she'd gone to see afterward. Not to a single family member or friend. Not to Peter. Not even to Adam, who'd cradled her in his arms after that horrendous night, his hot, angry tears falling into her hair. But the word hung there now and would always be branded into her psyche. It changed you, she thought. Even if something like that never happened again, your life would never quite be all your own again. And because of that, because she'd never been able to acknowledge that fact out loud, Darcy decided to ignore the warning in her head that told her not to go down this road with Lisa. There would be no way to unring the bell, but Darcy had to come out with it.

"There were times . . . ," Darcy started, and found herself fumbling. Where did she begin this story? With the too-tight grip on the arms? The "playful" shoving? The slapping? Or did she go straight to the smashing glass and the punch in the face?

"I never said anything about it," Darcy said. "Because I didn't want to admit it even to myself. I guess I didn't even believe it was happening. But Peter was . . . He was abusive, Lisa."

Now it was Lisa's turn to gasp. "*What?* Is that some kind of a joke, Darcy? It's not very funny."

"Why would I joke about something like that?" Her voice sounded small and flat.

"I don't know. But apparently that's not the only thing I'm in the dark about."

"It's the truth, Lisa."

In the pause that followed, Darcy could hear a door slamming and greetings being shouted on the other end of the line. The boys were home. And in the rearview mirror she could see a woman in bike shorts and a visor approaching her car. Darcy wondered what it was with people who had nothing better to do on a beautiful day than hassle a stranger.

"I don't believe you," Lisa said. But Darcy could hear a faint note of doubt in her voice. "And I don't know what purpose you think you're serving by making something like this up now." Darcy could hear the strain in Lisa's voice. She was so upset, she wasn't even talking to the boys, whom Darcy could hear clamoring for attention in the background.

"I'm not making it up. I told you, I didn't want to admit it to myself or anyone else, but it happened. And there's no purpose I'm trying to serve. I just want you to know."

"I saw the two of you together, Darcy! I know my brother. I *knew* him." There was a catch in Lisa's throat. "You would have said something. Or I would have sensed something. There is no way you were an abused wife. Peter *adored* you. I never understood—" Lisa stopped abruptly, but she'd caught herself a second too late. No, Darcy thought, Lisa would never believe that Peter was capable of anything even approaching violence toward her.

"Never understood why he married me in the first place?"

"That's not—"

"Yes, it is, Lisa."

There was a tapping at Darcy's window.

"Excuse me. Ma'am? You can't park here."

Darcy turned to the woman and pointed at her phone. The woman put her hands on her spandex-clad hips, having none of it. A scowl spread across her overly made-up face. "You need to move your car."

"Who is that?" Lisa said. "What's going on?"

"Just give me a second," Darcy said, and made a shooing motion with her hand before she rolled up her window. "I'm going to have to go now, Lisa."

"No, Darcy—you can't just drop that kind of bomb and then hang up. You can't say things like that—it's not right!"

"He *punched* me, Lisa! Do you want to see the doctor's report? Oh, wait—you can't because I gave a fake name when I went in. I was so humiliated, I wouldn't even go to my own doctor."

"I don't believe you. Nothing about this sounds right. Why are you saying these things?"

Darcy started her car. The scowling woman didn't move. Bitch. Darcy felt like running her over. It had been a colossal mistake to talk to Lisa about any of this. Just one of many mistakes. It was too soon to know what the implications of this one would be, but Darcy wasn't hopeful.

"I have to go, Lisa. You'll get your papers or whatever it is you need."

"This isn't the end of this conversation, Darcy."

"Please give Nick and Jeremy my love." Darcy ended the call and tossed her cell phone onto the passenger seat. She half expected Lisa to call her back, but the phone stayed silent as she turned the car around and headed back to the main road. It wasn't much of a surprise. Like Peter, Lisa wasn't one to beg for attention. Both of them expected others to come to *them*. But that didn't mean that Lisa was going to just drop it. Darcy had no idea how she was going to continue this particular conversation the next time she spoke to Lisa—who was probably running the whole thing past Bill at this very moment. Darcy could almost hear it. *Why did he marry her? Can you believe she said that? There is no way Peter was capable of anything like that . . .*

Had she really expected any sympathy from Lisa?

Darcy was suddenly engulfed in a black and bottomless loneliness. It came on without warning like a thick cloud descending on her, filling her head, choking her. She'd been fighting it, Darcy realized, pushing it back, but now it was impossible to ignore. She missed Adam so much, it felt as if her chest were collapsing. His absence was a physical pain, spreading throughout her body. She was successful, much of the time, in ignoring that pain—in not viewing the reel of memory that wanted to play behind her eyes. But now it was all jumbled together, coming at her in the same way as that glass smashing against the counter. She replayed the moment in her bathroom. The call. The whispered confession.

He hit me.

Where are you? Let me come and get you.

I can't believe he hit me.

It's going to be okay. Listen to me. I'm going to take care of you.

Please help me, Adam.

I'm going to take care of you. I love you, Darcy. I love you.

There had never been a place in Darcy's past—and she was certain there wouldn't be one in her future—that felt as safe as Adam's arms when she finally saw him after that night. She could still feel the roughness of his shirt against her face. She could still smell his skin. She'd closed her eyes, and he'd enveloped her, his chest rising and falling under her buried head. Nothing separating their bodies. Nothing between them. She would have done anything for him at that moment—anything.

There was so much more to their love than the physical, Darcy thought now, even though she still ached for his touch—for the feel of him under her hands. She could see how someone looking at the two of them would see it another way. He had nothing. He was a bartender and a musician—almost a struggling artist cliché. Those high cheekbones and curling locks. The stubble always just right. His skin always the perfect golden shade. And she was older, although not by so much that anyone could tell by seeing them together. She had everything—the money, the house, the willing body . . . and the husband. She wasn't stupid; she knew Adam attracted women by the flock, and she knew he'd spent time in many beds—and in cars and on tables and who knew on what other surfaces. She'd seen the way they looked at him at Poquette—the waitstaff and customers alike. Waitresses touched him when they came to the bar to pick up their drinks. She'd seen the little stroke of the fingers across his hand as he set cocktails up on the bar. That bar—it was always full of women when he worked, old and young, all staring at him like lionesses ready to pounce on a still-trembling piece of meat.

Darcy knew. She had been one of them.

So while she didn't think about whom he'd slept with before— or whom he rubbed up against in the kitchen—she knew he was no monk. She took his word—because she had to—that there was nobody but her when they were entwined in a sweaty, panting embrace, but she knew Adam hadn't passed up too many opportunities in his life. He was well aware of what his face and his body could get him. So she could also understand how someone else could see their relationship as just that—an opportunity for Adam to tap a rich, bored, sexually unsatisfied trophy wife. But that was not at all what they were for each other. He loved her. That night, when he'd pressed his lips so softly on her battered jaw, promising her that she would never have to experience that kind of brutality again, that he would protect her—save her—she believed him without question. She could feel his love. It was the most true and real thing she had ever known. To have experienced that moment with him, Darcy thought, was almost worth everything that came after it—almost.

Darcy had been driving on autopilot, but now she looked up and saw that she was about to pass Poquette. Her spine still tingled every time she saw the facade. It was a Pavlovian response, driven home by all the ties she had to it. It was first her place with Peter. Then it was all about Adam. And now . . . Well, thought Darcy, now there was Eden.

And Eden, Darcy decided, was exactly the person she wanted to see right now. She turned into the parking structure, pulled into a space, and took the elevator up to the third floor. All at once, Darcy's rattled consciousness felt soothed. Because what she needed now—what she had been missing for so very long—was a real friend. And although Darcy could not explain why, she felt that Eden could be that friend.

Meeting her had been the oddest experience—one Darcy tried to decipher for a long time afterward. The moment she'd looked into that girl's eyes, she'd seen something that had pulled her in.

And even though Eden had been fumbling with the bread and water, Darcy had caught a spark—a look of something like anger or . . . Darcy still couldn't work out the emotions flashing across Eden's face, but she'd found it undeniably intriguing. Later, Darcy thought maybe Eden had been schooled by the other waitresses who knew her from when she'd come in with Peter (and some of whom she was sure knew about her and Adam), but it still didn't make sense why Eden would prickle with what appeared to be hostility at the mere sight of her.

But Darcy had seen something else in Eden too. She'd seen the same attraction she felt for Eden (because there really wasn't a better word to describe it) reflected back at her when Eden looked at her. It wasn't anything creepy, nor was it the déjà vu feeling of running into someone you thought you knew. But it was an unusual type of connection. And Eden was different. Darcy could tell from that very first moment in Poquette that there was something going on with that girl—some secret or something that she was covering up. It was evident in every movement. There was the way she kept putting her hand to her chest, her quick, furtive glances. And then, strangest of all, there was that bizarre scene at Zulu's where she'd gone all pale and zombielike and had to leave the place after only a few minutes.

Of course, they'd gone out together a few more times since then, and Eden had been fine—she had appeared completely normal and had even apologized for acting so oddly before. But there was still a wall Darcy hit whenever she tried to get Eden to talk about herself, even though it seemed to her as if Eden *wanted* to talk about herself. There was something . . . *haunted* about her. Yes, *haunted* was the word, Darcy thought. And that *did* feel familiar to Darcy. Although there was really nothing similar about them—at least as far as Darcy had been able to tell—there was something, some experience or aspect of their lives that they shared. Darcy was sure of this. There was no other way to explain how she already felt linked to Eden despite knowing her only a short time.

Poquette felt uncharacteristically sleepy and slow when Darcy walked in. She could hear the distant clink of silverware hitting plates, but all the tables in the front of the restaurant were empty. Nor was there anyone immediately visible at the bar. Sometimes Darcy thought she was out of her mind to still patronize this restaurant. But appearances were important. As far as anybody was concerned, there was no reason for Darcy *not* to be here. And as Peter had once told her, the best defense was a good offense. Words to live by.

"Mrs. Silver, how are you?"

Jacques had materialized at her side, bringing with him the subtle but intoxicating scent of expensive cologne. He leaned in and air kissed her on both cheeks. Darcy had to admit that she didn't mind the fawning attention he lavished on her whenever she came in. Whether or not it was genuine didn't matter.

"Hello, Jacques."

"One for lunch today?"

"I think I'm going to . . . I might just have a drink and maybe something light. I was thinking I'd just sit at the bar. No need to take up an entire table."

"Whatever you like!" Jacques said. There was, perhaps, just a tiny bit too much exuberance in his tone. "You can order whatever you want at the bar, of course."

"Thanks, Jacques."

"Of course, of course."

He walked with her to the bar, which looked particularly dark and forlorn to Darcy today. She'd hardly ever seen it so empty. "The bartender should be back any second," Jacques said as if reading her thoughts. "He's downstairs checking in a wine order. I can send someone over—"

"Is Eden here today?" Darcy asked brightly. She lifted herself onto a bar stool. They were high but had plush backrests—all the better to wedge yourself into when you'd had one too many.

"She is," Jacques said. "Shall I send her over?"

"That would be great. If she's not too busy."

"Momento," Jacques said, and glided off.

Darcy put her hand on the shiny wooden bar top. It was warm, and she could feel a subtle vibration coming through it from somewhere below. At any given moment, something was always vibrating in California. The earth was in constant motion here. There was a still-wet circle on the bar from where a glass had recently been resting. Darcy trailed lines through it with her finger. Her shoulders felt tense and her stomach jittery. It took almost no effort at all to conjure Adam in the empty space behind the bar. He'd moved well back there, she remembered. She'd spent one entire afternoon watching him as she nursed a single glass of wine. He wasn't flashy—no spinning bottles or high pours—but he was as graceful as a dancer. He was showing off for her too, she knew, because by then they'd already exchanged that look, and both knew what would happen next. In a way, Darcy thought, that moment when the desire and assent passed between them was more intimate than when they made love for the first time. You were never as naked as when you saw yourself imagined naked in someone else's eyes.

Darcy closed her eyes and let the memory of it wash over her one more time. She'd thought she'd known what she was getting into, but of course she hadn't. No amount of sophistication or desperation or blind stupid love could have prepared her. Yet she would have done it again, Darcy thought.

"Hi there!"

Darcy's eyes snapped open, and she turned quickly to smile at Eden.

"Hey, Eden! How are you?" Darcy thought she sounded way too bright, overly chipper, and weird.

"Fine, fine." But she didn't look fine, Darcy thought. Her dark hair was pulled back into a haphazard ponytail from which several strands had come loose, her white shirt looked as if it had been on the losing side of an argument with a cup of coffee, and her apron pocket was torn. Worse, though, she had dark circles under her eyes and her fingernails looked ragged, as if she'd been biting them. "Are you going to have lunch?"

"I'm not really that hungry," Darcy said. "But I was driving by, and I thought it would be nice to come in and get a drink. And see—say hi. It's been kind of a rough day."

"I'm sorry," said Eden, and she looked as if she meant it. "Sticks should be back up here in a minute. I'd get you a drink, but he really doesn't like anyone to go back there. It's his territory. Can I get you something while you're waiting?"

"No, no, I'm fine. Really, I mostly wanted to come see if you were here and say hi. And . . ." And what? thought Darcy. See if you want to be my BFF? Have a pajama party? She was so bad at this. "Are you sure you're okay?" she asked. "You look a bit stressed."

Eden's hand reached up to her shirt collar, pulling it closed. Darcy wondered if she even knew she was doing it, because it seemed like such an automatic nervous tic. "It's been a weird day for me too," Eden said. "Super slow all day, but"—she looked down at her apron—"you'd never know it to look at me. It's been slow all week, actually."

"Really?"

"Yep. I guess the season is officially over now that the Del Mar racing meet is over. I didn't realize there would be such a drop off in business. I've been trying to pick up extra shifts, but everyone's in the same boat, so nobody wants to give anything up."

"What do you mean, 'same boat'?"

Eden gave her a small crooked smile. She was really very pretty, Darcy thought, though not the kind of pretty that could get a girl into trouble. Hers was that wholesome, fresh kind of pretty, especially when she smiled. You felt like you'd eaten a good breakfast just looking at her.

"The money boat," Eden said. "Fewer customers mean fewer tips. Fewer tips mean . . . time to look for a second job. For some of us."

Darcy felt stupid and clumsy. It had been so long since she'd had to worry about making ends meet that it hadn't even occurred to her that Eden was actually trying to make a living from waiting on tables. Here she'd come from a meeting where the sale of million-dollar apartments and trusts were discussed, and Eden was worried about twenty-dollar tips.

"I'm sorry," Darcy said. "I should have known that."

"It's fine. Don't be sorry, Darcy."

"Are you okay? I mean, are you managing?"

"I didn't think . . . I didn't really have much of a plan, I guess. Didn't really anticipate how expensive it would be to live here when I decided to move to San Diego." Eden sighed and looked away from Darcy for a moment, a squall of emotion passing quickly across her features.

"Are you in trouble? Financially, I mean."

"You know, I don't exactly live beyond my means, but the rent is pretty high. I didn't really think about that beforehand. I mean, I did, but . . . It's just expensive."

"So what does that mean for you?"

"Nothing. I don't know. I'm going to have to recalibrate my thinking."

"You know, you never told me why you moved here in the first place. These days, it's the other way around. I always hear how wonderful Portland is—people move up there by the droves." Darcy gave Eden a broad smile. She asked the question lightly, but the truth was that Eden had pointedly avoided answering it every other time Darcy had posed it.

"I used to like Portland too," Eden said. Darcy waited for more, but it wasn't going to happen because at that moment, the bartender, Sticks, appeared and took his place in front of Darcy. He was a big guy—Darcy was sure he could get hired as a personal bodyguard if this job ever fell through—and stingy with chitchat. He recognized her, there was no doubt, but she was almost positive he knew nothing about her. He and Adam hadn't worked together very often; when they had, according to Adam, they'd never been buddies. Not that Adam would have shared anything personal with Sticks—at least anything to do with her—even if they had been friends. If he knew nothing else, Adam knew to stay quiet.

"How are you doing today?" Sticks asked, putting a cocktail napkin down in front of her. "Sorry about the wait."

"No worries."

"Eden been taking care of you?" He looked over at Eden and gave her an affectionate wink. Well, thought Darcy, she had at least one friend here.

"I'm just going to have a . . . You know what? I think I'll have

a dessert!" Darcy didn't like dessert—or rather, had trained herself not to like dessert—so she didn't know why she was suddenly
in the mood for something sweet and creamy, but there it was.
"Do you guys still have that gourmet strawberry shortcake
thing?"

"We do," Eden said.

"Perfect. I'll have that. And a cappuccino. Decaf. And a glass
of port, what the hell? It's been that kind of day."

"Got it," Sticks said.

"I should go get ready to cash out," Eden said, pushing herself
off from where she'd been leaning on the bar.

"Are you just about done for the day?" Darcy asked her.

"Just about."

"Do you . . ." Darcy trailed off, not knowing how to phrase
the question or even what the question was that she wanted to
ask. Eden turned to her, eyebrows raised, that little smile still on
her face. "Never mind," Darcy said, "I forgot what I was going
to say."

"Okay," Eden said. "Well, if you remember . . ."

Eden rounded the bar and headed toward the kitchen. After
putting a napkin and fork next to Darcy, Sticks ducked back out
and followed her. Darcy watched as he walked up beside her
and put a hand on her shoulder. Even from afar, Darcy could see
how Eden shrank instinctively from his touch. Her whole body
seemed to tense up, and there again was the hand coming up to
her chest. Sticks didn't seem to notice, Darcy thought, because
as they walked through the swinging double doors to the kitchen,
his hand was still there—so large it covered her entire shoulder.
She leaned away from him so subtly that nobody would have
noticed—nobody but Darcy, who had once tensed up and shrunk
into herself exactly the same way.

Darcy stared into the garnet-colored glass of port that Sticks had managed to pour without her even noticing. Suddenly it all made sense. *Eden* made sense. That reticence, the cringing, the odd tics and panics. She'd been abused—Darcy was sure of it. She'd said something incredibly vague at one point about a boyfriend—or was it a fiancé?—but like almost everything else, Eden offered no details, and it seemed to pain her to even give up that much. Now Darcy knew why. She'd run away or escaped from him—that was probably why she had moved here and why she didn't want to say anything about it. Maybe she wasn't even using her real name. Every woman had her own way of dealing with this particular kind of trouble. Every woman had her own desperate measures. So there *was* something they had in common. And maybe that was what they had both seen in each other the first time they'd met. Darcy tried to avoid thinking in terms of fate and destiny—it was too cumbersome a concept for someone in her set of circumstances, but she did think now that meeting Eden hadn't been a complete accident. Perhaps the universe had finally thrown a little luck in Darcy's direction.

As she sipped her port, already half gone by the time Sticks got back from the kitchen with her strawberry shortcake and three-quarters drained when he put the frothing cappuccino down next to it, a plan began to form in Darcy's mind. It was the perfect solution to both her and Eden's problems. Win-win.

A few minutes later, Eden came back to the bar with a handful of canceled tickets and her apron folded over her arm.

"Done?" Darcy asked.

"Indeed I am."

"Are you busy for dinner?" Darcy asked. She kept her voice low, although there was no rational reason why she didn't want Sticks or Jacques or anyone else to hear her.

"No, just going home to my lonely can of cat food," Eden said, and then laughed when she saw Darcy's shocked expression. "I'm kidding, Darcy!"

"Let me buy you dinner," Darcy said. "What do you say?"

Eden smiled but hesitated, seeming unsure of how to answer. Darcy took a sip of her cappuccino and set down the cup.

"You know what—why don't you just come to my house, and I'll cook dinner?"

"Dar—"

"There's something I want to talk to you about. An idea I have. Come on, Eden."

"Okay, but you have to let me cook," Eden said.

Darcy smiled and reached for a cocktail napkin. "Do you have a pen?" she asked Eden. "I'll write down my address."

CHAPTER 13

I must be out of my mind.

Derek took a last look at his nervous reflection in the bathroom mirror. It had been so long since he'd been out on any kind of date—not that this was a *date* per se; they'd both been very careful to avoid calling it that—that he simply couldn't remember how he should look. He was clean shaven and wearing a jacket, but he was without either cologne or tie. Was that good enough for a casual dinner? Was it *too* casual? Trying too hard?

He shouldn't be doing this. No matter how relaxed he was as a boss, technically Wendy worked for him. If things went wrong . . . if she felt like it . . . well, it was a lawsuit waiting to happen, wasn't it? But no—it wasn't like that, and Wendy wouldn't

172

do something like that. It was just dinner. She'd been putting in many extra hours lately, and he was just showing his gratitude. At least that was the cover story. But Wendy was nobody's fool. They both knew what was really going on—and it was the same thing that now had Derek worried.

"Damn it," Derek said out loud, hating the way the word echoed off the walls. He shot his cuffs, grabbed his keys, and left his house before he could change his mind about the whole thing.

The restaurant was crowded, and Wendy was nowhere to be found when Derek walked in. He didn't mind; it meant more time to have a drink (or two) and push beyond what had become an almost full-blown anxiety attack. This was what came from listening to your poker buddies, Derek thought as he ordered a double scotch rocks. It was a small group—the few guys he'd gone to Lewis & Clark with who'd remained in Portland— but they managed to get together only once a month or so to play a few rounds of Texas Hold'em, talk, and drink and/or eat whatever it was that their wives or girlfriends wouldn't permit at home. It was mostly wives at this point, Derek admitted. They were five all together, but there was always at least one guy missing—at a birthday, an anniversary, and increasingly, soccer practices, late nights at work . . . Derek had attended these sessions faithfully until Eden had gotten sick, and then he'd dropped out for quite a while. It had taken him a long time to go back, but not because he didn't miss the companionship or the welcome break from seriousness. No, he was embarrassed about what had happened with Eden—it was as simple as that. He felt like a failure, and he just didn't want to show that side of himself to his friends.

It was Dave—never shy about speaking his mind—who'd finally convinced Derek to come back to the group. "Don't be an asshole, D.," Dave had said. "I know the story—we all do—but I'm gonna start taking it personally in a minute. And you know that's not like me. You need to deal with it. Besides, I'm sick to death of sitting between Mike and Pat. And Raul's been on some sort of wheatgrass bender or some shit, and he's trying to convert all of us. Help me out, dude."

So Derek had returned, expecting the guys to just fold him back in as they had before. To his surprise, they'd started in almost immediately about how he needed to get out and start dating. Dating! As if he were in some kind of Hugh Grant romcom.

"Seriously," Raul said as he checked his hand one night, "it's time. I don't want to sound gay or anything—not that there's anything wrong with that—but you're a good-looking dude with a lot going on. You know how hard that is to find? Just ask my ex."

"He isn't wrong," Dave said.

"Gotta move on," Pat added.

And so it went. Derek couldn't remember when or in what context he'd brought Wendy up, but they'd seized on it, hammering on about how he should take her out, "test the waters," and "She's that hot and you haven't done anything about it yet?" Finally he told himself that they were right. And then . . . Well, he had to admit that Wendy had made it easy. Once he actually started paying attention, he could see that Eden had been right; Wendy was "into him," despite her feminist stance. She wasn't, it turned out, anti-man.

"I was thinking the two of us could grab dinner," he'd told her. "If you like. Charles and Xander are pretty busy or I'd invite—"

"I'd love to," she said before he could fumble through the rest of the lie, and it was settled.

The scotch was working. By the time he saw Wendy glide through the big glass doors of the restaurant, he was well lubricated and ready, even looking forward to dinner. She smiled when she saw him and moved gracefully through the crowded tables to meet him at the bar. He couldn't help but admire her. Her hair caught the dim overhead light just so, creating a halo around her beatific face. But there was nothing angelic about the tight black tunic she was wearing or the matching leggings and the knee-high calfskin boots. She wasn't just hot—she was smoking. Why *had* it taken him so long to notice?

"Hey there," she said as she approached him. "Sorry I'm a bit late. I got stuck in traffic."

"No worries," she said. "I've made myself comfortable, as you can see." He held up his almost-empty glass and shook the melting ice. "Can I get you one?"

"Don't mind if I do," she said. "I'll have a lemon drop."

"Excellent choice," Derek said, and signaled the bartender. And then, without thinking, he said, "You look great."

Wendy smiled at him, those big blue eyes of hers wide and glowing. "Thanks," she said. Her drink arrived, and she took a long sip. "I lied," she said. "I wasn't stuck in traffic. I was . . . I didn't know what to wear."

"Well," Derek said, feeling a grin spread across his face, "you made the right choice."

Wendy took another sip and gently put her glass down on the bar. She looked at him and smiled. There was nothing flirtatious about it, but there, in the upturned corners of her mouth and the slightly guarded but searching look in her eyes, Derek saw desire and assent. It had been so long since he'd seen anything like it directed at him that for a moment he felt like an observer—a cultural anthropologist taking field notes on mating practices—watching the scene unfold from a distance. Wendy must have sensed this because she looked away from him and down into her glass. She tapped her fingers on the bar and then, so subtly he almost missed it, she shrugged.

"Shall we have dinner here at the bar?" she said. "They serve the whole menu here. And the drinks come quicker."

Derek just smiled.

Derek fumbled with the keys, his drunken hands refusing to obey the commands from his not-drunk-enough head. He grazed the lock and then dropped the keys on the ground. He wove like a wind-bent reed as he leaned down to pick them up. Behind him came the soft tinkle of Wendy's laughter. He remembered this scenario. The drunk entry into the house was followed by the sloppy kiss in the foyer. Then there was the staggering embrace to the bedroom or maybe just the couch, and then the stripping of clothes—as many of them as were necessary to remove to get the job done. *Stop,* he told himself. *It's not like that. It isn't.*

"Lemme help you," Wendy said. "Is it this one?" She held up something that looked like a fuzzy version of his house key. Derek nodded and watched as she fit it into the lock and turned.

"And we're in," she said softly.

How many drinks had he had? He'd lost count after the third, which might have been a double, but he couldn't remember now. Surely he'd switched to singles. Wendy had kept pace with him too. She had to be pretty tipsy, especially considering all she'd had for dinner was a glorified salad and a few pieces of bread, but she wasn't showing it. She seemed perfectly in control of all her faculties. Then again, he thought as he took her hand and led her into his house, from his vantage point that wasn't saying much. The odd thing was that Derek knew he was wasted—his swaying, slurring, key-dropping actions were proof of that—but his brain hadn't gotten the message. He had a beautiful woman in his house and he was, for the first time in longer than he wanted to admit, about to have what promised to be some very enjoyable sex; yet he couldn't shake the very clear thought that it was wrong. That was the problem, he thought—too much damned clarity.

Wendy walked into the middle of the living room and then stopped as if unsure of what to do next. Derek closed the front door and managed to lock it. He felt sorry for her suddenly. She looked lost. He walked toward her. It felt inevitable. He wanted it to feel good.

"Wendy . . ."

"Do you have anything to drink here? I mean . . ."

"I know what you mean," he said. He looked at her, holding her gaze for a moment. He couldn't tell if she was going to laugh or cry, so he took her face in his hands, tilted her face toward his, and kissed her. Her lips were so soft. He didn't know why he'd expected them to be firmer. She put her arms around him and drew him closer. Her mouth parted under his. She tasted sweet. He leaned into her, his desire building, his hands traveling the length of her back and then reaching down lower.

"Mmm." Wendy gave a small moan of pleasure and pressed herself into him.

"Let's . . . uh . . ." Derek broke away from her. He didn't want to. He wanted to keep going. He wanted what was next. But he had to get the two of them maneuvered into a bed; otherwise it was going to be the couch or the floor. He gestured toward his bedroom. "Over there," he said. She moved, walking now, in the direction he was pointing, and he followed her.

His bedroom was dark, and now he wondered what kind of state it was in. He couldn't remember how he'd left it. He hadn't been expecting this—hadn't planned for it. Not consciously anyway. He should have a candle burning—some kind of low light, nothing too harsh. He wanted to look at her. He wanted to touch her. She'd found the bed and was sitting down on it. Derek could see now that he'd at least straightened the covers before he'd left the house. Small mercies. He knelt down in front of her, his hands on her thighs. She stroked the side of his face and leaned over to kiss him again. Now his hands were moving, sliding up her legs, pushing her down gently, feeling the smooth stretchy fabric of her top, reaching beneath it, finding the soft skin, She was breathing harder, pulling him to her, tugging at his shirt, at the zipper of his jeans. This was the hard part, he thought. Once the clothes were off, it was so much easier flesh to flesh.

They were almost there, lips and tongues and hands connecting and releasing, the rustle and snap of tops and bottoms being shed. They were both bare-chested now, and as he lowered himself on top of her, he felt the heat and softness of her body rise up to meet him. It was going to happen. *Now.*

"Oh Derek," she whispered. "I've been waiting so long for this."

There wasn't enough alcohol in his system to wash away the memory of Eden that flashed into Derek's consciousness at that moment. The vision of her was so clear, it might have happened only hours ago. The day he'd asked her to marry him, when she'd shown up at the office and seen him and Wendy talking, she had automatically assumed they were sleeping together. The angry, hurt look on her face was incomprehensible to him. It would never have occurred to him that she thought he and Wendy were having an affair if she hadn't told him. That was how far removed he was from any attraction to a woman other than Eden.

She's into you. I know what I saw.

No, he would never have noticed had Eden not said it. But once she did . . . Well, he'd never forgotten, had he?

Derek's head spun. It was wrong—all of it. He was here not because his pals had put him up to it or because he'd suddenly developed a new affection for Wendy, but because this attraction was something *Eden* had noticed. He was, God help him, trying to make Eden *jealous.* It didn't make sense, but there it was. This beautiful woman on his bed was not the woman he wanted, and she deserved more and better. For a moment he debated carrying on because his male pride and, he had to face it, a portion of his male anatomy wanted Wendy in the most visceral way, but he wasn't even sure that his brain, now tuned in only to Eden, would even permit his body to see it through. It was over, and now . . . The next part was going to be horrible. He lifted himself off Wendy and rolled over onto his back. She gave a little gasp and began to turn to him, but then—that intuition of hers again—she stopped and sat up instead, crossing her arms across her lovely naked breasts.

"What is it?" she asked. "What's wrong?"

"Wendy . . . I can't do this. I'm—"

"Don't," she said quickly. There was a hard note in her voice now. "Don't say you're sorry. Please don't say that."

"It's not—"

"Also," she said, and now he could hear a tremble, "don't say, 'It's not you, it's me.' For the love of all that is holy, do not say that, Derek."

"You are so beautiful, Wendy. I never should have let this happen."

"Because you were the only person making decisions tonight?" she said. "I was there too, in case you hadn't noticed. But I guess you hadn't."

"Please don't be angry," he said.

Wendy sighed and got off the bed, fishing around for her clothes. "I suppose the thing for me to say now is that I'm not angry—that it's all okay, right?" She found her bra, slipped it on, and hooked it with impressive dexterity. "But it isn't okay, and I am angry."

"Let me explain," he said.

"No need," Wendy said. "You can skip that. It's not going to help either one of us at this point, believe me."

"Wendy, please . . ." He sat up, feeling he should put his clothes on, do something chivalrous, but he was at a loss. She seemed quietly furious and, worse than that, hurt. She was moving fast, fully dressed now and heading toward the door.

"I *am* pissed," she said. "But I'll get over it. You don't need to worry, Derek." She took a deep breath, and, to his horror, he realized she was crying. "I'm not going to make a scene or anything. Let's just pretend it never happened. Okay, Derek?"

"Wendy . . ."

"Please."

"Okay, but . . . Why don't you stay awhile? You shouldn't go like this. You can . . . You can stay here tonight if you want."

She turned to look at him. Even in the dim half-light of his bedroom he could see that she was absolutely incredulous. "Are you fucking *kidding*?" she said. "What the fuck kind of offer is that?"

It occurred to Derek then—this was the first time the entire evening he'd heard Wendy curse, something that was usually second nature for her. In a way, it was as if she'd entered the room for the first time just as she was leaving it.

"Good-bye, Derek. I'm sorry this didn't work out. I really am."

He couldn't move from the bed. He seemed to be rooted to it. He heard the front door close behind her and then, a minute later, the sound of her car pulling out of his driveway. Five minutes passed, then ten. Still he sat there, the room slowly spinning and Eden's eyes staring out at him from his memory. He wished the earth would open up and swallow him whole.

PART

3

CHAPTER 14

SAN DIEGO

This road, this road . . . It was bad in the rain. And it was raining hard—no end to the deluge. There was something about the name . . . the name of the road . . . You were in God's hands on this road. It was a freak storm—totally unexpected—but at the same time there was nothing surprising about it. It had to rain because . . . because it made this drive so much more dangerous.

She'd been here before—on this road.

She'd seen all of this before—the rusty rock on one side and a fall into water on the other. It was so beautiful, but it was also treacherous.

Just like *her*.

Water was pelting the windshield. Visibility was getting worse.

185

The windshield wipers were sticking. The outside of the car was a blur now—green and gray shapes blending and bleeding together. She heard the swish of tires in water—it wouldn't be long before the car started hydroplaning—and the racket of rain on glass. It could have been avoided—all of this—but now it was too late. And now there was this crazy dangerous drive.

It was true what they said about karma. It was a bitch. And so was she.

It was pouring hard now. Sheets of water were pounding the car. There was a bend coming soon. It was no more than a few yards away now. There would be a bend and then an SUV and then just inches between them.

No, no, no, she had to get off this road. She knew what was coming. The rain had become torrential—like a hurricane. Everything was going dark.

She had to get out of here—had to get out of this dream—but there was nowhere to get off. She was going to die here in this dream, on this road. The rain was a roar now. There would be one more turn and then . . .

But there—she could see it now—a patch of blue in the near distance. In just a minute, if she could only get there, the rain would stop, the car would stop, and she could get out.

She could hear a song, the lyrics just out of reach. It was louder now, even louder than the rain. If she could only get to that patch of blue, she could escape this road and this dream.

But now it was bright—too bright. The lights were drowning everything. It was the truck coming straight ahead—dead ahead. She was going to die—again.

Stop! Brake!

The car was going faster, speeding to certain death.

It was her fault. All of this was her fault.

The car was going faster. Swerving and spinning. No use. Impact was coming.

She didn't want to die.

Darkness.

Eden swam up through cloying blackness, trying desperately to reach consciousness. Colored spots of light flickered through the darkness. She pushed and turned, then grabbed at the air. She was at the edge of awareness but couldn't cross it. She couldn't wake. The darkness softened and rippled. Eden stopped struggling and floated. Gradually, as if a dimmer switch were being lifted from low to high, light entered, illuminating shapes she recognized. She was in Poquette, standing at the bar and staring out at the patio. The sun was setting, streaming yellow and orange through the windows and blocking her view. She needed to see . . . She shifted to the left. A glass broke somewhere behind her. She tried to move, but she was fixed, her feet rooted. She needed to see. She had to see.

Something was happening to her vision. She looked ahead, and her eyes seemed to telescope, zooming in on a table in the far corner of the patio. There she was. Darcy. She was playing with her long gold hair, twisting it nervously around her finger. Her black halter dress was cut low in front, the curves of her breasts highlighted by the lines of red piping on either side. The dress tied at the neck with the fabric hanging to the middle of her back and shoulders—the exposed skin soft and warm. Her eyes were wide and glittering green in the waning sunlight. Her hand came up to her face, covering her mouth, the scarlet fingernails the same color as her lipstick. She was frightened. Her other hand was in her lap, clenched into a fist. She leaned forward, her mouth moving. What was she saying? Her shoulders tensed and rose, making her collarbone sharply visible. She moved her legs under the table. The folds of her dress shifted and fell. She looked down. She lifted her glass and drank. Her heart was beating fast, blood pulsing at her throat.

A male hand reached over and covered hers. A wedding ring gleamed fat and gold on his finger. He squeezed her hand. The touch wasn't affectionate. The flesh of her fingers turned white under her scarlet nails.

Her husband. Peter.

Darcy pulled back but couldn't pull away. Her hair fell across her face. He was talking now. He held his arms loose and easy, but the muscles of his jaw were clenched. She turned her face away from him and stared at Eden.

Help me.

Eden could hear her calling.

Help me.

Darcy stood up. She was covered in sun. She lifted a hand to shield her eyes, and Eden could see the red semicircles where she'd dug her fingernails into her palms. Darcy turned and walked. Her face was a barely controlled storm. She came closer.

Help me help me help me help me.

Eden dived forward, and Darcy vanished into a pool of light.

"Where are you?" Eden could hear her own voice strangled in her throat. She threw out her arms, blindly searching for something solid to hold on to. "Help me!" she called out.

Eden opened her eyes. She lay still for a long minute, feeling the same way she used to feel after she'd run a marathon—spent, muscles aching, lungs drinking air, heart beating fast and steady.

Eden brought her hand to her chest and rested it there. She could feel the scar through the thin material of her T-shirt. She could feel the drumbeat—*notyourheart notyourheart notyourheart*—over and over again.

Familiar shapes—real ones—emerged. There was the long window on the eastern wall of the bedroom, dawn filtering through the palm fronds just beyond it. She was in Darcy's house—*her* house now, at least this part of it, where she'd been living for several weeks. There was the door that led to her bathroom. She'd left it ajar, and now she could see a sliver of the floor—the white octagonal floor tiles, the fluffy blue edge of a washcloth she must have dropped. There was the antique bedside table on which she'd left the contents of her apron pocket before getting into bed last night. She inventoried the items: a wine opener; a wad of ones, fives, tens, and twenties; coins; a book of matches; a tube of rum raisin lipstick; a cocktail napkin on which a man at least twenty years her senior had scribbled his *personal cell phone number* in digits that testified to the shakiness of his drunken hands; her car keys; a silver teardrop earring; and her cell phone—silent for now, but soon, she knew, vibrating with her mother's concern. The thought of her mother, brows knitted together with worry over her only daughter, brought Eden fully back into herself at last.

She sat up in bed, the heavy white linen sheets falling away from her body, and ran her hands through her hair. There was a dull ache in her forehead as if she'd banged it on something hard. Had she screamed out loud? When you slept alone, it was hard to tell what outward signs your nightmares produced. Derek's image skipped across her mind. He'd held her hand when she'd woken up like this back in the early days after her surgery. She'd never told him all the details of the car-crashing dream because she could never quite reach them after she was thrown out of it. Because that was exactly what it felt like—as if she were physically ejected. Then as now, when she woke up, screaming and drenched in sweat, she could remember only the vaguest outlines of the dream/nightmare—the car, the road, the rain, the blinding lights. There was paralyzing fear, but there was also . . . anger. Eden couldn't work out why. Anger seemed such an odd emotion to attach to these images.

She'd gone for a long time without this particular nightmare—so long, in fact, that she'd begun to think she'd imagined having it in the first place. And though her other dreams had been strange—places Eden had never seen but that were nevertheless familiar and people she didn't know speaking to her as if they were the best of friends—Eden had gotten used to them. There was no sense of danger in those dreams, no feeling of imminent death, and she didn't wake up from them feeling as if another person had taken over her soul. But then she'd moved in with Darcy, and the dream had returned.

It didn't come every night or even every week. But each time she closed her eyes and drifted into the space between wakefulness and sleep, a faint sense of dread followed her into unconsciousness. Eden turned her gaze inward, trying to reassemble the pieces of the dream, but she could capture only a few disconnected images—the rain, the blurry road, the oncoming lights. Much clearer was the dream she'd had right after it that featured Darcy in distress at Poquette. She could still see the suffering on Darcy's face and hear her pleas for help. Eden had never met Peter in life, but it didn't surprise her that as soon as she saw him in the dream, she'd known exactly who he was. This dream, at least, had an obvious genesis. Eden was living in Darcy's house, but it was Darcy who had moved into Eden's consciousness. The dream, Eden was certain, was an indication that Darcy was now spilling over into her *un*consciousness.

Darcy's house was very large—so big that Eden's room was really more of guest suite with its own bathroom, bedroom, and sitting area. The kitchen was the only space that the two of them needed to share, and if either one of them wanted privacy, the layout of the place would allow them to go days without seeing each other. Darcy had even made this feature a selling point when she talked Eden into moving in with her.

"I'll never bother you," she'd said. "You'll see. It'll be like having your own apartment."

"It's not you bothering me I'm worried about," Eden had countered. "I don't want to disturb *you!*"

"Not a problem," Darcy said. "Don't even think about it. Once I'm upstairs, I can't hear a thing. And you won't even know I'm here."

But Darcy hadn't invited Eden to come and live with her so that the two of them could rattle around separately in Darcy's elegant, empty house, and they both knew it. Darcy needed a friend, and Eden was tired of being alone. Not *living* alone. It was an important distinction. Eden didn't mind her own company, but she had grown weary of feeling so isolated. Every day, especially when she was working at Poquette, she felt as if she were moving through space behind a glass wall. And it was exhausting trying to push people away when they got too close. That her solitude was self-imposed made no difference in how cold and distancing it had become.

Eden had tried; she really had. She'd made a real effort to be more social, but, she thought wryly, her *heart* hadn't been in it—literally or figuratively. Eden knew she didn't possess the kind of beauty that inspired swooning or stalkers, but she was pretty, sometimes very pretty, and now that she'd adjusted to her medications and was getting regular exercise, her body had regained its shape and curves. Several waiters at Poquette had hit on her before she'd even completed her first month. The attention was balm for Eden's ego, but she knew they weren't looking for much beyond a hookup. But even if Eden had been predisposed to a sweaty, postshift encounter, the last thing she wanted was to have to explain her scar. It was bad enough that she felt like Frankenstein's monster. To have a man staring at her chest that way . . . The exposure was too much for Eden to even think about. She supposed that had she been avid enough, she could have found ways to do it in the dark, but since Derek, Eden just hadn't felt the urge. The last few times with him had been so awful. She'd felt dead. No, she felt worse than dead; other than guilt, she'd felt nothing but a vague distaste and a sense that she was missing something.

Still, Eden missed what she'd once had with Derek—that effortless communication, the understanding between the two of them, the *knowing* of who each other was. Of course, Eden was no longer sure of who *she* was, so she couldn't expect anyone else to figure it out. But that longing for connection was persistent— so persistent that it caused her to let down her guard. One night after work, Sticks asked her if she wanted to go have a drink. Even though her head told her not to, the words, "Sure, why not?" just came falling out of her mouth.

Sticks hadn't pursued her like the waiters at Poquette—he was much quieter, even taciturn toward her, but he'd acted so chivalrously toward her since she'd begun working there that Eden thought he was safe. Maybe he too had a walled-off place inside himself that he needed to open.

The "date" had started well enough. He'd taken her to a late-night wine and coffee bar that was practically on the beach. When it was warm enough to sit outside, you could taste salt in the air as you sipped your drinks. Sticks had ordered an Irish coffee for himself (a peculiarly old-fashioned drink, Eden had thought) and hadn't blinked at her decaf latte.

"I always think of that Ernest Hemingway story when I come here," Sticks said. "It's called 'A Clean Well-Lighted Place.' Have you read it?"

"Hasn't everyone?" Eden said, smiling.

Sticks shrugged. "It's weird, because the story is so deep and full of meaning, and this place is so shallow and empty." It was such an odd thing to say that Eden thought he was joking at first, and she laughed. But when he didn't crack a smile, Eden realized he was serious.

"In a way, that's the meaning of the story too, though," she said. "The light and the darkness, the carelessness of the young waiter . . . But then," she said, smiling, "maybe it's just because you're a bartender and I'm a waitress. It's the ideal story for service people. Kind of our Bible, isn't it?"

"You remind me of someone," Sticks said suddenly.

"I do." She'd meant it to be a question, but it didn't come out that way. There was something in his voice she didn't like—some note of desperation.

"Yeah," he said. A flash of déjà vu broke over Eden like a lightning strike and was gone, but in that moment she knew what was going to happen—she knew Sticks was going to lean forward, pull her face close to his, and kiss her on the mouth. And then when he did exactly that, she saw what *she* would do next—pull away and put her hand to her lips as if he'd burned them—before she could do it. It was the most bizarre feeling, as if she were traveling forward and backward simultaneously. It took several seconds for the sick-drunk feeling to pass and for the present, past, and future to align, but by the time she'd gained some control over her own body, Sticks had moved in for another kiss, his hands stroking her face and neck and then—

"Stop!" she said. Then, seeing his stricken expression, she said, "I'm sorry—you just surprised me." Her hands itched to go to her shirt and clutch it shut, but she kept them at her sides.

"I thought . . . ," he started. "But, no, why would you?"

"Sticks, I—"

"It's okay," he said. "I should have known."

"You just surprised me," she repeated. "I didn't mean to snap at you like that. I wasn't expecting that."

He shrugged. "I know," he said. "I didn't plan it. I don't really know why I did that. I mean, other than the obvious reason."

"The obvious reason?"

"You're hot." He smiled then and finished his drink.

"I should have—"

"No, it's my fault," he said. "I'm sorry." He stood up. "Shall we go?"

Although the evening had been a dismal failure, Sticks never mentioned it again. Nor did he seem to hold it against Eden. If anything, he was even more solicitous toward her after that. But there was something so *wounded* in his voice every time he spoke to her, even if it was something as banal as "order up," Eden felt as if she'd driven a stake through his heart. And it only served to underline for her that she wasn't ready—maybe she never would be—to open herself up to anyone else. But that didn't mean she wasn't lonely.

So when Darcy floated the idea of her moving in, Eden put up only a vague resistance. There were, after all, very good reasons to take her new friend up on the offer. She'd been unprepared for the big drop in tip income that came along with the end of the summer season at Poquette. She hadn't even known there *were* seasons in San Diego—it seemed as if everyone operated in a state of perpetual summer. And she also hadn't anticipated chewing through her savings as fast as she had. Her parents were more than willing to help her out, but Eden didn't want to ask it of them. They'd given more than enough as it was.

Then too there was Darcy's beautiful, luxurious house. Eden had fallen in love with the place the moment she'd walked through the big oak front door. They'd stood in the spacious kitchen together, Darcy roasting tomatoes and Eden peeling garlic for the pasta dinner they were cooking, and Eden had sighed over the loveliness of the tile and the garden view. She ran her hand along the cool, wide black granite counter and gazed up at the collection of pristine copper pots hanging over it. It looked staged, ready for an *Architectural Digest* photo shoot. And that was just the kitchen. Every room was beautiful and tasteful in its own way. Darcy had blushed with pride as Eden walked from room to room, complimenting everything from the furniture to the fixtures. It was nice to be appreciated, Darcy had said, because she'd spent a long time picking everything out and arranging it, and it hadn't been easy to get it to look this good.

"This house has a good feeling," Eden had told her. She thought about her old apartment in Portland—how much she'd loved it. At least four of those apartments could fit inside this house, Eden thought, and that didn't even include the garden and the swimming pool.

"I'm glad you feel that way," Darcy had said, "because I have a proposition . . ."

Eden hadn't wondered too much about why Darcy was drawn to *her* of all the people she might have fished out of a possible sea of potential roommates. She and Darcy had felt familiar to each other from the start. It wasn't as if Eden felt her to be a kindred spirit, but there was something about Darcy that she recognized—something they shared. That night, while they ate dinner at Darcy's kitchen table, Eden realized it was loneliness. Darcy must have sensed the same thing. There was no other reason to invite someone you hardly knew into your home to stay. Well, maybe there was one other reason.

Darcy was not miserly as far as Eden could tell, but she was no philanthropist—not the type to fund hungry children anonymously or volunteer at soup kitchens. So it wasn't a charitable act to take Eden in (although Eden wasn't living there entirely free; she was paying Darcy a small amount of rent for the sake of appearances). There was something Darcy felt she could gain from having Eden around. And that too was fine with Eden. She still felt that she'd been given too much—that in the grand scheme of things she would never be able to pay back all that she owed.

So she gathered her possessions—one small load was all it took—and moved into Darcy's house. It wasn't long before the two of them decided to cook dinner together once and then twice a week. And then, because neither one of them ever went out on anything resembling a date, dinners together became more frequent and were sometimes joined with television or rented movies. Eden was working as many shifts as she could at Poquette, but Darcy seemed always to be awake and ready for a chat when she came home. Soon the chats became conversations, and then they got even deeper than that. And that was when Eden realized what it was that Darcy needed and what she herself was being called upon to give.

Eden turned and swung her legs off the bed, but that was as

far as she got. She hated waking up feeling more tired than she had when she'd gone to sleep. But on nights when her dreams took over, it was as if her body were actually being used by some-one else—or, at least, someone else's heart. Again, Eden raised her hand to her chest. As if it had read her thoughts, her cell phone dinged with the sound of an appointment reminder. She'd almost forgotten.

She'd rescheduled twice, but this afternoon she absolutely had to go see her cardiologist. She wasn't looking forward to it. The appointment was at Pierce Memorial. Just walking through the entrance of any hospital sent adrenaline racing through Eden's blood, but the doctor required tests that couldn't be performed in a clinic. It would take Eden all day to prepare mentally for this visit because every time she saw a doctor—every time someone looked at the place where her body had been opened and her failing heart replaced—she felt the same rush of tangled emotion. And every time, without exception, she had to bite her tongue to keep from asking whose heart was beating inside her. It would never change, Eden thought. This was her destiny.

Karma is a bitch. And so is she.

Eden could hear the words in her head as if someone had spoken them in her ear. This too had been happening with more frequency lately. But these words—angry and defiant—also sounded familiar. She'd just heard them somewhere. Eden scraped her half-awake mind. The dream. Of course, that was it. But now Eden couldn't remember which dream it had come from. The only dream image playing across her mental screen was that of Darcy's face begging for help and Peter's hand squeezing her fin-gers in that small but cruel act.

Darcy hadn't told Eden a story that matched her dream ex-actly, but it clearly hadn't been hard for her subconscious to fill in the details. The table in Poquette where she'd dreamed them was the same table, Darcy had told her, where they always sat when they came in together. Aside from her hair being much longer than it was, the dream Darcy was the same down to the faint laugh lines around her mouth. Peter—that big wedding ring glinting on his finger—was Eden's creation entirely because Darcy had drawn only a sketchy picture of what he looked like. There were no photos of the two of them displayed anywhere in the house.

"For so long, he never did anything that could be considered violent," Eden remembered Darcy telling her. "He was just, you know, a big guy—masculine. He made a kind of joke out of slapping me on the ass or grabbing me. And he didn't do it that often. But then he got a little stronger. He would sort of push or shove me. It was still meant to be 'playful.' Because he hugged me hard too, and he hugged me all the time. I never thought . . . I would never have called it anything but affectionate. It's funny what you notice and what you choose to ignore. He never did it in public— at least not so that anyone would notice—and so I really thought for the longest time that it wasn't happening at all."

Eden couldn't remember what had triggered the confession from Darcy, but once she started talking about her abusive husband, it was as if a dam had been opened—as if she couldn't *stop* talking about it even if she'd wanted. They had been sitting at Darcy's lovely granite kitchen counter, drinking decaffeinated coffee and picking at almond biscotti that Eden had brought back from Poquette. Apropos of nothing, Darcy had launched into the middle of her story as if they'd been in the middle of a conversation already under way.

"I was embarrassed," Darcy said, "once I realized what was really going on. I mean, what kind of woman puts up with that?

Oh, I know—I've seen all the movies-of-the-week, right? But I wasn't one of those frightened wives. We had a good marriage. I *thought* we had a good marriage. We talked about things. But then I . . . Something changed."

"What was it?" Eden asked.

"Just . . ." Darcy became nervous at this point in the story, twirling her hair around her finger, biting her lip, crossing one arm across her chest in a protective gesture. "He got more possessive. Maybe he was having a midlife crisis; I don't know. He wanted to make decisions for me. I started to feel that I was one of his *things*. Something that he owned. And then it got worse. I couldn't ignore it or pretend it wasn't happening."

Eden said nothing. She'd had no experience with domestic abuse and couldn't fathom what it would feel like to be on the receiving end of it. She didn't know what words would be appropriate or soothing or if Darcy even wanted to be soothed. Darcy had been looking down, her eyes shaded and her face obscured, but she lifted her head at that point and stared straight at Eden.

"He punched me," she said. "It was as if I were some guy in a bar he'd gotten mad at. He just pulled back his fist and punched me in the face. I thought he'd broken my jaw."

Her eyes were on fire. Eden opened her mouth to speak, but there was nothing to say.

"I mean, that is unforgivable, isn't it?"

Eden nodded at that point, almost afraid to do anything less than agree with whatever Darcy said.

"Because some things *are* unforgivable," Darcy said. "No matter what. Aren't they?"

"Yes," Eden said. "I suppose."

"No, you have to be certain. Some things are unforgivable. That's all. Has to be."

"Did he . . . ?" Eden didn't know how to finish her sentence. Darcy was unnerving her. Bright red spots had appeared on both her cheeks, and her eyes looked glassy. "I mean, what happened? What did you do?"

"He punched me," Darcy repeated, as if she hadn't heard Eden at all. "He would have done it again."

"He would have—"

"Do you know how I knew he would do it again? Because he apologized." Darcy barked out a laugh. "One of the things I used to tell myself was that it couldn't be abuse because he never said he was sorry for any of the things he did. That was my movie-of-the-week education for you. Those women would always fall for the apology, right? When the husband says he'll never do it again and he's so sorry. That was what I was waiting for. A ridiculous justification if ever there was one. If he wasn't sorry, it never happened. But then, after he punched me, he apologized. He said those very words, 'It will never happen again,' and that was when I knew it would happen again."

"And . . . did it?"

"It would have," Darcy said. There was steel in her voice.

"But what . . . Did you leave him?"

Eden scanned her memory then. She didn't remember Darcy saying anything about leaving her husband. Quite the opposite. Everything she'd heard from Darcy indicated they'd been together—close together—until . . .

"I didn't leave him," Darcy said, and pursed her lips. Finally, she turned her eyes away from Eden and looked inward at some far-off point inside her own head. "He died."

"What happened?" Eden asked before she could stop herself. It had been nagging at her since Marisol had told her about going to Peter's funeral. Darcy had never said anything about Peter's being sick and had never made any reference to an accident. All she'd let on before this moment was that she missed him and that she had been at loose ends without him. It was a very different story from the one Eden was hearing now.

"He had a heart attack," Darcy answered after a long pause. Her voice became monotonous, as if she were repeating something she'd said before. "It was very sudden. There was nothing anyone could have done. It was unexpected."

"I'm sorry," Eden said. It was an automatic response, but Eden wasn't sure it was the right thing to say. Her own heart thumped uncomfortably under her ribs.

"Yes," Darcy said bitterly, "so was he." There followed a moment so strained and awkward that Eden felt her shoulders bunch with tension. But then Darcy seemed to snap out of whatever daze she had fallen into. Her face softened, and when her eyes came back to Eden, they were clear and focused. "It was very difficult," she said. "We never had a chance to work things out. Everything was left . . . unfinished. I don't know if he understood what he was doing. I don't know if I would have left him. And then he was just gone."

She'd finished her coffee then and took her mug over to the sink. Eden wanted to know more but was hesitant to ask. Darcy's revelations seemed to come without warning and end just as suddenly, as if they were on some sort of timer. Eden waited for her to continue, but instead she turned back to Eden and changed the subject entirely.

Darcy hadn't spoken about Peter's death again since then, at least not in specifics. Periodically, she made elliptical references to the funeral or to how different things became for her once Peter was gone, but that was all. Once she'd opened up about the abuse, though, Darcy took every opportunity she could find to bring it up again. Each time she embellished the original story, adding new details, more anecdotes. And each time she pushed Eden to respond a certain way. She wanted Eden to tell her that there had to be a line that couldn't be crossed under any circumstances and to confirm for her that some things not only couldn't but shouldn't be forgiven. A man laying hands on a woman in anger was one of those things. "Don't you agree with me, Eden?" she asked over and over again.

It was almost as if she were trying to get Eden to match her, confession for confession, but Eden could not give Darcy as much as she seemed to want. She'd told Darcy quite a bit about her parents and her childhood (skillfully avoiding her imaginary stay in California), but she could take it only to a certain point— that moment in Waterfront Park when she'd collapsed, and the sky, ground, and water all merged into one gray mass. The day she'd fallen down in one reality and gotten back up in an entirely different one—that was Eden's uncrossable line. Whenever Eden shifted the conversation after offering only the barest of bones about Derek and nothing at all about her surgery or her health, Darcy gave her an odd look. Eden sensed that she was getting suspicious about why Eden's stories were so truncated. But she just wasn't ready to share. And there was still something about Darcy that she couldn't trust.

Eden finally climbed out of bed and shuffled to the bathroom. The mirror showed dark half-moons under her eyes and pinched skin around her mouth. Had the dreams taken that much out of her? She felt as if she looked years older than she was. Splashing water on her face in an attempt to perk up, Eden realized she couldn't really remember coming home last night or getting into bed. It hadn't happened very many times, but in her college days Eden had gone to enough "parties" to recognize what a bad morning after felt like, and this was one of them. Of course, the one thing Eden was certain of was that she hadn't had anything to drink, because beyond a taste here or there, she didn't drink alcohol anymore. She'd been given the go-ahead from her doctors for "small amounts," but as far as Eden was concerned, that was simply another way of saying "none," so she just left it alone like so many other things she'd used to enjoy. So it wasn't liquor that had her feeling this way.

Then what?

She tried to retrace her steps from the night before. She'd worked the dinner shift but had been let off early because business was halting. It was so slow, in fact, that she'd picked up tables in the bar area. When it was really hopping at Poquette, the people at the cocktail tables were usually on their own unless they wanted to fight their way through a three-deep body stack at the bar, but last night those tables got premium service. At one of them was the old guy who'd scrawled his number on a cocktail napkin. That, at least, Eden remembered all too well. But then what? She'd come home . . . That was where things got very hazy. Darcy had been home, she was almost sure . . . Eden pushed her way through the fog. Darcy was sitting on the couch . . . They must have talked, but Eden could recollect nothing of the conversation. Her dreams were the next thing she remembered.

It was just as well she had an appointment, no matter how much she was dreading it. Eden felt fine most of the time, but ever since that moment in the park, she'd never had a full day when she hadn't thought at least once about dying. First the fear was about the old heart giving out; then it was about the new one failing. And whenever she felt even vaguely ill, as she did now, she wondered if it was the beginning of another end. The water-splashing technique wasn't working—Eden felt even more exhausted than before. And now her head was pounding out a steady beat of pain at her temples.

"What is this?" she said out loud.

Dragging her feet, Eden returned to her bed and lay down. It was only just past dawn—no need, really, to get herself out of bed yet. Her head swam as she placed it on the pillow. She grabbed the edge of the fluffy white comforter and wrapped it around her body. That was better—warm and soft. She closed her eyes and, behind them, fragmented dream images slid across one another. Blurry rain. Darcy's frightened eyes. Peter's hand moving to cover hers. Sunlight streaming into Poquette. His hand squeezing hers. Harder. *Sshhh* . . . Somebody was whispering. Somebody didn't want her to hear . . .

"Eden. Are you awake?"

The voice was soft, but there was no urgency in it. Eden ignored it. She was warm, and the dark behind her eyelids was comforting.

"Eden? Eden, wake up."

Now the voice was commanding, but Eden still couldn't be bothered. If she ignored it long enough, maybe it would go away.

"Eden!"

Eden startled and opened her eyes wide. "What?!"

Darcy was hovering over her, close enough so that Eden could smell her freesia perfume, but not so close that they were touching. There was no hand on her shoulder or anything like that. It was the sharp tone of her voice alone that had woken Eden. Unmoving, she stared up at Darcy, who was wearing a red one-piece bathing suit with cutouts on each side and a towel around her shoulders. But she hadn't been swimming. She was dry.

"Oh good, you're awake. I was worried about you."

"Worried?" Eden felt disoriented. She moved her hands under the comforter, clutching the fabric to her chest. She was wearing only a loose-fitting T-shirt, and the neck wasn't quite high enough to cover the scar. She didn't want Darcy to see it. She didn't have the words or the inclination to explain it.

"It's almost noon," Darcy said. "You never sleep this late. I thought I'd come check on you."

"Oh," Eden said, pulling herself slowly into an upright position while keeping the comforter folded around her body. The headache was gone, but she still felt thickheaded and woozy.

Almost noon.

"Shit!" Eden tensed, trying to figure out how to get out of bed without exposing herself.

"What's the matter?"

"I have an appointment," Eden said. "I can't believe I slept this late!"

"Well, you kind of tied one on last night, so I was wondering if maybe you—"

"I *what*?"

"You had a few." Darcy smiled. "I mean, I did too, but you don't usually drink, so I was wondering if it was going to hit you harder. I guess it did."

"I don't remember drinking anything." Eden felt a cold, crawling sensation running down her back, as if someone were melting an ice cube on her neck.

"Ouch," Darcy said. "You *must* be a lightweight."

"No," Eden said, running her hands through her hair. Her feet were cold and so were her fingers. "That's not what I meant. I couldn't have had anything to drink. I wouldn't—"

Darcy raised her eyebrows, her smile fading. Eden noticed she was wearing lipstick. It didn't go together—the lipstick, the towel, the dry bathing suit. "But you did, Eden. I'm sorry; I didn't think it was that strong. It was only port."

"Port?"

"Tawny. You don't remember any of this? I broke out the Quinta do Noval. It was one of Peter's. We talked about this, remember?" Eden shook her head. "You got home from work and said you were in the mood for an adult beverage. I said I had one that was *really* adult." She paused for a minute, tucking her hair behind her ear. "It's kind of a bummer that you don't remember. It was a really great port. Now I know why Peter paid so much money for it."

"I've never had port in my life," Eden said.

Darcy shrugged. "Well, you had it last night, my dear." She smiled again, slid the towel from her neck, and wrapped it around her waist. Why was she still standing there? "Where's your appointment? Do you want a ride? I'm happy to—"

"No, thanks. I'm fine. I mean, I don't need a ride. I'll be on time if I can just get my ass out of bed and into the shower." Eden attempted a smile and a look that she hoped would telegraph her need for privacy, but Darcy wasn't picking up on it.

"Where are you headed?"

"Just . . ." Eden didn't want to be rude. It was a natural question from a roommate. Housemate. Well, landlady, really. And apparently, they were even closer than Eden had thought if Darcy's tale of the port-drinking party was to be believed, which Eden didn't quite. Still, if Darcy didn't get out of her room soon, Eden was going to say something she'd probably end up having to apologize for later. "I'm just going down toward Mission Valley," she said, avoiding Darcy's question entirely.

"To?"

Eden's cell phone started ringing, and she almost swooned with relief. But that relief turned to dismay when she grabbed the phone off the nightstand and saw that the caller was Derek. Scylla, meet Charybdis. She looked up at Darcy, who was *still* unmoving, and said, "I'm sorry, but I should answer this."

"Oh," Darcy said. "Right, yes, of course." She turned, a little too slowly for Eden's liking, and finally exited the room, leaving the door wide open. Eden stared at the ringing phone for a moment and then pressed IGNORE so that it would roll over into voice mail. She couldn't talk to Derek, but she could pretend to talk to him.

"Hello?" she said, holding the phone to her ear. "Good, how are you? Yes, I know, I've been meaning to." Still clutching the comforter, Eden slid off the bed, walked over to the door, and closed it, all the while carrying on her one-sided fake conversation. "Yes, it's great. Oh, really? Yes, me too. Listen, can I call you back? I'm just on my way out. Do you mind? Okay . . ."

She didn't put the phone down until she'd gone into the bathroom and turned on the shower. Her phone chimed with an incoming voice mail message.

"This is ridiculous," Eden whispered to herself, and took the phone back to the nightstand. Any minute now, he'd be following up his voice mail with a text message, and she didn't want to see it—another plea to speak to her.

Why wouldn't he give up? Why wouldn't Derek just let her go?

Eden pulled into the Pierce Memorial parking structure fifteen minutes before her appointment, which was not enough time to navigate the labyrinthine entrance to the hospital, find her floor, and check in. But there was nothing to be done. She hated being late even more than she hated going to the hospital. Chalk another one up to bad judgment and timing, she thought as she ran for the elevator.

Pierce Memorial was nothing like the other hospitals Eden had been in. A new wing had recently been added, and the whole sprawling complex had been redesigned to look more like a luxury hotel than a place where the sick and injured came to stay. The marble-floored lobby was airy and full of original artwork. A large glass dispenser offered water flavored with real lemon and mint, and an upscale coffee bar sold pastries and lattes. In the center of all this was a long desk, with the word CONCIERGE engraved in black letters on a gold plaque. Eden had to stifle a chuckle at this detail. It could be a resort, except the smartly attired personnel at the desk would tell you where to find the Intensive Care Unit rather than which restaurant served the best Italian food. But they probably could tell you that too. All in all, the effect was undeniably soothing. It was clever, Eden thought, because you could almost forget what you were doing there.

"I'm not sure where I'm supposed to go," she told a sweet-faced woman at the concierge desk, who, without having to look on a computer or a printout, directed Eden to the fifth floor. Eden waited for the elevator alone. She imagined herself in a swank apartment building, on her way to a penthouse where she would be greeted by a scenario of perfection—a husband, lovely children, a dog, white wine chilling in a silver ice bucket and canapés ready for her on the coffee table. It was a life she would never have and a fantasy that she couldn't maintain for longer than a split second because entering the elevator with her was a priest, smiling and holding a Bible.

Please don't let him be going to my floor.

Eden pushed the number five button and looked over at the clergyman. "Floor?"

"Six, please." His smile was wider than before, but Eden wasn't comforted. She'd seen many clergymen come and go through the halls of the hospital in the months she'd spent there, so she knew why they were there. She knew it was only a matter of time before one of them came to visit her. The inside of the elevator was stuffy, and despite her hot shower and dash for the car, Eden's head was still fuzzy and her mouth was dry. Any other time, she'd have been sure she was coming down with something, but there was something so different about this feeling. As the elevator chimed her floor, Eden's eyes began to water, and she sneezed.

"God bless you," the priest said as Eden exited.

"Thank you," Eden said, and watched him disappear behind the closing doors.

The nurse at the fifth-floor desk didn't know anything about Eden's appointment, but she did know Eden's doctor.

"I don't know why you'd be here, though, dear. Dr. Morgan's in surgery today. Are you sure you have the right day?"

"Well, I thought I did."

"Hang on then," the nurse said. "Let me check." She gestured for Eden to take a seat near the desk. Eden sat, holding her purse close to her chest as if it would protect her. To her left was a waiting room where she could see an anxious family huddled, drinking coffee and speaking in hushed tones. To her right was a long hallway of private rooms. Eden could see the metal edges of the hospital beds and hear the faint pings and beeps of monitoring equipment—sounds that for so long had been an integral part of her world; so much so that when she stopped hearing them, the silence rang with their absence. She didn't want to focus her gaze in either direction—both scenarios were equally unappealing for the memories they brought. At a loss for where to look (because staring directly ahead at the nice nurse seemed rude), Eden dug her cell phone out of her purse and, reluctantly, checked her messages. Derek, she saw, had called twice.

"Eden, it's Derek. I really wish you would answer my calls. Look, I'm sorry about whatever it was I said the last time we spoke. I can't even remember what it was now—that's how unimportant . . . No, not unimportant. I meant . . . Okay, Eden, you know what I meant. I have something I'd like to tell you. I've been researching—looking into some things I think you'd find really interesting and, well, it's important that we speak, Eden. Don't . . . Just talk to me. Okay? I—I still care about what happens to you."

Eden sighed. There were two more voice mails. The first, predictably, was from her mother.

"Darling, I don't want to be a pest, but you haven't called, and you know that I worry about you; it's my job—as a mother. How are things going at work? What about with Darcy? Is everything okay with that? You sounded a little strained when you were talking about her last time, so I was wondering. I just want to say this one more time, honey, because I want to be sure you know. If you want to move out of her house for any *reason at all,* just tell me and Dad, okay? We will help you out, Eden. You don't have to do everything on your own. That's what family is for. I know you said everything is fine, but I just want to make sure. Call me, honey. Love you."*

Eden searched her memory for what she might have said to her mother about Darcy that would have sounded *strained*. It seemed an odd choice of words, but Eden knew her mother often picked up nuances in her tone or expression that gave away feelings Eden sometimes didn't even know she had. That had happened more often before the surgery, of course, when Eden had been closer to her mother in all ways, but she still had the ability to get inside Eden's head when she wanted to. As her phone switched over to the final voice mail message, Eden made a promise to herself to call her mother as soon as she was finished with her appointment.

"Hey, Eden. It's Dar." *What the hell?* Why was Darcy calling her? "*You ran out so fast, I didn't get a chance to ask you if you want to do dinner tonight. If you're still feeling hungover, we can go light. Maybe soup and sandwiches? Something like that? Anyway, let me know. Bye!*"

As Eden listened to the message, she felt unexplainable anger starting to burn as if a fuse had been lit within her.

It's all her fault. None of this would have happened if not for her. I never would have been here in this awful place. It was her; all along it was her. She made me do it, and nobody will ever know. It's not right; it isn't fair. It's all her fault. She's the one; she's the one. She's the one to blame, not me. There was no other way.

Eden couldn't stop the thoughts coming at her and overtaking her brain. Darcy's face—smiling, laughing—appeared in her mind's eye, mocking her. Her head was jumbled. Emotions and images swirled and competed for space. She struggled to regain control—no, *wrest* control away from someone or something that had taken over. But her rational side was losing, and mindless fury at Darcy raced through her, blinding her. *Her fault, all of it.* Eden dropped her phone on the floor. Bending over to pick it up, she saw that her hands were shaking. *She deserved to be punished.* She scrambled for the phone and tipped herself out of the chair. Now she was falling, the contents of her purse spilling onto the shiny hospital floor.

"Ms. Harrison? Are you okay?"

Eden looked up at the nurse, and something in the young

woman's calm, steady gaze centered her. She felt the tidal wave of anger begin to recede. But below it was another feeling—a cutting fear and a horrible sense of déjà vu. She'd been here before— she'd seen this nurse, this hospital floor, even those overhead lights. She turned her head sharply to the left where the family was still gathered together. She felt suddenly that she'd seen them before—that she'd been in that room, even though this was the first time she'd been here. Eden looked at the nurse and opened her mouth to speak, but no words came out. Her voice seemed to have been ripped out of her throat. She could feel her face flushing. It was like the dream—everyone's worst nightmare—of discovering that you were naked in public. Eden couldn't believe she was once again helpless on a hospital floor. Why was this happening?

The nurse stood up, her face creased with concern. Eden could see her training and caregiving instincts kicking in. She was making the decision now—whether to call for help or just get Eden off the floor on her own.

"I'm okay," Eden said. She sent up a silent prayer of thanks for the return of her voice and her senses. "I just lost my balance." Eden managed to right herself and get back into the chair (she didn't trust herself to stand up just yet), but the nurse was already out from behind her desk and had come over to Eden, her hand warm and steadying on Eden's arm.

"Are you sure? Do you want some water?"

"No, I'm okay, really."

"Are you fasting for a blood test today?"

"No," Eden said. "My blood sugar's fine." Once more, fear flooded through Eden's body, and she felt her adrenaline spike. She didn't want to be here. It wasn't going to turn out well.

"You look a little flushed," the nurse said. "Do you feel warm?"

"No," Eden said. "Really . . ."

"Okay," the nurse said, seeming, at last, to take Eden's word for it, and headed back to her desk. "Someone will be out for you in just a minute," she said. "Looks like Dr. Morgan wants you to see Dr. Baru today. You'll be in good hands, don't worry; Dr. Baru is terrific. My name is Michelle, by the way."

"Thanks, Michelle." Eden waited a few beats. "I've been feeling a little weird all day. I think it's just because I have a hard time with hospitals after, you know, spending so much time . . . It wasn't exactly a fun experience, even though it turned out all right in the end." Now she was babbling. Eden wondered if she was losing a sense of her own identity. Surely this was how madness set in. But if Michelle felt Eden was acting strangely, she didn't let on.

"You mean the transplant?" she said. "I understand what you mean. It's a blessing, there is no question, but what a difficult thing to go through. There's nothing like it—no comparison to be made. And I know it's about science and medicine, but it's still a miracle, isn't it?"

Eden had become so used to medical professionals toeing the line of rationality that it took her a moment before she was sure that Michelle wasn't having her on in some way. But the woman seemed completely serious and sincere.

"That's all been true for me," Eden said. She didn't stop to wonder how much Michelle knew about her medical record or that she knew anything at all. It was liberating to be able to talk to someone—anyone—without having to evade and construct alternative versions of her history. "Have you seen . . . Have you known many heart transplant patients?"

"Sure," Michelle said. "This is the place, isn't it? We have the best transplant unit in the state—and personally, I feel it's one of the best in the country. So I've seen patients, if that's what you mean. But I have a personal connection too. My father-in-law had a heart transplant in this very hospital." She smiled at Eden. "He's doing great."

"That's amazing," Eden said. "Such a coincidence."

"Well, not *such* a coincidence. He had the transplant before we were married." She paused and smiled at Eden. "That was how I met my husband is what I'm saying."

"Ohh." Michelle didn't seem at all disturbed about revealing such personal information, Eden thought, and she wondered if she'd ever feel the same way. "Did he . . . Does your father-in-law know the family? Does he know who his heart donor was?"

"He does," Michelle said. "It was a young man—very young. Not even twenty years old. A terrible shame."

"And did that help?" Eden twisted her hands in her lap. "I mean, with the adjustment after surgery? Because it's so hard if you don't know anything." Eden wondered if she was pushing too hard, asking too many questions, but Michelle didn't seem to mind.

"I can see how it would be," Michelle said. "You've tried to find out, I take it?"

"I did in the beginning. But the donor's family insisted on being anonymous. I don't know why. I'm sure they have their reasons. And I'm sure those reasons are really good ones. But . . ."

"You want to know. I understand. It has helped my father-in-law. He's been in touch with the family, and he's thanked them. I think maybe it helped them too."

"Is there a way to . . . I wish I knew even just something, any-thing. It wouldn't have to be a name. Even a location would be good. Just something. Anything."

"You didn't have your transplant here, did you?"

"No. It was up in Portland. Oregon."

"I see." Michelle gave Eden a long, searching look and then shrugged so subtly that Eden almost missed it. "If they want to stay private, there really isn't much you can do," she told Eden. "It's hard, but we have to respect their privacy. It's the least any-one can do, considering what they're giving. Sometimes, even at the last minute, they aren't ready to go there, you know? It's so hard to let go, and I think many of them feel that donating organs is . . . Well, they just aren't ready. But if they don't, well, you know what can happen."

Yes, Eden thought, she knew only too well what could happen. Eden looked down at her purse—at all the items she'd hastily jammed back into it. She noticed that she had a text message she hadn't yet read, and again, a surge of animosity rose inside her.

"Did your father-in-law feel different after his surgery? Not in the obvious way, of course. I'm wondering if he maybe had dreams or . . . liked different things or different people?"

"He still does," said Michelle. "There are all kinds of foods he didn't like before that he likes now. He even wanted to ride a motorcycle. Can you believe that?"

"I'm afraid I can."

"And that's happened to you?"

"Yes. Well, not the motorcycle, but similar things," Eden said. "I know there's no scientific evidence for the things I'm feeling. I've been told that, but it doesn't mean it isn't happening."

"I'm sure you've heard the term 'cellular memory'?" Michelle asked.

"Yes, of course I have."

"Look, there's science and then there's life," Michelle said. "What we see here every day and what I've experienced in my own life can't always be explained that way. There's a line between science and what goes beyond it. I'm not a religious person, but I believe . . . I have faith in a higher power. I think all of us here do. It's more than just a piece of a person you carry within you now. It stands to reason . . ." Finally, Michelle seemed to think better of what she was saying and halted. "You probably think you're going crazy sometimes," she said to Eden. "I'm here to tell you that you aren't. That's all."

"Thank you," Eden said. "I can't tell you how much I . . . Just, thank you so much, Michelle."

"I can give you my father-in-law's phone number if you like," Michelle said. "He comes here to speak to transplant patients regularly. I'm sure he would be happy to talk to you."

Eden was going to say yes, that would be so nice of her if it wouldn't be any trouble, but at that moment another nurse appeared from some unseen bend in the hallway and approached Eden.

"Ms. Harrison? Eden? We're ready for you now."

Eden stood, her heart lurching only a little and her legs finally steady enough to walk. "Thanks again, Michelle," she said. "Maybe I can get that from you on my way out."

"Of course," Michelle said. "Good luck."

"Thanks," Eden said, adding silently, *I need it.*

CHAPTER 15

Darcy had never attempted to follow a car before, and she'd found it much more difficult than she'd anticipated—a real stretch of her driving abilities. Like so many things, it wasn't as easy as it looked on TV where people routinely chased others through all manner of hazards at high speeds. She'd had a little luck, though. A fender bender on the southbound Interstate 5 had slowed traffic enough for her to catch up to Eden and keep her in view for the rest of the drive. Still, weaving through freeway traffic was not something Darcy was going to list on her résumé anytime soon. There was also the problem of trying to stay incognito. Darcy was pretty sure that being followed was the last thing on Eden's mind, but she'd prepared a decent story just in case she was found out: She was concerned about her friend—and she had good reason, considering how out of it Eden had been this morning—and so it was only natural that she wanted to keep an eye on her and make sure everything was okay. After all, she imagined herself telling Eden, there was that time at Zulu's when Eden acted so strangely and had to leave. Then today, she'd left in such a rush, and Darcy didn't want to pry or seem like an anxious mother hen, but . . . To further underscore her concern, Darcy called Eden's cell phone and left a voice mail message about having dinner together. *"When you didn't pick up, I got worried . . ."*

It sounded reasonable in Darcy's mind anyway, but she'd still taken whatever precautions she could to stay out of sight, especially after Eden exited the freeway. This meant a few dicey maneuvers ducking behind other cars and almost having to take a sharp left turn over a concrete island and into a gas station, but she managed to tail Eden successfully right until she pulled into the parking structure for Pierce Memorial. That move had surprised Darcy. She didn't know what Eden was doing at a hospital, but it made her uneasy. Hospitals were not for routine doctors' appointments. Either she was visiting someone or . . . Darcy eliminated the first possibility right away. Eden would have told her if there was someone she needed to see at the hospital—there was no reason to be circumspect about something like that. And Eden had clearly been in avoidance mode when Darcy tried to press her about where she was going. So what was it—an illness? Pregnancy? Drug addiction treatment? Darcy's instincts told her it was none of those things, but, realistically, it could easily have been any one of them. That was how little she knew about Eden's comings and goings.

Darcy couldn't follow Eden into the parking structure—it was just too small a space to avoid being seen—so she pulled off to the side in a fifteen-minute parking spot and waited, watching the entrance for Eden. If only Eden had told her where she was going, none of this cloak-and-dagger nonsense would have been necessary.

Darcy hated that she knew so little about Eden—it had been gnawing at her since the girl had moved into her house. Darcy had been so sure that once they started living together, Eden would open up to her, but what had happened was almost the opposite. If anything, Eden had become even more unwilling to reveal anything about herself since then. The odd thing was that Eden didn't seem excessively private. In fact, she and Darcy had spent quite a bit of time together in the six weeks they'd been living together, and Eden never locked her bedroom door or snuck around the house. So it wasn't that she didn't want to share her space or time with Darcy, but in all their conversations, Eden never offered Darcy even the most trivial details about her life or her past or even how she *felt* about anything. That, perhaps, was the most frustrating of all for Darcy because she sensed there was much more happening under Eden's mostly controlled surface than she was letting on.

It had taken a bit of convincing on Darcy's part to get Eden to move in. She could tell that Eden didn't want to feel beholden to anyone, especially someone she didn't know very well, and Darcy didn't want to come on too strong. It *was* odd, she supposed, for her to suggest the arrangement in the first place. But that day at the bar in Poquette, Darcy had looked at Eden and felt a connection to her that she couldn't explain or define. Even less rational, she felt it was important to keep Eden physically close to her. She would never have shared that information with anyone, let alone Eden, but it was at the core of her decision to offer Eden a room in her house. But no, not really a room—Darcy wanted Eden to feel that it was her house as well.

The one feature of the house that she and Peter had liked the most when they (well, *he*) had bought it was the self-contained guest bedroom. Peter imagined it as a nice place for his sister to stay when she came to visit, but Darcy loved it for its own sake, for the look and feel of it. She'd put a lot of work into decorating the room, down to the white tile on the bathroom floor, and had created a space that—she thought, anyway—felt cozy but elegant, calm but not sterile. And then, much later, she had reason to love the room even more. She and Adam had stolen time there—how many hours Darcy didn't know, but they would forever be seared into her sense memory. She would never have been with Adam in the bedroom she shared with Peter—or anywhere else in the house, for that matter—because the rest of it had always felt like it belonged to Peter. But that bedroom was different—it was hers, and then it was hers and Adam's. In that bed she'd felt what everyone should get the chance to feel at least once—that she could die happy. And when she'd pitched to Eden the idea of moving in, she'd used this room as a major selling point. Eden was already besotted with the rest of the house—Darcy could see it as she drifted from room to room, admiring all the furniture and fixtures—but Darcy could tell it was the bedroom that put her over the edge.

Eden seemed to fit into the house—and the room—immediately. It wasn't exactly as if she'd been there forever, but it was certainly a comfortable arrangement from the start. The routine they fell into was easy and happened quickly. Darcy really believed, in those first two or three weeks, that she and Eden were going to become very close friends. She also believed that once she told Eden about Peter—about what he'd done—that Eden would confess to her that the same thing had happened to her. But that was not how it went. Darcy still remembered the look in Eden's eyes when she'd told her that Peter had punched her in the jaw. There was a certain cold remove on Eden's face and behind that, a spark of something Darcy couldn't define except to sense that it wasn't sympathy. And as she'd gone on, pressing Eden to agree that what she had suffered was terrible and unforgivable, Eden had retreated further into herself. Darcy had found it strange and, oddly, almost hurtful.

But Darcy had kept going since then—kept telling Eden more and more about her life with Peter—because, even more than before, she felt that Eden was hiding something. And then, more disturbing to Darcy, she sensed Eden pulling away from her as if afraid of giving too much away. Maybe, Darcy thought, that was why Eden never drank. She didn't want to lose any part of that control.

Darcy felt a twinge of remorse. What she'd done last night would probably be considered wrong by almost any measure— almost. But she knew it wouldn't hurt Eden—it was such a tiny, *tiny* amount—and, in the long run, it would wind up being beneficial for everyone. Eden was so tightly wrapped—she needed to relax. It had been one of the warmest autumns on record in San Diego—the thermometer had even hit temperatures in the nineties for an entire week—but Eden couldn't even loosen up enough to take a swim in Darcy's beautiful—and very private— pool. Darcy had mentioned it several times, but Eden always had an excuse; she was too tired (who was too tired to lie by the pool?), she wasn't much of a sun worshipper, she didn't feel comfortable in a bathing suit. The last one was especially ridiculous because there was nothing wrong with Eden's body. Well, at least not that Darcy could see—she always kept it pretty well covered up. But—and here was something else that just didn't add up—Eden didn't seem to be a modest type. Darcy could see it in the way she walked, in the swing of her hips. Women who were self-conscious about their bodies did not sashay across a room or wear form-fitting clothes that highlighted all their curves. Eden did all those things, but she was always buttoned up, always fully clothed. So, no pool. No lounging. No cocktails and no . . . gossip. It wasn't good for one's health to be so bottled up. Darcy could often feel waves of intensity emanating from somewhere deep inside Eden, and she knew that whatever it was that Eden was hiding or protecting or ashamed of had to be eating away at her. All Darcy had done was help that process along a little. After all, she knew what it felt like to have buried shameful secrets. They corroded one's spirit as surely as acid ate through metal.

But Darcy hadn't expected Eden to be so strongly affected so quickly. Within minutes she was light-headed and weaving. And though Eden seemed slightly more jocular than usual, she didn't react in the way that most people did when under the influence. She didn't volunteer any true confessions. But Darcy kept talking, leading her, not knowing how much of the conversation Eden would remember in the morning, and Eden seemed to follow. There was a moment when Darcy thought she'd finally broken through—Eden had leaned back into the couch, her arms crossed against her chest, and said, "It's so hard sometimes, you know? Nobody really understands what I'm going through." Darcy, sitting next to Eden, inched a little closer to her. "What is it," she said, "that you're going through? Tell me." Eden turned to look at her as if summoning the courage to speak, but her eyes glazed over and she slumped. "I'm so tired," she said slowly. "Feel . . . exhausted." Darcy had tried again, gently prodding Eden for more, but it was too late and Eden was too out of it. Minutes later, she pulled herself up and staggered into her room.

There was no harm done, Darcy thought. Eden had slept late and she was a little hungover, but that was the worst of it. She'd been slightly concerned about *how* late Eden had slept, actually, which was why she'd gone into her room to check on her—twice. The first time, at about nine or so, Eden seemed passed out so solidly that she didn't even hear her cell phone buzzing with that message from Derek. Darcy had taken a peek at the message only because it might have been someone important trying to reach Eden, and, as it turned out, it was important—to Darcy anyway. The area code was 503, which Darcy knew was from Oregon, so whoever Derek was, he was connected to her past. He really wanted to talk to Eden, and, judging by the message, she'd been blowing him off for quite a while. Darcy quickly committed Derek's information to memory just in case—because you never knew when information like that might come in handy.

When Eden still wasn't awake by eleven, Darcy started to feel very nervous. But it hadn't taken much to wake Eden up in the end, thank goodness. Eden was absolutely no worse for the wear. A little pale, maybe . . . Darcy had a momentary flash of panic thinking that Eden had come to the hospital now because the aftereffects of the drug had made her feel so ill. If she thought . . . But no, when Darcy had seen her before she'd left the house, she'd seemed fully recovered—or back to normal. And she *had* said she had an appointment. So this hospital visit was clearly planned, and now Darcy was determined to find out the reason why.

She didn't have to wait long. Fortunately, there was no entrance to the hospital through the parking structure, so anyone coming into the hospital had to pass directly across from where Darcy was parked. She'd been sitting there less than five minutes before she saw Eden walk through the pneumatic front doors. Feeling only slightly ridiculous, Darcy waited a few beats and then followed Eden into the building, hugging the walls and keeping an eye on the exits as she went so that she could duck out if she needed to. She ran through her story once more—*I was concerned; you didn't answer your phone; you weren't feeling well*—and hoped for the best. She hovered at the coffee bar while Eden consulted with someone at the concierge desk and then waited until Eden got into the elevator before she ran up to the desk herself.

"I'm so sorry," she said. "I'm with that girl who was just here? Eden Harrison? It took me so long to find a parking spot! She told me to meet her, but I don't know which floor she's gone to. Can you tell me? Thank you!"

If the woman at the desk was in any way suspicious, she didn't let on. She directed Darcy to the fifth floor and turned back to her computer without a second thought. Darcy thanked her profusely and dashed off before anyone could ask her any questions. But once at the elevator, Darcy decided not to get in it. Following Eden from afar was one thing, but if she ran into her on the actual floor, it wouldn't be as easy to explain her presence. Instead, Darcy checked the board next to the elevator bank where the hospital's wards and units were organized by floor. It didn't take Darcy very long to figure out that the fifth floor housed the hospital's extensive cardiac care unit.

Darcy became progressively more confused as she stared at the list of subunits on the floor. Why would Eden be visiting a cardiac unit? And it wasn't just any cardiac unit. Pierce Memorial, Darcy now remembered, was known not just as having the best cardiac center in San Diego, but also as having the *only* transplant center in the county. Darcy's confusion turned to uneasiness fluttering in her stomach. She had the sense of being on the verge of making an unpleasant discovery—something that was right in front of her but that she couldn't yet see. The sensation was unsettling and a little frightening. Feeling a strong need to get out of the building, Darcy hesitated, trying to decide whether to leave the way she'd come in and run the risk of the woman at the desk seeing her or find another exit. Remembering that she was in a fifteen-minute parking spot, Darcy put her head down and sprinted for the front door. The last thing she needed was to get ticketed or towed.

Immeasurably relieved to find her car where she left it, Darcy pulled out and headed home. She'd hoped the mindless maneuvering through freeway traffic would help soothe her, but instead she became increasingly rattled the closer she got to home. What was Eden hiding from her (because now Darcy was convinced that Eden was definitely covering something up), and how did it involve the cardiac unit of Pierce Memorial? She ran images of Eden through her mind, looking for any clues that Eden might be sick. There was something unusual about her friend but nothing that would suggest she needed cardiac care. She was healthy, she ate well, she wasn't pale . . . Darcy had never seen her work out, but that didn't mean she wasn't fit. She put in long shifts waiting on tables and running around.

Running.

Darcy remembered a tidbit Eden had given her once when Darcy had suggested that the two of them take a run together in the mornings.

"I don't run anymore," Eden had said. It was the "anymore" that had piqued Darcy's interest.

"You used to run a lot?" Darcy asked. "Did you get bored? Injure yourself?"

"I used to be . . . I used to like it," Eden said. "But then, yes, at a certain point, like you said, I did get bored."

"I wouldn't be boring," Darcy said, smiling.

"I just don't do it anymore," Eden said. "Sorry."

Darcy wondered now if Eden's giving up running had something to do with her heart. But surely if that were an issue, she wouldn't be able to handle working in a restaurant. None of it made sense, and something about it felt wrong—a puzzle piece that didn't fit. Darcy didn't know why she felt such a strong need to know the details of Eden's past or why in the last couple of hours it had all taken on such importance for her, but she couldn't stop thinking about it.

A shock of realization suddenly hit Darcy so hard that she almost forgot she was driving and started to drift into another lane. She needed to know more about Eden because she was worried about how much—and what—Eden knew about *her.*

Eden talked about Poquette all the time—funny anecdotes about customers who came in, stories about the shouting and cursing that went on in the kitchen, and how slow or busy it had been, but she never discussed or even mentioned anything about Adam. It was true he'd been gone from Poquette a long time and many of the staff had turned over in that time, but Darcy knew there were still servers and bartenders at Poquette who remembered Adam. Of those, there had to be at least one or two who knew something about their relationship. She hadn't worried about Adam talking early on, but then, later, when things took that turn . . . she wasn't sure what he might have let slip. And although Eden had told her once that nobody at Poquette ever discussed Darcy beyond her being a regular customer, Darcy wondered now if Eden had been holding something back.

Yes, she was being paranoid, but there was that old expression—just because you're not paranoid doesn't mean people aren't talking about you. Or something like that. Darcy needed to figure out a way of getting Eden to reveal what she knew without seeming as if she wanted to know. Darcy realized it sounded ridiculous when phrased that way. In a perfect world, she should just be able to ask Eden about it and then be able to accept whatever Eden told her. But it wasn't a perfect world, and Darcy couldn't be kept in the dark about anything—there was too much to lose. She'd thought that telling Eden about Peter would get Eden to open up to her, but it hadn't. Maybe, Darcy thought, she should tell Eden about Adam instead. The best defense, after all, was a good offense. Maybe. But not just yet.

Darcy's house felt a little too still. She had gotten home so fast that she had to consider herself lucky to have avoided getting a speeding ticket. She'd been so preoccupied, she hadn't even noticed how fast she was going or, for that matter, anything about the drive. Muscle memory alone had guided her here. But now that she stood in her kitchen listening to the silence—not even the slight buzzing of appliances to break it—she felt a tickle of fear at the back of her throat.

"Hello?" she called out. It was such a stupid thing to say—why was that always the first reaction of someone alone in a house? If there were home invaders around, it was like calling attention to the fact that you were home, you were by yourself, and you were scared. Darcy walked lightly into the living room, peering into corners, and then into the family room. Eden's room was separated from the main living area by a long hallway. Darcy looked down into the shadows, hesitating. "Eden? Are you home?" No answer. It was dead quiet. Spooked, Darcy reentered the living room, grabbed one of the heavy, showy iron pokers that never got used because it was never really cold enough in San Diego for a fire big enough to require a poker, and crept down the hallway toward Eden's room. Another ridiculous move, she told herself as she inched down the passage, because if there was someone down there with a gun, a poker wasn't going to be much help. Nor was she likely to be able to overpower anyone—any man—even slightly larger than she. Yet Darcy kept going. The larger part of her brain told her there was no danger in her house, but the small and completely irrational part made sure she kept a firm grip on the poker.

"Eden?"

But of course Eden wasn't there. Eden was in a hospital doing who knew what. Darcy walked tentatively into Eden's room for the third time that day. Eden had left in a hurry—the bed was unmade and clothes were draped over the splash-of-red loveseat in the corner. Loose change lay scattered all over the nightstand, and a pair of rejected shoes had been tossed haphazardly in front of the bathroom door, which Darcy noticed was open. Her gaze traveled across the room and along every surface, stopping and lingering on the bed. Darcy experienced a pang of desire and loss so intense, it made her stomach hurt. She could feel Adam's presence as strongly as if he were standing in the room next to her; she could remember the last time they'd been in that bed together, his hands in her hair, his lips on her neck. They'd stolen time in this room only a few times, when Peter was out of town, and the rest of the time it had been either his place or the classic no-tell motel quick stop. But their time here had been the sweetest. Adam never allowed Darcy to talk about karma, even though she knew he believed in it, California boy that he was. He said it didn't matter, because you had to create your own destiny; otherwise you were just a victim. But what had happened . . . well, it felt a lot like karma, didn't it?

Darcy put the poker down behind the bedroom door. There was obviously no intruder. Her senses and instincts were off-kilter from all the skulking around she'd been doing. But it had been worth it, Darcy decided, because she now knew *something* about Eden—and she was about to figure out the rest. Darcy crossed the bedroom and walked into the bathroom. Here too, the memory of Adam permeated the space. Darcy looked into the vanity mirror and could picture him standing behind her, his naked limbs entwining hers as the steam of a hot shower filled the air and turned them into misty shapes. Darcy sighed and ran her hand over the edge of the medicine cabinet she'd designed herself. It was white and wooden with intricate scrollwork on the top. Darcy opened the cabinet. It wasn't an invasion of Eden's privacy. Technically, this was Darcy's house, and the door was wide open. The cabinet was empty save for Eden's toothbrush, toothpaste, and rinse cup. Darcy was vexed—what kind of girl had *nothing* in her medicine cabinet? Not a bottle of ibuprofen? Vitamins? The odd prescription? Everyone kept *something* in her medicine cabinet unless she was . . . hiding it.

It took Darcy a few minutes. Eden had done a good job of squirreling it away, and Darcy was trying to go slowly so that she didn't overturn anything or put it back in the wrong place, but eventually she found the stash in a metal box almost camouflaged underneath a makeup case and behind some towels under the sink. Darcy held up the prescription bottles one by one, looking at the drugs she'd never heard of before: CellCept, Prograf, Lasix, Clonidine. They'd all been filled recently at a local pharmacy. They all had refills. Behind those were a five-hundred-count bottle of low-dose aspirin, a bottle of multivitamins, and a large container of Tums. On the bottom of the box, still full, was an older and, it appeared, unused prescription for Zoloft. Well, that one—an antidepressant—Darcy was at least familiar with.

Now Darcy had started to perspire, and a different kind of fear began tingling at the base of her spine. Who knew she was taking all these damned medications? That Klonopin she'd slipped Eden last night could have interacted with any one of these things, whatever they were, and created all kinds of problems. Darcy sent up a silent prayer of thanks that the worst of it seemed to be that hangover. But she knew now that she had dodged a big fat bullet and that she should have been more careful. The things one didn't know could be one's undoing. She laid the pills back in the box as carefully as she could, because now she was in a tremendous hurry—if Eden walked in on her, she'd be screwed. There was certainly no way of explaining *this*. As soon as she'd gotten everything back in its place, Darcy dashed upstairs to what used to be Peter's office, but which she had now reimagined as her own, closed the door, and sat down at her computer. She typed the names of the drugs she'd found in Eden's bathroom and watched the results come up. Darcy felt her own eyes widen in surprise as she read. Eden was taking anti-rejection, immunosuppressant drugs. There was only one reason for her to be taking such potent medications in this particular combination.

She'd had a heart transplant. But *when*?

It all made sense now—her keeping covered up all the time, those weird little gestures she made, clutching her shirt collar closed and raising her arms to her chest. Why she didn't run anymore. Why she didn't drink.

Fuck.

Why was Eden keeping this such a big secret? Darcy could have killed her last night. Why wouldn't you *tell* people, especially a friend, especially someone you *lived* with, that you'd had a damned heart transplant? It wasn't as if she'd had a breast augmentation or some other kind of elective surgery that you wouldn't want to tell people about. What the hell?

Darcy was angry and more than a little shaken, and, beneath all of that, she was deeply disturbed. This wasn't the end of it. There was more. Darcy didn't know what it was that she wanted to find out, but she knew she had to keep looking. She needed a drink—or, something stronger but less likely to make her slur and appear like a midday lush. She rummaged through her own medicine cabinet, dug out the same bottle of Klonopin she'd unburdened into Eden's drink, and popped a pill in her mouth. It was so small, she didn't even need to drink water.

Darcy went back to her office and paced until she felt the drug start to kick in and her mind slow down its spinning. She sat, finally, in the comfortable leather chair that Peter had picked out and that she'd never replaced. She felt the knot in her stomach release and send warmth radiating throughout her body. Better. Much better. After a few minutes Darcy had had enough time to figure out what to do next. She signed into an e-mail program she'd established long ago to communicate with Adam that belonged to a completely fabricated and anonymous person. It was fortunate, she thought, that these days you could actually send an e-mail as a text message to someone's phone. Technology was amazing. That girl had someone else's heart inside her chest; yet you'd never know it. Darcy stared at the blinking cursor for a moment, the Klonopin starting to make her just a bit drowsy, and then she began to type.

Hi, Derek. You don't know me, but I'm a friend of Eden's . . .

CHAPTER 16

Eden was standing at the bar in Poquette. But there was something different about the place. It looked . . . dimmer, and there was something else. She turned her head to the left. When had they installed that giant fish tank? It was way too big and took up way too much space. You could fit at least three tables there. Eden didn't know what they'd been thinking or why she hadn't noticed them putting it in. It must have taken a long time to get it all set up and filled—surely she should have noticed. The reflection of the overhead dining room lights bounced and shimmered in the water, which was teeming with fish of varying colors, shapes, and sizes. Eden could identify only the slippery flickering lights of the neon tetras.

It wasn't just the fish tank that was different, though. The bar itself looked older, scuffed, and beaten up. The lights were low, and Eden couldn't see very well as her eyes scanned the bodies and faces at the bar. But she recognized one of them instantly. There she was. Darcy sat in the middle of the horseshoe, her black dress cut low, a single diamond sparkling at her throat, and an amber drink in her hand. She was laughing, her long luxurious hair tucked behind her ear on one side, loose and flowing on the other. She was talking to the man sitting next to her, but her eyes kept darting down to where Eden was standing. She was trying to look as if she weren't looking. She did that all the time and never thought anyone noticed. Darcy wasn't nearly as discreet as she thought she was; that was the problem—well, one of the problems. Eden had customers to serve, but she couldn't move. She couldn't take her eyes off of Darcy.

"Hey."

Eden turned her head. Sticks had appeared next to her. He was scowling. "She's not worth it," Sticks said.

"What do you mean?" Eden asked.

"You know what I mean. You know who I'm talking about."

Eden shook her head slowly at first, but then harder back and forth as if someone had taken control of her body. The room started spinning, turning the bar, the fish, and Darcy into a bright blur. *Make it stop.* The blur became brighter. She could hear the echo of Darcy's laughter and then . . . nothing.

Eden waited in the soft darkness for her vision to come back, but it was as if her eyes had been glued shut. She wanted to wake up, to be out of this dark, senseless dream.

Finally, there was sound. Rain beating on metal like thousands of tiny drums. Eden felt as if she could hear each individual drop as it hit. There was nothing to see. Her vision was drowned in inky blackness. There was another sound—broken glass shifting and falling, the noise sharp and amplified in the dark. She could hear wind and the rustle of something that could be paper flapping. The caw of a crow. And now, something else. Cars. The noise of a road.

A dim light filtered through the darkness, turning the black to gray, but there were no shapes yet—nothing she could see. Something shifted and released her. She began to float up. She rose but could feel nothing—there was no sensation, no body. The sound of the raindrops grew softer. A new sound came in—sirens approaching.

Wait. Not yet. I don't want to go.

Like a Polaroid developing, forms began to emerge from the gray. She was looking down at a smashed windshield painted red. No, not paint. Blood. Glass and blood everywhere. She floated higher.

Not yet!

There was an open hand, the palm full of blood. The arm, twisted and broken. A head thrown back. She was drifting up, drifting away. Above her was sky, thunderously dark save for a bright and sparkling patch of blue directly overhead. She looked down and saw the face. His eyes, open and dark. Lifeless.

"No! No, no, no!" Eden screamed and screamed, but now the sound was gone.

Eden jerked awake, her body cold, her heart racing. "Goddamnit," she said out loud. These dreams were going to kill her. No, these dreams *had* killed her—once. But those dead eyes she had seen, floating above what had to be the aftermath of the crash she had been dreaming about since her transplant, were a man's eyes.

Who was he? Who had owned those dark, dead eyes? *His* heart . . .

It was a man. She had a man's heart.

How could they say it didn't matter whose heart you received? How could all of these experts Eden had seen keep telling her that any evidence of cellular memory was anecdotal? The only person who had been straight with her since the beginning of this ordeal had been Michelle, the nurse at Pierce, and this was probably only because her own father-in-law had gone through the same thing.

Eden sat up, and the book she'd forgotten about slid off her chest and fell to the floor. She was on the couch in the living room and hadn't meant to fall asleep, only to relax a little. But she'd been able to pick up more night shifts and had been working late and often. Her body was tired, but it was her mind that really needed to shut down. But every time it did, the dreams came in. It was like that movie *Groundhog Day* where the Bill Murray character had to repeat the same day over and over again, but this was a particularly hellish version.

No rest for the wicked.

Eden snapped her head around in the direction of the voice, but there was nobody there. This had to stop, or Eden was going to wind up like one of those laboratory mice that were fed experimental drugs while researchers watched them run through mazes until they collapsed and died from exhaustion. She needed a therapist. No, more than a therapist she needed a psychic or a medium—someone who could speak to the dead. Or at least someone who could interpret what the dead were trying to tell *her*. She sighed. It was a pity she didn't believe in that kind of thing—and for a nonbeliever, it would never work. Faith was at the root of all miracles. If nothing else, her heart transplant had taught her that much. And as far as therapy went, Eden had *lost* faith. These doctors had saved her body and shown her how to take care of the physical organ that now beat inside her, but they had done nothing for her metaphoric heart. Eden stretched her legs and checked her watch. She had two hours before she needed to be at work, plenty of time to get ready, but she was still shaken and wiped out from her dreams. She would have thought that after enough of these, she would have gotten used to them but no—they were vivid and real every single time. At least when she was inside them. Even when Eden knew she was dreaming, she couldn't pull herself to consciousness and was forced to see the scene over and over again. But what was more frustrating was that when she woke up, those scenes blurred and slid together. The details disintegrated under the glare of consciousness.

She hadn't had the crashing dream for a few weeks—not since the Blackout Night, as she'd now privately dubbed it—and she'd never had this dream in the daytime before. She was working too hard, and she knew it. Eden was sure Dr. Morgan wouldn't approve, and her mother would have a fit if she'd known about it, but among other things, Eden needed the extra cash.

There was nothing specific that Eden could point to as wrong with her housing arrangement, but after living with Darcy for less than three months, she was ready to have her own place again. The two of them hadn't been spending as much time together as they had at first simply because Eden hadn't been home as often, but Eden felt Darcy was somehow insinuating herself even deeper into her life. Again, there was nothing tangible Eden could come up with to support her theory—they weren't exchanging clothes or jobs, and nobody had cut her hair to match the other. They weren't becoming more like each other, and they weren't even talking as much anymore. And since Eden's hospital visit a few weeks ago, Darcy had backed off with the intense stories about her marriage. She'd taken a greater interest in what went on at Poquette, but other than that, she didn't seem to be prying into Eden's past as much either. But all of this had only served to make Eden more suspicious of Darcy, because in Eden's mind, the best reason to stop asking questions was if you'd found the answers. If Darcy had found out something about Eden, there was no longer a need to pry.

This was where slivers of doubt became shards for Eden. For some time—she couldn't tell exactly when it had started, but it hadn't been more than a couple of weeks—she'd felt as if she were being followed. It wasn't anything as dramatic as a tail or anything like that, but she just sensed a presence near her as if someone were keeping an eye on her. And that someone felt very much like Darcy. She'd come home a couple of times and felt that her room had been occupied in her absence. There was nothing out of place, but the air felt disturbed. Her things felt . . . *touched*. And then there was the mysterious appearance of the poker that Eden had discovered behind her bedroom door.

"I wondered where that had gotten to!" Darcy had exclaimed when Eden showed it to her.

"You didn't, um, leave it in my room?"

"Why would I do that?"

"I don't remember bringing it in there. I can't imagine why I would."

"Well . . . ," Darcy had begun, and then just shrugged and smiled, which was the way Darcy ended quite a few conversations that held no interest for her. Eden flashed on the piece of her dream where Darcy was smiling and tossing her hair. *Trying to look as if she weren't looking.*

Eden stood up and leaned over to pick up her book. Her bones were aching. She needed a hot shower and a reason to look alive. She heard the front door opening, and Darcy breezed in, holding fresh flowers and shopping bags.

"Hey, you!"

"Hi, Darcy." Eden stifled a yawn.

"So, you cannot believe the deal I got on these heirloom tomatoes at the farmers' market," Darcy said. Her voice was light, and her eyes were shining, that bright green color Eden had seen the first time they'd met. *So beautiful,* Eden thought suddenly, and with the thought came a wave of wistfulness that Eden couldn't even begin to understand.

"I bought at least five pounds," Darcy continued. "You have to see these things; they're *gorgeous.* I was thinking we could have dinner tonight? We haven't cooked anything together for a long time, and I have this great recipe for an heirloom tomato tart that I'm dying to make. Tomatoes are really good for"—Darcy shifted her packages and nervously tucked her hair behind her ear—"for whatever ails you. Or so they say. So, what do you think, Eden?"

"Sounds really great, Darcy, but I'm working tonight."

"Wow, again?"

"Girl's gotta make a living, right?"

"Well, sure, but you've been burning the candle at all kinds of ends, girl. You've worked like six nights in a row or something like that, haven't you?"

"I don't know. Maybe." Had she been keeping count? Eden hadn't known that Darcy had been paying such careful attention to her work schedule.

"Can't you take a night off?"

"No, not really. But thanks for the offer, Darcy. It really sounds great."

Eden thought that would be the end of it and started to make her way to her room, but Darcy wasn't taking no for an answer. "Well, what about later, then? I could make dinner, and we could at least eat together when you come home?"

A portion of Eden's dream flickered in and out—Darcy laughing, tossing her hair—and was gone. "I can't, Darcy. I'm . . ." What excuse would work? What would sound even remotely plausible? "I'm going out for drinks with a couple of girls from work. They've been asking me forever, so . . ."

"But you don't drink, I thought."

Eden turned her head to look at Darcy, whose eyebrows were raised.

"I'm just going along," Eden said, that odd irrational anger sweeping through her again. "And I do drink, just not a lot. Anyway, I'd better get going."

Darcy said something in response, but Eden, walking so fast it was almost a jog, couldn't make it out.

It wasn't a total fabrication, Eden thought as she cashed out her last tickets of the evening. Melissa and Marisol *had* asked her to go out with them soon after Eden started working at Poquette, but she'd begged off so many times that they'd given up. Eden had tried not to make herself seem standoffish, because she knew how important it was to be on good terms with the people you worked with in a restaurant. The quarters were close, and the tension was always high. Any friction between coworkers had a tendency to spark and erupt into flame with little provocation. Eden didn't want to be on the receiving end of that, so she tried (perhaps a little too hard) to ingratiate herself to the waitresses she worked with. She didn't know what Marisol and Melissa thought of her reticence to go out and party, but she made sure they had no reason to think it was because she didn't want to spend time with them. Tonight, all that chumminess had paid off.

It had been so slow that all the servers had been cut early except for Eden, Melissa, and Marisol. When a party of fifteen showed up at nine p.m., Eden and Marisol decided to split the table and let Melissa pick up whatever other diners came in until closing. The three of them were kept very busy (and it was difficult to get up to full speed after you'd spent most of the evening dawdling and folding napkins), but they had worked together like connected pieces of the same machine. Each one of them had wound up making much more money than she'd anticipated at the beginning of the shift and had had fun doing it. It had also given Eden the opportunity to suggest that the three of them go out for a celebratory cocktail after they finished. If they were surprised by Eden's sudden offer, they didn't show it. And neither Marisol nor Melissa needed much convincing. They were good-time girls, Eden thought as she stapled her tickets into an orderly packet. Neither one of them could be much younger than she was, but they both seemed so much, well, *happier* wasn't exactly the right word, but . . . maybe happier *was* the right word. Eden sighed, wondering if she'd ever stop feeling like a specimen and be able to step outside that wall of glass surrounding her.

"Ready to go?" Sticks eyed Eden from his spot behind the bar. His arms were crossed and his brow furrowed. Eden could tell he was eager to leave, but as the person who had to collect all the servers' tickets and cash them out, the bartender was always the last person to go home.

"Yes, all done. Here you go." Eden held out her tickets and smiled.

"Turned out all right for you in the end, didn't it?" Sticks asked, opening the cash register and fishing out an assortment of bills.

"What do you mean?" Instinctively, Eden brought her hand to her chest, clutching at her shirt. What was he implying? *She's not worth it.* The Sticks from her dream merged suddenly with the live version standing in front of her. He had said that to her in the dream, but it was as if she *remembered* him saying it. She thought back to the ill-fated evening they'd spent together. Had he said something like that then?

"Your night," he said. "Looks like that party treated you guys okay."

"Oh, right, yes." He was referring to her credit card tips, ten percent of which were going straight to him. So that was it—he was just angling for a good tip-out. But no, there was something more in his tone. Eden couldn't work out what. She peeled two twenties off the stack he'd given her and pushed them over to him with one finger. "This is for you." His eyes widened, and he gave her what Eden assumed he intended to be a smile but what looked more like a grimace.

"Even better than I thought, then."

"I'm feeling generous." But she wasn't feeling generous; there was something about Sticks that was making her nervous. She felt as if she owed him something or . . . he *thought* she owed him something. And it wasn't just his extortionate tip-outs she was thinking of; it was something less overt than that. Something emotional. A sort of blackmail. But of course, Eden thought, shaking herself mentally, that made no sense at all. He'd been nothing but civil to her, if not warm, since their night out.

He knows.

There was that voice again—hers but not hers.

"Well, then, I thank you." Sticks shoved the bills in his pocket and shut the cash register drawer with a flourish. "Now, if the M&Ms could just get their asses in gear, I could shut this place down."

"They're just about done," Eden said. "Any minute."

Sticks grunted and drained the glass of spiked orange juice he kept sitting behind the bar. *He hasn't changed at all,* she thought. Once again, the dream version of Sticks appeared in her mind's eye. But this time she also saw the detail she'd forgotten earlier—the fish tank.

"Hey," she said, "was there ever a, um, a fish tank here?"

Sticks rinsed his glass in the bar sink before turning to her with a look she couldn't interpret—some weird mix of anger, surprise, and . . . longing, but not really any of those. "Right over there," he said, pointing to the spot in the restaurant where she'd seen the tank in her dream. "It was there for years. They finally took the stupid thing out just before you started here. Redid the bar too. Finally. Why do you ask?"

"A customer mentioned it," Eden said, inwardly complimenting herself for her quick thinking, "so I was just wondering. I couldn't really picture it."

"It was totally cheesy," Sticks said. "We used to laugh at it back here all the time. I can't tell you how many people walked right into it."

"I know, right?" Eden said, and quickly caught herself. Because she didn't know. She couldn't. And yet she did. Eden wanted to believe her dream was caused by a subliminal suggestion. Perhaps someone had said something about a fish tank at some point. Darcy could easily have offered that nugget of information without Eden even noticing. But in her heart—that foreign, demanding heart—she knew she had seen that fish tank because somehow she'd been there. Somehow she remembered it. Sticks didn't seem to pick up on Eden's thoughts. He was nodding, even chuckling, as he gave the bar another wipe with his towel.

"Nobody was sad to see that thing go," he said. And then, unexpectedly, he winked at her.

"Hey, hey, hey!" Marisol circled the bar and slapped her ticket down in front of Sticks. "Do me, babe!"

"Yeah, yeah," Sticks said. "Big talk. One day you're gonna have to make good on that, girly." He scooped up her tickets and opened his drawer again.

Marisol looked at Eden and rolled her eyes, but she kept up the flirtation. "Be careful what you wish for, big man. I don't know that you could handle all this."

"You think. Try me, darlin'."

Eden listened to the two of them carry on as Sticks counted out Marisol's money, and it occurred to her that of all the waitresses at Poquette, she was the only one Sticks *didn't* flirt with. His quips with the other waitresses varied from sexy banter to borderline sexual harassment, but there wasn't a single one who escaped it entirely except for her. He was always serious with her—always giving her those searching looks. For the first time, she wondered if anyone else had noticed.

"Whatever, boyfriend. Here you go, my lord. Thanks for doing what you do."

Sticks snorted. "What's this? Your girl here did me much better." He nodded at Eden.

"Really?" Marisol said. "Well, then, I guess drinks are on you, Eden."

"You guys going out?"

"As soon as Mel gets her butt out here," Marisol said.

"Oh yeah?" Sticks tried for another smile. This one looked more like a smirk. "Want some male company? Keep you girls protected. You know."

Eden cringed inwardly. What was with him? He hadn't asked her out since that night at the coffee bar. Then again, she wasn't alone now, and maybe he thought crashing her party with Marisol and Melissa was less threatening. She didn't want Sticks to come with them, unaccountably anxious that he would hear something she didn't want him to know. There was that feeling again—that he had something on her. She just couldn't shake it. Nor could she come up with a good enough reason why he shouldn't come with them, and she had no idea how to put him off.

"It's just a girls' night tonight, babe. You know how it is. We're going to talk about cramps and shoes. No offense."

"None taken," Sticks said, but Eden could tell by the scowl creasing his face that he had. "You girls be careful," he said, slamming his drawer shut. "Wouldn't want you to get in trouble." He turned to Eden and stared at her full on before ducking out from behind the bar and brushing by her on his way to the kitchen. That last comment had been intended for her, and she didn't know why.

"Damn, what crawled up his ass?" Marisol said.

"I don't know," Eden said, "but I think it's time for us to go, don't you?"

"Never been readier," Marisol said, untying her apron and crumpling it into a ball. "Let's grab Mel and blow this pop stand."

"You should have seen him!" Marisol said between sips of her tequila sunrise. "I thought he was going to bite Eden's head right off. And she wasn't even the one who shot him down—I was!"

"He can be a real dick sometimes," Melissa said. "I swear, his name should be Dicks. Sticks the Dick. Stick the Dick. Dick-stick!" She dissolved into laughter at her own witticism, clutching her stomach and slapping her hand on the table. She'd had only one drink, but it was a Long Island Iced Tea, and she was well on the way to being completely in the bag. One of them, Eden thought, was probably going to have to drive Melissa home.

They hadn't gone too far from Poquette. There was a bar across the street—the Olde Delmartian it was called—and what it lacked in charm it made up for in convenience, since it was one of the last in sleepy Del Mar that actually stayed open past ten o'clock. The tables were greasy, and the walls were still coated in old cigarette smoke even though smoking in public places had been banned in California for more than twenty years. But the drinks were strong and the lighting dim, and after a certain hour that was all anyone needed or wanted. Eden had ordered a greyhound—it seemed an appropriate drink for a place like this—and she was taking tiny little nonsips of it, hoping Marisol and Melissa wouldn't notice that she was still on her first drink when they were about to order their third.

"Seriously," Marisol said, "I'm getting sick of his shit too. Fucking bartenders!"

"Ha!" Melissa laughed even harder. "That's your specialty, girl!" Alcohol giggles got the better of her then. Breathing when she should have been swallowing, she started to sputter and cough.

"Jeez, Mel, pace yourself," Marisol said, swirling the ice in her glass. Although Melissa seemed to try, the only thing that managed to quiet her convulsive laughter was a round of convulsive hiccups.

"Has he always been like that?" Eden interrupted. "Sticks, I mean. He's been working there how long?"

"I think Sticks came with the place," Marisol said, unpinning her long dark hair and letting it cascade down her shoulders. "Oh, that feels good. He was there when I started anyway."

"He seems to like *you*, though."

"He's all right," Marisol said. "But he drinks too much—that's for sure. And he's always lusting after women he can't have, so I guess that makes him bitter."

Eden had a flashback to Sticks stroking her face, his lips on hers. "What kind of women?"

"Waitresses. Customers. I've seen him go for both—it gets ugly."

"Customers . . . ," Eden said, repeating, not asking.

"He even made a play for your friend one time," Melissa said, having finally recovered from her giggling fit.

"Which friend?" Eden said, a cautious smile on her face. Melissa's pronunciation of the word *friend* implied something else entirely.

"You know, your pal Mrs. Silver. The *widow*." Melissa gave Marisol one of those meaningful glances that spoke volumes Eden couldn't read because she'd not been privy to their personal discussions. Marisol shrugged as if to say, *What do I care,* and then looked over at Eden expectantly.

"Well, she's not my . . . I mean, I don't really consider her . . ." Eden had never told anyone at Poquette that she'd moved in with Darcy. She'd worried that Darcy might have taken offense to that, but she needn't have worried. Darcy was the one who suggested that they should "keep it quiet."

"It might be strange for you, considering I'm a customer and all," Darcy had said. "I wouldn't want you to get in trouble. Not that you could get in trouble, but you know what I mean."

"Yes, you're probably right," Eden had said at the time, grateful that Darcy had brought it up first and happy to let her think it was her idea. So all Marisol and Melissa or anyone else at Poquette knew was when Darcy came in (not very often anymore), she usually asked for Eden to wait on her. Apparently that was enough to warrant Melissa's undisguised sarcasm. "Why do you call her *the widow* like that?" Eden raised her drink to her lips and toyed with the straw between her teeth.

"She's one of those women," Melissa said. "I'm sorry to say it, but he had all the money, and it was obvious that was what she married him for. You see them around here, you know." Melissa drained her drink and started looking around for their server to order another.

"I don't know if it was all that," Marisol said. "You know what Adam said. And she did come in wearing those big dark sunglasses all the time."

"Not sure if I'd take Adam's word for anything," Melissa said. "You know how much that's good for."

"Hey, he never promised *me* anything."

"You sure about that? You didn't seem so okay with it at the time."

"Yeah, well . . ."

They were slipping into some sort of private conversational shorthand, and Eden was almost desperate to bring them back out of it. She needed details. She needed the story. The skin on her scalp was prickling, and she felt she might finally be honing in on something important.

"What do you mean about the sunglasses?" she asked. "Who's Adam? Help a girl out, will you?"

"Adam," said Melissa, "used to tend bar at Poquette. Hot guy. Superhot guy." Eden noticed she was starting to slur her words. Marisol, not yet drunk enough to be oblivious to Melissa's inebriation, frowned slightly but didn't interrupt. "Not just hot, though. Ever meet one of those guys who has it all? Adam had this thing about him—he could turn on the charm and make you seem like you were the only person in the room even though he was scoping out *everyone else* in the room at the same time. Good bartender too, as if that mattered. That's probably why Sticks is such a dick. He never got over working with the dude. Because Adam really could have had anyone he wanted. He *did* have anyone he wanted. I think half the guys wanted to do him too. Fucking worked his way through the waitstaff pretty quick. I mean fucked the working staff." Melissa almost started giggling again but managed to catch herself. "Whatever. No offense, Marisol."

"None taken," Marisol said drily, finishing her drink and pushing it to the edge of the table with Melissa's glass. Eden gave Marisol a quick glance. Her color had risen, and she was looking for something to do with her hands. Eden felt a pang of sympathy for Marisol—*it was too bad about that*—but for what she didn't know.

"But he was extremely fond of our Mrs. Silver, wasn't he?" Melissa said. "I don't know how they thought they were going to keep *that* quiet."

"He was having an affair with Dar—Mrs. Silver?"

"Well, he'd never admit it, but everyone knew. *I* knew anyway. And you knew." Melissa looked at Marisol.

"Can we get another round?" Marisol said, almost grabbing the cocktail waitress as she walked by. Eden debated whether or not to "accidentally" spill her drink, but it didn't appear that she needed to—Marisol and Melissa both seemed preoccupied with other things.

"What was he like, this bartender?" Eden asked.

"Tall, dark, handsome," Melissa said. "But kind of scruffy too. In a sexy way. And of course he was in a band because possibly the only thing that could make him hotter would be playing guitar."

"A band?" It was not just Eden's scalp that was prickling now. It felt as if thousands of tiny pinpricks were pressing into her back, traveling down her spine.

"He recorded a CD, I think, didn't he, Mar?"

"A demo," Marisol said. "They recorded a demo."

"I went to see them a couple of times," Melissa said.

"At Zulu's?" Eden asked.

"That was one of the places," Melissa said. "They were pretty good. They were called . . . I can't remember. What was it, Mar?"

The Proxy, Eden thought.

"The Proxy," Marisol said.

"Fuck, he was hot," Melissa said.

"Yup," Marisol said, adding, "What can I say? I fell for it too. But not for long."

"So, both of you . . . ?" Eden said.

"Not me!" Melissa said too quickly.

Their drinks arrived, and Eden did some shuffling of the glassware so that it looked as if she had only the fresh drink in front of her.

"But I was the only one, I think," Melissa said. "Some of them fell pretty hard too. There was this one waitress who followed him around like a puppy—rearranged her whole schedule so that they could work the same shifts and then had to quit when he blew her off."

"I remember her," Marisol said, chewing her ice. "Lulu. That was pathetic."

"So where does he work now?" Eden asked as lightly as she

could muster. "I'd love to meet this gorgeous dude." Her heart was thumping so loudly, she was sure everyone could have heard it if the room had been just a little quieter.

"Yeah, well, that's the thing," said Melissa. Eden realized that in about three more sips, Melissa was going to be unintelligible.

"He quit," Marisol said, "and went off to pursue his recording career."

"Really?"

"And you know she helped with that," Melissa said.

"Who?"

"The widow. The husband died, and then all of a sudden he finally had the money to go make a record." Melissa was talking, but it was Marisol's face that darkened. "And then she stopped coming in for a while. It was very weird."

"So you think she gave him the money?"

"Kind of a coincidence if she didn't. You can tell when two people are doing each other. Remember that funeral, Mar? Fuck, it was so obvious."

"But we don't know everything," Marisol said.

No, nobody knew everything. Nobody knew that it was all her fault.

"What were you saying about the sunglasses, Marisol? You said Adam told you . . ."

"He said her husband—Mr. Silver, Peter—used to hit her. And she did come in with those big shades on sometimes. She could have been covering a black eye. That would be the classic cover-up, right? But I don't know. Maybe it was just her fashion, because she came in plenty of times on her own too and looked just fine when she was sitting at the bar."

Smiling, tossing her hair. Looking as if she weren't looking.

"She's not worth it."

"Oh fuck."

Eden and Marisol turned to Melissa just in time to see the remainder of her drink land in her lap as the glass fell and smashed on the floor.

"Oh dear," Marisol said. "I think it's time to go home, sweetness."

"I could just get another one," Melissa said with perfect drunken logic.

"I really don't think you should drive, Melissa," Eden said, mopping up what she could of the sticky drink with the few cocktail napkins on the table.

Marisol looked at Eden. "I don't suppose you want to volunteer? Mel and I live in opposite directions, and I have to get up early to—"

"I don't mind," Eden said. "I'll take her home."

"Hey," Melissa said, "doesn't someone ask what I thought I want?"

"Yes," Marisol said, patting her hand. "Exactly."

Melissa lolled in a state of semiconsciousness in Eden's car for most of the ride back to her own house, but toward the end, she sat up and attempted to pull herself together.

"I really should get something other than a Long Island Iced Tea next time," Melissa said. "I don't think they agree with me."

"I don't think they agree with anyone," Eden said.

"Maybe. Thanks for the ride, Eden. You're a doll."

"De nada."

Melissa laughed a little. "He would have *loved* you."

"Who?"

"Adam. You've got that kind of cool thing going on. He liked that shit. That was why he liked the widow so much. Also why he didn't like me."

Eden was starting to feel nauseated. She would have blamed it on the alcohol, but she'd had less than a quarter of her drink—barely enough to taste it. No, there was something else turning her stomach now. "I thought you said you were never with him," she said, quickly looking over at Melissa.

"Yeah, I lied about that. I didn't want Marisol to know because she doesn't know, and I know she slept with him only once, but she liked him more than she said. Pretty gross, isn't it? But, listen, I was drunk. And he was so hot." She sighed. "It was worth it, Eden. And there aren't too many assholes you can say that about."

"Oh God, Melissa."

"What? I'm serious."

"Is this your place?" Eden turned onto a particularly dark street in Leucadia. It was hard to see the street signs and even harder to make out numbers on doors.

"Yeah, that's it," Melissa said, pointing into the darkness. "I think." With some difficulty, Melissa clambered out of the car.

"I'll wait until you get inside," Eden said.

"You're sweet," Melissa said, and instead of walking to her house, she staggered around to the driver's side of the car. Eden rolled down her window.

"Don't tell anyone, okay?" Melissa said in an exaggerated whisper.

"Okay," Eden said. "Drink lots of water. Get some sleep."

"Thanks, babe." Melissa leaned in and then, before Eden could stop her or pull away, she planted a long, alcohol-scented kiss on Eden's lips. "Bye-bye."

Eden did wait until Melissa got inside, but just barely. It was late—after one a.m.—but something told her that Darcy was still awake, perhaps even sitting with her homemade tomato tart at the ready. But tart or no tart, Eden was finally ready for that conversation Darcy was so desperate to have with her. Only this time it was Eden who wanted answers from Darcy.

CHAPTER 17

From: Derek
To: proxy438

Hi there—it's been a while since I've heard from you, and I'm wondering what's going on. I still haven't spoken to Eden. If you're a friend of hers, please tell her it's important that she get in touch with me. I don't know if she's told you what we've been through together, but it was a very difficult time for both of us. Maybe she feels I didn't do enough for her or tried to shut her out. I said some things that weren't very sympathetic at one time when she was going through some difficult stuff. But I need her to know I'm on her side. She's a strong person, but I think she needs more support than she lets on. You obviously care about her, so I'm glad you are there for her. You'd be doing me a huge favor if you'd tell her to get in touch with me, and I think it would be in her best interest also. I'd love to talk with you— or even just to know your name! Let me know. Thanks, Derek.

From: Derek
To: proxy438

Hi again! I hope everything's okay over there, and I hope I haven't said anything to offend you. I really do appreciate your getting in touch with me. Just wondering why you haven't written back, and I'm starting to get a bit nervous. I don't know if you've mentioned anything to Eden about our correspondence. Have you? You probably haven't since you haven't even told me what your name is. Please write back. Thanks, D.

From: Derek
To: proxy438

Hi there. Look, I know this is starting to feel a little stalker-ish (even to me), so I'll try to lay off, but I'd really appreciate it if you could give me an update, okay? I assume you wrote to me for a reason. Unless you are actually Eden and this whole thing is some kind of weird prank. I really hope that's not it. D.

From: proxy438
To: Derek

Hi, Derek. I'm sorry I haven't been in touch for a while. Things have been hectic in my own life, and I really haven't had a lot of time. It may have been premature of me to write to you, and I apologize for any inconvenience it caused you. I assure you I am not Eden, so please don't tell her about this. I think she would be upset with me if she knew I had reached out to you since she has told me that she doesn't wish to have any further contact with you. I don't know her reasons for this, Derek, and I don't want to push. In fact, I haven't seen much of her lately. But the last time I did see her, she seemed absolutely fine, so I don't think you need to worry. Again, I probably rushed into this (contacting you) and didn't mean to tread on anyone's toes or privacy. For that reason, it's probably best if we don't write to each other at this point. All the best to you.

Derek cursed and hit the REPLY button on his e-mail. But even as he sat watching the blinking cursor and trying to compose a response, he knew it would bounce back marked as "undeliverable." This last message was a kiss-off if ever he'd seen one, and he suspected the e-mail address associated with it had probably been deleted already. He'd waited too long with this mystery correspondent, and now he was going to lose her. Of course, proxy438 could be a "he," but Derek's instincts told him the author of the anonymous e-mails was a woman—there was something about the way she phrased things, something about the whole "I've got a secret" tone of the messages that seemed

female to him. Not that he'd admit that publicly because, as
Wendy would hasten to tell him, there was no way of telling who
was male and who was female simply by looking at word choice.

Hi again,

he began.

I'm really sorry that you feel this way. I thought we

Thought we . . . what? Had a great rapport? Were friends? This
was ridiculous. Derek dashed off the rest of the e-mail, barely
paying attention to what he was saying. Something about please
don't make any hasty decisions; we both care about what happens to Eden, etc., etc., and hit SEND before he could give it too
much thought. Just as he suspected, it took all of three seconds
for his e-mail to come right back to him: **Error. Mail returned.
Recipient e-mail address does not exist.**

Derek leaned back in his chair and studied the light coming in
from the window in his tiny home office. The sky was full of
those soft, flying saucer–looking clouds that he used to know
the name of, and somewhere behind those was the sun. It would
have been a pretty picture if he could allow himself to appreciate
things like nature anymore. But his vision and his world had
become impossibly narrow. The fact of it was that he should be in
his "real" office downtown, not here pretending to work while he
immersed himself ever deeper in Eden's life from afar. He trusted
his staff implicitly, but it was his business and he was neglecting
it. He didn't even have that much to show for his efforts, for all
they were worth, and Derek was bitterly disappointed.

For a moment there he'd really thought he was going to be

able to make contact with Eden through proxy438 and work his way back into her life. He should have known better. He'd been surprised but oddly not suspicious when he'd received the first message.

You don't know me,

it had said,

but I'm a friend of Eden's. I found your contact info through Eden, and I know you must be important to her. I wanted to let you know I'm concerned about her. We are not that close, but I do know about her medical issues. I don't know much about her life before I met her, though, and I think there is something troubling her. I am wondering if you can help me understand what that could be. Eden doesn't know I am writing to you, and I hope we can keep it that way. I wouldn't want her to think I am trying to invade her privacy. I just want to help her. Thank you.

Derek had written back right away (maybe too quickly, now that he thought of it), thanking the author of the message for getting in touch with him, agreeing to keep their correspondence confidential, and seconding her concern about Eden. He said something about adjustment, how difficult it had been for Eden, and he mentioned that the two of them were "working things out." He asked what Eden was doing or saying to create the impression that she was troubled. And then he started asking questions. How do you know Eden? Who are you? What is your name? That, perhaps, was the second mistake. He knew next to nothing about proxy438, but the one thing that was perfectly clear was that she didn't like to answer questions—she preferred to ask them.

As their correspondence progressed, Derek found himself giving out much more information than he was getting back. It happened almost without his knowing it, and by the time he realized he'd shared his name, his professional information, and his innermost feelings about Eden with a person who wouldn't even reveal her identity, it was too late to pull back. And then, as soon as proxy438 got what she was after (whatever that was—Derek couldn't tell), the e-mails started tapering off. And now, this.

He should have put Xander on the case, Derek thought now, but he'd already asked for too much help that wasn't work related. Not that he'd had to push them. Since Derek had confessed to them his obsession about finding Eden's donor, Charles and Xander had taken almost immediately to sleuthing. Of course, Derek had told them not waste their time on it, and, of course, they'd all told him that they wouldn't. He told them he meant it; they said they did too. So finally he just admonished them—in the strongest possible terms—not to do anything illegal. The last thing he needed was federal investigators checking him out for hacking into sensitive computer databases. And then, despite himself, he waited for one or all of them to come up with something more than he'd been able to dig up. Somewhere in the middle of all that, proxy438 started sending him e-mails. Xander might have been able to figure out where they were coming from—that was one of his "hobbies"—but Derek had stayed true to his promise not to tell anyone about his correspondence. He didn't want to break what he saw as a fragile thread linking him to Eden. But now here he was, staring at . . . lenticular clouds— that was what they were called—back to square one.

Well, not quite square one. Eden had obviously found herself some kind of nosy, sneaky friend down there in San Diego—exactly the kind of person she'd never have been friends with before, when she was who he now thought of as the "real" Eden—so he knew at least that much about her new life. Also, the real Eden would have answered at least one of his damned voice mails or text messages. He knew now that someone had been reading them—proxy438. Derek felt a momentary pang, imagining Eden gossiping about him to proxy438. What had she said—that he was a lovesick loser who couldn't stop hounding her? That he was insensitive? Too sensitive? A shitty lover? Was this person someone she worked with or someone she'd met while walking or strolling on the sand or . . . It annoyed him more than he wanted to admit that he didn't even know what Eden did for fun anymore. He didn't know if she had fun at all. He pictured Eden with the mystery correspondent (whom, in his mind, he'd conjured as a paler version of Eden because he had so little else to go on) sitting at a café table with palm trees swaying outside the window, sipping decaf lattes and talking about how difficult it was to rid herself of this guy who wouldn't leave her alone. The real Eden would never do that, he thought. But he hadn't seen the real Eden for quite some time. Eden 2.0 seemed capable of anything.

Stop that, he admonished himself. It wasn't really Eden. Well, it *was* Eden, but now more than ever, Derek was convinced that Eden was operating under the influence of her donor's heart—the heart she now owned. Derek sighed as a tune started playing into his head. He had avoided—or at least tried to avoid—songs about hearts since Eden's surgery. It hadn't been easy—he'd been astounded at how many of the songs he'd been listening to for most of his life had titles or lyrics that involved hearts—but he'd managed. Every so often, though, one would come sneaking into his consciousness via the radio or just regurgitated by his memory. Now it was "Owner of a Lonely Heart" by Yes, a song he hadn't even liked in the first place, that had somehow wormed its way into his inner ear.

"That's it," Derek said out loud, and stood up. He needed a break. He needed human interaction. He decided to call the office and let them know he'd be coming in today after all. Wendy picked up right away, and Derek felt his stomach drop. She'd stayed true to her word and had not mentioned their aborted encounter once. Nor had she displayed even a hint of the anger she'd shown him after he'd so unchivalrously left her lying half naked on his bed. If anything, her attitude was even more professional than it had been before they'd gone out that night. And if either Charles or Xander suspected that anything had happened between the two of them, they were giving an Oscar-worthy show of playing dumb. For his part, Derek treated Wendy exactly as he had before, or at least he tried. He couldn't help the oily sludge of guilt that seeped into his brain whenever he looked at her, and he wondered not if, but when she'd realize what an asshole he was and exact some sort of revenge—or just quit. He didn't want to lose her.

"Hi, Wendy."

"How's it going, boss?"

"Okay, thanks. Listen, I'm going to come in today after all. Just wanted to give you guys a heads-up."

"Okay," Wendy said, but Derek could hear the slight hesitation in her voice.

"What?" he said. "Is there something wrong?"

"No, not at all. But . . . Derek, I think Charles wants to speak to you."

"I'll be in shortly."

"No, I think he wants to talk to you now. He seems to be waving at me."

"Put him on," Derek said, barely able to get the words out before Wendy transferred him four feet over to Charles's desk.

"Hey, D. How are you?" Charles said after a too-long pause during which Derek heard absolutely nothing. That was another thing he needed to attend to—hold music.

"Okay, Charles. What's going on?"

"Yes, so okay, I have something for you," Charles said in a near whisper.

"Charles, you're making me nervous."

"No, no, everything's fine." His voice was now even lower. "I've been looking, and, uh, I found out something about, you know, the, um, transplant." By the time he got to the last word, Charles's whisper was so light that Derek could barely understand what he was saying.

"Charles, do you want to wait until I come in or what?"

"Derek, what I'm trying to tell you is that I found out something about the donor."

Derek felt his back and shoulders tense up. "You know who it is? How—"

"I don't know who; I'm sorry, Derek. I'm still working on that. But I did find out *where*. The heart donor came from San Diego."

Yes, Derek thought, of course. Why else would Eden be drawn there? He wondered why he hadn't thought of that first, but then he realized that Eden's heart could have come from anyone anywhere in the United States. They'd told him and Eden that repeatedly.

"Are you sure about that, Charles?"

"Yes, I am."

"Do I want to know how you came into possession of this information?"

"Probably not, D. Just saying."

"Anything else I should know?"

"Not yet. But I'm—I'm working on it."

"Okay." Derek paused, rubbing his suddenly tired eyes. "Thank you, Charles."

"No problem." Charles hung up without a good-bye, but Derek was used to that. He hadn't hired Charles for his social skills.

Now what? Derek paced in front of the window, looking at but no longer seeing the sky. He had real information now, not just hunches or good intentions. These was something substantive that he could offer Eden along with admitting that he'd been wrong about denying her feelings and telling her to forget about whose heart she had. He didn't know that she hadn't already found this information out herself, but he doubted it. The last time he'd spoken to her, she'd seemed determined to give up that quest permanently and move on. And then there was the mystery correspondent whom he could no longer contact and whom he no longer trusted. Although he didn't understand why, Derek was starting to feel he was running out of time. Whether it was just his impatience talking or an instinct that needed paying attention to, Derek felt that he really needed to get through to Eden, but short of making a menace of himself, he didn't know how. He'd been shut out by her and now by her "friend."

After musing on it for another five minutes, Derek made a decision. He went into his kitchen, opened the freezer, and pulled out the bottle of vodka that had been chilling there since much happier and more festive days. One drank vodka in fancy mixed drinks when one was happy and about to be married. One switched to scotch when one was bemoaning one's fate and the girl who got away. This was why the vodka was mostly full and there was no scotch in the pantry. Derek poured himself a short shot, slugged it down, and wiped his mouth. There. Now he was ready. He picked up his phone and punched in the number.

"Hello?"

"Hi, Patty. It's Derek."

Derek could hear her draw in her breath as she decided, no doubt, what tone to take. Would it be sympathetic and kind or tired-of-this-crap? "Hi, Derek. How are you?"

"I'm okay, Patty. How are you doing?"

"I'm fine, Derek." She waited, giving nothing more. She wasn't going to make it easy, then. Well, that was fine; he was fortified with Absolut Peppar.

"Listen, Patty. You know I don't want to make a pest of myself. I also remember that when we had lunch a while back, you told me to get on with my life."

"I don't think I put it exactly like that, Derek."

"Okay, well, maybe not. I know you meant—I know you mean well, Patty. I know you love Eden more than anything, and I know you understand how I feel about her."

"Where is all this going, Derek? Have you found another girl-friend? It's okay, you know, if you have."

"No," he said with a sigh, "I haven't. I'll be honest with you. Eden hasn't spoken to me for a long time—months, I don't know. I've been trying to get in touch with her. I've sent her text messages, left voice mails—not that many, don't worry; I'm not harassing her or anything—but she hasn't been responding." Derek wasn't about to frighten Patty off by telling her about his mystery correspondent, so he chose his next words carefully. "I just don't think she's happy, Patty. I know you said she was fine and everything was okay, but it isn't. I can tell. It hasn't been since . . . well, you know. And I still care about her. I can't help it."

"I know that." Her voice had softened ever so slightly. Derek was encouraged.

"I've thought about this a lot. I've spent days and nights thinking about it, actually. It wasn't something I've come to lightly is what I'm saying."

"I don't know what you're saying. Get to the point, Derek."

"I think Eden is unhappy because . . . I think it has really hurt her not to know who donated her heart. I know what you're thinking and what you're going to say, Patty. I felt the same way too, at first. I agreed with everyone, and I told Eden that she should forget about it, that it didn't matter. But it does matter. And there is a thing called cellular memory. I don't know if you've heard about it?"

"I'm familiar." Her voice shifted again to short and clipped. Or, Derek thought, maybe she was just anxious to hear what he had to say.

"I really think Eden is different . . . no, not different . . . I think she's making decisions based on what her heart is telling her. And I mean that literally. It's because she doesn't know anything at all about the heart donor. If she did, I think she'd have some peace—some kind of closure." He inhaled, held his breath for a second, and breathed out. "So I did some research, and I turned up some information." Lies, lies, lies, but Patty didn't need to know that his staff was also involved in this formerly private business.

"And?"

"And the donor came from San Diego. And I think that's why Eden moved there."

"But, Derek—"

"Hear me out, Patty. I think if Eden knew that and even if she just knew that we—that I don't think she's crazy, that we validate those feelings of hers instead of denying them—"

"Look, skip the psychobabble, Derek. Why are you calling, really? What do you need from me, dear?"

The endearment at the end of her sentence was such a relief to Derek that he almost dropped the phone. It meant that even though she might have been angry at him for doing exactly what she'd told him not to do, she was on his side. She was going to help him.

"I just need to talk to her. I need you to tell her to talk to me. That's all."

Patty was silent for a few beats, and Derek began to worry that he'd misinterpreted what she'd said. He'd always had an amenable relationship with Eden's family, but he'd felt a special bond with Patty. Whether it was a mother's instinct or just her personality he didn't know, but Derek had always felt that Patty understood his feelings for Eden even better sometimes than Eden herself.

"Derek, I have to tell you," she said finally, "I'm not entirely thrilled that you've been pursuing this. We all came to an agreement about it, and I really thought you were going to honor that. But"—she sighed heavily into the phone—"I can't fault you altogether. I don't think you're wrong about Eden is what I'm saying. She isn't happy, it's true, and I've been worried about her too. Oh, she says everything's fine—she's really good about calling me so that I won't worry or show up on her doorstep—but I know better."

"Is she okay? Patty, is she?" Derek was seized with panic. Had something happened? Was her body rejecting the heart? She'd been doing so well, but there was always a chance . . . He couldn't lose her. Not again.

"Physically, she's fine. You don't need to worry about that. She wouldn't take any chances with her health, not now."

"So . . . ?" Derek said, relaxing his grip on the phone.

"That girl has been through so much. I don't have to tell you. I want so badly to give her the space she needs, but . . ."

"Patty, I—"

"No, let me finish. There have been a few times her father and I have been ready to fly down there and try to help her out, but I know it would just piss her off. If nothing else, she's been perfectly clear about wanting to establish her own life. But since she's moved in with that woman—"

"What woman?"

Patty sighed again. "I guess she didn't tell you. She made a friend down there, Darcy. Some woman she met at work who apparently lives alone in a huge house. Eden moved in with her a few months ago, which I thought would be a good thing. She needs a friend, someone to . . . Everyone needs a friend. But I don't think it's working out. Not that she's said anything to that effect, but I can tell. But she won't . . . Look, she's my daughter, and I love her more than I can say, but she has not been herself lately. I don't know if she resents me now or what, but . . ."

Derek waited for her to finish the thought, but the pause lengthened and he had to fill it. "But what, Patty? What is she—"

"She's not been very nice. That sounds silly, and I shouldn't even be telling you this—she'd be so angry at me—but I just don't know who she's turning into lately."

"What do you mean? How is she acting?"

"I think it may be that woman. I think she's being influenced—"

"Which woman?"

"Her friend. Darcy."

"Does this woman have a last name, Patty?"

"Silver. Darcy Silver. Now, Derek, don't—"

"I'm not going to do anything, Patty. You're right to tell me this. We're on the same team here. I really think I can help her. I just need to talk to her." Derek did not suffer a single pang of conscience by not telling Patty about his anonymous correspondent, whose identity he now felt he knew. It was obvious that Patty was struggling, and Derek knew if she'd taken the extraordinary step of revealing her feelings to him, she had to be very anxious about Eden. He wasn't going to do anything to make her feel worse.

"I will tell her to talk to you, Derek. I promise you I will. I don't know if she'll listen to me. She hasn't been paying much attention to what I say these days, but I will let her know she can't shut you out like this. I hope you can do something to help her."

"I'm going to try my best, Patty."

"I really hope you can," Patty repeated. Derek heard a muffled sound that he hoped wasn't a sob.

"It's going to be okay, Patty." It sounded so feeble. How many times before had he told her the exact same thing? "Thank you for this."

"You're a good guy, Derek," she said. "I mean that."

Derek thanked her again, told her that he would call her very soon, and hung up. He looked at the vodka and briefly debated taking another slug before putting it back in its frosty bed. He decided that now wasn't the time, but he was glad, all things considered, that there was still so much of it left. He wondered how long it would take for Patty to talk to Eden and then how long it would take for Eden to talk to him. Patty hadn't sounded hopeful, but Derek planned to be armed with all kinds of information when he next tried to get Eden on the phone. Part of that would be what Charles had just discovered, but another part of it was going to be what he could find out himself right now. Derek headed back to his computer. Work was going to have to wait just a little longer.

Derek's search for **Darcy Silver San Diego** yielded instant results. The woman herself didn't have much of a profile, but her husband, Peter Silver, was all over the Internet. There were dozens of articles in the financial trades that mentioned him, and his name came up even more frequently in the pages of various charities. There were society events, dinners, amateur golf tournaments. In all, Silver's wife, Darcy, got a mention, usually as **Silver's lovely young wife**. Derek continued scrolling, sometimes clicking on links but mostly scanning the descriptions. Then he found the obituary.

Peter Silver, longtime San Diego resident, entrepreneur, and philanthropist, died suddenly Thursday evening at a North San Diego County hospital. Silver, 51, was an investor in several local businesses and a regular contributor to the area's charities, including Food for Life, Children's Hospital, and Beach Restoration. Silver was a regular emcee at the Golden Club Variety Gala and Banquet. An avid golfer, Silver had recently participated in the San Diego's "Run for the Cure" marathon, finishing a respectable seventh place in his age division. "It is a shock and a terrible loss," said Silver's attorney and business partner, Lawrence Putterman. "There is no way to express how devastated I am personally and what a tremendous loss this is to the community." Silver is survived by his wife, Darcy. A private memorial service will be held on Sunday at Fieldstone Gardens. The family has asked that in lieu of flowers, donations be made to one of the many charities Peter Silver supported.

Derek stared at the screen for a long time, the wheels in his brain spinning, before he went back to his original search and clicked on **Images**. Photos of Peter and Darcy Silver appeared in miniature all over the page. Derek chose one of the higher-resolution images and opened it. She was wearing a long black cocktail dress, diamonds in her ears and at her throat. She had long, blond fairy-tale hair—the spun-gold kind little girls envisioned when they dreamed of becoming princesses—sparkling eyes, and an adoring, alluring smile for her husband on whose arm she rested a bejeweled hand. His other arm was wrapped protectively around her waist, pulling her in toward him. Derek wasn't surprised that he held her so close. You wouldn't want a woman like that to get away.

Proxy438 was a real beauty.

CHAPTER 18

Eden hadn't bothered going home after work to change clothes, and she regretted it because now she was stuck wearing the not-terribly-clean jeans in which she'd worked her lunch shift and the too-tight black T-shirt that she'd hurriedly thrown in her purse on her way out the door this morning. She'd changed in one of the stalls in the Poquette restroom—very little privacy there and certainly no time for the fine details of wardrobe management—balled up her apron and work shirt, and headed straight for Zulu's.

Now she parked her car in almost the identical spot she'd picked when she and Darcy had come here for their first "date," pulled down her visor, and checked her face in the mirror. Even in the waning "magic hour" light, Eden could see the dark circles under her eyes and the hollows in her cheeks. She'd been eating well, if not plenty, and her shifts at Poquette absolutely counted as exercise, but Eden's interrupted sleep and constant nightmares were really starting to take a toll. She supposed there were some who'd consider her madwoman look sexy, but she found it very unappealing. She was tired, and she looked it.

Eden fluffed up her hair with her fingers. It was a new haircut, and she still wasn't quite used to it. Eden had kept her hair in the same shoulder-length straight style for her entire life, but last week, directed by a sudden, strong urge to change it, she'd walked into a salon that Marisol had recommended and asked the stylist to cut it all off.

"Are you sure, really?" the stylist had asked her so many times that Eden found herself getting irritated.

"It's just hair," she said finally. "I need a change. It'll grow back if I don't like it."

"But that's such a *radical* change," the stylist had said. "If you don't like it, you'll have to wait a long time for it to get back to where it was."

In the end, Eden started to see the logic in the stylist's argument, and they compromised. There was a big pile of her dark tresses on the floor when all the cutting was done, but Eden didn't look shorn. It was short but not boyish. There was a sort of swoop happening on one side and some feathery thing happening on the other. The girls at work had been complimentary ("It really makes your eyes pop"), but Darcy had seemed startled when Eden walked in with her new hair.

"What?" Eden said. "Don't you like it?"

"No, it's not that at all," Darcy said. "You just look so different."

"Well, that's what I wanted."

"I did that once," Darcy said.

"Did what?"

"I made a major change with my hair. It used to hang down to my waist. All that hair. I could tie it in knots if I wanted to. I could hang it out the window and let someone climb up on it. But then I cut it short. Not as short as yours is now, but short."

"And?"

"It didn't go over well," Darcy said.

"Nobody liked it? Was it a bad cut?"

"My husband . . . Peter loved my hair. He loved it so much, I sometimes thought he loved it more than he loved me. He told me never to cut it. He made out as if it were a joke—don't cut it or else—but it wasn't really a joke. He wasn't good at jokes, Peter. Anyway, I cut it, and he freaked out. No, he didn't freak out exactly. He said he didn't care." Darcy gave Eden a long, defiant look. "But that was when he punched me in the jaw. Over hair. He knocked me out over hair."

"I'm sorry about that, Darcy," Eden said, and she meant it. But though she was sympathetic to Darcy and believed what she said about Peter's abuse, Eden's simmering unease and distrust of Darcy weren't blunted by this story. If anything, they had only gotten stronger since she'd found out about Adam from Marisol and Melissa and then heard Darcy's own version of what had happened between the two of them.

It was funny, Eden thought now, how Darcy seemed to anticipate Eden's finding out about her affair with the bartender. She'd come home that night—really, early the next morning—and found a generous slice of Darcy's homemade heirloom tomato tart on the kitchen counter wrapped in foil next to a small bowl containing a fresh green salad with dressing in a ramekin on the side. On a small square sheet of paper next to the meal, Darcy had written, *Thought you might be hungry anyway.* The house was quiet. Eden hadn't been prepared to feel as moved as she was by Darcy's gesture. She pulled up a stool, sat down at the granite counter, and ate under dimmed lights. The tart was delicious. Eden didn't realize how hungry she was until she'd polished off the entire slice. Her almost manic desire to find out what Darcy had to say about Adam had ebbed away by the end of the meal. But the next morning, when the two of them arrived in the kitchen for coffee at the same time, it was Darcy who seemed to want to spill the entire tale.

"You were out late last night," she said after Eden thanked her for leaving the plate of food.

"Well, those girls can really tie one on," Eden said. "I had to give Melissa a ride home—she was too drunk to drive—so that made me even later." Eden had flashed back briefly to the long kiss Melissa had planted on her lips and decided to pretend it had never happened.

"Melissa," Darcy said thoughtfully. "Which one is she?"

"Olive-skinned, pretty skinny, dark eyes, long ponytail?"

Darcy shrugged. "I'm not sure I know her."

"You've seen her. I'm sure she's waited on you."

It must have been there in her tone, Eden thought, because Darcy then said, "She knows *me*, then."

"Yes. Both she and Marisol. I'm sure you'd recognize them if you saw them."

"So," Darcy said, artfully stirring cream into her coffee, "I suppose they've also mentioned that I knew other people who used to work there as well."

Eden had looked at her then, trying to gauge what kind of reaction she was going for or what she expected Eden to say. In the end, she decided to just come out with it. "The bartender," she said.

"It's true," Darcy said, leaping right into the middle of it. "Just so you know. But whatever they said—whatever they think they know about what went on between the two of us probably isn't."

"I'm not judging," Eden said. But she was—oh, she was indeed. She'd already been judge *and* jury.

"You can't help who you fall in love with," Darcy said. It sounded as if she'd rehearsed that line many times. "The thing was, I really did love my husband, and we *were* happy together for a long time." Eden had put her head down. She didn't want to see the desperation in Darcy's eyes, and there was something about this speech that felt very familiar to her. "I never intended for anything to happen. I didn't go out looking for trouble. One day I was there and he was there and . . ." She'd paused for so long, Eden looked up again and saw that Darcy was staring at her with the same kind of blazing intensity she'd had when she'd first told Eden about Peter hitting her. It was just a moment, but Eden felt thrown off balance and almost frightened by that look. They were standing very close to each other, and Eden had to fight to keep her hand resting on the table and not shooting up to her chest to cover and protect that scar.

"It's not any of my business," she told Darcy. But it was. Of course it was, but in what way, Eden was only just starting to understand.

"It's not your business, but you want to know about it," Darcy said. Eden didn't bother denying it. "In the greater scheme of things, an affair isn't a worse moral violation than hitting your wife," Darcy said. "Not that I did one thing because of the other. But still, if we're casting stones . . . I'm sure I know what those girls had to say about me. Rich woman, slumming with the help. Something like that? The way they looked at me sometimes . . . Eden, you have to understand what it was like for me. He would have killed me in the end—I'm sure of it. One way or another. There are all kinds of ways to crush a person."

To Eden's shock, Darcy's eyes started to fill with tears, and she bit her lip. "I *loved* him. It was a real love. And he loved me." Eden no longer knew whether Darcy was talking about Peter or Adam. She seemed both lost in her thoughts and tortured by them. *What happened?* Eden wanted to ask. *Why couldn't you just let it go?*

"You remind me of him," Darcy said.

"Who do I remind you of, Darcy?" Pieces of her dreams slid and splintered in Eden's mind. Darcy laughing and tossing her hair. The bar, the fish tank. Sticks saying, "She's not worth it." And then that patch of blue, rising as it had out of that gray and red twisted metal.

"Adam. I know that sounds strange, but you have the same kind of, I don't know, determination. There's something so strong about you—inside. I always felt safe with Adam. I always felt I could trust him. And I felt that way about you too, Eden, from the moment I first met you. Do you remember that day? As soon as we were introduced, I knew you were someone who would be a friend. You can't say that about many people, can you? I felt that way about him too." Darcy's eyes were glittering, whether from tears, fever, or madness Eden couldn't tell.

What does she want from me? Haven't I given her enough?

"Can you?" Darcy repeated. "Didn't you feel that too? That we would be *friends*? Didn't you?"

And at that point, Eden remembered, Darcy had leaned in toward her so close that Eden could see the pulsing of blood in her neck. Just like the dream she'd had before. Darcy sitting at that table with Peter, that hand gripping hers. *Help me.*

"I have to go," Eden said then. She had to get out of the conversation and out of the kitchen. She felt as if she were suffocating.

Now Eden flipped up her visor and took the keys out of the ignition. Her feelings about Darcy had become impossibly tangled, and so much of it was based on swirling half-realized dreams and intuitions. She was drawn to this complicated, beautiful woman and repelled by her at the same time. She was angry at Darcy for no real reason but also felt a deep understanding and empathy for what she'd been through. And she alternated between feeling dismissive of Darcy's wealth and beauty (she hadn't earned any of it—all of it had been gifted to her) and desirous of it (there was a woman with a whole body and not a material care in the world). Often she felt all of these things simultaneously. It made talking to the woman very difficult. And then, when she wasn't in Darcy's presence, Eden felt spikes of distrust (which made it even odder that Darcy kept hammering on about how much she trusted Eden), splinters of fear, and something else—that same sense of recognition she'd had the first time she met Darcy and the feeling that they were hurtling toward something together that she was powerless to stop.

And all of it had something to do with Adam. Eden was sure of that now. She didn't know how, and she could prove nothing; but she was convinced she was on the verge of being able to connect the dots. That was why she was here at Zulu's—a place she hadn't visited since that time with Darcy. Something about this innocent little coffeehouse had scared her off every time she'd thought about it. But now she was determined to sit here until something happened—some trigger, some emotion or memory or dream. There was something here she could use.

Eden was halfway to the entrance when her phone began to vibrate in the pocket of her jeans. Muttering a curse, she pulled out the phone and checked the caller ID. *Mom. Not now,* Eden thought, but she answered the phone anyway. Her mother's radar had been buzzing lately, and Eden had to assure her that she was fine, that everything was okay. If she wasn't successful, she'd find both parents outside her door as they'd threatened, and Eden didn't want to see them. It wasn't that she didn't love them or that she didn't appreciate their concern, but Eden didn't want to be told what to do or how to feel. Her mother still spoke to her as if she were the Eden she'd been before her surgery, and Eden was becoming increasingly frustrated—almost angry—with trying to be that person. The old, sick-hearted Eden existed only in pieces now, but her mother would never be able to accept that, which made it very difficult to talk to her.

"Hi, Mom."

"Finally!" her mother said. "My long-lost daughter."

"Sorry, Mom. I've been so busy at work. I've been picking up extra shifts, so it's just been go-go, you know? I don't know what happens to the days."

"I know you don't want to hear this, Eden, but you should take it easy. There's no reason for you to work so hard. You should—"

"Mom, I'm fine. I just saw Dr. Morgan—I told you that. Everything's fine."

"I don't know, Eden. I think—"

"Mom, I'm actually on a break from work right now, and I have to go back in. I'll call you later, I promise."

"Eden, I don't understand why you won't talk to me. What have I done to make you so angry at me?"

"I'm not angry." Eden sighed into the phone. "I have to get back to work."

"If you say so. But just give me one more minute. There's something I want to tell you."

It was easier to yield than argue. "What is it, Mom?"

"I want you to talk to Derek."

Eden's annoyance edged into anxiety. Her mother hadn't been pleased about her breakup with Derek, but she'd never pushed Eden to stay with him. And though Eden knew that for a while her mother had been in better touch with Derek than she had, it had been months since her mother had even mentioned Derek. So why now?

"Why, Mom? Is there something wrong? There isn't really much to talk about. He wants . . . I can't give him what he wants. Has he been complaining to you? I wouldn't have thought he'd do something like that, but—"

"Eden, just listen for a second. He hasn't been complaining to me. There's no conspiracy here." The testiness in her mother's voice surprised Eden. "I understand that you're living your life and I know you want to make your own decisions and I know you're tired of people worrying about you, Eden, but . . . Sometimes you have to give a little too, even if you don't think you should. Just call him. Okay? Do it for me if not for yourself."

"Okay."

"Promise me, Eden."

"Okay, Mom. I really have to go now."

This time her mother didn't put up a fight. She told Eden she loved her and hung up before Eden could say the same. For a moment, Eden hesitated. She could call Derek now—do her duty and satisfy her mother and her own curiosity. She pictured Derek, his handsome face smiling at her, and for the first time in months, she felt a twinge of longing for him. But it was as if she were seeing him from across a vast distance that couldn't be breached. And the longing was for the feeling she'd once had for him—a feeling that seemed now irretrievably lost. Eden put her phone back in her pocket. She would call him. Just not now.

Eden walked into Zulu's and, once again, took a table outside. This way, if she became dizzy and faint, she could pass out quietly in the bougainvillea and be back on her feet before anyone noticed. When the waitress came around, Eden ordered a café mocha, which wasn't her usual drink and one she really wasn't supposed to consume, but this was not a usual situation. She needed something that might revive her if things started to go the way they had when she'd been here with Darcy.

"D'you want anything to eat?" the waitress asked. "We have a great menu."

"Sure, okay, I'll take a look," Eden said. The waitress was short, perky, and spoke with an English accent, which Eden imagined garnered her plenty of extra tips. It was amazing how much people loved foreign accents. It made you wonder what it was about dropped consonants and slippery vowels that got people so excited.

"Splendid!" the waitress said. "I'll be right back with that. My name's Suze, right?"

"Thanks," Eden said, smiling in spite of herself. It was an uncharacteristically humid day, and the air hung heavy over Eden's shoulders. She stole a glance at the ministage where the bands set up and played. She'd known about the Proxy before either Marisol or Melissa had had a chance to tell her about them. And now she could almost hear the sound of their music in her ear. That song fragment she'd heard in her dreams—something about water and the moon—had to have come from the same band. She was willing to bet her afternoon's tips that she'd find that demo CD somewhere in Darcy's possession if she looked hard enough.

Eden still felt fine—no spinning or dry mouth—so she tried to concentrate on that small square space where Adam had once played his guitar and . . . feel something. But after a minute, the only sensation Eden had was of her eyes tearing up because they were staring so fixedly into space. Of course.

Where is the fucking help when you need it?

Eden startled. Suze was standing next to her with a menu and a basket of bread.

"Here you are, luv."

"Thank you."

"So, listen—I have some recommendations if you want."

"No," Eden said, "but can you tell me . . . Is there a band playing tonight?"

"Not tonight, sorry. But tomorrow—"

"Have you ever heard of a band—I mean, do you know a band called the Proxy? They've played here, right?"

"Oh yeah, sure," Suze said. "But it's been a long time now. They haven't been here in forever."

"Did you know any of the people in the band?"

"Yeah, we got to know them a bit. The Proxy was a regular band here, so yeah." Suze shook her head and rolled her eyes at the same time. Eden had never seen anyone manage to look quite so dismissive.

"What?" Eden laughed a little, trying to make Suze think that she was cool, that Suze could tell her anything. "Didn't you like the music?"

"No, nothing like that," Suze said. "They were pretty good, actually. People liked them. Probably could have been big if they'd stayed at it long enough. But . . ."

"But what?"

"Nothing, nothing." Suze pressed her lips together. It was the oldest sign there was that she was finished giving out information, and Eden was stricken. She had to know—she had to know more. "Have you decided? Shall I give you another minute?" Suze asked.

"Did you know Adam?" Eden asked, just giving up the caution and throwing herself into it. What did it matter? "The guitarist of the band? He—"

"Oh, I know who you're talking about!" Suze's reaction was instantaneous. Her animated face was speaking volumes; mouth turned down at the corners, one eyebrow raised, and a nose wrinkle just for good measure. She tilted her head and gave Eden a searching look as if trying to figure out whether or not she could be trusted. "How did *you* know him?" she asked Eden.

Eden scrambled for what to say that would sound authentic and truthful. Her brain was in knots and nothing was coming to her, so she reached for the first thing that seemed believable. "I used to . . . date him. It was a long time ago."

"Jesus," Suze said, shaking her head. "Was there anyone he *didn't* screw?"

Eden blushed, a deep hot red that she could feel starting at the bottom of her scar and flooding into her face. She couldn't control it or the overwhelming feeling of shame that came with it.

"Shit, I'm sorry, luv. Didn't mean it like that at all. I'm always sticking my foot in my mouth. I just meant—"

"No, it's okay. Don't apologize," Eden said. "I'm not offended. It was a long time ago, like I said, and it really wasn't for long. I've been gone a long time. I just moved back to the area, you know, and . . . Anyway, I was just wondering. Did you . . . ?"

"Oh, I never," Suze said. "Could see that coming a mile off. Didn't turn out well for those girls who were so in love with him. He was a right prick. Sorry, but I have to say it. He cheated on *all* of them. People who say men can't be total slags don't know what they're talking about—he was top of the list! And he hit the jackpot too. You'd have thought he would have quit hounding after that, but no."

"He hit the jackpot? He won money?"

"No, of course not. He was a total gold digger, that one. He always turned on the charm, you know, and they always fell for it. I never could figure out why. I mean he was good-looking and all, but that's not enough to—unless he had some kind of magic going on between the sheets, but still. Actually, maybe—"

"He was a gold digger," Eden said, trying to gently push Suze back on track. She couldn't afford to have Suze drift off on a tangent and then realize she had tables she was neglecting and run off to serve them. Eden got the impression that once Suze left this table and this topic, she wouldn't come back to it again, and that was completely unacceptable because Eden felt that she was so close—so damned close.

"Yeah, and that was how he hit the jackpot. But you probably know all this already, yeah?"

"No, I don't. Please tell me." Did it sound like she was begging? She hoped not. *Go on, Suze, go on. Tell me.*

"He got in with this rich woman—a ton of money. She was married, but that didn't stop him. He bragged about it, even. Said the husband was totally loaded and gave her everything she wanted except what he could give her. He had a problem with people who had money. Thought he deserved it more than they did. He talked about her like that too, even if he said she was gorgeous. I don't know—it was hard to tell with that one. He loved himself so much, I can't imagine how he managed to get any love in for anyone else. And then—how bloody lucky—the husband kicked off and left her all the money. Adam fell with his ass in butter, he did. Oh, you should have heard him go *on*. He was off to LA; he was going to record an album. Managers, recording deals—whatever else. The band didn't like it, and he didn't like them interfering with his shit. He got that Lead Singer Disease thing." Suze shook her head again, making tsk, tsk noises. She seemed to have fallen into a reverie of indignation, and Eden needed her to stay in the moment just a tiny bit longer. "You'd have thought that would be enough for him, wouldn't you? See, the thing is, I just can't stand these men who treat women so shabbily. I know they have free will and all that, and nobody's twisting their arms or anything, but shit. That woman with all the money? He cheated on her too. And then as soon as he had a piece of that cash, he ditched her. Ran off with some waitress with a really hot body. I don't think that lasted either. But I don't know—he was out of here by then. The band was so pissed off, they never came back here again. Probably all became fucking accountants or some shit like that."

"Wow," Eden said. "I didn't know all that."

"Then you probably don't know . . ." Suze took an uncharacteristic pause and looked at Eden questioningly. There was doubt in her eyes now. A sudden chill ran up Eden's spine. Her skin was tingling. Her heart was beating fast, and the scar on top of it felt tight, almost painful.

"I don't know what?" But Eden did know. Her dreams had told her.

"He was a dog through and through," Suze said, "and some would say it was fitting." She took a breath and let it out as a sigh. "It was still sad, though, what happened to him." She looked at Eden again. "I'm sorry," she said again. "I've upset you. I shouldn't have said anything. You're not going to complain, are you?"

"What happened to him?" Eden asked. It was back—the dizziness, the parched throat. Her words sounded dry and ragged. She felt as if she were about to pass out. *Not yet. It's too soon. Please not yet.*

"That car accident. Terrible. I hate that bloody road."

"Road," Eden said. She was going to have to leave. She couldn't stay here anymore. "That road."

"Yeah," Suze said, "Del Dios Highway. So dangerous. You won't catch me—"

"God's Highway," Eden said.

"What?"

"Del Dios. God's Highway." *There was something about the name of the road—something to do with God. That sudden storm. God gave the rain. The twists and turns. That patch of blue.*

"Yeah, okay. Listen, are you ready to order?"

"I'm going to have to go," Eden said with great effort.

"Oh shit," Suze said. Eden thought she actually sounded angry.

"It's not you. It's nothing you said." Eden tried to summon all her strength—or whatever of it had been left for her. "I'm just very tired, and I think I ate something that . . . I'm a waitress. I work in Del Mar, so I know what it's like with difficult customers. I'm not going to complain or anything. I would never do that. I'm sorry."

Now Suze looked hopelessly confused, and Eden didn't know how to help her understand. "I'm sorry," she said again. "I just have to go. Thank you. You have been very . . . helpful."

"Yeah, okay." Suze picked up the bread basket and put it back on her tray. "I hope you feel better," she said, and walked off, leaving Eden alone outside.

Eden fished out some money to cover the café mocha she hadn't consumed plus a ridiculously large tip and headed back out. She felt more clearheaded if not less heartsick once she got to her car. But even after she'd taken several long, slow breaths and three generous sips from the bottle of water she kept in her car, she still wasn't ready to turn the key, start the car, and drive. It wasn't every day you discovered that you'd died while driving, even if you'd been crashing in the same car over and over again in your dreams for months on end. It was just a heart—just an organ, one of many in the body. It had no mind. The heart was merely a piece of a person, not the soul of a person.

And yet it wasn't.

Eden had become an unholy creation—a glued-together version of two people. One sat in her car trying not to dissolve into tears of anger and self-pity and the other refused to accept that he had died at the bottom of God's Highway.

It was all her fault. She's the one who caused this. Beautiful and treacherous. A cruel mistress, just like this road. She did it. She's the one.

The voice in Eden's head wouldn't be quieted. It whipped through her brain like wind and rain, forcing her to listen.

"What is it you want from me?" she said out loud, but it was only those same three words she heard in response.

She's the one.

Eden tried, but she couldn't ignore it. That voice was with her, in her head, in her ear, inside and out. It didn't stop until she got home.

CHAPTER 19

"Adam, please. Please, I don't know what to do."

"Darcy, what is it? What's wrong? Are you crying? Darcy, what did he do?"

"He hit me, Adam. He p-punched me. I d-don't know what to do."

Her face felt huge, like an outsized balloon. She was afraid to look in the mirror and thankful that steam from the running water was starting to fog all the reflective surfaces. She was afraid to touch her jaw. It hurt so badly. How was it possible to be in so much pain?

"Where are you?"

There was steel in his voice, but he was keeping it quiet. She could hear bar noise in the background—people laughing, glasses clinking, someone shouting an order. It was the buzz and hum of a good time, something she felt sure she would never know again.

"In the b-bathroom." She was whispering. She didn't want Peter to hear. He could be standing outside the bathroom door at this moment; she didn't know. She didn't know anything about him anymore. All she knew was pain—and shame.

"Are you okay, Darcy? Do you need an ambulance?"

"No! No, Adam, I don't want—p-please, Adam."

"Darcy, God, you're crying. Darcy . . ." There was pain in his voice too—she could hear it. He was hurting for her. He had to help her.

"I—I—I . . . okay, okay . . ." She drew in a big breath. Her face throbbed. She needed to control herself—she couldn't fall apart. *"I'm okay, Adam. No, not okay, but I don't—"*

"Where is he?"

"He's downstairs." A sob escaped her, and she struggled to pull herself together. *"He said he was sorry. He knocked me out."*

"You lost consciousness?" He made a sound—like an animal trying to escape a trap—and then she heard the background noise fade. He must have moved out from behind the bar. *"Darcy? Did you pass out?"* When he spoke again, there was a faint echo. They were both hiding in bathrooms. If she hadn't been in so much pain, she might have thought that was funny.

"For a minute. Not long."

"You need to go to the hospital, Darcy! Let me come and get you."

"No! You can't do that, Adam. You know you can't. Please."

"Can you leave? I can meet you somewhere."

"Adam, we can't . . . I'm scared."

He made that sound again. Darcy pictured his face, the shape of his cheekbones, his mouth.

"I love you, Darcy. I love you."

"I love you. Please help me. Can you help me?" Darcy didn't know what she was asking until much later, but Adam knew right

then. There was never a doubt. He hushed her, told her he loved her again, and then he told her what to do.

A few minutes later, Darcy went back downstairs. She'd splashed water on her face, avoiding her jaw and not looking at the mirror. She'd changed clothes. Even though there was no reason to wear something different, Darcy couldn't bear to be in the same clothes. She knew that as soon as she could, she would throw away the top and pants she'd been wearing when Peter had raised his fist. He was in the kitchen when she came down, sitting at the counter with his head in his hands. Darcy couldn't tell if he was ashamed or sorry or drunk or even angry. Her hands were trembling, so she kept her arms rigid at her sides. She couldn't let him see how frightened she was. Adam had told her what to do, what to say.

"Peter."

"God, Darcy." He looked up. His eyes were red. Had he been crying? She didn't care if he had. Nothing could make her care about his feelings now. Nothing could convince her to try to understand why he had done what he had. He would do it again—but only if she let him. She knew that now. "Babe, I am so sorry. I didn't mean to do it—I don't know what came over me."

"Tell him you need to see a doctor," Adam had said. "And tell him you want to go alone. Don't let him go with you, Darcy. If he insists, tell him that somebody might see and put two and two together. He's a bully, and bullies are cowards."

Darcy knew what she had to say, but the words wouldn't come. She was temporarily paralyzed, staring at him as if she were an animal in the middle of the road and he were coming toward her. "Are you okay, honey?"

"I need to go to a doctor."

He looked torn, as if he disagreed with her but was afraid to say so out loud. How long would the contrition last, she wondered, be-

*fore it turned again into anger? A month? A day? "It's not broken,"
he said. "I can tell."*

*"I need to go to a doctor, Peter," she repeated. Tears were welling
up behind her eyes. She couldn't cry—that wasn't part of the plan.*

"Okay," he said, standing up. "I'll drive you."

"I don't think that's a good idea, Peter."

He hesitated, giving her a quizzical look. "Why not?"

*"What would they say? How would I explain this? Somebody
might recognize you. I can't say I walked into a door. Not with
you sitting there next to me." It had been very difficult to keep the
tremor out of her voice for that last part, but she'd managed. It was
working—she could see the expression on his face change. He was
thinking about it. He could see the logic in her argument.*

*"But . . . Jesus, Darcy. I'm so sorry about this." He shook his head,
but he sat down again. The bastard sat down.*

"So I'm going to go now."

"Let me at least drive you. I can wait in the car."

*"I really think it would be better if you didn't. I'm going to go to
Urgent Care. Not the one around here. Another one."*

"Darcy . . ."

*"I'm going to go now." But she still wasn't moving. What was she
waiting for?*

"I'm sorry. It will never happen again."

"Okay, Peter."

*Finally, she was able to leave—to walk out of the house, get into
her car, and drive to the clinic that Adam had told her to go to. She
started crying again when she saw him.*

*"He's never going to hurt you again, Darcy. It's going to be okay.
I promise you. I promise."*

*"How do you know that? You don't know that. What if he kills
me next time?"*

"I'm not going to let that happen, my love. We aren't going to let that happen."

"I can't leave him. He won't let me. He'll find a way to make me stay."

"You don't have to leave him."

"What do you mean? Adam . . ."

The rest of it seemed to happen so quickly. In fact, if anyone had asked Darcy for the exact sequence of events—even for the relative times that things happened—she wouldn't have been able to say. The moment she saw Adam waiting for her outside the clinic, she let him take over. He huddled with her, letting her sink into him without speaking for a long time. She felt his tears fall into her hair and the strength of his arms around her. And then his idea, his plan, and his love for her made up the security blanket that Darcy needed. She wrapped it around herself, covering her ears and eyes and mouth with it. She gave herself over to him.

"We'll have to wait awhile," he said. "He needs to think you're okay with everything. He needs to think you've forgiven him. It isn't going to be easy, Darcy."

"Yes," she said. "Okay."

"You're going to have to . . ." He bit his lip, and his hands clenched into fists. "You're going to have to pretend to like being his wife and do—"

"I know."

"And you have to heal. He's not going to want you to go out in public like this. It's going to be bruised." He kissed her carefully, gently. "I hate him so much, Darcy. If I could . . ."

"Adam . . ."

"You have to pretend it never happened. Don't tell anyone about it—make him think it never happened. You have to be the perfect wife."

"He's going to move us, Adam. He's—he's going to sell the house."

"Don't worry. It hasn't happened yet, and we still have time. But you have to tell him you've changed your mind—that you're happy to move. Tell him it's a great idea. Tell him you want to celebrate. Tell him you want to go to Poquette. Tell him you want to sit at the bar." Adam paused. Darcy looked up at his face. She saw the muscles working in his jaw. "I know how to make his drinks just the way he likes them."

"Yes," she said.

Adam looked down at his hands as if he'd just noticed how tightly he'd balled them into fists. "Does he . . . Has he ever taken Viagra?"

Darcy trusted Adam with her life. She didn't ask why he wanted to know. "No," she said. "I don't think so."

Adam sighed. "The only fucker over fifty who hasn't, then. You're going to have to convince him to take some. Before you go out. I'm sorry, Darcy. I'm so sorry, love. I'll get you some. Just tell him—"

"He has some already," Darcy said, remembering Putterman's gift. The pills were still there, in the drawer of the bedside table. "I can do it," she said. "I'll make sure he takes it."

"Okay," he said. "It's going to be okay."

"Adam—"

"You're going to have to go back there now, Darcy. Are you going to be able to do this? Baby, are you going to be okay?"

"Yes," she said. She'd been given pain medication at the clinic, but that wasn't what was making her feel as if she were floating, weightless, in warm water. It was him. She was safe.

It wasn't as difficult as Adam thought it would be. But, Darcy thought, that was probably because she was in a daze—her mind and heart detached from her body and all that it was doing.

Adam had given her a charm—a small heart made out of rose

quartz on a silver chain—and told her to keep it with her all the time. "Quartz is one of the hardest minerals in the world," he said. "It will remind you to be strong, and you'll know my heart is there with you." Darcy kept it close to her skin, held it in the palm of her hand, touched it so many times every day that she worried she would wear it away. Peter never asked about it. He never noticed that it lay between his body and hers when he pushed himself inside her. He didn't feel it brush across his skin when she leaned over him. He couldn't tell that it was a shield, that it protected her from feeling anything when he touched her.

She cooked him breakfast. She covered the bruises on her jaw with makeup until they faded. She wasn't unnaturally cheerful. She played the part of a wife who had seen the error of her ways. She went back to the salon and spent hours in the chair while a stylist glued extensions into her hair. She bought new clothes and a few pieces of very expensive lingerie. She took every one of the pain pills she'd been prescribed, and then she renewed the prescription. She was very careful. Adam got messages to her and they spoke—stolen phone calls on prepaid cell phones that Adam instructed her to buy—but she hardly needed the directions. She could hear his voice in her ear—the blanket of his love wrapped tightly around her.

Peter loved the idea of going to Poquette—of course he did. Darcy thought Adam was a genius—he'd called all of it exactly right. Magic man. She made a big deal out of it. She promised him the best sex of his life.

"What do you have planned, woman?" Peter asked her.

"I've been doing some research of my own," she said. "You'll see. I'm going to show you a really good time. A really good time."

"Honey, I don't know how much better it could get," he said, his hand reaching down over her hip and coming to rest on her backside in a gesture of ownership.

"Well, you ain't seen nothin' yet," she said. "Remember these?" She opened up her hand to reveal the blue Viagra diamonds in her palm. Peter raised one eyebrow and smiled.

"What are you doing with those?" he asked.

"We're both going to take one," she said.

"Holy shit," he said. He grabbed her hand then and rubbed it on his already bulging crotch.

"I can't wait," she said.

She wore a low-cut black dress—elegant and revealing at the same time. She wrapped Adam's heart around her wrist so that Peter could stare at her bare chest. She dusted her skin with gold-flecked powder. She sparkled; she smiled. She sang along with him when he broke into the Rolling Stones's "Happy." It wasn't until they got to Poquette—inside the door and to the bar—that the adrenaline hit her and she started to shake.

"Sit, baby. I'm going to have a word with Jacques," he said. "I'll be right back. Hold me a seat."

Darcy's stomach roiled and flipped when she took her place at the bar. She held a seat for Peter on one side of her, but there was an unctuous bar hound on the other who leaned over and tried to make conversation. Adam greeted her with a smile that was not too big, not too familiar. She felt hot and cold looking at him as if someone were flipping switches on and off inside her. He put a cocktail napkin in front of her and another in front of the empty bar stool.

"How are you doing tonight?" he asked. His eyes said, Is everything okay?

"I'm great, thanks." She smiled. It's all good.

"What can I get for you?" Where is Peter?

"My husband is just talking to Jacques," she said, gesturing to the hostess stand. "He's going to join me in a second. I'll just have a glass of water while I'm waiting for him."

"Okay, sounds good," he said. She put her hands on the bar. His eyes flicked to the heart around her wrist and back up to her face. And then he had to turn away because he couldn't afford to let anyone else see what was there. Darcy shuddered.

"Nice place, huh? Really hopping tonight."

Darcy turned to the man on her left. "Great place, yes. My husband and I come here all the time."

He laughed. "Yeah? Your husband likes it too, does he?"

"Sure does."

They went on like that for how long Darcy couldn't tell. It could have been seconds or hours—time had lost all shape and dimension. She watched Adam from the corner of her eye, the way he moved gracefully around the other bartender whom she couldn't even see because she was so focused on Adam. Everyone else in the room turned into flat gray forms, leaving only him three-dimensional and in color—the only real person in the restaurant. He didn't look at her full on, but she could see that he was stealing glances at her, and, when he did, there was a slight nod of assent—it was all going according to plan.

Finally, Peter joined her at the bar. This was the first tricky part. If he insisted on ordering a bottle of wine, it wouldn't be easy . . . She couldn't come on too strong.

"Have you ordered something, babe?" Peter looked across her at the bar hound who took his cue at last and shifted his attention from Darcy.

"I was waiting for you."

"Shall we do a bottle of bubbly?"

"Let's have a drink, Peter. I'm in the mood for a fun drink." Did she sound too bright? Too eager? But Peter was nodding. It was all good. Adam managed to appear in front of them before Peter could even think about looking for him.

"Evening," Adam said. He gave his best smile and showed not a trace, not a flicker of nervousness in his eyes. "What can I get for you folks?"

"What do you feel like, Dar?"

"Whatever you're having. You choose."

"Do you know how to make a good Manhattan?" Peter asked Adam, and then winked at Darcy.

"Of course," Adam said. "Two of those? Rocks?"

"Darcy?"

"Yes, sounds great."

Her body was trembling now, but she couldn't let it show. She had to stay perfectly calm. She had to remember what she was supposed to do. Her hands were cold. Peter was talking. She strained to listen carefully and answer appropriately. The drinks came. For a moment, Darcy thought she wasn't going to be able to lift her glass because of the tremor in her hand, but somehow she managed. Now it would start. She looked up, found Adam, and their eyes met for a second. It was okay. It was going to be fine.

"Distract him. You'll know how. It won't take long, so you're going to have to get him out of there after the second drink."

Darcy leaned into Peter and rubbed her thigh against his. "It's working," she whispered. "I'm getting so hot . . . I don't think I can wait."

"Mmm. Baby, have I told you how beautiful you look tonight?"

He drank, and she pretended to drink. Adam asked if he'd like another. Darcy held her breath, willing him to order one. "Go on," she told Peter. "You've earned it. I'll drive tonight." *Peter nodded at Adam. She could see that Peter was already slowing down. Just a little longer. She reached her hand under the bar and started stroking Peter's thigh—light touches and then a little harder, moving up. She knew how.*

"I mean it," she whispered again. "I don't think I can wait." She had to move fast now. She had to get him to the car.

"I'm feeling it," Peter said. "What you do to me, baby." His words were slurry. The window was closing.

"Let's go down to the car," she said, her voice low and full of promise. She squeezed his crotch. "Just for a minute."

It was essential that he agree to go. There was no room for improvisation now. She needed to get him out of the restaurant.

"Remember that time," she said, so close to his ear that her lips were touching his skin, "on our first anniversary? We parked at the beach?" Peter grunted softly. "Let's go," she said. "Just for a minute."

"Mmm . . ."

"We'll come right back."

Peter didn't need any more convincing. It was working. Adam had known it would.

"Get him to the car and then drive across the street. Park in the alley."

Peter was already out of it when they got to the car. He didn't put up any kind of resistance when Darcy told him to sit in the passenger seat. Even though he was under the control of a one-pointed desire, as soon as he sat down, his head began to loll.

"He should be out by the time you park. Get out of the car. Leave it unlocked. Go to the convenience store on the corner. Find something to buy. Take your time choosing and paying for it, but not too much time."

She had to hand it to Peter—he tried mightily to stay awake for his reward, even managing to get his pants halfway unbuttoned, but then, just as Adam had predicted, he couldn't stay conscious. She watched him breathe, slowly but surely, until she was sure he was completely out. Then she buttoned up his pants and got out of the car.

It was strange, Darcy thought, that the most difficult part was trying to decide what to buy in the convenience store. She drifted from the candy to the bottled water and then to the small and over- priced boxes of laundry soap and paper towels. Who came to a con- venience store looking for paper towels? She was dressed for a dinner out. What would a person dressed this way want to buy? Something small. Finally, her nerves about to overtake her, Darcy settled on a pack of gum and a ballpoint pen. She dropped change on the counter and the clerk sighed. The whole procedure took longer than it needed to, but Darcy thought that was probably a good thing.

Peter was very still when she got back into the car. She didn't look at him—she couldn't, not yet—but she could sense the difference. He wasn't breathing. He was already dead.

"Drive up the Coast Highway. Take fifteen minutes. Then go to the hospital."

In a way, that drive was the most peaceful fifteen minutes Darcy had ever experienced in her life. She rolled down her window and drove slowly north along the coast, listening to the crash of the ocean and feeling the warm salt breeze as it swirled around her. She kept her eyes fixed on the road. Traffic was light, and the ride was espe- cially smooth. She felt no emotion at all. The nervousness was gone, but there was no calm in its place. There was just a vacuum—a quiet emptiness she'd never experienced before. She had the sense that she could just keep driving like this—that night would never turn to day and the road would just loop over itself—and that it would be fine. But fifteen minutes was all she needed.

Finally, she turned her head to look at Peter. His head had fallen forward, chin to chest. The seat belt held his body in place. He could have been just sitting there, dozing on this scenic drive.

"Peter," she said softly, "what's the matter? Do you need a doctor? Well, do you, Peter?"

Darcy steeled herself. She lifted her wrist, kissed Adam's heart, and steered the car in the direction of the nearest hospital. She hadn't expected how horrible Peter would look in death. When she pulled into the brightly lit Emergency entrance, her shock was genuine.

"My husband . . . ," she said. Her whole body was shaking. "Please help me."

Darcy sat at her desk, holding Adam's rose quartz heart in the palm of her hand and staring at her computer. It was very late, but she couldn't sleep. Eden had come home hours ago but had spent the whole night in her room. Darcy didn't know what to make of Eden's strange expression as she walked through the front door. The girl looked haunted and pale. Darcy had offered to make her a cup of tea, but Eden had said, "I don't think so," and had walked directly to her bedroom.

You didn't have to be a highly evolved or sensitive person to feel the waves of kinetic emotion emanating from Eden. Whatever it was that she was keeping trapped under that surface of hers was about to come boiling over. It worried Darcy—frightened her just as Adam had frightened her when he started to get pushy at Peter's funeral. How desperately she had wanted him then. If she had been in better control of herself, if she hadn't been so madly in love with him, she might have seen what was going on. She would have understood what it was that *he* wanted. But she had gone along with it. She'd given him everything he asked for, just as she had gone along with the plan because it allowed her to be free. And it allowed her to be blameless—at least at the time. Adam had thought of everything. He had backup plans and worst-case scenarios. He'd instructed Darcy to find a way to slip it into a drink in case Peter had refused to take the

Viagra. And if Peter hadn't wanted to order a drink at the bar, Darcy was to give Adam a signal and he'd tell her what to do. Only later did Darcy realize that he had to have been thinking about it for a long time—certainly before Peter punched her in the face; maybe even since the first time they'd made love. He must have charted it out. Maybe there were diagrams some-where with color-coded tape and 3-D simulations. That would be the kind of thing he would want to do just so he could see evidence of his own brilliance. The Greeks called it hubris, and it had been the downfall of men for thousands of years. But that wasn't the only thing that could bring a person down.

In the end it was the stupidest things that got you in trouble, Darcy thought—stupid crimes, stupid criminals, and trails of evidence left behind that almost glowed in the dark. People developed a certain blindness when they were in the heat of the moment and then assumed the rest of the world had that same lack of vision. It happened all the time. In the old days, there was lipstick on the collar; now there were e-mails on the computer. She should do away with them and scrub her hard drive, but Darcy couldn't bring herself to delete them. They were disguised; none of them actually came out and stated anything specific. Still, if you were careful—if you wanted to read between the lines—you could put it together. It hadn't mattered before— who would go looking, after all? These were relics of another life that nobody even knew about. She'd gotten rid of every-thing else, but these . . . Even as she sat at the computer, her finger hovering over the DELETE key, Darcy knew that these she couldn't bear to part with.

There weren't just . . . instructions. There were also song lyrics—songs he wrote for her. Her favorite, "Water on the Moon," would have been Adam's breakout hit. That was the title track of the album she'd funded. What a beautiful job they'd done on that album—everything from the mix to the artwork on the CD—but that was no surprise. Darcy didn't know the average cost of studio time or graphic artists or music producers, but she did know that Adam had spared no expense. Those long sessions in LA required hotel rooms too—and food. And, Darcy later found out, they also required another girl to share in all of those fine things. When had it all started to go bad? Darcy still couldn't tell. There was nothing she could do about it either. She had to remain the grieving widow. There was a time period for these things.

He didn't desert her entirely. No, he was too smart for that. He was the culpable one—they both knew that. It was the one condition that Darcy had laid down when Adam first whispered the plan in her ear. She couldn't know and she couldn't see. She would come back to the car and it would all be over. They could waterboard her and she wouldn't be able to give up any information because she didn't have any. That too was part of the plan. In the emergency room, Darcy went into a very real state of shock, which was entirely convincing. When they asked her if Peter was taking any medications, she said he wasn't. When they asked her if he had a heart condition, she said he didn't. They wanted to know where she and Peter had been and what they had been doing.

"We were on a date," she said. "We were . . . We were in the car . . ." She started to cry, and the tears were genuine. "What's happened to him?" she said.

When at last an unlucky doctor came out to tell her that Peter was gone, she was trembling in a plastic waiting room chair, her arms crossed against her chest. It wasn't an act.

Lisa, in her comfortable house with her well-behaved husband

and children, could speculate all she wanted, but she would never find anything. There was nothing to find. The autopsy concluded the cause of death was cardiac arrest. A toxicology screen came back clean. Peter was cremated before Lisa got off the plane, his ashes neatly divided into three brass jars. When Lisa, tears streaming from her eyes, asked, "What happened to my brother?" Darcy answered honestly, "I don't know." Only one person knew what had happened after Darcy left the car for the flickering neon light of the convenience store, and that person was dead.

Darcy wasn't stupid. Once the numbness wore off, she began to put the pieces together. There were warnings in bold black letters on every Viagra ad. There were interactions—things could cause "a dangerous drop in blood pressure." And when blood pressure dropped that low, a person could pass out. A person could stop breathing. A person could die, especially if another person obstructed his airway for a minute—or five.

Adam had told her once, "It took both of us, Darcy. We will always be in this together. Forever." He was right. But forever came much sooner than he was expecting.

Darcy sighed. Her eyes were stinging and felt dry. She'd been awake too long. Every fiber in her body cried for sleep. But to-night it had been impossible. She'd lain in bed for two hours, her eyes open and visions of Adam superimposed on the darkness. Finally she'd given up and come in here to these secret files just to see—to feel—and remind herself that she had been loved and that she hadn't imagined all of it. Darcy often wondered if it was strange that she missed Adam more than she missed Peter. She had been with Peter for so long and even though the end was grim, she'd have thought that what had come before—the sheer familiarity of living side by side with someone all those years—would have filled enough of a space so that it would have felt empty once he left it. And for a while Darcy did feel Peter's absence. But it was Adam she missed. She missed him still. Even now.

There were so many things she hadn't known about Adam—things she would never have expected to be important. She hadn't known his blood type. She hadn't known whether he was an organ donor. Darcy opened her palm and looked down at Adam's heart. She never wore it anymore, but she often brought it out and touched it. He had given it to her so that she'd always know his heart was with her. She hadn't expected that he would be quite so literal. Adam was dead. But his heart had come back to her. There was no way she could know this and no way she could ask, but Darcy knew. Now that she'd found out about Eden's transplant, it was the only explanation that made sense to her. It wasn't so strange—she'd been drawn to Eden from the moment she met her. There was something she recognized, some connection they'd shared. And Darcy could see the same thing in Eden's eyes too, although the girl had been so guarded from the start. It wasn't an accident that she and Eden had wound up living together. Now, late at night with her nerves stretched taut and the weight of the past pressing down on her, Darcy almost believed—no, *did* believe that Adam had found his way back to her.

There was a sound coming from downstairs, but Darcy couldn't tell what it was. Maybe Eden had gone into the kitchen for a late-night snack, although that wasn't like her. Maybe someone was at the door. Maybe she was hearing things again. She didn't want to get up, go downstairs, and check it out. She didn't want to be vulnerable in any way, even if this was her house and it was probably nothing. But once again Darcy was hit with that strange compulsion to walk into the middle of danger just as she had when she walked down the hall to Eden's room carrying a poker for protection. She stood up and walked out into the hall. There was the noise again. It sounded like a moan. Darcy walked down the stairs, listening for more, but, by the time she got to the landing, the noise had stopped. She stood there like an idiot, wearing only a tank top and underwear, one hand on the banister. She should have at least put on some shoes—a pair of flip-flops—before coming down here and confronting God-knew-what. She thought about going into the kitchen and checking to make sure everything was turned off, but she was frozen in place.

Something has to change, Darcy thought.

And then she heard it. It was coming from Eden's room—a wail that seemed to be coming from the bottom of her soul.

"No, no, *no!*"

Darcy turned, quivering, in the direction of Eden's room.

"Darcy! *Darcy!*"

Darcy started moving, walking right into the middle of it. Eden was calling her.

CHAPTER 20

Del Dios Highway was a bitch in the rain.

This beautiful road didn't get traveled so much anymore now that they'd put in the SR-56 freeway. It used to be the main thoroughfare for traffic going east to Escondido. It was always a stunning sight—the deep blue of the lake (it was man-made, but so what?), the pink and sandy rocks. It was as if you were driving through the heart of a mountain. Del Dios. God's Highway. Because it was beautiful. And also because it was how so many went to meet their Maker. Had they known about this when they'd named it? Had they foreseen all those accidents? Had they known that when it rained, this road would be even quicker to offer up its travelers?

It wasn't supposed to rain. There had been nothing in the forecast about precipitation—it was to be another cloudless, gorgeous day here. But here it was—pouring down, turning Del Dios into a roller coaster waterslide. It was so beautiful, all these merging grays, greens, and blues. So beautiful and so dangerous. Del Dios. Del Darcy.

It rained harder, buckets of rain hitting the car. Nowhere to go here but straight ahead. The windows were fogging. He had turned the windshield wipers from high to low and back again, but they were doing nothing to clear the rain. The car might as well have been going through a car wash.

"Goddamn," he said out loud. "How could this get any worse?" He was laughing now, but there was fear in it—a sharp edge slicing the thick air inside the car. And the fear was there because it could get worse and he knew it. But that was what you got with her—just a long slide downhill off a cliff. He should have known when he got involved with her that it would end up here. He had almost gotten away from her—out of her clutches and the sway of her siren's song—but then something had happened, a shift in his brain. She'd put a spell on him with her body and her beauty and her money. She beckoned, and he fell.

But there was more to it than that, wasn't there?

He still loved her.

He would always love her.

And that was why he was here on God's forsaken two-lane highway, careening to his fate. The SUV would come next, almost sideswiping them. And then there would be more rain—so much more of it.

Goddamn Darcy. Goddamn her, goddamn her. None of this would have happened if he hadn't been so weak. He'd gotten away—why hadn't he been able to see that? How had she managed to pull him back in?

It was so wet. There was so much rain. You could feel fate closing in on you, you could understand the inevitable, but it was still frightening. Your body and mind still tensed for fight or flight. You couldn't stop the fear from taking over. It was an automatic human reaction—like falling in love.

There it was—that bright and beautiful patch of blue. There was visible sun and sky just a mile off. A believer might have said it was God smiling. But there were no believers here because to believe, you had to pick either free will or fate. You couldn't have both. Yet this road, this rain, and that glowing patch of blue sky were the perfect combination of both.

He punched a button on the CD player, and the car filled with a song in midplay—*her* song, "Water on the Moon." But it was just a fragment of sound, a splinter and not there long enough to hear the love he had for her pouring out in verse and chorus. Because now the lights were here—that truck, all eighteen of its wheels screeching, bearing down. Now there was no sound at all—the lights drowned everything else out.

He was hitting the brake hard, but the car didn't slow at all. No resistance, no grip. No brakes. He jammed them again. Now the car was hydroplaning on all that water. The car was going faster. Now swerving, now spinning.

He knew so much about so many things one would never expect. Like cars and how to drive in any condition. He was proud of all that knowledge he'd accumulated, and he shared some of it with her. He'd showed her how easy it was to cut the brake line and make it look like an accident. He knew about accidents too. He'd told her once, *Do you know you could make almost anything look like an accident? Think about how random the universe seems. Everything has the potential to look like an accident.* Well, they both knew about accidents now, didn't they? They were both experts. Now he knew what had happened. He knew what was coming.

It was her fault. She was the one.

Darkness.

Eden's eyes were open, the sound of her own scream still echoing in her ears. *Where am I?* She couldn't see anything—it was all still dark. She waited for the light to come back in—waited to see that tangled mess of blood-covered glass and twisted metal. That heart was beating as if it wanted to leap from her chest. His heart. She raised her hands, almost surprised to find she still had a body, and felt the scar on her breastbone. *Who am I?*

She couldn't escape the dream that was not a dream. She was still there in the rain, in the car, those impossible lights coming toward her. Eden struggled. She couldn't catch her breath, couldn't control that wildly beating heart.

It was her fault.

A door opened, and light splashed into the room. Her bedroom. She was in bed, tangled in sheets wet from sweat. She could see now. Her thin cotton shirt had fallen off her shoulders. The yellow light from the hall shone right on her chest, right on that scar, exposing the heart that didn't belong to her. And there *she* was—Darcy—standing there, taking it all in.

"Eden, what's wrong?"

All of it was her fault.

"Are you okay? I heard you. You were calling my name."

Eden wanted to speak, but the words were trapped in her throat. The fear from the dream gripped her, tightening around her. Darcy strode into the room, over to Eden. "Eden," she said. Then, louder, "Eden!" Her throat felt raw and tight. She'd been screaming Darcy's name.

"Are you all right?"

Eden wasn't yet all the way out of the dream. The images had never persisted this long after waking before. She could still see the inside of the car—his foot hitting the brake and finding no resistance. The brake line had been cut. Darcy put a soft hand on Eden's shoulder, then leaned in close. Too close. Eden could smell her perfume—those lovely white flowers—and feel her long gold hair brush across the naked skin of her shoulder. The sensation made Eden tremble. Her heart—his heart—had quieted a little, but adrenaline was still coursing through Eden's veins.

"What can I do to help you?" Darcy asked. "Can I get you something?"

Darcy's voice was soft and sweet. Eden could feel the heat of her skin and the whisper of her breath. There was genuine concern in her voice. *You were calling my name.* That was how she'd heard it—as a summons for help. But Eden knew it to be a scream of rage.

"I'm okay," Eden said. "I had a dream—a nightmare."

"You had a nightmare about me?"

"No, it was just a dream. It wasn't about you, no."

It was her fault.

"I'm here," Darcy said. "I'm here for you, Eden. What do you need? Tell me what you need." There was an urgency in her voice now and a note of pleading. Eden didn't understand why she was so close, why that hand was still on her shoulder.

"I really am fine," Eden said. "You don't need to do anything for me. It was just a dream, Darcy." Eden tried to smile at Darcy, but it was hopeless. There was nothing to smile about here. She wasn't nearly as good as Darcy at pretending to be light and carefree.

"But you were calling me." She'd lowered her voice as if this were some kind of confession—a middle-of-the-night secret.

"I was dreaming. I don't know why I was calling you. I'm sorry if I woke you up. What time is it?"

"You didn't wake me up, don't worry. Eden . . ." And then Darcy looked down. It was only for a second and they were both in half dark, but Eden saw her eyes go to the exposed scar on her chest and then come back to Eden's face. Eden felt rather than saw the emotion coming from Darcy. She was vibrating with a combination of need—though for what or whom Eden wasn't sure—and fear. There was no reason for Darcy to be afraid of Eden—no reason for her to hover at her bedside so close that she was almost in the bed with her—unless she thought Eden knew something she shouldn't.

The brake line had been cut.

"What do you need?" Darcy asked again. Eden shrank into herself. It was almost a rhetorical question the way Darcy was asking it—a riddle. Not *What do you need?* but *What do you know?*

That was it. Darcy knew.

Somehow she had found out about Eden's heart transplant, although how long she had known Eden couldn't yet tell. It was a shocking thing, that scar. Derek was the only person who had seen it like this, and even he had been awed by it. There was no way a person like Darcy would see what Eden had been hiding all this time and not draw in a breath, not comment, not ask,

What is that? Unless she already knew about it. Unless she knew whose heart Eden had.

It's her fault. She's the one.

"Are you sure you're okay?" Darcy sat down on the edge of the bed. She reached over to Eden.

"Stop!" Eden's pulse was racing. She felt weak and frightened.

Darcy froze, then dropped her hands to her sides. But she didn't get up. "Sorry," she said. "I didn't mean to scare you. I just want to help. Do you want me to stay with you for a while?"

"No, Darcy, I really don't." Eden grabbed the sheets and pulled them up to her chest. It was too late to cover anything up now, but the reaction had become instinctive. She needed to protect herself. "I'm sorry—I didn't mean it to sound like that. I'm just . . . I'm fine."

Go away. Please go away.

"Okay." Darcy stood up. Even in this half-light Eden couldn't help but notice Darcy's beauty. So effortless. She understood why Adam had not been able to let go of his attraction to her even as it pulled him into disaster.

She's not worth it.

"Thank you for checking on me."

"Of course, Eden."

"Why are you still awake?" Eden asked. She wanted Darcy to leave her room, and she needed desperately to organize her thoughts, but she couldn't stop herself from asking. It was almost as if Darcy had been waiting for this opportunity. Maybe she really *had* been standing outside the door, listening.

"I couldn't sleep. I guess there must be something in the air. Maybe the ions are magnetized or whatever that is. I don't know." She headed for the door. "I'm going to try again," she said. "I have another appointment with—I have to go somewhere to-morrow, early. I'd better try to get some sleep."

"Good," said Eden. "I mean, yes, you should."

"If you need anything," Darcy said, "I'm here."

"Thanks," Eden said.

Darcy walked out of the room. A few moments later, Eden heard her climbing the stairs. Eden lay where she was for a long time, staring at the empty rectangle of light Darcy had left behind, before she finally got up and closed the door.

Eden knew she was taking a chance, but it was worth the risk. She hadn't been able to fall asleep again after Darcy left her room, but she was too physically exhausted to get out of bed. She'd lain there until well after dawn filtered through the window, listening for Darcy, making sure to catch her before she left the house.

It didn't seem as if Darcy had fared much better in her own bed. There were dark smudges under her eyes, and her face looked sharp and pinched. Eden suspected that both of them had been kept awake by the same thoughts—or at least by different sides of the same thoughts.

"How are you doing?" Darcy asked her as she prepared her coffee. Eden had managed to arrive in the kitchen at exactly the right time. Darcy was already dressed, wearing a conservative pantsuit and minimal makeup, and about to get going.

"I'm okay," Eden said. "Just a nightmare. They happen from time to time."

"I can imagine," Darcy said, and then caught herself. "I mean, yes, everyone has nightmares. I used to have them when I was a kid. There was one recurring nightmare I had that I was being chased by a clown, and I couldn't run away because I was carrying this gigantic heavy book."

"Huh," Eden said.

"I suppose it's normal to be afraid of clowns when you're a kid. Every kid has a bit of clown fear, right? And yet clowns exist for kids. I always thought that was strange. How about you? Do your nightmares repeat? Do you have the same one, or are they different?"

"Different, I guess. I can't really remember them when I wake up, so I don't know for sure." Darcy was on some kind of fishing expedition, but Eden wasn't going to bite. "So, where are you off to?" she asked Darcy.

"I just have some business to take care of," Darcy said, a small smile playing at the corner of her mouth. Two could play the evasion game. "Hopefully it won't take more than a couple of hours, but you can never predict the traffic."

"That's true," Eden said. "You never can."

There was more small talk—so small Eden couldn't even remember it now—during which Eden could feel the rising tension in the kitchen grow thick with subtext. Darcy didn't seem to want to leave. But after fussing through cabinets looking for a travel mug in which to pour her coffee, digging through her purse to find her car keys, and applying a fresh coat of pale pink lipstick, there were no more little tasks to keep her there.

"So I'll see you later, then," she said.

"Okay. I'm working lunch," Eden lied, "so I'll be headed out soon too. See you later."

The scent of Darcy's white flower perfume was still lingering in the air when Eden raced upstairs. Eden tried to imagine how the scenario would play out if Darcy came back suddenly to pick up something she'd "forgotten" or just decided not to go wherever it was she was headed and found Eden going through her things, but every time she tried to picture what kind of confrontation might ensue, Eden's mind went blank. There were too many variables, and she was starting to realize she didn't know Darcy at all.

She was sure now that Darcy had rummaged through her room while she was at work. She'd concealed her medications but hadn't hidden them. If a person was looking and determined to find something, it wouldn't have taken too much effort to find those drugs. And after that, it would have been downright easy to figure out what they were for.

There wasn't as obvious a trail of bread crumbs for Eden to follow. Nor was she sure exactly what she was looking for. But, Eden thought as she entered Darcy's office, perhaps her heart would help to lead her.

The first place to look was always the most obvious. Eden didn't have time to search through locked drawers or look for false bottoms and encrypted files. She was counting on one of the most basic tenets of human behavior—that people gave themselves away with the simplest things. It was the same principle that made "password" the most popular choice of password for most people. Eden scanned the room, taking everything in. One wall was dominated by built-in bookshelves. A long L-shaped desk took up the rest of the space. There were some papers stacked at the far end of the desk, assorted knickknacks placed haphazardly along the long end, and a large laptop in the middle of the short end. Conveniently, the computer was in sleep mode, so Eden would be able to check it out without having to boot it up and power it off again. She went there first and watched as the screen came to life. Her theory about the simplest things was already proving true; Darcy's computer wasn't even password protected. Eden glanced at the folders and files, trying to decide which ones were worth opening. If there was nothing to be found there, she would try Darcy's Internet search history.

Eden started in Darcy's "Documents" folder. There weren't too many subfolders, but none of them screamed to be opened. Eden began, again, with the obvious—a folder labeled "Peter." Inside were some photos, which Eden opened one at a time. There was one taken on what must have been their wedding day. Darcy looked not much younger than she did today—breathtakingly beautiful in a diaphanous wedding dress—looking beyond the camera at something or someone else. The next photo was of the two of them sitting poolside with umbrella drinks at what must have been a resort. Darcy was wearing large sunglasses, and her long hair was wavy with humidity. Peter leaned in toward her, a grin on his face and his hand resting on hers—the same face and the same hand Eden had seen in her dreams.

She closed the photos. Opening a document titled "Wines," she found exactly that—a list of wines, divided by red, white, and sparkling, with prices and ratings. Other documents—tax forms, receipts, information about various charities, lists of donations—were just as unhelpful. Worried about time, Eden started clicking fast, opening anything that might lead anywhere, which was how she arrived at a folder titled "Miscellaneous Receipts," which, when opened, revealed another folder, titled "Proxy." Eden opened the folder and looked through the contents, her eyes widening at the dollar amounts Darcy had shelled out for the production of Adam's CD. She wasn't surprised that Darcy had kept these items in her "Peter" folder. It was Peter's money, after all, that had funded Adam's would-be career.

There was a surprising lack of any other documentation on the computer, at least from what Eden could see. There were no letters, or random bits of prose (everybody had a novel in progress or a poem or two on the computer), or a journal . . . A journal. Eden closed all the open files and folders and opened Darcy's browser. While the page loaded, she stood up and walked slowly around the room, giving the bookshelf particular attention because these weren't books that Darcy had ever read or probably even knew about—books about golf and biographies of billionaires, a smattering of classics reissued in expensive leather-bound volumes, first editions of several Ian Fleming novels. Then there were collections arranged by topic—bridges, the human body, vineyards, war. These had been Peter's books. From the look of them, he had been an omnivorous reader and a meticulous organizer. Someone like that would document things the old-fashioned way, in a ledger or a journal.

It had been smart of Darcy not to box these books up and toss them out or donate them. She wouldn't want it to look as if she couldn't wait to be rid of the man, would she? The shelves went all the way up to the ceiling, beyond where Eden could reach and where she was almost sure she would find something. Climbing carefully on what Eden suspected was a very expensive antique chair, she scanned the shelves. There, in the middle of a shelf where a six-foot-plus man would just be able to reach it if he extended his arm as far as it would go, she found what she was looking for and pulled it down. It was a thick oxblood leather journal with gilt-edged pages and a cloth bookmark tucked into the pages. Eden opened the journal and knew right away that she'd hit a jackpot of sorts. Peter had been as meticulous about documenting his activities as he had about organizing his books.

July 27—Sunny, temp. 76°

Good day for golf but Larry's out. Breakfast this morning: Blueberry muffin, black coffee, sliced mango. Used paper filter. French press coffee is bad for cholesterol. Learn something new every day.

July 28—Sunny, temp. 74°

Breakfast this morning: Fruit bowl (strawberries, blueberries, cantaloupe, banana), whole wheat toast, black coffee.

Lunch: Grilled salmon, small tossed green salad. Lemonade.

Dinner: Poquette!

At the mention of Poquette, a quiver ran through Eden's center. Her nerves were starting to take over. She wouldn't have enough time to leave the room and look as if she'd never been there if Darcy came home suddenly. Eden had no reason to be upstairs at all. The one disadvantage of her self-contained suite was that it was ill-designed for spying. She flipped through more pages. Peter had documented every food item he'd ever put in his mouth, but some entries didn't list what day they were written on—and none of them listed the year. Unless, Eden thought, shuffling through the journal, this was all the same year—the year that he died. Eden turned to the back of the journal—to the last pages he'd written.

August 31—Hazy, temp 85°

Gorgeous day. Closing on NY property. Darcy's not happy about moving, but she'll get over it.

September 1—Sunny, temp 82°

Annual physical this morning: Looking good. Working out

and good diet must have paid off. BP solid at 120/75. Cholesterol numbers and triglycerides well within range. No prostate trouble at all. Dr. Carter says most men my age already have issues in that department. Not this guy. Darcy not impressed with this news. Still pouting over the move.

Eden felt the seconds ticking away. She didn't have time to stand there and read the entire thing. She looked at the space where the journal had been on the bookshelf and made an executive decision. She would go back to the computer and check Darcy's search history; then she would take the journal with her and read it somewhere else. Eden moved the books together so that the journal space was filled, then got down from the chair. She felt as if she'd been looking through the office for hours instead of the few minutes it had been, and she was starting to perspire. Adrenaline and lack of sleep had made her neck stiff and her tired eyes sting. She wiped her moist hand on her leg and was about to start hitting keys on Darcy's computer when she noticed that Darcy hadn't signed out of her last session. The page that had come up when Eden opened the browser was an e-mail program with a cache of messages back and forth between two people who were using pseudonymous e-mail addresses but who Eden knew immediately were Darcy and Adam.

And she knew because she'd seen these e-mails before.

Subject: Water on the Moon

I haven't been able to stop thinking about you. At night I lie awake and stare at the moon, and all I can see is your face. Do you know they found water on the moon? Water, like frozen tears. I think it would make a good song. How much longer?

Subject: Re: Water on the Moon

I have to be careful. There are still people here—my sister-in-law and her kids. I don't want her to think I'm in a hurry to get rid of her. She's already a little edgy, and this morning she brought up the cremation again—asked me why I was so insistent on getting it done so quickly. I miss you. Not much longer.

Subject: Re: Water on the Moon

You don't have to explain anything, and you don't have to worry. You told me he wanted to be cremated. Your sister-in-law should know that. If she keeps pressing, remind her that the tox screen came back negative. I don't need to tell you how to act—you know what to do. You always know what to do. I've seen how strong you can be.

Subject: Re: Water on the Moon

She's leaving the day after tomorrow. You know where to find me.

Subject: A song

I wish you wouldn't fret so much. It isn't like you to be jealous, and it isn't becoming. I will always love you—forever, no matter what, all of those things. There is nobody else, and there never will be. I'm working hard on the songs. Here's the single. It's for you.

"Water on the Moon"

I felt your tears/they made me cry/I felt your fear/had to say good-bye

We're in this thing together/you can't forget so soon

Our secret and our pleasure/safe like water on the moon

Subject: Re: A song

I love the song. I love you. Please don't make me regret that.

Subject: Re: Us

I am sorry, but the thing is, I don't think you get to decide what happens. It's like your song says, "We're in this thing together." I thought that was the deal. Who has more to lose here, you or me? And why do I have to ask this question? You say you love me, but what you do says something else. Do you think I don't know about the girl? I can't prove it, no. But then, nobody can prove anything, can they? Wasn't that always the point?

Subject: Re: Us

I do love you. Forgive me.

Eden felt as if she were standing on a ticking time bomb. Her overtired senses were sharpened to a knife edge, and every tiny rustle and puff of air made her jump. She was shaken by the e-mails, and her knees felt weak. Darcy must have thought these messages were so cleverly camouflaged—song lyrics, elliptical references, fake names. No need to delete them. Even if someone managed to find them here, who could figure them out? But Eden didn't need a decoder to understand what was being said here.

Eden thought about Peter's journal entries. No wonder Darcy had been unimpressed with the hearty state of Peter's health. It must have taken some planning to send a man as hale as Peter into cardiac arrest. But Eden had spent so much time in hospitals, so much time hearing about what the heart could and could not stand, that she knew how easily it could be done with the right tools and the opportunity. All one needed was the will to do it and a little research. The rest was easy. It wasn't at all unusual for a man in his fifties to suffer heart problems, even if they hadn't been detected before, Eden knew. And a standard toxicology screen would look only for drugs of abuse—cocaine, amphetamines . . . Nobody would think to look for something like nitroglycerin, for example.

Clever.

It would have worked, Eden thought. Darcy could have had her happily-ever-after with Adam. They could have waited awhile and made it look as if Darcy really was a grieving widow, taking her time to get over the loss of her husband. But ultimately nobody would have blinked if she'd sold the house and moved away to start a new life somewhere else. She was still young. Nobody would have expected her to spend the rest of her days wearing a black veil. But Adam was greedy. And Adam couldn't wait. Eden placed her hand on her chest. The scar felt warm but still. She couldn't feel that traitor's heart beating under her skin.

"What do you want me to do?" she said out loud. "You deserved to die. Why couldn't you stay dead?" Now there were tears forming in her eyes, but whether they were from frustration, sadness, or just exhaustion, Eden couldn't tell. She felt herself splitting deep inside, as if the two parts of her—the part that was Eden and the part she knew now was Adam—were tearing and separating like wet tissue.

For the first time since she'd emerged from anesthesia with a new heart in her body, Eden felt a longing for her old self so intense it almost took her breath away. That girl who'd drawn unicorns in her notebooks, who'd loved the color pink, who'd taken such joy in running through Portland's city streets, seemed impossibly simple now—a sweet, simple, lucky girl. She'd never been a great beauty, like Darcy, and she'd never had a gift for creating the kind of high drama she was involved in now. The love she'd felt for Derek was warm and strong and sustaining. It didn't scorch; it didn't destroy. It wasn't *tragic*. It had been enough for her. And then it wasn't. The transplant had given her back life that she would surely have lost without it, but it hadn't given her back her own life. Her body kept the heart, but her being rejected the person who had been Eden. It wasn't Derek she fell out of love with, she now realized; it was herself. And at this moment she missed both desperately.

Eden pictured his face now—not the face that had become so lined and sharp with worry but the one that had been so full of hope and love and just a touch of nervousness when he asked her to marry him. And then she remembered that cold rainy night a lifetime ago when she'd curled up inside Derek's embrace, so content it seemed an affront to nature, and thought, *I can die happy now.*

Maybe she was being punished, after all, Eden thought. One wasn't supposed to think—even for a moment—that one could die happy.

Eden heard a sound, and for a second she thought her own jumpy, twanging nerves had created it. But her brain wasn't capable of creating the exact crunch of car wheels on the driveway or the hoist of the garage door opening. Eden's thoughts scattered like a frightened flock of birds. *Out!* She had to get out of the room. Her fingers shaking so badly, they were almost uncontrollable, Eden tapped a few keys on Darcy's computer so that it would look exactly as it had when Darcy had left it. She tucked Peter's journal into the waistband of her leggings and pulled the loose T-shirt over it. She had only seconds to get out of here and down the stairs. Darcy was back already, which meant that Darcy suspected she was up here, or was trying to trap her, or . . . Eden's heart was leaping, the fight-or-flight response kicking in and flooding her body with adrenaline. Had the lid of the computer been up or down when she came in? For an agonizing moment, Eden froze, unable to decide what to do. *Up or down?*

Shitshitshitshit!

Eden flipped the lid of the computer down and walked out of the room, closing the door softly behind her. Her muscles were stiff from tension. She could hear the garage door closing. She had to get downstairs. *Run!* She took the stairs two at a time. Darcy's key was in the front door. The journal slipped, almost fell, but Eden grabbed it in time. She rounded the corner at the foot of the stairs and sprinted down the hall. The front door opened just as Eden closed her bedroom door.

"Eden?" Darcy called. "Are you here?"

Eden sank to the floor, knees up, back pressed against the door, and put her head in her hands. Her entire body was shaking. It would be ironic, Eden thought, to survive something as traumatic as a heart transplant and then die of fright in her own bedroom, but for several seconds, it wasn't difficult to imagine that scenario. Even though the rush of blood through her veins finally began to slow, Eden knew she would feel the physical effects of all that stress for a long time to come. A scene from a half-forgotten movie flashed through her head—a character waking up the day after getting the shock of his life and looking in the mirror only to find that his hair had turned completely white overnight. Eden could almost feel the roots of her own hair blanching.

"Eden?" Darcy's voice was coming closer—she was walking down the hall.

Eden pulled herself up and half staggered into the bathroom. She closed and locked the door. Darcy knocked on the bedroom door.

"Eden? You here?"

What did she want? Why was she here? Eden didn't move or speak. She waited for Darcy to come in and . . . what? Eden didn't know what was next. She closed her eyes. Tears she'd forgotten about fell and rolled down her cheeks. A minute passed. Then two. Darcy hadn't come in and didn't knock again. Maybe she had gone to the kitchen or upstairs. Maybe she was in her office at this very moment, wondering why the lid of her computer was down when she'd left it up. Or maybe she was still standing outside the door, waiting for Eden. How long could she stay here wondering, a prisoner in the bathroom?

She had to leave this house, and she had to confide in someone. Eden needed help. She hadn't wanted to ask—for so long this foreign heart of hers had turned her away from the one person who cared about her the most—but now she realized how much she needed Derek. Eden could only hope that he would still be willing to help her.

She unlocked the bathroom door and stood in the middle of her room. Nothing. No Darcy waiting for her. No rustling by the door. Eden changed her shirt and put on a pair of jeans. She put Peter's journal in the big bag she took to work, burying it underneath a change of clothes, and hoisted it over her shoulder. She gave her hair a few swipes with a brush, checked her face to make sure it hadn't frozen into a rictus of wide-eyed panic, and headed out.

"Eden? Is that you?

It sounded as if Darcy was in the kitchen, but Eden couldn't be sure. She kept moving.

"Eden, I want to talk to you. Can you wait a minute?"

No. No, no, no.

"Eden!" She could hear Darcy's voice getting louder, moving toward her. The front door was right there.

"Hey!"

Eden didn't stop, didn't answer, didn't turn back once she'd left the house. She could pretend not to have heard Darcy, but if she made eye contact, it would be over. Her hands were trembling as she unlocked her car. Forcing herself not to push the gas pedal to the floor, Eden drove and didn't stop until she got to the beach. She parked at the edge of the sand, rolled down her window, and for a moment let her senses absorb the sound of the waves, the taste of the salty air, and the light dancing off the water. Almost reluctantly, she pulled Peter's journal out from her bag and began going through it more carefully.

Then she picked up her phone and called Derek.

CHAPTER 21

Derek was in his office, booking his flight to San Diego on the computer when his cell phone rang. His first impulse was just to ignore it. It had been a ridiculous day already, and it wasn't even noon. Wendy was out with some kind of god-awful sinus infection (or perhaps, he thought, looking for another job), and the phones had been uncharacteristically busy. So much of their business was done via e-mail that the phone was almost unnecessary—a sort of quaint atavism that nobody thought to use first—but this morning the ringing had been ceaseless. And somehow Wendy's absence had served to make Charles's and Xander's social skills diminish by negative exponents. Their conversations this morning had been snippy, then rude, then tongue-tied. It had been driving him mad and setting his teeth on edge. But he couldn't blame them entirely. They were overloaded and

329

understaffed. Even if Wendy managed to recover enough to drag herself back into the office in the next twenty-four hours, it was still a bad time to leave them on their own. And, of course, part of the reason it was a bad time was because he had been neglecting his own business for months.

But he had to go.

It was going to be for two days only—and not even that if he could just find a return flight to get him back to Portland at around lunchtime. Which he would do if that phone would just stop ringing. After the fourth ring, Derek finally picked his phone up and looked at the caller ID.

Eden.

After waiting all these weeks and months for her to call, he almost didn't believe it was her. Even Patty hadn't been able to convince her to take his calls. He was taking a big chance flying down to San Diego—she could refuse to see him, she could accuse him of harassing her—but he knew it was the only way he would be able to get her to listen to him. But now, here she was. He managed to answer just before it rolled over into voice mail.

"Eden?"

"Hi, Derek." She paused for a moment. Derek could hear the sound of the ocean in the background. "How are you?"

He'd been trying to get through to her for so long and had imagined the conversation they'd have so many times. He had whole conversations plotted out in his head—in all of them he was calm and reasonable and nonthreatening. Not too emotional—nothing to scare her off. And in these scenarios, he'd imagined her as warm and sweet, telling him that she'd been thinking about it, that she'd decided she never should have left, and that there was a chance for them . . . But none of that happened now. The endless days and nights of frustration, of searching, of giving up and starting over, of breaking all his own promises to himself, all came crashing over him, and when he spoke, his words came out cracked and broken. "It's so good to hear your voice, Eden. I'm so glad you called. I have missed you so much. You don't know . . ."

This was not how it was supposed to go, but he couldn't seem to control himself. He couldn't rein in those messy, wayward feelings.

"Derek, I'm sorry. If I could take back the hurt I've caused you—if I could undo it somehow, I would. I've said this before, I know. And it wasn't that I didn't mean it before, but I'm just starting to understand what it's been like for you."

Derek was torn. Speaking to her was like a balm. Just knowing that she had finally called him was enough to lift his mood higher than it had been for months. But her voice was strange, and the sound of it scraped at him. Her words, which were kind and meaningful, didn't match her tone, which was hard and a little detached. It was almost as if Eden were speaking through someone else.

"It's okay, Eden. There's nothing to be sorry for. I'm the one who hasn't understood. But I do now. That's what I've been wanting to talk to you about."

"I've just not been myself, Derek." Now her voice sounded as if it were collapsing, flattening out into monotone.

"Edie . . ." Calling her by her pet name was something else he hadn't intended to do. But he was trying to bring her back, to keep her there long enough to tell her what he knew.

"I've been such a bitch," she said with sudden vehemence. He could hear her sighing and rustling paper. A seagull cried somewhere in the near distance. "I wouldn't blame you if you didn't want to talk to me ever again." Her voice had shifted again. Now she sounded petulant.

"No, no, I would never do that," he said. "Please, Eden, don't even think like that. I have something important to tell you. That's why I've been trying to get in touch with you. I know you didn't want to talk to me, but I've found something out, and I think it's going to make such a huge difference for you."

"My mother said I should call you," she said, "and I didn't. I should have. I'm in over my head here, Derek." She laughed, a tight, shrill sound. "I thought I could handle all of this, you know, but it turns out that it's much bigger than I am. When they said I shouldn't go looking for my donor? Well, there are good reasons for that."

"I'm coming down to San Diego, Eden."

"What?"

"I'm flying down tomorrow morning. I should be there by eleven or so."

"But why?" Eden said. She sounded genuinely confused, but not, to Derek's surprise, upset by his announcement.

"Well, you wouldn't talk to me on the phone." He laughed. "So I thought I'd come down there and talk to you in person. It's been too long, Eden. I still care about you." He held his breath for a moment. "I always will." She didn't say anything for a long time, so he forged ahead into the silence. "What do you mean you're in over your head? Is something wrong, Eden? Are you okay?"

"I don't even know how to start," she said, "so I guess I'll jump right to the end. I have the heart of a killer. And I'm living with the woman who killed that killer. And here's the best part—I think she knows all of this. And I think . . . I think she's probably going to try to kill me again."

She sounded lucid and more present than she had a few moments before, so Derek knew she wasn't drunk. Her sentence construction made sense, and there was even a thrum of amusement in her words, so she wasn't having a psychotic break, but what Eden had just said didn't make sense. But what really alarmed him was what she'd said about living with a woman who wanted to kill her.

"Are you talking about Darcy?" he said. "Darcy Silver?"

"How do you know about Darcy, Derek?"

"Your mother told me you'd moved in with her, but don't be angry at her. She—"

"I'm not angry," Eden said. "Besides, she doesn't know anything about Darcy."

"But I do," Derek said. He sighed. This was going to be the tricky part. If Eden took offense at his digging around in her life, he'd be in a worse position than he had been before he picked up the phone. "I did a little investigating." He waited a beat, but Eden said nothing. "I know that she's a widow and that her husband was much older. And that he died suddenly. And that she inherited a whole lot of money from him. That house you're living in is worth a fortune."

"I think he killed her husband," Eden said after a long pause.

"He? What are you talking about?" Derek's anxiety had ratcheted up. He felt Eden slipping away again—her voice growing distant and atonal.

"But not alone," she said. "Darcy was a part of it too."

"Who? Who are you talking about?" Derek tried to keep the panic out of his own voice. *Stay with me,* he begged silently. It was a phrase he'd used too many times before with Eden, and he hated to even think it.

"I have his journal here," Eden said. "I've been looking through it. He was very healthy when he died—there was nothing wrong with him. He was planning to move—he was going to take her away to New York. He says it right here—'Darcy doesn't want to go. She's putting up a great resistance. There must be a reason.' But then, later, right before he stops making entries, he says she's had a total change of heart. See? They came up with a plan. And then she had him cremated right away. But it was him—*he* was the mastermind. And now I have his heart."

"Whose heart, Eden?"

"Darcy's lover. They killed her husband, and then she killed him. Adam. I don't know what to do. I think—"

"No, that's wrong. Look, I was going to wait until I got there so I could tell you in person, but . . . please don't be angry at me. I found out who your donor was. I know for certain, Eden. It wasn't a man."

"No, Derek, I know—"

"Your donor had nothing to do with Darcy, except that she lived in San Diego and once worked at that restaurant where you're working now."

"She," said Eden. It wasn't a question.

"Yes, she. Her name was Louise Green, but she went by Lulu. She was twenty-five when it happened. It was a car accident, Eden. She was on life support. The family didn't want to let her go. They thought maybe . . ." He stopped to gauge her reaction, but all he heard was the sound of the ocean in the background. "I spoke with her mother, Eden. I saw a photograph of her. She looked a little like you." He paused again and waited for her to speak. He hadn't wanted to tell her this way. He'd had a plan for this conversation too. He was going to ease into it—save the part about talking to the mother for last. And the photo . . . He hadn't planned to mention that at all. He'd wanted to be able to see her face, to read her expression. But he hadn't expected that she'd have come to her own conclusions about whose heart she'd been given, and he certainly hadn't anticipated the strange and frightening things she was saying about killing and being killed.

"Eden, please say something."

When she spoke, it sounded as if she were mumbling the way people do when they are drifting into sleep, and it was difficult for him to understand what she was saying. "I was in that car with him. We were together."

"The car?"

"*He* was driving. Not me."

"Are you talking about the accident, Eden? Are you saying you remember it? There was somebody else with her that day. It was—"

"Adam," Eden said. Her voice had become dreamy and somnambulant, but it was clearer now. "It was her fault. Darcy. She's the one."

"Eden—"

"It was *her* fault."

"Eden, I don't understand what you're saying. What do you mean it was her fault? What did Darcy have to do with it? What do you know about this, Eden? Tell me."

"I have to go now," she said.

"What? No. Where are you going? Eden, please—"

"It makes sense now," she said. "I should have put it together, but it was difficult to see in the dream, and I always forgot when I woke up. I didn't know what I was looking at." Derek heard the sound of a car starting. "I know what to do now."

"Wait," he said. "Don't hang up."

"I have to go now," she repeated. He started to tell her again to wait, not to go, but before he could get the words out, she said, "Thank you," and hung up.

Derek called her back instantly but wasn't surprised when her phone went to voice mail. He tried again and then a third time. On the fourth try, he didn't even get a ring—she'd turned off her phone. He typed out a quick text message, telling her to call him please, it was urgent, but he knew it was a futile gesture before he even pressed the SEND button. She was gone—in the wind—and headed who knew where.

"Boss, we have a bit of a problem."

Derek turned around and saw that Charles was standing behind him as if he'd been beamed in. Derek wondered how long he'd been there and how much of the conversation he'd heard.

"Yes, we do," Derek said. "A major problem."

"I have our distributor on the phone. There's an issue with that last shipment, and I—"

"I don't suppose it's anything you can take care of, Charles? I'm just in the middle of something here." Derek looked down at his silent cell phone, realizing he was holding it in a kind of death grip.

"Bad time?" Charles asked.

"You could say that."

"Eden? You want to talk about it?"

Derek released his grip on the phone and put it on his desk. "I'm really worried about her," he said.

"Did you tell her about the, you know?"

"Yes, I did."

"She didn't take it well?"

"No, it's not that. She seemed . . . okay with that part of it. I wasn't going to say anything until I got there, but she was going on—rambling about how she thought she had the heart of a killer, this guy who was the lover of the woman she's living with."

"Darcy Silver. The hot widow."

Derek sighed. Charles knew way too much about all of this, but he couldn't help that now. "Yes, Darcy. And then she said Darcy had killed her too—I mean, *him*. She wasn't surprised when I told her about the girl—Lulu. That's the thing . . ." Derek rubbed his eyes.

Charles looked over at the multiline phone on Derek's desk. Three of the four lines were blinking insistently. He gave a small shrug and said, "D., why don't you start at the beginning?"

His eyes continually darting to his cell phone, Derek recounted his conversation with Eden as exactly as he could remember it, leaving out the parts where he'd almost sobbed with relief at the sound of her voice but including how strange she'd sounded and how detached and dreamy her voice had become by the end of the conversation.

"I don't want to sound like an alarmist," Charles said at the end of it, "but I think she may be in danger."

"Yes," Derek said. "She said something about being killed again. It was just so hard to figure out what she was saying. I'm trying to put it together."

"She said it was Darcy's fault, right?" Charles said. "The car accident?" Derek nodded. "I mean, she could be imagining it, but . . . If she's figured out that Darcy did something to her husband, and if Darcy knows that she's figured it out—even if she suspects that Eden suspects . . . Well, accidents can happen. But maybe that car accident really wasn't an accident. And maybe there could be another accident."

Derek turned back to his computer and began hitting keys.

"Derek?" Charles said. "Do you—"

"Fuck it," Derek said, and stood up. "I don't have time for this. I'll just go."

"To?" Charles asked as Derek brushed by him on his way out the door.

"The airport. I'm going to San Diego." He was walking so fast that Charles had to trot to keep up with him. There was a flight leaving for San Diego in less than two hours, and Derek was determined to be on it. "I'm sorry, Charles," he said. "I'll call you."

"Okay, listen, we—" But Derek couldn't hear the rest of the sentence. By the time Charles had finished it, he was already gone.

Del Dios was a bitch in the rain. But it wasn't raining today. No, today God's Highway looked like the sparkling stairway to heaven that it was. Eden had never been on this road before—not as Eden anyway—but she knew exactly where to go. She didn't need directions to find the exact spot where the car and truck had collided and been sent, crushed and twisted, off the edge of the road.

Let's go for a ride to the Elfin Forest. It's so beautiful out there. Remember how we used to go there all the time?

He hadn't argued, even though the sky looked heavy and low. It wasn't the ideal day for a picnic or a walk in the woods or quick, hot sex outside under the trees, made so much more exciting because anyone could see them at any time. He'd loved that once, but not as much as she—never as much as she. He knew that none of those things were going to happen, but he agreed to the ride anyway. He agreed because he was guilty and maybe because he was a little afraid of what she might do when he told her the real reason they were in San Diego. Not afraid enough, it turned out. He'd said it was just to take a break from the Los Angeles craziness. He said he wanted to spend a couple of days near the beach and relax, but she knew what it was really about. He was going back to Darcy. She'd known it was coming, but she wasn't going to make it easy for him. She insisted on going with him, and he'd been restless and nervous since the minute they'd crossed the county line. She could see him twisting in his own skin—wanting to tell her, to get it over with, but afraid of her tears. He hated big emotional scenes unless he was the one controlling them. So when she'd suggested the ride, he went along.

The rain had been a surprise. It had made everything a lot more frightening, but it had helped, because until that last moment, she still hadn't been sure it would happen.

You sure picked a great day for a ride. He'd tried to laugh—to make light of it, but after a while the rain became so heavy that they both lost the will to speak. There were no words between them for the longest time. But *she* was there—as she always had been—a permanent presence between them, dividing them and snaring him in that net of her golden hair.

He had never stopped loving Darcy.

It was coming to Eden so easily now, all the little details of the dream that she'd never been able to remember before. She wondered if she would have figured it out on her own eventually or, if she'd taken this drive sooner, if her heart would have told her where she was and what had happened here. But Eden didn't think so. Lulu had submerged herself so deeply into Adam that she wasn't even able to make herself known as a distinct entity in Eden's dreams. She was there but not there. It wasn't until

Derek had told her—not until the moment he mentioned the name Lulu—that Eden understood what she'd been seeing. She felt bad about hanging up on Derek and worse about turning off her phone, because she knew it would probably drive him mad with worry, but she couldn't hear it ringing now; she didn't want to be distracted. She needed to be focused. The puzzle was coming together, but there was one piece still missing. As soon as she'd turned off her phone, she'd turned the car around and headed here. It was ironic how close Del Dios ran to Darcy's house. Darcy was always close by, wasn't she? Just as she had been that day.

Eden was finally able to see it all from the correct perspective. All those dreams she'd had of Darcy had been what Lulu had seen when she'd worked at Poquette. Lulu had known about Darcy and Adam from the beginning, but she hadn't been able to change her feelings for Adam. *She's not worth it,* Sticks had said, but he didn't know the half of it. That was the night Darcy had come in with her husband and the two of them had sat at the bar. She was supposed to wait on them when they sat down for dinner, but they never made it to her table. That was the night Peter died. Adam hadn't spoken to Lulu the entire night, and while she was there, sitting at his bar, he hadn't taken his eyes off Darcy. Eden could see Darcy again in that low-cut black dress, looking as if she weren't looking.

Why didn't he love me more than her? Why couldn't he?

She could see it all again—sitting next to Adam, watching him drive, watching the fear start small as it flickered at the corner of his mouth and grew like a dark, spreading stain across his face. But she'd been so close to him—so connected to him—that she might as well have been driving herself. She could feel what he felt, know what he knew. That was what Eden had seen and felt in her dreams. That was why, even as Lulu drifted up and away from her body, it was Adam's face she looked for in the wreckage of the car and not her own.

Eden had driven through Rancho Santa Fe and was wending her way toward Lake Hodges. She was driving slowly, taking great care with every turn in the road and waiting until she got to wherever it was she was being led.

It was all her fault, Eden thought. And then, just as the sparkling blue water of the lake came into view, Eden thought, *It should have been her. She's the one who should have died, not me.*

She's the one.

She should die.

CHAPTER 22

Darcy sat alone at her lovely granite kitchen counter—the one she'd spent so much time picking out, the one Peter had smashed his glass into before he'd smashed his fist into her face, and the one at which she'd now shared several meals with Eden. She put her head in her hands and wept. She'd been holding back these tears for so long, and now that she'd let them start, they flowed like water from a broken dam. She hadn't wanted to let go like this. She'd known that for the rest of her life she'd have to remain strong and keep her secrets frozen deep inside her (like water on the moon), and until now she'd been able to pull it all off.

But she hadn't expected Eden to come along and home in on that inner hiding place of hers. And she couldn't have imagined how seeing the scar on Eden's chest and knowing what lay beating beneath it would trigger the grief she'd been holding in for so long.

It wasn't just that she missed him, though she did. And it wasn't regret for what she'd done—what they'd both done—that she wished now had never happened, though that too gnawed at Darcy. What she felt now was a black and bottomless sense of loss. It hadn't been that way with Peter. She'd been in a state of shock and numb when she'd driven through the night with his lifeless body in the car next to her, but even at his memorial service and later, at home, when the permanence of his absence finally became real to her, she still hadn't felt the enormity and finality of death the way she did now. It was like falling—that sick sensation you got when the ground gave way beneath you—and never hitting the bottom. Just an endless, hollow loop of dread.

She'd been at Eden's bedside when it had first hit her. The light had hit her chest in exactly the right place so that her scar practically glowed in the dark. She was pale and shiny with perspiration—still half in her dream—and Darcy had felt the weight of Adam's death fall on her with a crushing heaviness. She had begged Eden to let her help, but it was Adam she was really talking to. For the first time since the accident, Darcy visualized Adam bloody and broken on the side of the road, and she felt as if a wound that would never close were opening inside her. It was almost as if the full understanding of what had happened to him hadn't hit her until that moment because, when she'd first heard the news, it wasn't just Adam they were talking about—it was the girl too.

They hadn't released her name at the time, stating only that she'd been pulled from the wreckage with him, but Darcy didn't need to be told who it was. She had shut herself down then. She had folded up the pieces of herself that had loved Adam and had hoped until the last minute that he would come back to her—that he loved her *the most*—and had put them away as neatly as she would a letter in an envelope. Of course she thought of him and of course she had to contend with the memories and the knowledge of what had died with him, but until she laid her hand on Eden's trembling shoulder, she hadn't allowed herself to feel the pain of losing him. And now it wouldn't stop.

She'd wanted to tell Eden about everything. Last night, before Eden's defenses all rose up again and she sat there open and exposed, Darcy came so close to spilling it all out. But Eden, like Adam, had shut her down, and she'd had to go. She hadn't slept at all after she'd left Eden's room. For the rest of the night, images played themselves over and over again behind her closed eyes—the car on the road in that rain. Why was he even there on Del Dios Highway? What had brought him back to San Diego? She'd wondered about that many times. He hadn't told her he was coming down from LA. Then again, why would he? Those questions were difficult for Darcy, but even harder to contemplate were the others: What were they talking about at the end? What was he thinking? Did he feel any pain? Darcy couldn't help wondering, as selfish and pointless as it was now, if Adam had thought of her in his last moments—if she'd been there in some way. That was when the tears started, and Darcy didn't get up until her pillow felt soaked with them. She'd had to put a cold compress to her face for almost an hour this morning to get the puffiness around her eyes to go down. She had another appointment with Putterman, and she didn't want him to see her like that. She couldn't afford to show the man any weakness—any sign that she was broken. She must have done a good enough job, because Eden didn't seem to notice that anything was wrong when the two of them met in the kitchen before Darcy left the house.

Darcy had expected Eden to be embarrassed or maybe even angry when she saw her again because, despite seeming almost pathological about not needing anyone or anything, Eden had woken up in the middle of the night calling Darcy's name. It was perhaps the only time Darcy had ever seen Eden completely un-guarded. And Darcy knew Eden had seen her eyes go right to the scar. Darcy had given herself away by not saying anything about it—not acknowledging in any way that she knew what that scar was and why it was there. So Darcy had thought—even hoped—that Eden would make some reference to it herself. She'd tried to get Eden to talk about her dreams. She'd tried to get behind that locked-down exterior of hers and find the person she'd lost.

Adam.

In the end, she couldn't make it to Putterman's office. Half-way there, she burst into tears again and started crying so hard that the road in front of her actually became blurry. She had to pull over and park in a beachfront lot and let some of it out so that she could drive again. This wild, uncontrolled grief was like a poison, Darcy thought as she sat with her head on the steering wheel, her whole body shaking with sobs. It had in-vaded her mind and her body, and now she couldn't shake it or purge it from her system.

When, after a mighty effort and half a bottle of water, Darcy felt she could trust her voice again, she called Putterman to can-cel their appointment.

"Are you all right, Darcy?" he said. She could almost feel his disingenuousness ooze through the phone like an oil spill. "You sound a little hoarse."

"I'm really not feeling well, Larry. You know there's that flu that's been going around. I don't know if that's what I'm getting, but if it is, I'm sure you don't want to be exposed to it."

"Riiight," he said. "That's thoughtful of you, Darcy." How she hated him. Every small dealing she had with him, every paper she had to sign, every barely concealed dig he directed at her, was like Peter reaching out from the grave to punish her. Maybe he had planned it that way, Darcy thought, because he'd seen it coming. Not his death—Darcy was sure that up to the very end, he never had an inkling of what was happening to him or he would have locked everything up in trusts and bequeathed it all to his sister—but Darcy separating from him and going after his money. It was ironic, Darcy thought now. When they'd first discussed getting married, Darcy was so intent on proving that she wasn't marrying him for his money that she had told Peter that she wanted him to have a prenuptial agreement. Even though she hadn't intended it to, her suggestion worked in reverse. Peter had told her that he would never consider such a thing. He loved her, he was going to take care of her, and what was his was hers too. But somewhere along the line, he'd put Putterman in charge so that he'd be placed directly between Darcy and Peter's money like Cerberus guarding the gate to the underworld. Putterman couldn't keep her from the money after Peter died, but Darcy was absolutely certain that had she left Peter or even if he'd left her, he'd have seen to it that she got nothing.

"Darcy? Can you hear me?"

"Yes, I'm sorry. Reception's a little spotty. So can we reschedule, Larry? Would that be okay?" She could feel the tears starting again and knew she'd be unable to hold them back.

"Sure we can. But listen, Darcy, I can come over to the house. I'm not afraid of catching the flu, you know."

"Larry, I'm losing you. I'll call back and reschedule," Darcy said.

"I really think it would be better if I came over," he said.

"Why?" There was a new note of warning in his voice, and it alarmed Darcy enough to dispense with any niceties.

"Well, as you know, Lisa's decided to fly out, so I thought you'd want to . . . talk to me before she gets here."

"Lisa is *what*?"

"Oh," he said, "you weren't aware?" Of course she wasn't *aware*, and he knew that, damn him to hell. Darcy had wondered why Lisa had gone so quiet lately, but she had been too preoccupied to give it much thought. So this was the plan . . . She was just going to show up? And then what? And why was Putterman telling her this? He wanted something.

"No," Darcy said, "I wasn't. But you already knew that."

"I assure you—"

"What's this really about, Larry?"

"Why don't I tell you in person?" he said. "You're sounding better already. Lisa has some problems, Darcy. I can help you work it out before she gets here. I'd be doing you a favor. I'll come over to the house. If I leave now, I can be there—"

"No," Darcy said. "I have to go now. Do you understand? I. Have. To. Go."

She hung up before he had a chance to say anything else. Darcy knew that canceling her appointment with Putterman, not to mention this contentious conversation, was going to have repercussions, especially now that she knew Lisa was not only re-involving herself, but actually showing up in San Diego. She would have to call Lisa and put her off or make nice or . . .

Fuck Lisa, Darcy thought. *And fuck Putterman*. Though fucking Putterman, she now realized, was exactly what he wanted.

It was all going to fall apart, this emotional house of cards she'd built. But at that moment Darcy didn't care.

For what felt like a long time, Darcy just stared at the section of beach grass and sand she could see through her windshield. The tears came and went, smearing and then clearing the landscape in front of her. But it wasn't the parking lot she was seeing through her wide-open eyes; it was Adam the last time she'd seen him before he died.

They'd met at Zulu's because, he'd said, he didn't think it was a good idea to come to her house. "Neutral ground," he'd said, "is what we need." They hadn't seen each other for weeks at that point, and Darcy knew what he was going to say as surely as if she'd been given a script. But even so, the conversation had flattened her. She was unprepared for the impact of his words. It was like being run over slowly by a bus.

"I think we need some space and time away from each other," he had said. He'd done something to his hair, Darcy noticed. It wasn't any shorter, but it was slicked back into a wet look that didn't particularly suit him. And the patchy beard was new too—a sort of carefully cultivated grunge.

"That's all we've had, Adam. Space."

"You know what I mean. I need to think about where we go from here."

"You're with someone else." She stated it as fact, not a question.

"No," he said, but it was the worst lie he'd ever told. He couldn't even meet her eyes with his—he couldn't even make the attempt. "I know it's been hard for you, Darcy. You've had to go through some things that would have destroyed a weaker person, and you've handled it all . . . But it hasn't been easy for me, either. I'm carrying a lot of weight here too, and sometimes when I'm with you . . ."

"*You're* carrying the weight, Adam? I didn't realize I was so very heavy."

He'd looked at her then, and she could see there were tears standing still in those dark eyes of his. But she couldn't tell whom they were for.

"I'm going up to LA for a while," he said.

"Who's in LA?" she asked.

"Darcy . . ."

"I hope she's worth all of this, Adam."

"Just a little time," he said. "That's all."

She'd stared at him then—taken as long a look as she could before he had a chance to say anything else—drinking in every detail of his face, the set of his shoulders, his beautiful, graceful hands. She wanted to imprint every line and curve of the way he was right then, before she asked him the question she could never take back and before he answered it.

"Was it always about the money?" she said. "Please, Adam, just tell me. You owe me that much."

Surprise flashed in his eyes, but there was hurt there too and anger. He said nothing, his mouth slowly compressing into a thin line, his jaw set. "How can you ask me that, Darcy?" he said finally.

Darcy got up and walked away without saying another word. She never saw him again. He called her once, but she hadn't recognized the phone number that showed up on her cell phone and she hadn't answered. The message he left was brief and hollow. *"I just wanted to say hello,"* he'd said. *"There isn't anything else."* She erased the message. A few months later, she received a flurry of e-mails from him. The last one said that he wanted to talk—that he had something he needed to share with her and that he had to tell her in person. She answered it, telling him that he knew where to find her. When he didn't answer, she assumed he'd changed his mind. And then—two weeks later, maybe less, maybe more—he was dead. As Darcy started her car and headed home, she wondered again how differently it might all have worked out if he'd reacted another way to her question about the money. If he'd managed to convince her with a word, a look, or even the touch of his hand, that Peter's money hadn't been on his mind from the very beginning, she would have fought for him. She would have found a way to be with him. If the money was an afterthought and if it really had been love that motivated him, Darcy could have handled anything—even the girl. As she had so many times before, Darcy tried to work out what it was that Adam wanted to tell her before he died—what secret had perished with him that day. And then, like a bright balloon rising up and sailing free, the thought came to Darcy. Eden would know. Whatever had been in Adam's heart was there now inside Eden. Darcy clung to that hope. Eden could tell her. By the time she got home, Darcy— wrung out and exhausted from weeping—was desperate to know.

But Eden had run out of the house like a frightened cat as soon as Darcy had come home. No response, no good-bye, just like Adam that day at Zulu's. So, unable to even think in a straight line any longer, Darcy sat down at the granite counter and waited for Eden to come home. Bowed by the weight of her grief, she leaned over and rested her hot cheek on the cool granite. *What does it feel like to be dead?* she thought, and closed her eyes.

Darcy startled and yanked herself into a sitting position. The front door had slammed, and someone was calling her name. She was disoriented, and her neck was sore and stiff. How long had she been out like that?

"Darcy!"

"What?" Darcy said. "Who is it?" The voice was high and shrill—angry.

"It was you!" the voice screamed again, and then its owner appeared in the kitchen. Eden. She looked wild and disheveled, her hair tangled and loose as if she'd been in a windstorm and her eyes wide and blazing with ferocity. Her shirt hung loose and was pulled off one shoulder. It was the first time Darcy had seen Eden dress in a way that exposed her chest. Her scar was visible, and her hands were in fists at her side. "Why couldn't you just leave him alone?"

Instinctively, Darcy shifted herself off the stool and gripped the edge of the counter. Eden had had some kind of psychotic break. Was she on drugs or drunk? She seemed to be vibrating with rage.

"What are you talking about?" Darcy said. "Why are you looking at me like that?"

"You couldn't let him go. You had *everything*, but you had to take more. He was with me, he was going to stay with me, but you had to have him. Why?"

"Who? Eden, please, you're scaring me!"

"*Adam!* You know who I'm talking about, Darcy. It was your fault—all your fault. He wouldn't have had to die. I wouldn't have had to die. If you'd just left him alone."

Eden stopped and looked down at her own hands, confused,

as if she didn't know who she was. She really was having a psychotic break, Darcy thought, and Eden needed a doctor. But Darcy had no idea how she was going to make that 911 call with Eden standing over her like that, nor what she'd even say to the operator.

"Eden?" Darcy asked. "What's going on? What about Adam?" She kept her voice low and nonthreatening. Maybe it was working, because the rage seemed to leave Eden's eyes, replaced by a glazed-over blankness.

"I changed my mind," she said. "At the end. When I knew we were going to die. I changed my mind. It was a mistake. But then it was too late."

Darcy caught her breath. *When I knew we were going to die.* "When you knew who was going to die?"

"Adam and I," Eden said. "Adam was good at so many things, you know. He knew cars as well as he knew drinks and guitars. He was proud of that too. He showed me how easy it would be to screw with the brakes and really hurt someone. Nothing obvious, of course. Adam was always talking about how easy it was to make anything look like an accident. He loved the idea of getting away with things without anyone knowing what you'd done. It was a risk because what if I didn't do it right? What if it didn't work? But I didn't care about anyone finding out. I was going with him, wasn't I? That's why I picked Del Dios. The rain helped. It helped a lot. There was probably an easier way of doing it. I could have shot us both in the head, I guess. But I would never have been able to go through with that. I was too weak. That's why I was with him in the first place. God, I knew he didn't love me enough."

"The girl," Darcy whispered. "Not Adam."

"You didn't even know my name, did you?" Eden said. "Did he even tell you? Did he ever mention the name Lulu? No, of course he didn't."

A filmstrip of images unrolled in front of Darcy—Lulu, the waitress at Poquette serving her a salad, glaring at her from across the restaurant, huddling with the staffers at Peter's funeral. Who could forget a name like that or the scowl that was always on her face? Lulu was a favorite of Peter's, but Darcy felt uncomfortable around her because of the resentment that always seemed to be pouring off her. Lulu. It was true; she hadn't known.

"What are you saying?" Darcy asked. "He was *with* you. Adam left me for you. For . . . Lulu. He left me for Lulu." Darcy was looking right at Eden—seeing the flesh-and-blood friend who lived in her house—and yet it wasn't her.

"He was coming back to you," Eden said. "He always loved you the most. Maybe he didn't want to, I don't know, but he did. I knew that. We were together, but I was always second best. He said he wanted to come back down here for a rest, to take a break, but I knew why he was here. He wanted to see you. And that would have been the end. He loved you and he wanted you and Adam always got what he wanted. I couldn't live without him, and I didn't want him to live without me."

He was coming back to you. Was that what Adam had wanted to tell her?

Eden was like a sleepwalker now, Darcy thought. Her shoulders slumped, and she looked down, up at Darcy, and then down again. She walked across the kitchen, took a glass from the cabinet, and filled it with water. She drank a sip and then looked at the glass as if she didn't know how it had gotten into her hand.

"I changed my mind," Eden said. "It shouldn't have been me, and it shouldn't have been him. I didn't figure that out until it was too late. But I'm here now. It's a second chance."

"Eden," Darcy said cautiously, "are you talking about your heart transplant?"

Eden's eyes flashed. "It should have been *you*," she said, and the sound of it sent a chill up Darcy's spine. "You are the one who should have died."

"Eden . . ." Darcy began to back up. She needed to get out of the kitchen. She needed to get to a phone.

"It should have been you," Eden repeated, and hurled her glass of water in Darcy's direction. Darcy sidestepped the glass just in time, and it smashed on the wall behind her. But now Eden was coming toward her, fury contorting her face. "You should be dead!" she screamed. Darcy turned and ran into the living room, but Eden was on her heels. Frantic, Darcy grabbed the first heavy thing she could find—the poker—but before she could turn around to wave it at Eden, she felt her legs go out from under her. Eden had grabbed her ankle and tripped her. Darcy fell hard, sprawling to the floor, and within a single heartbeat Eden was on top of her, holding the edge of the broken glass at Darcy's neck.

"Eden, don't!"

"You're the one," Eden said, and lowered her voice to a ragged whisper. "It was always you." She pressed the sharpest point of the glass into Darcy's skin. Her hand was trembling.

Darcy closed her eyes.

CHAPTER 23

The grave site was at the far end of the cemetery, which itself was at the end of a long, winding road, up and over a rolling jasmine-covered hill. It took some doing to get there—even if you parked as close to the main part of the cemetery as possible, it was still a trek—but once there, you could see why it was, as the attendant had put it, "a first choice for a last resting place." The graves faced west and caught every ray of the setting sun with golden precision. There were bouquets of every kind of flower laid on and around the headstones, but it was the jasmine that scented the air—light and sweet.

Derek had worried about the length of the walk and the steepness of the hill, but then he reminded himself that Eden had once been a runner and that despite his constant worries about her stamina, she was probably in better shape than he was.

In fact, it had been his pace, not hers, that had slowed as they crested the hill. She pushed forward, turning once to give him a small reassuring smile but then moving ahead of him into the glowing sunlight. He stopped for a minute, letting her make her way to the grave—letting her have a moment there by herself.

He'd wondered about the wisdom of making this pilgrimage, and he'd mentioned that to Eden. There was healing, and then there was healing. She'd survived the physical part of her transplant, but the emotional part of it had nearly destroyed her. He didn't want to take even the smallest risk of losing her again—ever. But, Derek thought, it was likely that he'd always worry this way about Eden. It was going to be his cross to bear for as long as he loved her. And that, he was certain, would be until the day *he* died. At least she seemed to understand that now and, more reassuringly, she allowed it. Eden had let him back in the moment he'd arrived at Darcy's house and found the two of them together, and although he didn't know for certain what the exact shape of their future would look like, he felt that she was now going to let him stay.

There were many days in Derek's life with Eden that he would always remember—their first date, the day he'd proposed to her, watching her open her eyes for the first time after receiving her new heart—but none of them would ever compare to the day he arrived in San Diego, frantic and nearly paralyzed with the fear of what he might find. That day would become a new anniversary for them, but it was one they would never celebrate.

Derek didn't want to think about what might have happened if he had arrived as few as five minutes later than he had, but that too was going to be something that would haunt his imagination for a long time. He wanted to believe that she wouldn't have done it—that the person she was deep inside wouldn't have allowed it—but he would never be sure. As it was, he had barely made it there at all. The whole effort was a comedy of errors—if one could even use the word *comedy* to describe it.

It had started at the airport. He'd paid an exorbitant sum for his last-minute flight to San Diego, the ticket for which the woman at the counter hadn't even wanted to sell to him until he was able to reasonably prove he wasn't some sort of terrorist. He had no luggage, he asked for a one-way ticket (foolishly thinking this would be less expensive than the round-trip ticket), and he was sweating bullets as he emptied the contents of his wallet, looking for the right credit card. Then she sent him to the wrong gate where he waited exactly long enough to feel the sinking desperation of a missed flight as he ran down hallways, through strollers and happy travelers, to get to the right gate at the exact moment they were shutting the doors. His pulse hadn't slowed at all for the duration of the flight, despite the bad airplane scotch he consumed on the way.

His mind kept whirring through possible scenarios, and Eden fared well in none of them. He kept hearing her voice at the end of their last conversation—that flat affectless tone, as if she'd been put to sleep. And then that line—"I know what to do now"—made the hairs on the back of his neck stand up. There were things he hadn't told Eden when he'd spoken to her on the phone—things he hadn't planned to tell her ever. Sitting in that too-small airplane seat wedged between a hygiene-challenged teenager and a buxom woman who sang out loud and off-key to the music on her iPod, Derek couldn't stop thinking about what they meant.

Lulu's mother had been nearly impossible to find because of

the anonymity she'd insisted on, but once Derek made contact with her, she seemed to want to talk about her daughter. No, *talk* wasn't exactly the right word—*unburden* was more accurate. She said what a good, sweet girl Lulu had been—and so beautiful. *Oh, if you could have seen her as a baby—she looked like a little china doll. But something happened to her. She fell in with a bad crowd—she was so easily influenced—and then it was the boys, always the boys. She would do anything they asked her; that was the problem—she was always selling herself out for a boy. And then the last one—Adam—the one driving that damned car. He was never any good. But she was so crazy about him—never seen anything like it—she would have killed for him, no question. In the end, she'd died for him. Such a waste.*

She would have killed for him, Derek kept thinking. Had she killed for him?

And if she had, and Eden was in possession of more than just her physical heart, who had the woman he loved become?

Derek had never been to San Diego before and wasn't prepared for the plane's descent into the city—so close to the buildings of downtown that he could almost see people at their desks. He would never admit it to anyone, but his hands still hadn't stopped shaking by the time the plane taxied to the gate and his legs were still unsteady as he walked down the Jetway. This was probably why he got so confused getting out of downtown in his rented car. He had directions and he had Darcy's address, but he lost precious minutes looping on and off exits before he managed to get himself pointed in the right direction.

There were no mailboxes and no house numbers on Darcy's street. Somewhere in the middle of the street he thought he was supposed to be on, he realized he was lost and had no idea which way to turn. He'd been dialing and redialing Eden's number, but her phone was still turned off. He decided to turn back to the main road and retrace his route on the map. It would have taken him at least twenty minutes out of his way. But then, like a sudden mirage, he saw a jogger appear on the road—a woman running easily, wrapped in the sheer joy of movement—and he rolled down his window and waved to her.

"Can you help me?" he said. "I'm looking for this house." He pointed to the address on his map. Without interrupting her pace, the woman pointed to a spot a few yards down the road. "You're on top of it," she said. "Turn left at that eucalyptus tree and it's right there."

It wasn't exactly *right there*, Derek thought as he drove down the long, recessed driveway, but he had come to the right place. He tried to imagine how Eden had wound up in this opulent place with its beautiful landscaping, and he couldn't picture it. Not for the first time he wondered who it was he had come so far to find.

He knocked at the door; then he rang the bell. Nothing. There was a car in the driveway—a gray Toyota that looked as if it had seen better days. Derek assumed it was Eden's. Darcy Silver would not drive a car like that. He was surprised it was even allowed in this posh neighborhood. He knocked again—harder and louder this time—but still nothing. And then he heard something inside the house—a noise that could have been a sob or a scream or laughter—and his stomach fell. He pushed at the door and, by another intervention by fate, discovered it was unlocked.

It didn't take him long to find them. This was the image Derek would never be able to erase from his memory. Eden was straddling Darcy, leaning over her, holding a jagged piece of glass, and whispering a mad string of curses in her ear. Darcy was sobbing but lying curiously flat and motionless beneath Eden. In the moment he didn't register it, but later Derek would realize that she had already given up. She wasn't even trying to fight.

He didn't call her name, and he didn't yell for her to stop. He just ran full force into her, knocking her off Darcy and covering her with his body. She let out a huge sigh as if he'd knocked the breath from her lungs, and he felt her go limp. The glass fell out of her hand, and she looked up at him. She was very far away, but he could see that she was there somewhere behind her wide-open, staring eyes.

"Eden."

He watched her come back to herself, her emotional body swimming up to the surface of her consciousness.

"What happened?" she said. "What have I done?"

Derek looked over at Darcy, who hadn't moved but who was breathing and alive. Even with her face distorted with terror and wet with smeared makeup and tears, she was beautiful. Too beautiful, Derek thought. The photographs he'd seen really hadn't done her justice. In the flesh, she was luminous—so much more than the sum of her individual features. Looking at her lying there, the tears still shining wet on her cheeks, he understood how beauty of that magnitude could lead to danger.

"Are you okay?" he asked her.

Darcy nodded and opened her mouth to speak, but nothing came out. She lifted herself up to a sitting position but then stopped moving, as if unsure where to go or what to do next. Derek looked down at Eden and realized he was still pressing the full weight of his body into hers. He shifted off her, still keeping his hands on her arms. She was giving no resistance, but he was still afraid to let her go.

"Why?" he asked her.

"She's angry," Eden said in a small voice. "She's still angry."

Derek turned to look at Darcy, who was touching her neck, looking for a wound. He was almost giddy with relief to see that there was nothing there—no mark, no injury. "Is she talking about you?" he asked Darcy. "You're angry?"

"No," Darcy said, "it's not me. The girl . . ." She got on her hands and knees and crawled over to Eden. The two of them exchanged a look full of meaning—unspoken words in a language he couldn't understand—and then Darcy reached over to take Eden's hand. "Not the girl," she said. "Lulu. Her name was Lulu."

Eden squeezed Darcy's hand. "I'm sorry," she said. "Darcy, I'm so sorry."

Darcy closed her eyes, leaned forward, and pressed her lips to Eden's forehead.

Derek crested the hill and saw Eden in the distance, crouching beside the grave. She'd laid the two bouquets of flowers—roses that she'd picked out and lilies from Darcy—on the ground and rested one hand on the headstone. As he got a little closer, Derek could see her lips moving. She looked intent but not upset. He walked slowly, dawdling, wanting to give her whatever time she needed.

Derek wondered again why Eden had felt the need to travel to this place—why she needed to speak out loud to someone who was more of a presence inside her than six feet below her in the ground. But Eden had told him her sleep had been dreamless for days and that, even when she spoke to Darcy, she felt nothing except a pulsing, overwhelming sadness. The confrontation, violent as it was, seemed to have released Lulu's restless, unhappy spirit from its place inside Eden. Or maybe, Eden said, she had been able to separate herself from Lulu now that she knew the truth. She still felt Lulu's presence, but she no longer felt haunted by it. He had suggested, though without much conviction, that she reconsider and see a therapist, but Eden had just shaken her head and given him a small tired smile.

"You can't stay sad forever," he'd told her. "You deserve to be happy, Eden."

"I know," she'd said. "I'm trying."

And now they were here.

He couldn't pretend to walk anymore, and he didn't want to simply stand like a scarecrow in the middle of a graveyard, so Derek finally followed Eden to Lulu's grave and went to stand beside her. She was quiet now, staring at the headstone, though there was nothing much to read there—just the name, the dates, and the simplest of phrases, *Beloved Daughter.* Derek slid his hand into Eden's and gave it a light squeeze. She turned her head to him and smiled—that pretty Eden smile he'd spent so many nights dreaming of.

"Are you all right?" he asked.

"Yes," she said. "I'm fine. I needed to do this, but I won't need to come here again."

Derek nodded.

Eden fussed with the flowers for a minute, arranging them this way and that until she was satisfied, and then she stood up and looped her arm into Derek's. "We can go now," she said.

"I'm in no hurry," he said. "We can stay here as long as you need to."

"I know, but it's okay. I'm ready to go."

Derek steered her gently toward the edge of the hill. The air was as thick and sweet as honey. The light of the sunset caught in her hair, bringing out reddish tones he'd never noticed before. It occurred to him suddenly that there were probably a great many more things he would discover about her that would be new to him—as long as she let him. They walked for a few minutes in silence, their steps finding a rhythm. It was peaceful, and Eden seemed calmer than he'd seen her for a very long time. But he found himself unable to let it be. He had to ask.

"When you were back there," he said, "I saw you talking."

"Yes," she said. Her voice was soft. There was no rancor in it, no defensiveness.

"What—what did you tell her?"

Eden raised her hand and placed it gently on her chest.

"I told her that it's time to forget."

ACKNOWLEDGMENTS

My grateful thanks to the following people for sharing their time and expertise with me and for answering my questions: Brad Nichinson, MD; Daniel Fertel, MD; Michael C. Martin, MD; Robin Hutton, RN; Kirsten Dickinson, RN; Karen McKeon; and Maya Ginsberg.

PHOTO BY GABRIEL R. BARILLAS 2012

Debra Ginsberg is the author of the memoirs *Waiting, Raising Blaze,* and *About My Sisters,* as well as the novels *Blind Submission*; *The Grift,* a *New York Times* Notable Book and winner of the 2009 SCIBA T. Jefferson Parker Mystery Award; and *The Neighbors Are Watching,* an Indie Next Great Reads pick. She lives in San Diego.

CONNECT ONLINE

www.debraginsberg.com
facebook.com/debraginsbergwriter

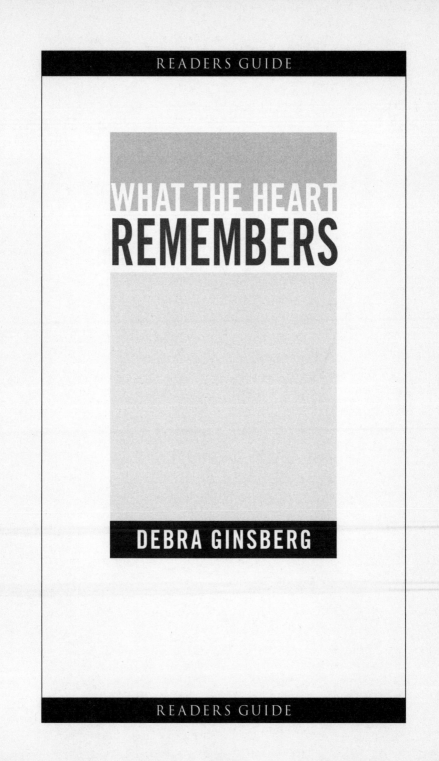

WHAT THE HEART
REMEMBERS

DEBRA GINSBERG

A CONVERSATION WITH
DEBRA GINSBERG

The ideas for my novels usually simmer just below the surface of my consciousness for years before emerging as structured stories. But in the case of *What the Heart Remembers*, I woke up one morning with the characters, plot, and question—*What would it feel like to be someone else?*—fully formed and wanting to be told. I was especially interested in exploring the idea of friendship between two women, Darcy and Eden, each with something to hide and neither of whom would befriend the other had fate not thrown them together. As in all my novels, this story features characters who live in the gray zone between good and evil, their actions constantly wavering between right and wrong. Eden and Darcy are complex and flawed—as are we all—and this is what makes them eminently human. Each has the capacity for kindness, cruelty, and love. Eden, the transplant recipient, struggles to reconcile what she feels (literally) in her heart with what she thinks she knows to be true, all the while coping with survivor's guilt and the need to (re)establish her own identity. Darcy is likewise complicated: a strong woman who has nevertheless been victimized to varying extents by two men, a woman with a damaged moral code, yet one who is desperate for love and connection.

And as with my previous novels, this one wraps fiction around real events. In this case, the core concept is cellular memory—the idea that memories, habits, desires, and inclinations are stored in all the cells of the body—not just the brain. There is plenty of anecdotal evidence that transplant patients experience some of the characteristics and memories of their donors—though, so far, no hard scientific studies to back this up.

It was one such story, that of Claire Sylvia, that first piqued my interest and led me to research this topic further. Soon after her 1988 heart-lung transplant, Sylvia began experiencing changes in her attitudes and habits. She liked different foods, developed a new taste for beer, and even started walking in a more masculine manner.

She began dreaming, too, about a man named Tim, whom she was sure was her donor. It turned out that Tim, an eighteen-year-old who had been killed in a motorcycle accident, was indeed the person whose heart she had been given. There are many other such anecdotes as well: an eight-year-old transplant patient who repeatedly awoke from nightmares of being shot and whose family subsequently learned that the donor had been murdered in this way; a young boy who received his donor's love of the violin along with his heart; and, most striking, the man who married the widow of his donor and then shot himself in the head in exactly the same manner as the widow's former husband.

Science is always skeptical of such ephemeral, unproven connections, yet they are difficult to deny. I explored such a theme in my novel *The Grift*, the tale of a fake psychic who wakes up one day to find she truly has the "gift" of second sight. With its exploration of cellular memory, *What the Heart Remembers* delves further into the space between fact and fiction—that nebulous area between what we know and what we believe.

The connection between Eden and Darcy, however, is at the "heart" of this novel. I wanted very much to take a close look at female friendship through these characters as well as the slippery nature of love and loyalty. Is it possible to truly *know* another person? What defines friendship and to what ends should one go in its service? What sacrifice is too great to make for love? What is the real nature of one's *self*—does it reside in our cells or in our (figurative) hearts? These were the questions that presented themselves as I sat down to write *What the Heart Remembers*. My hope is that through the twists and turns of Eden's and Darcy's stories, readers will discover some surprising—perhaps even shocking—answers.